I0761338

THE SONG LEADER

OTHER BOOKS BY JAN REID

NOVELS

Sins of the Younger Sons
Comanche Sundown
Deerinwater

NONFICTION

Let the People In: The Life and Times of Ann Richards
Layla and Other Assorted Love Songs
Rio Grande
The Bullet Meant for Me
Close Calls
Vain Glory
The Improbable Rise of Redneck Rock

EDITED

Splendor in the Short Grass: The Grover Lewis Reader, with W.K. Stratton

THE SONG LEADER

A NOVEL

JAN REID

FORT WORTH, TEXAS

Library of Congress Cataloging-in-Publication Data

Names: Reid, Jan, author.

Title: The song leader : a novel / Jan Reid.

Description: [Fort Worth, Texas] : [TCU Press], [2021] | Summary: "Haid Shelton is his small-town church's song leader as a teen and dreams of becoming a rock singer. His enduring gifts are in his tenor voice and success as a Golden Gloves boxer. Hoping to evade Vietnam, Haid joins the Marine reserves, gets into serious trouble, and is sentenced to four years in the brig. There he's recruited as the sparring partner of future heavyweight champion Ken Norton. Haid's knockout by his new friend Kenny gets him routed to the war as an infantry grunt in 1968. Back home, bitter, with a disabled hand and a Purple Heart, he's surprised and signed to a recording contract by the rock star Leon Russell. He rejoins his friendship with Norton on the eve of Kenny's famous upset of Muhammad Ali, who's an important character along with George Foreman, Joe Frazier, and Mike Weaver. Later their lives are brought together by a horrendous accident and by Kenny's guardian angel Virginie Nalula, a child refugee from eastern Congo. The tale embraces themes of race relations, friendship, and the American culture of violence"—Provided by publisher.

Identifiers: LCCN 2021007050 | ISBN 9780875657776 (cloth) | ISBN 9780875657837 (ebook)

Subjects: LCSH: Tenors (Singers)—Texas--Fiction. | Boxers (Sports)—Texas—Fiction. | Race relations--Fiction. | Violence—United States—Fiction.

Classification: LCC PS3568.E47655 S66 2021 | DDC 813/.54--dc23

LC record available at https://lccn.loc.gov/2021007050

TCU Box 298300
Fort Worth, Texas 76129
To order books: 1.800.826.8911

Design by Preston Thomas

For

RICK HENDON

And in memory of

GARY CARTWRIGHT

He had the punch lines, I was the joke

Every shot felt like something broke

It was all much more than a man should stand

And I finally went down to a big right hand

Now let me go home, got to lay in ice

And I don't want to hear no more advice

Just give me my clothes

Get me out of this place

How many more stitches in my face?

—MARK KNOPFLER, "BROKEN BONES"

CONTENTS

TCU Press actively promotes civility, respect, tolerance, consideration, and professional conduct. It fully commits itself to advocating for diversity, equity, and inclusiveness in all of its undertakings and will not condone any forms of discrimination or harassment. TCU Press does not tolerate bigotry of any kind but occasionally does publish works of authors who employ racist language to expose and condemn the bigotry of particular places and times.

THE SONG
LEADER

PROLOGUE
GOD'S GIFT

My first stop in the brig was a solitary confinement cell that had a pair of gold-painted footprints on the floor. My orders were to keep my boots planted on them unless told otherwise. The iron door had only a food slot but guards could see in, and they came around quietly. If they caught you sitting on your rack, elsewhere known as a bunk, it was two weeks' rations of rice cereal and all the cold water you could drink. I know I'll never eat another Rice Crispie.

The light bulb overhead was never turned off, and I lost all track of time. Why they call it the Hole. You come out of it disoriented and blinking. They finally moved me to a one-man cell. I heard the red-line brigs originated on navy ships, where deck space was tight for the likes of me. Red lines were painted in the middle of all the corridors. If you met a guard coming, you took one step to the right, waited until he passed, took one step forward, then left back on the line. In the rare event you met another convict coming, you both went through that routine in passing each other. One time I met a black kid coming, and my mind wandered. He gave me a quick hard shove that made me stumble across the parallel yellow line. The guard didn't see the shove but he saw my transgression. They leaned me hands against a wall and whipped my butt and backs of thighs with a length of fire hose, then wrote me up for attempted escape.

Some of the guards were sailors. They'd been trained as medical corpsmen to accompany combat marines, but they weren't handed out aspirins and bandages now. The inbred animosity of the navy made them the most sadistic ones, in my experience. I don't know how else to account for it. We had to ask the guards' permission to do anything.

"Corporal, request permission to take a piss."

"Use the Marine Corps language, fella. It's called 'use the head.'"

"Corporal, request permission to use the head."

"Do it, do it now."

"Corporal, request permission to take my pecker out."

"You mocking me, Private?"

"No, Sir!"

"Then do it. Do it now."

In the chow hall we stood with boots planted wide, consuming the slop. After evening chow, our orders were to sit on our racks, elsewhere called bunks, and with boots on the floor until they turned the lights out, we were to study the Marine Corps Manual, otherwise known as The Little Red Book. Most of the busted marines came in, were broken, and soon went back to be obedient parts of the war machine. Convicts with sentences as long as mine were usually routed to the all-service brig in Fort Leavenworth, Kansas. But the marines couldn't tolerate the kind of crime I'd committed. They thought if it wasn't punished with great severity, the discipline and whole system of the Corps might start to break down.

Camp Pendleton's red-line brig sat amid golden brown southern California hills miles away from the white barracks called Mainside. In the dry season, a little more than half the year, with black helmet liners on our heads we jogged out through the hills with twelve-pound sledgehammers on our right shoulders. The helmet liners symbolized our guilt and shame. A sergeant trotted along with us, warbling yodels of cadence. Dump trucks delivered us piles of rocks, and it was our job to break them up. I don't know where they got all those rocks, or what they could do with them after we made them smaller rocks, but the shards and sediment were scooped up by front loaders and put back in dump trucks to be hauled away.

It was regimented madness.

The tedium and exhaustion of the rock pile would have made me run just to have them shoot me, if we hadn't been allowed a tradition born of convicts in state prisons and field slaves on cotton and sugar cane plantations. It was music of American blacks—songs and hollers that had gotten their grandpas and great-grandpas through the days of dragging long cotton sacks or chopping down trees. They were a kind of talking blues, the tunes monotonous and irrelevant, made up as we went along. New black guys often gave me a look. What you think you're doing, white boy? I'd just been there long enough to know some of the lines and rhythms. I was the song leader once more, that's all. I'd voice a line and sling the hammer, and the others would sling their hammers and answer.

They give me ninety years
Fortune it weren't no century
I come by it naturally
What they say about Stagger Lee
My papa was an evil man
Only excuse he's got
He killed my mama just to have something to do
His nine brothers and sisters too
They accuse me of burglary
He don't know the way in
They accuse me of forgery
He can't sign his name
They accuse me of murder
He never knew the man
I got me a high yellow woman with three gold teeth
Lies of this man defy belief
Oughta be down on Shiloh Street drinking wine, wine, wine
Give me that woman, she be on cloud nine
Tell you now, the truth need be told
Tell it 'fore these rocks turn gold
Girl say come on here, you don't need to worry none
Baby I'm sorry but I got me worries some
He's been on this rock pile since nineteen oh one
I been overloaded for the crimes I done

Rocks and rain, those were our seasons. When the rainy season came, out in the world mansions broke up and fell to the ocean in mudslides. For us it was hard-time prison, much like any other, only there was no hanging out and lifting weights in the yard. There was no yard. If we weren't assigned to work details we marched in the brig's corridors, did pushups, and climbed ropes. Arm strength only, no help of our boots allowed.

On the work details we scrubbed trays in the chow hall, swept and mopped the floors, and in the wing of the officers and ranking sergeants we used a smelly kind of wool to keep every brass fixture gleaming. The guards' attitude toward me softened because I held up under the labor, caused no trouble, and they began to know me as a person, not just another scum. On occasions when a navy doctor came around, I carried his clipboard and wrote notes for him. A sergeant assigned me duty as the brig's barber. I learned to be gentle with the shears. But the rock pile was always out there waiting on me.

The only regular respite was Sunday morning chapel. I listened to recorded sermons of a navy chaplain and thought, ye gods, what a job. When the program played hymns, I sang along, trying to repair my vocal chords. Ever tried singing in a whisper? It sounds like a frail distant whistle. When I got the vocal cords working, the sounds ranged from whines to croaks, and the effort hurt. In time I taught myself to sing again. But my voice had a rough edge it didn't have before.

One day a sergeant ordered me out of the cell and marched me, calling cadence, to the part of the building that housed the offices of the brass. The commanding officer of the brig was a tall, bald black man named Johnstone Bullick. I had seen him at a distance and had hoped to keep it that way. He returned our salutes, dismissed the sergeant, came to his feet, and left me at attention as he walked around me with an air of formal inspection.

"Nice spit shine on your boots," he said. "That shows a little effort."

"Thank you, Sir."

"How do you do it?"

"One of the guards gave me a can of polish. I use water and toilet paper. Sir."

"Not as efficient as cotton balls."

"No, Sir."

"Guard ought to be written up. Does it bother you to call me sir?"

"Not at all, Sir."

He made another circuit and eyed me with his hands clasped behind his back. "I can tell from your speech more or less where you're from. It's a town, right? Not no farm or ranch or something."

"Yes, Sir, it's a town."

"Does it have a name?"

"Yes, Sir. Deerinwater, Texas."

"What kind of town is it?"

I considered how to describe it. "About ninety thousand people, Sir. Rednecks and roughnecks. Would-be cowboys. Quite a few rich people because of the oil."

"Rednecks and roughnecks—people that talk like you?"

A rivulet of sweat slid down my spine. "I guess so, Sir."

"In this town is there a section where people of color live?"

"Yes, Sir."

"What's it called?"

"The Eastside. Sir."

"Anything else?"

I tried another evasion. "Some call it Shiloh Street, Sir. It's the main street through there."

"Private, you know what I'm asking. What do people of your color call this place? Say it, do it now."

"Niggertown, Sir."

"There you go. Now we're having a genuine conversation." He pronounced the adjective like wine. "Stand at ease." No one else in the brig had allowed me any better than parade rest. "Are your parents decent people?" he asked.

"Yes, Sir, they are."

He walked back around the desk and sat down. "Did you hear that word used in your home?"

"No, Sir. My mom says it's not Christian."

"Where'd you learn it then?"

"It was just how things were in that place. Way they are. Sir."

"Any other use of that kind of language comes across your tongue? Words that took to growing in your fertile mind?"

The worst ones sent a shiver of terror down my spine.

"I can only think of a couple, Sir."

"Let's hear them. Say it, do it now."

I let my breath out and said, "Some kids called slingshots nigger-shooters, sir. They called Brazil nuts niggertoes."

The colonel laughed. "I never heard that last one." He rocked back in his chair. "People in Vietnam have a saying: *Binh nang, thoc mang.* Means big illness, strong medicine. That's what you got yourself into, Private. Beating up that gunny sergeant was just an impulse, am I correct?"

"Yes, Sir."

"Were you drunk?"

"No, Sir."

"Was he your drill instructor?"

"No, Sir. That night was just the second time I saw him."

"Then why'd you do it?"

"He abused and hurt me bad, Sir. He didn't have any call to."

He rocked back and forth. "So you anointed yourself Genghis Khan."

"I don't know how to answer that, Sir."

"Well, you made a bonehead decision. And look where it got you. Tell me, are you dissatisfied with the mail delivery system here?"

"No, Sir." I never had used it.

"Your private's pay is set aside to provide you with stationery, envelopes, pencils, a little sharpener, and stamps. That correct?"

"Yes, Sir."

"You're fond of your parents. At least respect them. Correct?"

"Yes, Sir."

"Then why have you never once answered their letters?"

"I'm ashamed of myself. I wasn't raised to be in this situation."

"'Be in this situation.' All right, say it your way. For a while the mail was bringing these packages addressed to you. They had metal inside and the packages had to be opened to make sure they didn't contain explosives or firearms. They found tins containing carrot cakes and other geedunk in carefully wrapped cellophane. Regulations don't allow you to have them. So the guards enjoyed the geedunk your mother baked her very own self."

He watched me let that sink in.

"Your parents don't know whether you're dead or alive. They are concerned about you. There's a war on, getting bigger all the time, and they don't know if you've been killed or captured or declared missing in action. They have communicated with their congressman. They're asking questions that are a bother to the Marine Corps. It's not our job to tell them where you are and what you did. That's your job."

I offered no reply.

"Let me put it this way," said Colonel Bullick, his voice rising. "I am not going to stand for some general coming down on my ass because you're too twisted up in that bonehead of yours to write your parents a letter. You are going to write them and ease their fears. When I send for you in a week, you're going to bring the letter to me. I'll decide whether you've said what it ought to say. Is that understood? It's an order."

"Yes, Sir." I paused. "Do I have to tell them where I am?"

The colonel threw out his long arms and hands in exasperation. It struck me how white his palms were. "I guess not," he said. "As long as you don't tell them you're in Vietnam. Anything mailed from you identifies Camp Pendleton and the code of numbers of this Correctional Unit. You are not hearing this from me. We never had this conversation, and my reputation for telling the truth is superior to yours. I don't care what you tell them, if you can't admit to being a common low-down thug. Make up something. Lie. But God help you if any more shit comes down on me."

I composed a letter reassuring my parents I was in good health, we were in the same hemisphere, I was on a secret intelligence assignment, and I'd be calling them as soon as possible. As I waited for the next summons of the colonel, I think it was more like two weeks, I tried to write my girlfriend Ann, but once more the words failed me. I couldn't lie to her or tell her the truth either. I was brooding on that when the cell door whanged open and the sergeant ordered me out and marched me back to the officers' quarters.

Colonel Bullick returned our salutes like he was waving off a fly. He dismissed the sergeant and told me to stand at ease. He pushed back against his polished wood chair. "Private," he said, "how long have you been here?"

"Fifteen months, Sir."

"How much of your sentence is that?"

"Thirty-three months to go, Sir."

The colonel leaned on his forearms and clasped his hands on the shiny desk. "Have you ever heard of Carmen Basilio?"

I was startled. "The fighter? Yes, Sir. Ugly little guy, fought in the day of Sugar Ray Robinson, Jake LaMotta, Tony Zale, Gene Fullmer, Rocky Graziano, Marcel Cerdan. Tough bunch. Probably the best ever, that size. I think Basilio beat Sugar Ray once."

"That ugly little guy was the best fighter the Marine Corps ever had."

My tongue froze on the roof of my mouth.

"I didn't call you here to shoot the breeze. The marines have a guy now they think is better than Carmen Basilio. He's won three All-Corps titles, national and international tournaments, and they're trying to get him to re-up and try for the Olympics. He was an all-state football player somewhere. He's got a nice easy job that doesn't interfere with his training. He's a corporal in charge of photocopy. But he's hard on his sparring partners, and marines can't just go up to Stockton and hire them out of the onion fields. Marines aware of your court martial and sentence noticed something about your civilian background. When you filled out your form at boot camp you said you won a state Golden Gloves title in Texas. You girls in boot camp lie about things like that, thinking it will get you some kind of break. But a sergeant here keeps up with amateur boxing, and he found out it was true. Was that fun?"

"Except for one or two fights, yes Sir, it was."

The colonel sat back and said, "The commanding officer of your court martial has agreed to give you a chance to work off some of your sentence. You sign on with the sergeant and this boxer as a sparring partner, then every day, week, or month you last, that will reduce two days, weeks, or months of your sentence."

Once more I had the sensation I was falling in a well.

"Sir, if you don't mind my asking, how big is this fighter?"

The colonel smiled. "He's a heavyweight. You don't have to do it. We've got lots of rocks and sledgehammers."

I swallowed. "Do I have to make up my mind right now?"

"No, we got other business to attend to. Do you have that letter to your folks?"

"Yes, Sir."

"Let me see it."

"Sir, request permission to—"

"Just give it here."

I pulled the folded letter and envelope out of my pocket and put it on the gleaming desk. The colonel read my lies while stroking his chin with his thumb and middle finger. He smoothed out the paper and put it back on the desk before me. Then he opened a drawer and brought out two more sheets of paper, one blank and the other in typescript, along with a sharpened pencil. He lined up the three sheets neatly, turned the one with typescript toward me, and told me to read it out loud. He said I could lean over the desk if I needed to. I began.

> *Dear Mom and Dad, I have to tell you that I am in a Marine Corps brig at Camp Pendleton, California, serving a four-year sentence for aggravated assault. I ambushed an older Marine, a gunnery sergeant and decorated combat veteran, and hurt him pretty bad. I threatened to kill him. I am disgraced and you'll probably want to disown me . . .*

I straightened up and considered the man. He pushed the blank sheet toward me and offered the pencil, eraser first. "You'll need to put that in your handwriting."

I stared at the pencil like it was some kind of snake. An angry fer-de-lance.

"Private," he said, "I'm not just offering you another chance. I'm offering you a choice. If you choose not to go help this boxer, the letter you just read is the one that goes out. Now which one of the letters would you rather send your parents?"

In the athletic complex, a hodgepodge of Quonset huts, gyms, and ball fields recognizable only by rusted backstops and goalposts, I was received by a sergeant with a mess of twisted nose whose exact rank wasn't apparent, and never would be, because he didn't state it and always wore faded utility trousers, an olive-green T-shirt or sweatshirt, and ring shoes or flip-flops. The gym had a boxing ring, heavy bags hanging from chains, and speed bags bolted to the walls. I set my duffle down and looked around. The sergeant scooted out from his office in a battered office chair that clicked on cracked rollers. The chair's upholstering was shored up with duct tape. He moved his head at the surroundings. "Look familiar?"

"Like any other gym, Sir. The usual." Framed and hung on a wall was a single tattered fight poster from 1957, the one in which Basilio won a split decision over Sugar Ray.

"Don't call me *sir*. I ain't no officer. Call me Sergeant."

He never offered me any name. He was just Sergeant, nickname Sarge.

"Aye aye, Sir."

"And shitcan that navy talk. I never liked the sound of it."

That made me think I might like him a little. "All right."

"State champion in Texas, you were. Knockout artist."

I shook my head. "I just trained hard and got lucky one week."

"Why didn't you go to the Nationals, if you blew through Texas like that? Knocked out one of the top amateurs in the country. Why didn't you just give it a shot?"

"I'd flunked out of college and was about to get drafted."

"I see. Well, I don't care how or why you got here. My duty is being a boxing trainer, and they don't expect anything else from me. Not anymore. You'll see other jarheads out here on occasion. Don't even speak to 'em. You're the full-time partner of just one. When he runs in the morning, you run with him. When he stretches and lifts weights, you stretch and lift weights. I'll get you sweats, jockstraps, socks, shirts, hand wraps, a mouthpiece, and a headgear. Pick out a groin protector that fits you."

"Headgear," I mused. "I've never had one of those."

"Backward out there in Texas, huh? That's no surprise. You'll be grateful you have one here. What size boots you wear?"

"Ten and a half."

"I've got a pair of old ring shoes you can use. Our guy runs in boots. So do you. I'll take you to your quarters in a while. Just a crib in a Quonset hut, but better than where you've been. When you're not working out, you wear utilities and boots and a cover on your head outdoors just like everybody else. You do your own laundry and salute officers. When you're off-duty you can do whatever you want, as long as you don't leave this compound. There ain't no fences. If you take off from here, you're AWOL, whether you make it off the base or not. Understood?"

I nodded. He said, "You know much about the fights?"

"I've watched them since we first got a TV."

"Who are your favorites now? Guys that inspire you."

"Muhammad Ali. Nino Benvenuti."

The sergeant snorted. "You don't admire any Americans?"

"Ali's American," I said. "He won the light heavy Gold for us in the

Olympics. He just changed his name for his religion, no insult meant to his folks. Benvenuti won the welterweight Gold for Italy the same year. He's won two title fights and last I heard he's sixty and lost none. One time he was fighting a guy and was getting every bad call the ref could think of, so his corner threw in the towel. Nino kicked it out of the ring and kept on fighting. I like to watch those guys, that's all."

"Okay, but in this gym your favorite heavyweight's name is Cassius Clay. Do not ever again call him Muhammad Ali in my hearing. Got it?"

"Yes, Sir." Lots of people hated Ali over his draft refusal, his name change, and his conversion to Islam. Black Muslims threatened them.

"I said don't call me *sir*. You know who Billy Conn was?"

"Yeah."

"Think of your job that way. You are Billy Conn in the ring with Joe Louis. Kenny's about the size Louis was."

Oh, that helped. "I hear your guy murders sparring partners."

"Our guy," Sarge corrected me. "Murder's not the right word. All good fighters got a mean streak, but Kenny's not cruel. He's just trying to take advantage of his ability and the training the Marine Corps provides him. You'll get to like him, if you last."

When the fighter came in, I tried not to gape. He was two or three inches taller than me and outweighed me at least twenty-five pounds. He wore sweats, a dust-caked pair of combat boots, and no cover on his head. He was handsome with an air of knowing it. I got a strong handshake from him, and he introduced himself as Ken. Sarge had called him Kenny.

"I'm Haid," I said.

He grinned and pointed at his temple. "You mean like the knots on yo' head?"

"No, like my name, the way I said it. People aren't necessarily stupid because they don't talk like you."

His grin broadened. "Wise guy, huh? Where are you from?"

"Deerinwater, Texas. It's just a place."

He nodded. "So's Jacksonville, Illinois. Welcome to the house. We'll have fun."

"Can't wait."

He hadn't offered his last name, and it wouldn't have meant anything to me if he had. Any more than mine would have meant anything to him.

But I was raw meat being fed to Ken *Norton,* one of four great heavyweights in a spectacular generation of them.

"They tell me you're the Corps' best since Carmen Basilio."

He made a sound of equal parts pride and contempt. "Yeah, they say that."

"I saw Basilio on TV a few times. I thought he was ugly as a creosote bush. But not just anybody could beat Sugar Ray."

He tilted his head. "What's a creosote bush?"

"Desert plant in the Southwest and Mexico. They grow up three or four feet, bloom yellow flowers, and put out the smell of creosote, like a new telephone pole. It leaks that stuff out in the soil to discourage plants that want its water and critters tempted to browse it. Indians think the sap helps things like chickenpox, snakebite, and the clap."

My new boss chuckled. "I need a sparring partner and they send me a botanist."

"Not me. I'm a college dropout. I just read a lot. Or I used to."

"Basilio," he mused. "For a long time, they introduced him in Madison Square Garden as 'the Upstate Onion Picker.' Sarge has these old fight films he lets me watch. Makes me watch. If you stick around, I'll show you some. I'll tell you the fighter I think the most about. Benny 'Kid' Paret. Heard of him?"

"Yeah."

"You ever see that fight with Emile Griffith? Twenty-three unanswered punches, the ref just let it go on. The Kid looked dead before they carried him out of there. First rule of boxing—you're not in there with anyone but the other guy, and you're all the help you're gonna get. Second rule—don't call a fighter a faggot and then get in the ring with him."

I laughed. "Good thinking."

"Look at this face," he said. "Is it not pretty? God gave it to me. I mean to keep it that way. I like the way it looks and the brain behind it even more."

PART I PIPE TOWN BLUES

CHAPTER 1

One night my mom and my sister Virginia laughed and took a picture of me whaling away on a pair of Dad's coveralls hung out man-shaped on the clothesline. He'd wear those things every time he went to work, the rest of his life. They wouldn't have thought it so funny if they'd known I was trying to work up courage to resume a fistfight that erupted on a sidewalk right beside a bus stop downtown. My opponent was a boy who went to another school. A woman shooed us off the sidewalk in front of the Kress's five and dime, so we made a date to finish it at a Boy Scout meeting at a Presbyterian church. Out behind the church we flung fists at each other until the scoutmaster hustled out and broke it up. I don't remember who started the fight downtown, but I sure lost the rematch.

The name on my birth certificate is Haid Wallace Shelton. I was born in 1944 and started school in 1950. After the first two weeks the principal of the Patrick Henry grade school and my teacher called my mother to the school. The teacher said all they had gotten out of me were sobs of frustration and explosions of fury. They said I was too immature to start school, that it would be better to hold me back now than let me fail the first grade. Mom and Daddy didn't like it but they said all right.

The setback got me called *Retard* at the school and on its playgrounds. Every time I started a new grade at Patrick Henry, I swore this year I was not going to cry in front of the others. But I always did, and the setback and the tears marked me as easy pickings. On vacant lots and in alleys after school I *had* to fight. I would back up with older boys crowded close around and yelling at me until something snapped and my wild swings now and then made a bully back off. But what good did it do if I won a fight crying like a baby?

The year I turned sixteen Nikita Khrushchev threw a fit at the United Nations. The Russian leader wore a pair of shoes that didn't fit well that day, and he had taken them off. Infuriated by a Filipino delegate's insinuation that the Soviets were as guilty of colonialism as powers in the West, he started banging his fist on his desk so hard his watch flew off on the floor. Reaching for it, he touched a shoe and so he banged with that.

During Christmas season that year the Russians launched a rocket that contained two dogs and a cage of mice. The rocket failed at an altitude of two hundred miles. In fiery descent the capsule's ejection device also failed, and it crashed somewhere in Siberia. The Russians had a sixty-hour backup demolition device on the capsule. A frantic search located the capsule in night that was forty-five degrees below zero. The capsule was frosted over, and the searchers didn't have enough light to spring the capsule open. They heard no barking but returned at daylight. The mice had frozen to death, but now the searchers heard barking in the capsule.

The rescued dogs were longhaired little mutts, yappers. One was named Kometka or "Little Comet" and the other Zhemchuzhnaya or "Pearly." Wrapped in layers of fur and fleece, they were rushed to Moscow for veterinary observation and public adulation that got them paraded past the capital's gaudy minarets. I saw it on one of those newsreels that used to run with movies in theaters. The space race was in full gear, and the Russians never missed a chance to let the world know they were winning. A year later the Soviets detonated "Tsar Bomba," a hydrogen bomb that exploded in three stages with ten times the explosives set off by all the countries in World War II. The mushroom cloud rose forty miles up, the flash could be seen sixty miles away, and just looking at it would boil the insides of your eyeballs.

On the north side of Deerinwater triangle tails of B-52s poked up in the sky from runways at Allred Field. The tails were painted bronze, word had it, as a signal that they were armed with SAC atom bombs. Ours had been an odd conceit—*we're number six on Russia's list.* But now people in town were saying, "Holy shit, those Russians are crazy." Ones made rich from the oil boom had fallout shelters excavated under their mansions. Cheaper models looked like big silver footballs on the lots of former used-car salesmen.

None of that made our hoodlums grateful for the service of airmen stationed at Allred Field. Deerinwater in those days was a street-fighting town. The street fighters kept contraband Crayons moving inside the city jail so they could autograph and brag on the cell walls where they spent some nights. Kids whose dads were stationed at Allred Field went to school in small-town districts like Peach Orchard that were scattered around the base, because they knew how they'd be treated at Deerinwater High. The girls would be called whores, and boys wasted their time going out for the Antler athletic teams. They would get their asses kicked even though they weren't airmen themselves.

Airmen were treated like occupiers of a foreign land, and there was nothing for them to do at night but catch a bus into an ugly and dangerous downtown. The fighting got so bad that the base's commanding general declared the town off-limits to junior enlisted personnel. I didn't want to fight an airman or anyone else. In the high school's hallways, I just wanted to be invisible. By the end of my first few weeks there I could spot the boys to stay away from. The fighters loaded up both hands with big heavy rings to make them jerry-rigged brass knuckles. Beer can openers known to us as church keys were being used as cruel defacing claws. I supposed ball bats, switchblades, and guns were coming next. The violence scared me and moved with me like a shadow. But the time came when I had to own up to the fact that the shadow and I were one and the same.

As we grew older my sister Virginia and I stopped getting along. She was four years older, but because of my first-grade setback she was five years ahead of me in school. She sided with our mother in scolds and tried to boss me using Mom's tone and expressions. *I've got a bone to pick with you.* One year I got hold of an old tennis racquet and some balls, and in the backyard I was trying to mimic the serves of Pancho Gonzales, the champion who'd caught my eye on TV. Virginia was out by the back fence picking apricots off Mom's trees. My smash bounced the ball off Virginia's head and ricocheted into the alley. She threw the bowl of apricots at me and ran toward the back door. "You're dangerous!" she shrieked.

"I'm sorry!" I yelled. "You think I could *aim* that?"

Across the alley some neighbors had a little guesthouse next to a large cedar or juniper tree. The tree and its nettles were magnets for my tennis balls. One afternoon I got tired of it and set the tree on fire. I was unaware of the oil content of cedar. It roared up like an oil well fire. I panicked and ran over to those neighbors, crying that their tree was somehow ablaze. I grabbed their garden hose and turned on the hydrant but the hose didn't reach. The tree had burned itself out by the time the fire truck got there. Three charred tennis balls and the kitchen matches I'd used to light the fire lay half-burned in the smoking soot—stark evidence, if anyone had cared to pursue it, that I was a juvenile arsonist.

A sorry weed called puncture vine thrived on the sunbaked clay soil where I ran barefoot as a child. It replicated itself by making nasty stickers that put out five or six spikes as sharp as two-penny nails. We called them goatheads because they sort of looked like that. The thorns didn't break off in your foot because they were so hard, but if one spiked you, the wound reddened and swelled up for days. Church was the goathead in my heel.

Our sect was known for claims of being the one true church, the one that stayed alive in caves and catacombs during the takeover of the faith by popes and the so-called Protestant Reformation. All truth and creed were to be found in the New Testament. All the people on earth who were not baptized into our faith were going to hell. That didn't make us real popular with our Methodist and Baptist neighbors, though Mom never looked down on them or tried to convert them. Daddy had been raised a Baptist, but now he stayed out of that thicket of emotional and psychological hazards by never going to church.

Mom rode Virginia and me hard on matters of religion, but she had a good heart. She had grown up on tenant cotton farms in a part of the world where there just wasn't enough rain to sustain them. She was haunted by the time during the Depression when her father, whom we called Grandpa Nichols, had to give up farming for a few years and take up barbering. An uncle on her side of the family told me he remembered seeing them arrive in Deerinwater in a freight car with their plow horse and milk cow. She just wanted to go to heaven when she died, hoped the people she loved would be there with her, and meantime she never wanted to be poor and hungry again.

Mom took to bed one Sunday with a bad cold, but that didn't mean Virginia and I got a church holiday. Daddy was working a shift at the plant, the little congregation at Seventeenth and Keeler was five blocks away, so Virginia and I walked to church that evening. I don't know what the preacher said that night, but the song leader, a young plumber named Joey Carrigan, chose "Just As I Am" as the invitation hymn.

In my lifelong hunt for useless information, one time in an Episcopal seminary I looked up the origins of my favorite song in the Broadman Hymnal. "Just As I Am" began as a poem written and published in the 1830s by a woman in London who had been a pampered daughter of a minister. According to one author, the words came to Charlotte Elliott as she lay in her boudoir feeling sorry for herself. I wondered how many boudoirs there were in the catacombs of London. The poem was put to several melodies, but the lasting one brought the Reverend Billy Graham weeping down the invitation aisle after hearing a sermon in Charlotte, North Carolina. America's most famous preacher made it his altar song, his signature hymn.

That night Joey Carrigan sang it with such feeling that I bolted down the aisle to be saved and forgiven of my sins. Deacons took me in a classroom, shed me of my clothes, and put me in a white cotton gown. In the baptistery the preacher said a short prayer, bent me over backward, and dunked me with a handkerchief pressed against my mouth. I knew my hind end was showing pink in the thin cotton when the preacher, who wore deep fishing waders, helped me up the steps of the baptistery. I was already digging in my heels by the time we got home and Virginia pulled me toward our parents' bedroom. Daddy was working a shift at the plant that night. Mom turned on a lamp and looked up at us.

"Tell her, Haid," Virginia said. "Tell her."

"I got baptized," I said.

Tears welled up in Mom's eyes. "Oh, son, I'm so proud of you."

I was just getting it over with. I lied a great deal and there was that burnt cedar tree, but I didn't really think I'd sinned all that much at age thirteen.

CHAPTER 2

The turnover in our preachers was frequent. One year we got Brother Borbino, a converted Catholic from Queens, New York, who found his way to Deerinwater from a mission in Fremantle, Australia. Nothing got him going like John F. Kennedy being elected president—the pope was going to rule us all! The first time I tried to talk to Brother Borbino, I asked him if he liked the music of Dion and the Belmonts, whose song "Runaround Sue" was my favorite pop tune at the time. I thought all New York Italians had to know about Dion DiMucci, like all Texans knew about Lubbock's Buddy Holly. Or I assumed they did. The preacher frowned and moved on without answering. He seemed to think I mocked him.

That preacher had arrived soon after Allred Field's commanding general declared Deerinwater off-limits to low-ranking airmen. The general's rebuke got the attention of the Chamber of Commerce, the city council, and the police department. The street fighters were no longer free to maraud the downtown bus stops and roller-skating rink without cops and consequences. Brother Borbino decided to extend the hand of fellowship to believers at Allred Field. Maybe he hoped to cool off the hostility between town boys and airmen. About a dozen came around in their blue uniforms. They crowded in pews where the teenagers sat. That's how I got an airman for a brother-in-law.

Tall and of angular build, a pretty girl when she smiled, Virginia was the A-student in our household. To our mom's delight, she had a scholarship waiting for her at a Bible college in Abilene. But she had never had a boyfriend who asked her to do more than go to a movie or play Putt-Putt after Sunday night church, and all at once here was this short, cocksure pretty boy bringing her home with her lipstick smeared and her eyes sparkling.

Darrell Raines was a redneck from Tuscaloosa who washed out driving long-haul trucks. His flyboy friends said he flipped and broke up a refrigerated trailer full of chicken livers, hearts, and gizzards on a freeway through downtown Shreveport one August day, and the bloody mess cooked up fast and got a lot of local TV coverage. Relieved of his truck-driving prospects, he joined the Air Force. He was an airman first class, but before he rolled the truck and broke up the trailer, he had put away enough cash to buy a 1957 Chevrolet Bel Air, the larkspur-blue model with the white flare out the fin. But what moron would buy that classic as a station wagon?

Virginia announced that she wanted to marry Darrell before she graduated from high school. Mom at last negotiated a compromise and wrung consent out of Dad. Mom was distressed that Virginia gave up the scholarship at the Bible college, but she would graduate from high school before she married him. From my bedroom, I watched Daddy standing at the kitchen sink, staring out the window at the backyard, wringing his hands and drinking glasses of water as the celebration carried on in the living room. If he'd been a drinking man, he would have been knocking down shots of Old Crow.

After the wedding Darrell and Virginia moved into her bedroom on the other end of the house. One of Darrell's friends parked a broken-down Nash Rambler in our backyard. It was excruciating. Darrell kept taking me out in the bottoms of the Red River to teach me how to shoot a gun. If you never master that, he said, you aren't really an American man. I got tired of it one day and tossed his prized Smith & Wesson .38 in the sand. Darrell turned red and yelled that I was going to break the thing down and clean it when he took me home. I said, "Who do you think you are?"

Trouble was brewing between us, no doubt about it. I thought about moving to Ponca City, Oklahoma, where my Uncle Jack worked for a Conoco plant, and I would live with him and Aunt Mamie during my senior year and play for their high school teams. Up there I might be a star. It was only Oklahoma.

One week everyone in church was thunderstruck by mug shots that appeared on the front page of our paper, the *Standard-Patriot,* under the headline "Rob and Roy Robbers Nabbed." Joey Carrigan, our song leader, was the masked Rob who helped his partner Roy hold up several small grocery and liquor stores and one satellite bank. The masked robbers dodged the cops long enough that they acquired a Robin Hood aura, though there were no reports of them sharing the loot.

Joey's dad was an elder in our little church and a mechanic on the city's fleet of garbage trucks. You could tell from the looks on the faces of Joey's dad and hankie-twisting mom that they were humiliated and heartbroken. They walked down the aisle the first Sunday after the news broke and asked to be restored, as if Joey going bonkers or showing his true nature was their fault. I wasn't all that surprised. I figured Joey thought there had to be more excitement and reward in life than mopping asphalt on a roofing job in 102-degree heat and leading the singing at church. He pled guilty and went off to do his time in the big rodeo.

A passage in Psalms commanded the Israelites to make a joyful noise unto the Lord, but no mention of musical instruments could be found in the New Testament, so in our one true church there could be no lyres, Pandean pipes, pianos, organs, guitars, oboes, flutes, clarinets, harmonicas, the works. Didn't matter that King David was a skilled musician himself. The song leader might blow a discreet note on a pitch pipe in his hand, but the songs had to be sung acappella. Those gospel songs were about all of my faith that stayed with me.

My voice had slipped like a car clutch when my soprano deepened into a tenor, but now my Sunday school teacher bragged on it. Occasional Wednesday night services were set aside just for singings. One Wednesday night, Brother Borbino called me to the pulpit and told me to choose and lead two songs. I didn't think he really knew my name. With a gulp I found the numbers in the hymnal, called them out, and closed my eyes. It wowed the church leaders, who thought I was praying, but I was concentrating on trying to hear the first note. For me the staffs and clefs and quarter notes on the hymnal pages could have been Mayan hieroglyphics. Singing to me was all about ear. I got off to a wobbly start and rushed the congregation through "There Is a Fountain Filled with Blood," but I caught on the wonder of hearing myself in a microphone in "The Sweet By and By," and I fantasized having a whole damn band behind me.

After several painful auditions by other men I was coerced into being the church's new song leader. It didn't change how I spent most of my hours at church. After Brother Borbino said all his nice things about the aged and the ill and started in on his fire and brimstone, I tuned him out and didn't hear another word. My daydreams roamed far afield until I heard the tone of his sermon change again and people made scraping noises removing hymnals from the wooden racks on the backs of the pews. It was time for me to go back up to the pulpit for the invitation hymn.

At first I enjoyed it. I was working on my chops.

My favorite invitation hymns were "Just As I Am" and "Softly and Tenderly Jesus Is Calling." One Sunday I startled some people by singing the third verse of the latter.

> *Time is now fleeting, the moments are passing*
> *Passing from you and from me; shadows are gathering*
> *Deathbeds are coming, coming for you and for me*

Brother Borbino told me afterward that he didn't think that added one thing to his sermon, and it upset some members. Because it reminded them that they were going to die? I thought the hereafter was what Christianity was all about.

One Sunday night Daddy put on a dress shirt and tie and came along to see what all the excitement was about. Of my song leading he never offered a comment one way or another. His favorite singer was Perry Como.

I got some breathing room at home when Virginia and Darrell moved into an apartment out by the base. But Brother Borbino extended the fellowship further. Guest sermons began to be preached by a chaplain at Allred Field who wore silver captain's bars on his uniform. Chaplain Dingus was a short man of bland good looks. He left his blue service cap with his wife on the same pew up front where I sat. The chaplain's wife wore bright red lipstick and her blonde hair with the sort of tousled look of Marilyn Monroe. She gave me a firm handshake and smile on our meeting and said, "My name is Susan. Don't ever call me Sister Dingus."

Boy howdy. That chaplain had to have something going for him to be married to a woman like that.

As if there weren't enough church in my life, Brother Borbino announced a new Young People's Meeting on Sunday afternoons to be taught by Chaplain Dingus, and Mom said I had to go. I sulked, but the chaplain was a hard man to dislike. One Sunday he had been reflecting on the meaning of Christ's Sermon on the Mount when he stepped over to the classroom window and stared out. "Does anyone know who James Garfield was?"

A girl named Sandy spoke up. "A president?"

"Yes, for five months in 1881. I grew up in Ohio, where he was from. When I was in the seminary, I wrote a thesis about his use of Scripture in his speeches. My wife and I got married while I was researching that. Garfield was quite an orator. He had been a Union general at Shiloh and Chickamauga, bloody slaughters, both of them. He was a powerful state politician, an abolitionist Republican. People said he spoke Latin and Greek and could write either one with either hand."

He smiled and nodded at our murmurs of disbelief.

"A lawyer named Guiteau thought Garfield ought to appoint him ambassador to France, though he spoke no French and had no qualifications. When Guiteau didn't get the job, he shot the president twice as he was about to go on vacation. One of the bullets lodged in his spine. Doctors dug around trying to find it with unwashed fingers."

"Yuck," some girl said.

"Exactly. In medical practice back then they thought they had to get the bullet out because lead is poison. They didn't try to sedate him, and all they did was infect him. He lasted eighty days and lost a pound every day. It had been sixteen years since Lincoln's killing. People forget now that Booth shot him just five days after Lee surrendered the Confederate army. Northerners thought it was the last tragedy of the Civil War. I guess Southerners thought Lincoln had it coming. But Garfield's killing shocked the country. Was this the kind of nation we were going to be?"

He tapped his Bible on his hand. "Garfield's the only president who shared our beliefs, who relies on Scripture as we do. When the president and his wife went to worship in Washington, the driver dropped them off at our congregation in the capital, then moved the team and carriage beside a church that wasn't so beneath the dignity of the president's office. People thought we were snake handlers speaking in tongues."

In a church that held all faith is rooted in New Testament Scripture, I thought that if I couldn't believe Jesus was born to a virgin and rose from the dead, I couldn't rightly call myself a Christian. That gave me a good deal of leeway in my moral behavior. After the song leading one night, I got my first real feel of a girl's body in the back seat of a kid's old DeSoto. Another Sunday night when the service was over and people were moving out of the church, in the foyer the foxy mom of the McConnell sisters put a breast against my arm and murmured, "You sing just like Hank Williams." My word, that felt nice, and she smelled so good. For the most part I hated country music. To me it was like the dust storms that rolled in off the Panhandle. It clogged your sinuses and got all over you. But I gave Hank Williams a pass and made a mental note to learn "So Lonesome I Could Cry" and "I Saw the Light." If I couldn't make it as a major league ballplayer, I was going to be a rock and roll singer. Why couldn't I be both? Out of this pipe town I'd fly away.

CHAPTER 3

I was a fairly normal kid in that place and time. Sports were important to me, some more than others. They helped keep my mind off Russian hydrogen bombs, the B-52s parked with atom bombs at Allred Field, and the fistfights that awaited me sure as sundown. The game I loved most was baseball, because I could play that, in large part thanks to my dad. During the oil boom Deerinwater had a team called the Roughnecks in the Texas League, high minors in those days. One day Daddy saw Babe Ruth hit a home run high over Roughneck Park's center field wall in a spring exhibition game. I respected the Yankees he always rooted for, but my favorite hitters were the San Francisco Giants' Willie Mays and Orlando "Baby Bull" Cepeda and the Cleveland Indians' Rocky Colavito. The pitchers on my dream roster were the Giants' high-kicking Juan Marichal, the Dodgers' great southpaw Sandy Koufax, and the Indians' Herb Score, who was Koufax before he gained control of his stuff and became Koufax. They say a line drive off a Yankee bat left one of Score's eyes attached by a filmy ligament to his skull. He came back but was never the same. Who could have been?

My dad was a burly red-haired man, a refinery worker and son of a wildcatter who had mostly drilled dry holes. Though he was a little old he could have been drafted, but his job at the Pioneer refinery won him a critical industries deferment. He never meant to end up going out to work day after day carrying soggy sandwiches in a lunch pail. He had wanted to go to college, teach school, and coach. He never let us forget his sacrifice. I grew up hearing angry slams of the front door when he had to go take his turns on the graveyard shift.

My relations with him were not all peace and love, not by a long shot. But when he was working the day shift, he got home about the time school let out. Across Keeler Street and a railroad right-of-way was a Lutheran school, and afternoons on the playground he began to coach the best baseball he could get out of me. He got the only fungo bat I ever saw and spent hours with me schooling me to play the outfield. How to read the trajectory of fly balls and take a knee to avoid letting any ground balls get past me and come up throwing.

I played for a YMCA summer league team called the Roustabouts. Because of his shift work he could only be the assistant coach. When we were eleven-year-olds we rode flatbed oil trucks in a downtown parade that honored all the teams in the age brackets that made the town's Little World Series. I went three for three that night we won the city championship. And though we didn't always win as we moved up through the age brackets, we were always in the hunt.

There's a perception in baseball that right field is the lowest position, the last stop before the bench, but I liked it out there, chewing on stems of grass and in night games watching fireflies when nothing was going on. I matured into a line drive hitter with power to right center. I could lay down bunts with a light touch, and I had a knack for delivering base hits in the clutch. And I had an arm. When I cut down runners trying to reach third base or home plate, sometimes they'd get up and stare at me in disbelief. And one day my arm would count for more than boyhood conceit.

A man named Cleon Embry was the baseball coach at Deerinwater High. One summer night I hit and fielded with flair in one of our Roustabout games. The Stallions' pitcher was a lefthander and a good one, but I believed I owned southpaws. I thought I could have hit Koufax or the Yankees' Whitey Ford. This kid had a big curve but it swooped, it didn't break sharply. You could time it. He threw hard enough that his fastball hopped a bit before it got to the plate. He struck me out with it my first time up. My hits were usually line drives, but that hop made my bat strike it just under the ball's center, and it took off down the left field line and soared over the fence. Late in the game I threw out a Stallion runner trying to stretch a double into a triple—the longest throw a right fielder can make. After the game Coach Embry came up to my dad and me and said he wanted me to play for the Antlers the coming spring. I'd never made Daddy prouder.

Coach Embry was also head coach of the football B-team called the Spike Bucks, or just the Spikes. Football was king in that school and town, and I was as indoctrinated as any boy growing up there—you were nobody if you didn't play football. I hadn't gone out for it in junior high, but I told Coach Embry I wanted to play for the B-team. The first day I ran out of the field house toward the practice field I tripped and fell on my face. Cleats. I hated those endless August two-a-days. The coaches' idea of accommodating 106-degree heat was to make us eat salt tablets and drink no water until practice was over. I imagined brains leaking out the ear holes of our helmets.

The varsity's head coach, Pete Silver, was a tall man who favored coaching togs with pants like knickerbockers and the kind of ball cap worn by Ty Cobb. Coach Silver's trap-blocking single wing offense was so obsolete it was revolutionary. The coach had few close friends in town, for he had little interest in men who were not coaches, and he hired them, ran off some of them, or signaled their failure by shuttling them off into school administration. Because he was athletic director, he didn't have to teach or mix with kids who weren't the chosen forty-three. I doubt I ever passed in the focus of that man's gaze.

Black kids and coaches competed on Thursday nights in Antler Canyon for the George Washington Carver Jaguars. Antler Canyon was divided from the stands by a chain link fence and an asphalt walkway where fistfights were always breaking out on Friday nights when the Antlers played. Standing along the fence on the press box side of the field, we'd watch the black kids and the cheering sections of both schools in the stands across the field. Jaguar games got no coverage from the *Standard-Patriot,* so the press box behind us went unclaimed. The stands on home team side were empty except for about a hundred white men who shouted vile slurs at the black players. I guess it got them out of the house.

Across the way the black cheering sections were dancing to both bands, rocking and rolling, throwing up their hands. We laughed at the Carver players who wore mismatched uniforms and hand-me-down pads and slouched in lazy stances. Then a quarterback launched a spiral that carried forty-five yards and a receiver plucked it out of the sky without breaking stride. No way you could laugh at that.

On our B-team, Coach Embry let me try out at tailback—the passer, play caller, and one of two primary running backs in our single wing. After I adjusted my delivery for the shoulder pads, I could throw a football nearly as well as I could throw a baseball. But it was an airy night in Deerinwater if the Antlers or the Spikes threw ten passes a game. And in the wind sprints at the end of practices I could outrun only the blocking backs.

In practice when I got my chances, I leaned over in my stance three yards behind the center, the fullback a step to my right, the blocking back and wingback close behind the right side of our line. In the huddle the tailback called the plays, and when we broke the huddle and jogged to the line of scrimmage, the blocking back yelled a singsong "Down, *set!* One and *two* and . . ." I knew college and pro quarterbacks tried to lure defenses off sides with varied snap counts. One time in a practice huddle I told the blocking back to make it a count of *three*. The left half of our line plunged forward, a linebacker knocked over the center just as his snap of the ball shot over my head, and the linemen and wingback on the right of the center rose from their stances and stared at me, hands on their hip pads. Every coach was screeching his whistle.

Coach Embry demoted me from tailback to right end, which in our system was called the six-end. Ends on our team never got to split wide and learn to be real receivers. The corresponding "six-hole" was the one square yard of hard bare dirt and red ant beds I was supposed to own as a blocker. One day I leaned over in my stance and saw a spike-headed lizard we called a horny toad staring up at me. It didn't act disposed to get out of the way.

And the real world got in the way of my football development. My first October in pads coincided with the Cuban Missile Crisis. One day in the hall between classes I heard a cheerleader wail, "There won't even *be* a State Game." But America and Russia didn't blow up the world, and the football seasons ended with both the Antlers and the Spikes undefeated. The future didn't look bright for a fourth-string six-end on the

B-team. I shouldn't have been out there. I should have been happy just playing baseball. In a further slight Coach Embry put me on the field at safety against the first and second team offenses. "Dummy defense!" he'd yell, and we'd trot out to offer ourselves as animated blocking dummies. More than once I lay down pretending to be hurt because I didn't want to get up and be run over again. Coach Embry pegged me for a malingerer. He was right.

I was surprised and elated when he told me I was still on the baseball team. We played our games in Roughneck Park, which sat at the start of Shiloh Street, the main avenue into our town's black slum. The wind was almost always blowing on those plains, and it carried to our games and practices the stench of a rendering plant. I pinch-hit well for Coach Embry in a couple of early games, and after seeing my throws he put me in the starting lineup at right field. I hoped I had redeemed myself with the man, but against the Grand Prairie Gophers one day I hit a ball almost to the right center field wall. Their center fielder lost it in the sun and collided with the right fielder, and I chugged around the bases for an inside-the-park homer. Except the base umpire called me out. The three runs I had produced were scratched, and because of that we lost the game. Coach Embry came running at me in a rage.

"Did you *try* to do that? You missed touching every goddamn base!"

My summers then consisted of playing baseball, keeping Mom's tomatoes and other garden plants watered, catching city buses downtown, and bringing home armloads of library books. Too soon came my second tour of August two-a-days. Most players on the B-team were sophomores. A few of us were juniors—late-bloomers or discipline problems who might still make the grade. I was two years older than most of the Spikes' starters. The only coach I liked was a native son that people still called by his boyhood nickname, "Don Don" Morris. At practice one day Coach Morris got me aside and astonished me. "You're the best form tackler on the team. You could play linebacker if you'd just jump up in there and do it."

By late October, nearing the end of our eight-game season, we were undefeated and played in Frederick, Oklahoma, against its varsity. They were a fixture in the playoffs up there so they expected us to be a breather. Everyone on the team got to make the trip to that game. Like most scrubs I had been given old high-top cleats I likened to clodhoppers—no wonder

I never hit my stride as a running back. So I bought myself some classy low quarters. But I didn't get the elaborate ankle taping given other ends and running backs. In our locker room Coach Embry looked at me with a grunt of annoyance and told me to put my socks back on. Straddling a bench in the locker room, he gave me quick figure-eight wraps with a cigarette hanging out the side of his mouth, then gestured me on with his thumb.

When we got to Frederick and the visitors' locker room, Coach Morris went outside for another cigarette while Coach Embry gave us our pep talk. He ended it with a grin and a leer. "Now you're going to get you some of those *night fighters.* See if they show up in the lights or if their teeth just shine."

He meant black kids, which startled me. I didn't know coaches talked that way.

In the third quarter we were leading Frederick's Bombers 28-6 when Coach Morris sent me in on offense. We grunted and pushed and made three first downs. Then on third and eight, in the huddle the third-string tailback called a hook pass that might come my way. I dodged a linebacker and spun around hoping for the ball. The tailback threw it toward me but a pass rusher got a hand on the ball as he released it. The ball flopped crazily, and the Bomber safety and I jumped for it. I bumped him with my hip, made the catch, and loped about forty yards before they ran me down. I heard teammates yelling on the sideline and saw Coach Morris pumping his fist at me, but the drive ended with the fullback's fumble two plays later.

The clock was running down and the crowd had cleared out. If I was going to show my promise as a linebacker I'd better hurry up. Then Coach Morris sent me in on punt coverage. It was hard to time a collision if you were running flat-out. But the ball hit the ground and tumbled at the returner, who bobbled it and no doubt wished he'd let it roll. Here was my chance. I never saw the blocker for the Bombers. The black kid didn't clip me. His blindside whack sent me flying in a heap and my helmet came off. I flopped like a fish on land for a bit, thinking I'd never breathe again, but I got myself up. I looked around for the helmet in a daze. The black kid picked up the helmet and, grinning, offered it to me. The image wasn't lost on me. He handed me my head.

CHAPTER 4

My ribs ached as DeWayne Holland and I climbed steps up into the bleachers of the gym for the pep rally. DeWayne was a lean strong tackle who could have played with the young lords on the varsity, but Coach Embry had told him he was through with football because he'd gotten arrested that fall for Drunk in Public. I figured I had no chance of making the varsity. We didn't mind seeing the cheerleaders' legs and satin buff and blue panties, but neither one of us could get exercised about yelling "Two Bits, Four Bits." DeWayne and I kept our seats, drawing looks from other kids. He leaned over and murmured, "Two bitches, four bitches, there you go."

That night the Antlers were playing Arlington for the district title and ticket to the playoffs. The Colts weren't a huge concern. They just tried to look the part, with blue horseshoes painted on their white helmets like their pro namesakes in Baltimore. Our Antlers hadn't missed the playoffs in fourteen years. Suddenly some girl cried out near us and ran from the stands. Kids pressed transistor radios against their ears. DeWayne and I looked around as a louder buzz of voices rose and a couple of girls shrieked. President Kennedy had been shot in Dallas.

The pep rally dissolved and kids walked out of the red brick school with coaches and teachers yelling at us to get back inside. A dry cold front blew through town right after Walter Cronkite said the president was dead. The weather dropped thirty degrees the first hour and kept falling all day. DeWayne had use of his dad's pickup—his old man had a hangover and had taken a sick day off from the Cosden refinery. We consumed greasy burgers at a drive-in and rode around all afternoon, with DeWayne banging the dash, trying to make the heater work. We heard on KDWT that the school superintendent and Coach Silver said the game had to go on as scheduled that night. If not, the playoffs would be all out of whack.

DeWayne and I went to the game because we didn't know what else to do with ourselves. Antler Canyon was dug into a red clay bluff on the north side of town. A club of girls called the Goal Post Decorators always wrapped the uprights with crepe paper in our colors, buff and blue, and on the other goalpost the colors of the visiting teams. That night they had wrapped both goalposts in black crepe paper, and the streamers were snapping straight out in the frigid gale. The crowd would react to a play but then fall into a hush until there was another snap. The Antlers lost and missed the playoffs for the first time since 1949.

A norther's wind never seemed to blow quite so cold.

Two mornings later, Brother Borbino didn't say a word about the assassination. He hated Kennedy so much. In leading the prayer before the sermon, Chaplain Dingus defied him and prayed for the president's soul and his family. In my song leading I had started doing something with my right hand, trying to speed things along. I raised my index finger and then I swung my arm with a quiet snap of my fingers. It was a Sinatra affect, but I lifted it from Dion DiMucci's cool manner of singing "Runaround Sue" on *American Bandstand.*

Brother Borbino drew his sermon from the passage in Acts about how Saul the fanatic persecutor of Christians became the apostle Paul. No one came down the aisles as I led the invitation hymn, which kind of surprised me. I had listened to his sermon for a change, and it moved me, which added to my confusion. After communion trays and donation baskets were passed along the pews, I led "Blest Be the Tie that Binds." I loosened my tie and was having some charitable thoughts about the man. But then the preachers told me to come into a classroom, where Brother Borbino tore into me.

"You blasphemed the house of the Lord this morning."

"Beg your pardon? Everybody sounded good to me. Into it, you know."

"It wasn't the quality of the singing," Chaplain Dingus allowed in a kinder tone. "It was the way you led 'Leaning on the Everlasting Arms.'"

"This church is no juke joint on the Mississippi River," Brother Borbino piled on. "You can't snap your fingers leading our congregation in joyous noise unto the Lord. It was shameful. It's percussion. God's church does not allow musical instruments in our worship because no scripture in the New Testament supports it."

The hothead in me took over. "Snapping my fingers where nobody can hear it is an instrument? Sir, you want body percussion, this here's called the hambone." It was one of my new specialties. When I got rolling with it, I was a one-man rhythm section, slapping my thighs and chest and my open jaws, making popping sounds in the cavern of my mouth.

"Stop that, young man!" he snapped. "You're an inveterate sinner, and you've been given notice. Don't ever do that again." He turned on his heel and walked off.

The chaplain put his hand on my shoulder. "Don't let this get you down. You were experimenting. Just having fun."

"Sir, I don't know what to call you."

The chaplain smiled. "Call me Paul."

That set me back a beat, thinking of Brother Borbino's harangue about the apostle Luke. "Chaplain Paul, what does 'inveterate' mean?"

"Habitual. Incorrigible. You're not an inveterate sinner."

"Well, sir, I didn't volunteer for this job. I was drafted. Only I can quit this anytime I want."

"Of course you can," the captain said. "But you're gifted. Depriving these brethren and sisters of that gift would be a shame. And it wouldn't be a service to the Lord."

I got home and turned on the TV set, eager for the escape of a Dallas Cowboy game. All three channels showed a jammed crowd of reporters and photographers in some dark basement. Then a cop in a Stetson moved along a balding, handcuffed little man who needed a shave. On live TV Jack Ruby jumped out wearing a fedora and shot Lee Harvey Oswald right below his diaphragm. He let out a groan I can hear all these years later.

The killings cast a pall on Christmas, and all the churchgoing was getting me down. Christmas couldn't be mentioned in our church because no scripture said Jesus was born on December the 25th. One afternoon I was watching a *Lassie* program on TV. The collie and his boy pal had come upon a sleigh overturned in a snow bank. The bearded fat man trapped under it was, of course, Santa Claus. An escape route dawned on me.

The Broadman Hymnal had all the Christmas songs in it. After Brother Borbino's sermon the next Sunday I took over the pulpit and said I'd changed my mind about the song page numbers I had posted. I led them through "O Little Town of Bethlehem," "Silent Night," and my favorite, "O Holy Night." I could see Brother Borbino holding himself back from storming up and yanking the mike away from me. But people were singing, singing.

My stunt did the trick. I was the song leader no more. Chaplain Dingus approached me with a smile. "Nice work. That was your *Schwanengesang.*"

"Sir?" I said.

"Swan song. The expression originated with Franz Schubert's last seven songs. Great composer. Look him up."

CHAPTER 5

KENNY

He knew who his real dad was because they lived just a few blocks away from each other in a working-class shabby part of Jacksonville. Kenny and the man whose last name was Florence would see each other out and about on the streets. They'd nod, and that was the extent of their relationship. It didn't occur to Kenny to try to make any more of it. Neither did his dad. Kenny's mother Ruth never talked about him. Why should their son?

Ruth's mother had died when she was small, and she was brought up by her mother's sister Mary. The Florence boy was sixteen and Ruth was fifteen when they got her pregnant. Aunt Mary was a large, jovial woman with a booming laugh who went to church every Sunday, didn't take guff off anybody, and she didn't raise her niece for such a thing to happen. Ruth's most difficult obstacle was overcoming her shame. She scraped along at low-paying short-lived jobs, helping clean people's houses and the like, but in her twenties, she got hired as the activities director at Jacksonville's hospital. She worked long hours, making the best of having that job, so Kenny was mostly raised by his great aunt Mary.

Half the kids in that neighborhood called her Aunt Mary at one time or another. She raised and doted on Kenny just as she had his mother. When he was not quite four, Ruth had started dating a man named John Norton. She had known him since first remembering. They married and changed Kenny's last name to Norton. John formally adopted him. For a long time that didn't alter day-to-day growing up too much for Kenny. Pop was always on the run from his boyhood of poverty. He had to quit school in the worst of the Depression and at first became a shoe-shine boy. He had seven brothers and sisters, and there were that many mouths to feed and pairs of growing feet that needed shoes. Pop said he thought about trying his luck in Chicago but feared he might lose his way there, so he studied and got a high school equivalency certificate because he knew that would help him find work. He was the first black man hired by Jacksonville's fire department, and he passed a written civil service test to qualify. Pop would shovel and haul coal, sweep out a barbershop, and drive a fire truck, all in the same day. Kenny was closer to Aunt Mary than either parent because he was around her more. Because of her, he said the rest of his life he thought the world owed him a breakfast of Cheerios, milk, and sliced bananas.

Jacksonville, Illinois, was a history-rich town of about twenty thousand people. One of its native sons was Stephen Douglas, the Northern Democrat lawyer who was the other contestant in the seven debates that got Springfield's gangly Republican lawyer Abraham Lincoln on the road to being elected president. History teachers at Jacksonville's high school found it hard to explain how debates between two Illinois lawyers who lived in small towns thirty-five miles apart spawned a national election in which they were the nominees of their parties. In any case Lincoln's election ensured the Civil War.

Another Jacksonville man was an abolitionist who owned a prosperous farm that was a hub of the Underground Railroad. Runaway slaves tracked by bloodhounds were escorted by white men across two creeks and through a system of tunnels under the town to temporary safety in orchards on the Huffaker Farm. A generation later another native son, William Jennings Bryan, made his famous youthful speech about not being crucified on a cross of gold. His passionate call was for a monetary system based on plentiful silver mined out West. He thought devalued money would help people working for wages. Bryan was nominated by the Democrats for president three times and lost every race. Those were all white men, of course. The most prominent black man to come out of Jacksonville was Kenny Norton, but there were speed bumps along the way.

John was a no-nonsense dad who quelled acts of rebellion with use or threats of his belt. The worst one happened when an uncle dozed off in a nap in his house one day and Kenny found his pistol in a drawer. He took the gun, and on the pews at church he was showing it off to friends and letting them handle it. One boy told his own dad, a Monday-morning phone call ensued, and Pop's rage and belt were waiting for Kenny when he got home from school that afternoon. Kenny: "I thought he was going to whip me half to death."

He was prone to daredevil stunts like jumping on the rear of a garbage truck and hanging on as the driver raced sixty miles an hour to the day's last haul at the city dump. The owner of a drugstore caught him trying to steal the first issue of *Playboy* with Marilyn Monroe on the cover. Pop was furious at having to plead with the white pharmacist not to have Kenny arrested for shoplifting. Kenny's lies about how it happened were so elaborate that Pop would have laughed if not for the seriousness of the matter.

John Norton stood five-feet-seven and then weighed about 130 pounds. By the time Kenny was fifteen he was five-eleven and weighed 160. On Pop's nights off from the fire department Ruth always made them supper. One of those evenings the phone rang just as they were sitting down, and Ruth had to attend to some matter at the hospital. She told them to go ahead and not let the food get cold. Kenny was in a testy mood, and he started smart-talking his dad. "You'd better cool off, boy," said Pop.

"Plan to. I'm gonna be so cool I'll relieve myself of this town and make something of myself. Not like you."

Pop flung his glass of iced tea in Kenny's face. Kenny threw his glass of tea right back. Ruth saw none of this. She was just outraged to get off the phone and find what they'd done to her roast beef and potatoes and left her a floor to mop.

Pop started to backhand Kenny but caught himself. Kenny jumped up, knocking his chair over in a clatter, and said, "Let's settle this in the yard, little man."

Pop wiped off his face with a dish towel, picked up the chair and set it back upright, went through a little room where he kept his toolbox, and kicked the screen door open, sending an orange cat running. As soon as they squared off Kenny started having second thoughts. Pop said, "Are you sure you want to do this?"

Kenny swallowed and said, "Yes, sir."

"Then raise your hands."

Kenny raised them and closed them into fists but made no move.

Pop shot a quick right between them and clipped him on the jaw. Dumped on the seat of his jeans, Kenny was at first stunned by how much the punch from that little man hurt. Then he continued to sit on the grass and hung his head, ashamed. Pop stuck out his hand to help him up and said quietly, "Come on, son. Let's go inside."

One night the firemen on Pop's truck were called out for a blaze that roared up through a two-story house. If there had been enough margin of soil around the house, they would have just let it burn itself down. But other homes were built too close. The crew was inside, coughing from the smoke and braced against the heat, when a support beam of the second floor collapsed on Pop and brought some roof down with it. When the others freed and hauled him out, he had second- and third-degree burns on his right leg. The knee, fibula, and tibia were crushed, and infection from the burns could bring on sepsis or gangrene and kill him. Surgeons at the hospital amputated John's leg above the knee.

Pop refused to stay in the wheelchair the hospital provided. It was a source of constant frustration anyway because doors weren't cut wide enough to allow the thing through. He learned to get around on crutches, then needed just one crutch, then a sturdy cane, and funds raised at church paid for his prosthesis. With wonder he told Kenny about the pain he felt in the lower leg and foot that were no longer there, but he didn't whine about being a cripple. He couldn't be a fireman but he had to work. Jacksonville came through for him because of the way he was hurt. He got hired as a dispatcher for the police department. Kenny gained an admiration of Pop that ran deep, but he was caught up in himself.

As Kenny was coming into his teens, Jacksonville's school board accepted the Supreme Court ruling that outlawed segregation in the schools, which benefitted its athletic teams. Kenny was an exceptional athlete, but he knew blacks couldn't enter the town's few restaurants and hotels unless they came in the back to change the bedclothes or work in the kitchens. When he went to see his first movie, *High Noon* starring Gary Cooper and Grace Kelly, an usher at the town's theater pointed him to the balcony reserved for blacks.

His feats were almost legendary in the town, true or not. He could walk on his hands the length of a football field. He could throw a baseball ninety miles an hour. By the time he reached the Crimson varsities he was six-three and weighed 195 pounds. His height and physique were the gifts, the only gifts, of his birth father. A high school coach named Al Rosenberger said Kenny was the best athlete he'd ever seen. Coach Al was an assistant coach in football and the head coach of the track team. Jacksonville was a football powerhouse in its mid-sized enrollment division. The Crimsons went undefeated and won state championships during Kenny's sophomore and senior seasons on the varsity. He was big, tall, fast, and had long arms. He was a ferocious pass rusher and tackler, and he was also the Crimsons' star running back. Coach Al told him that if he'd lower his helmet and shoulders a little carrying the ball, he could be the next Jim Brown. He said, "Coach, I like to see where I'm going, and what's coming at me."

He was breaking sixty-yard runs and pulling away from smaller kids trying to chase him down. How could you coach that? Voted all-state on defense after his senior season, Kenny played forward on the basketball team, and the spring brought on his real love, track and field. He came within a second and a half of the national record cruising over the 180-yard low hurdles, and he kept breaking his own records flinging the discus.

At the end of that season they had a one-on-one meet against Eisenhower High in Decatur, a bigger school and town. Coach Al entered him in the low hurdles, the 100, 220, and 400-yard sprints, both relays, and three field events. They won six of the nine events the coach entered him in. Eisenhower's track coach filed a protest with the muckety-mucks in the state capital, Springfield, on grounds of unfair competition. They instated a "Norton Rule" that limited all athletes to four events in any track meet, and the rule stayed on the books under that name. Coach Al thought the ruling might have gone his way if Kenny hadn't jogged up to the high jump pit and cleared the bar, winning the meet for the Crimsons, without bothering to shed his sweat pants.

CHAPTER 5

The sports editor of the *Journal-Courier* kept up a stream of news tips and rumors about the parade of collegiate recruiters coming to Jacksonville to court Kenny and John and Ruth Norton. It came as a surprise when Kenny signed with Northeast Missouri State, which had a good small-college football program, but still. Coach Al thought for all his bravura, he didn't want to get too far away from home. Jacksonville and Kirksville, Missouri, were just 160 miles apart, and they were about the same unthreatening size.

Kenny got to the college campus and saw dozens of pretty girls all around him.

The year was 1961, Missouri had been a bloody border state in the Civil War, and Kenny stirred resentment on the Bulldog squad with his cocky self-assurance chatting up white girls. He blew off classes and dated and partied every night he could. The head football coach didn't have scholarships to burn, and he decided Kenny was a bust.

He already knew his grades were going to be a disaster when he went home for the Christmas holidays. One night, Coach Al took Kenny out for hamburgers at a Sonic drive-in. That way they could talk in privacy. "You're having the time of your life and good for you," the coach said. "But you're screwing up this deal, kid. When you get back over there, you've got to go to class and make an effort. You're not dumb. It's a liberal arts college, for heaven sakes. You could be somewhere they're loading you down with math and languages."

Kenny wagged his head and started to explain. "That coach they've got "

"Doesn't matter," Coach Al interrupted. "He's the coach *you've* got. You'd better play for him like you're able in spring training. If you do those two things, you can turn this around and go on having all that fun. If you don't, you'll be right back here in Jacksonville."

Kenny listened and nodded through the chewing out, but his eyes and thoughts were on the girls who brought out the orders on roller skates. They had on thick jackets and a couple wore earmuffs. Their breath fogged when they exhaled. But they wore shorts and didn't get the jobs if they weren't in trim and good condition. Shades of brown or white, it didn't matter to him. All in all, that reprimand just made him horny.

His grades improved, but spring training didn't raise his standing with the Bulldogs' head coach. Back in Jacksonville that summer, he hated being in the same bedroom, the same town. He went back to the college in August, but no matter how hard he tried, he couldn't please that head coach. Two-a-days and the first three games of the season passed. One afternoon in front of the rest of the varsity, the coach got all over Kenny for missing a tackle and told him to start running laps. Kenny threw his helmet on the ground and told the coach, "You're a no-account peckerwood."

That was the end of his college football, and the coach got his scholarship back. Kenny rode the bus home to Jacksonville sure he'd made a mistake. He should have just run the laps and told the coach why he was missing those tackles. After a few months Pop blew up at him. "I'm tired of you sleeping to noon, running around in your underwear, and doing nothing but talking to girls on the phone. If you're going to live here, you can start paying rent. Either get a job, find a way to get back in school, or join the service."

Coach Al told him the marines would make a man out of him, so he took that advice and enlisted for four years. Aunt Mary's diabetes and weight brought on congestive heart failure, and she died in the hospital with Ruth holding her hands. No way Kenny was going to miss Aunt Mary's funeral, so he missed his obligation to get on a bus with an envelope containing his orders to Parris Island, South Carolina. Pop sighed and explained the situation to the marine recruiter. "He shoulda let me know before he went to the funeral," the sergeant grumbled, but he arranged a three-month delay in the orders.

Because he was big and athletic and the debacle at college had taught him to keep his mouth shut, the DI's at Parris Island gave Kenny a fairly easy ride. After a month of infantry training at Camp Lejeune, North Carolina, Kenny chose to pass up his two-week leave and keep the airfare money. The marines routed him on to Pensacola, Florida, where they taught him to be a field radio operator. After that, he got orders back to Lejeune and figured he was soon bound for Vietnam. Then he found out that Lejeune had a football team that competed against other service teams and small colleges. He went to see the coach, a master sergeant, who asked Kenny what he wanted to play. Football had made him tired of trying to fight off blockers and make tackles. "Halfback," he said. The next Jim Brown.

The coach said, "Well, we run the I formation, so there's only one running back on the field at a time. But you've got the size and I've already called your coach, and he told me about your speed. You can at least give us depth." The season got along toward the end, and Kenny gained the team's most yardage. The starting running back was a white captain who had fair moves but was smaller than Kenny and had nowhere near his speed. The coach cow-towed to him because of his rank. Kenny and the captain disliked each other from the start.

On offensive drills one afternoon Kenny was the running back and the captain took his turn on defense at cornerback. The quarterback called a roll-out that was a fake pass and had Kenny kicking out on the captain. Kenny lowered his helmet and flattened him. The captain jumped up and said, "You really think you're hot shit, don't you, nigger?"

"No, sir. I think you're an asshole."

The coach and master sergeant yelled, "Hold it right there, Norton!"

Kenny said, "I don't need this, coach. Running him up to command for calling me that or kicking his ass ain't gonna change a thing. He'll still be an asshole."

He gave his helmet a heave of about thirty yards and stomped off the field. By the time he got to the locker room he was thinking, "This is getting to be a pattern. I just gave up all those nice steaks at chow and punched my ticket to Vietnam."

An old retired jarhead called Pappy hung around the athletic complex. He saw Kenny throwing pads and cleats in his locker and asked him what was going on. Kenny said in disgust, "I just quit marine football."

"Well," Pappy said, "I just got named the boxing coach. You interested?"

CHAPTER 6

Mom was exasperated by my behavior at church and only Christmas prevented a major blow-up between us. After the holidays, my best friend Chuck Mercer was back in town and school after a summer and fall semester away. He had been taking liberties with a country club girl and her father called Chuck's mom while drunk and said, "I'll blow his head off if I see him around here again." Instead of calling the police on a belligerent drunk, Mrs. Mercer borrowed and dipped far enough into their savings to ship him off for spring and summer semesters to a military school in Roswell, New Mexico. If she thought a dose of military discipline would change him, she was wrong. He returned to us the same Chuck, only now he had a blond streak of peroxide swept back with one of his ducktails. And he came back to us a boxer.

He told DeWayne and me that he'd been reading about the Boxer Rebellion in China. He said it was started by a secret organization that liked to kill Europeans and Americans, especially missionaries. It was called the Society of Righteous and Harmonious Fists. They once pinned down marines that were trying to keep them from overrunning the US embassy. Some thought their power made them immune to bullets, which didn't work out too well for them. Chuck wanted to fight in that winter's Golden Gloves, and DeWayne was game for it, too. I tagged along.

CHAPTER 6

The GI Forum gym where Chuck, Dewayne, and I trained was the old clubhouse of Roughneck Park. I told my folks that I had signed up to play basketball for First Presbyterian in a youth league. Mom stared at me and I said, "Why didn't our church sponsor a team? It doesn't have anything to do with religion. We don't pray before tip-off or things like that. They just buy us some jerseys and basketballs for practice."

"Well," she warned, "if you bring home a bad report card . . . "

We ran laps around the darkened ballpark and banged the heavy bags until we were tired, and I thought that was fun, but I never sparred anyone. The most we learned was not from the laconic coach, Mr. Guerrero, who missed a lot of sessions because we were his excuse to escape the house for poker games, but from two small, fast Latino kids, or Mexicans as we called them lightly in those days, who were good enough to enter the open division and go on to the state tournament in Fort Worth.

The fighters wore no helmets or padded groin protectors in our tourneys, only a jockstrap and shorts of the team's colors and whatever shoes they thought would not skid on the canvas. I was certain I couldn't go through with it. You were practically naked with a howling mob all around you. I decided I would fake a broken hand. Yet Coach Morris had told me I had a chance to be invited to varsity spring training. I was "on the margin." That went back and forth in my mind. Maybe this could help me overcome my fear in football. And I kept failing to fake the hand injury that would get me out of boxing.

I lollygagged until I thought I couldn't back out. I forged Daddy's signature on a release Mr. Guerrero handed out. Our black trunks had white trim and a logo of the GI Forum. I had bought a pair of low-quarter red shoes made for running indoor track. With the white socks and red shoes, I didn't mind the look of myself shadow-boxing in front of a mirror at the gym. Mr. Guerrero gave me a mouthpiece that I boiled soft and then while it was still warm, I chomped down to mold it to my teeth. Mom heard the bang of me putting her saucepan back in the cabinet and asked me what I was doing. "Just boiled an egg," I said as she arrived, trying to make my upper lip conceal the mouthpiece.

She cocked her head and said, "Well, where is it?"

"I *mum mum* ate it."

She glanced at the garbage can for the shells and sighed. Some days I was a good liar and some days I was not.

The night the Gloves began, Mom made three of my favorites for supper—chicken and dumplings, speckled lima beans, and banana pudding. I ate just enough not to alert and alarm her with my nausea, then I loaded my cloth sack and said I was off to play basketball. "Done your homework?" she asked.

"Yes, ma'am. Knowing the game was tonight."

"Who are you playing?"

"First Methodist."

"Do I know any of these boys?"

"No. May have heard me mention them. Just some guys at school."

"I'd like to see you in your uniform," she said, smiling. "I hope you launder them. I never see them on the clothesline."

"They have a laundry room and do that, too. Like at school."

"I thought you said they just gave you uniforms and basketballs."

Why did she make me lie over such small matters?

"Anyway, have fun," she said. "Hope you win."

What happens if I win? To bring home the trophy in my Novice weight division I'd have to win three fights on three consecutive nights. I couldn't make up enough lies to cover that. I was throwing the fight before it began. I just hoped I wasn't humiliated. I feared the chairs more than the licking I was going to take. In the tournaments a row of two metal folding chairs was lined up angling away from a corner post. Several fights before yours began, you had to sit beside your opponent and move up chairs as each prior fight ended. What was the point of that? What could you talk about? Middleweight, they classified me. What that meant to me was some kid that stood six-one and weighed 155 pounds. Skinny and weak. Skin the color of milk and pimples on my back.

I walked down the street some distance because Mom would recognize the noise of Chuck's Cushman Eagle, the vehicle of choice if you didn't have a car. Another norther had blown through that day, and I was shivering on back of the scooter by the time we reached the Boys' Club. The number of police cars startled me.

I understood what was going on when we showed our passes and walked in to look for DeWayne and the other GI Forum fighters. It would be years before black kids were allowed to compete in the Deerinwater Golden Gloves. Pressured by city fathers trying to make peace with the commanding general at Allred Field, the Boys' Club's directors had ruled that airmen could compete in the tournament as long as they were not Negroes or of Asian descent, could prove they were the proper age, disclosed any past boxing experience, and competed for a team coached by officers or sergeants. Off the record the directors said they feared lawsuits, which of course meant they wanted the record spread all over town. If something bad happened, it wasn't their fault.

For the biggest tournament of the year, the invaders and occupiers had a cheering section up against one corner of the rafters that was Air Force blue. And though they observed safety in numbers, they bought sodas and popcorn at the concession stands. I saw some of the most feared hooligans in town roaming the floor. I had never seen so many cops in one place. It was a powder keg waiting for one flip of a cigarette butt.

I was stunned to see that sharing ringside with the judges was a broadcast duo who called Antler football games from the KDWT radio station. In a room smelling of an over-chlorinated swimming pool, Chuck, DeWayne, and I changed and locked up our street clothes, shoes, and wallets. DeWayne had come with his dad, who was eager to see his boy slug somebody. Chuck was talkative and in a fine mood. "Remember who we are—the Society of Righteous and Harmonious Fists." While the spectators wore Air Force blue, I watched to see if any of their boxers dared show up in Air Force uniforms, and none did. There had been fights in the locker rooms in past years, and wanting none of that this year, the Boys' Club's directors had paid an off-duty cop to sit in a corner reading a paperback.

A little space behind the rafters was cleared for us to loosen up. Chuck was a welterweight, and DeWayne was a small heavyweight. DeWayne shook his head and said, "Don't need it. I'm ready." He had worked himself into an ugly mood, possibly a good idea.

In the workout space Chuck and I were moving around, shadow boxing, flicking jabs at each other's wrapped hands, when someone tapped my shoulder. It was Darrell. He had tipped the bill of his airman's cap back and was chewing gum.

"Hey, *bruddah* in law, I just wanted to say good luck."

Other fighters and the cop perched on the folding chair eyed us. It occurred to me Darrell was drunk. "Thanks. Listen, I'm kind of busy."

When the Pee Wees were done, the crowd got noisier. Our coach came for Chuck, and off they went in the corridor of shoulders toward the blazing light. Novices fought two-minute rounds, and the ref was stopping a lot of mismatches, so things sped along. Mr. Guerrero came for me and laced on my gloves, securing them with two tight wraps and an ex-sailor's command of knots. He led me into light so harsh it made me think of the apostle Paul on the road to Damascus. Two opposing corner poles were fitted with red and blue light bulbs that announced the judges' decisions. I took a chair beside a fighter who had a great deal of hair on his chest and had broken a sweat warming up. I glanced and saw a strong-looking jaw and shadow of dark beard. He probably had to shave every day. I felt as pale, naked, and ugly as a possum. Mr. Guerrero said, "All right, you brought your mouthpiece. Hang on to it, and don't let it get dirty. When the fight starts don't get tired and spit it out. They'll let you fight without one but it's not a good idea."

"He won't need it long," said the airman in the other chair.

The coach snorted and walked off, leaving that kind of talk to me. I left my gloved hands in my lap, holding onto the mouthpiece. "Haid Shelton," I said.

"Tony Pereira," he answered with a nod.

"You from around here?"

He laughed and sneered. "Shit, no. Taunton, Mass. See, I'm Portuguese. Grandparents came to this country. My mom wanted to change our name to Perry. The old man said, 'No chance.' He's a proud man. Got a boat and a lot of lobster pots."

Trying to visualize a lobster pot, I said, "I'm Scotch Irish. Maybe some Comanche. One of my grannies was born in Oklahoma when it was still Indian Territory." That last was bullshit, but I thought maybe Pereira had heard of the dread Comanches.

He said, "Don't try to buddy up to me, pal. I don't care about you or your granny." If he was trying to intimidate me, he was doing a fine job.

"You mind if I ask how old you are?" I said.

"Twenty-one. You?"

"Eighteen." He gave me a glance of contempt.

I said, "Don't think you have to go easy on me."

"Don't worry." Pereira changed the subject. "I hate Texas. After I'd done basic at Lackland in San Antone, I said get me somewhere that don't feel like a frigging blast furnace. All the places they could have sent me, they picked this asshole of the earth. They got whirlwinds here composed of dirt. Wrote my girlfriend about it. I've seen 'em."

Above us in the ring, a kid with a toad face was walking through everything Chuck was throwing. As the fight wore on, I winced and raised my hands like I was in there with him and shouted a couple of times. A Gloves official frowned and told me to cut it out.

"That's my best friend," I told Pereira, who shrugged.

The ref raised the ugly kid's hand, and Chuck came through the ropes and down in a hurry, his face aflame from the beating he'd taken. He's also my ride, I thought. I hope he doesn't tear out of here and leave me stranded.

"That's gonna be you," said Pereira.

"Keep talking, flyboy, maybe you'll start to believe it."

He grinned. "There you go. Let's give 'em a show."

Mr. Guerrero led me up the steps and I stepped through the ropes, gaping at the crowd. The blue-clad airmen were on their feet and cheering Pereira, who danced around and rolled his shoulders like a pro. Boxes of popcorn and cups of ice and soda pop were being hurled at the section of blue uniforms. The phalanx of cops rushed toward the crowd's hot spot. I saw a Deerinwater thug handcuffed. The bell rang.

Two long minutes later I sat on the blue corner stool in bad need of the water Mr. Guerrero poured in my mouth. "Okay, Shelton," he said, "you waltzed out there like a fairy and got the shit beat out of you. Pardon my French. You forgot everything and windmilled when you did anything. He oughta be fighting Open division but he's not. You gonna quit and cry?"

"No, sir."

"All right. You gotta do better right away or the ref's gonna stop it. You've got a long left arm that's connected to a fist. Lock your elbow and wrist, it's called a jab. It's your best defense, use it. Straight punches, lefts and rights, nothing fancy. This guy's not as good as he thinks he is. Get your legs under your punches, back him up. They score it more or less by rounds. You're down one to nothing. But you're still in the fight. If you want to be."

Two more minutes later, the Deerinwater fight fans were shouting down the airmen. "Hey, not bad," said Mr. Guerrero. "Look at that guy. He didn't get that nosebleed from the altitude. You won that round. You're spearing him with that jab, but you telegraph your right. He starts doing that cute stuff, switching his feet, now he's right-handed, now he's left. You don't understand. Look, when he shuffles like you're looking at a mirror, that's when he's switched to southpaw. When he does that, bomb him with that right hand. I mean bomb him. Every time he wiggles." He put my mouthpiece in. "Try and relax."

Pereira and I touched gloves and started trading long-range. I was getting belted, too, but I had him backed up and cornered on the ropes at the end. The bell rang with the crowd bellowing and standing up. We collapsed against each other to keep from falling down. I heard one of the radio announcers yelling, "Kickapoo County, what a fight!"

Yanking off my gloves, Mr. Guerrero yelled, "You mighta won that!"

Gasping, I looked up and saw that standing on the ring apron with him was my brother-in-law Darrell. Some dog's always going to come along and piss on the flowers.

The ref called us to center ring and held my right glove and Pereira's left. The red light came on and the ref raised the airman's hand. A loud and ongoing chorus of boos resonated in the hall. "Tough kid, Tex, you're a tough kid," said the Portuguese. He wiped some blood from his nose on a hand wrap.

"Want to tell you . . . " I began, then had to gulp more air.

"Yeah?"

"I envy you that ocean. I aim to see one someday and eat me a lobster."

As I stepped out through the ropes, Darrell put his arm around my shoulders and said close to my ear, "First time you ever impressed me." He hefted my hand to the crowd then raised his own. Jeers came our way.

On the floor were street fighters and jailbirds of my slight acquaintance. "You won that fight," one said. "You had him out on his feet the last thirty seconds."

"You got robbed," another thug agreed. "Those flyboys thought their guy's the world *champeen.* But who's the one that got up there with you on the ring?"

"He's a moron. Some people in my family sort of know him."

Chuck was in a good mood, considering the beating he'd taken. DeWayne was a heavyweight, but tipped the scales at a modest 185. His opponent was fat and ill-trained, but even an ill-trained novice can land a serious haymaker if he weighs 210. DeWayne walked around rubber-legged after looking great the first thirty seconds. Chuck and I eyed the crowd and decided to console DeWayne the next morning at school. Fights were breaking out everywhere. Cushman Eagle, do your stuff.

CHAPTER 7

"Haid, wake up," my mother said. "Your eggs are ready."

That morning more than ever, I wished she would work a few minutes in between those sentences. I noticed some traces of blood on my pillowcase, pulled a T-shirt over my pajama bottoms, and gimped into the kitchen.

Mom's mouth was a grim tight line. "Look at you," she began. "I've cringed every time I've seen a baseball zoom by your head. I've seen you so sore from football I had to pull you out of bed. But this . . . this was disgusting."

"I'm sorry, Mom," I shot back, wondering how she knew, since Chuck and I had ridden around in the cold jabbering about our fights, and my parents were asleep when I came in the back door, crawled in bed, and turned out the light, still replaying the bout over and over in my mind. "The crowd liked me. They were cheering me. But I'll never do it again. If they'd said I won, I would have forfeited tonight. That make you happy?"

Daddy was at the dinette table wearing one of his undershirts with no sleeves and a deep cut for the neck. "Don't talk to your mother like that," he growled.

"Of all the ways to get your name in the newspaper," she continued. "Like opening it one morning and seeing what Joey Carrigan did to Eldon and Lizzie."

Daddy frowned. "Hold on. You're talking about that kid at your church? There's a world of difference between competing in a refereed boxing match and sticking a gun in the face of somebody who's just operating a cash register."

"I knew you'd take up for him," she said.

"I'm in the paper?"

Wary of a row, Daddy grumbled, "What if you'd really gotten hurt?"

"We'd have been paying hospital bills," Mom said.

"No, you never," I said. "The refs stop fights too fast lots of times."

Daddy said, "I probably could have gotten off to come see you. I was making my last round at the catalytic unit when Elmer come running with one of those little radios upside his head. Saying, 'Booger Red, you gotta hear this.' I didn't know they put the Golden Gloves on the radio. Heck of a way for a dad to find out."

"I didn't know that either. The radio was a complete surprise to me."

Mom threw a wet dishrag on the table with a splat and left the kitchen. Daddy lowered his voice and said, "We probably ought not to talk about it when she's close around."

Chuck rolled up on his Cushman Eagle with a bag of books slung across his lap and a classic black eye on the right side of his face. I had some abrasions and a swollen lip. Though it was still cold it was a pretty morning, and I told him I'd walk. Chuck grinned, yanked the gearshift in low, and took off like he was riding a Harley.

There were two thousand kids in that high school, and until that day the only ones who didn't seem to look past me in the halls were a handful of friends and the few who paid any attention to the baseball team. In just eight minutes I had ceased being a nobody. I lost the fight but it won me a reputation. Thugs trailed along complaining that I won the fight. "Can't get off slow in a three-round fight," I said, looking for an algebra book in my locker.

One said, "Why don't you skip lunch and come to the smoking lounge?" It was a rectangle of brick walls with a concrete floor but open to the sky. They could smoke in there and smoke they did. "Like to but

I can't," I lied. "Gotta take care of my wind."

In sixth period Don Don Morris called me in his office and told me to sit down. "I heard about your boxing match," he said. "You going to keep on doing that?"

"No, sir. Too much grief at home."

The coach grinned and put his feet on his desk. "Fella has to factor that in. But listen, Coach Miles was there last night."

"He was?" Coach Miles was the defensive coach of the Antler varsity.

"Oh, yeah, he loves the fights. Talks about them all the time. He's high on that loudmouth Cassius Clay. Don't know why, but he is. Anyway, Coach saw your fight, and he liked what he saw."

A rush of excitement surged through me. "He did? I'm flattered."

The coach waved that off. "You know what he liked? It wasn't your skill so much. Or the mean streak, we'd seen that before. The only time we saw your potential was when you got mad in practice. You'd do something that made us give you another look. But you can't play football that way. You can't get mad, then calm down, and then get mad again every play. You stay in control. You find out it's fun."

He went on, "Think about it, son. That fight won you a ticket to spring training in a program that's won four state championships in the last seven years. Losing district this year was an embarrassment. Put on a few pounds, get a good manual labor job this summer, run a lot, you might even start."

I said, "When does spring training start? I mean, the baseball . . ."

"Don't worry your bruised little head. The spring game's played when the baseball team starts district play. There are seven other schools in our district and you play them twice. You'll miss the early games, but I guarantee you Coach Silver is not going to let you lose your place on the baseball team."

At school I put up my bat and glove and started lifting weights for football spring training. My jubilation lasted two weeks. At Allred Field Darrell Jaines was learning a new job skill. A group of airmen were climbing telephone poles using rigs over their combat boots that had spurs pointing inward that looked like halves of railroad spikes. They weren't told if they were being trained to cut wires or string them. They just had to climb poles.

When Darrell was fifteen feet up on an untethered climb, his left spur skidded off a knot in the wood. That boot and spur swung loose, he tried to clutch the pole, but there was nothing to grab, and as the other spur was coming loose, he shoved outward with his hands. That resulted in a partial back flip that turned him upside down. He landed with a crack at the feet of a sergeant and the other climbers.

I disliked the guy but didn't hate him. I wouldn't wish a broken neck on anyone. But the consequences in my life were staggering. Mom had never driven a car. Virginia didn't know how to drive either. She and Mom agreed that she was obliged to be at Darrell's bedside and comfort him every single day. And Virginia couldn't ride an Allred Field bus surrounded by a bunch of shaved-head recruits.

I had a driver's license, though Daddy never let me drive the family's '56 Mercury after the day we went practicing for the state's driving test. I told him I was going to make a quick stop and did it so expertly it flung him against the dashboard. Daddy tried to get out of this crisis with the alibi of his shift work. Under intense pressure, he told me I'd have to drive my sister in her husband's station wagon to the Air Force hospital every day after school, on Saturday, and after Sunday church. Three months, the rest of the whole spring semester.

I didn't help my case by making calm suggestions of other ways Virginia might get her rides and fulfill her duty as a wife. I jumped up and down, almost caved in the grate of the floor furnace. Unable to shout us all down, Daddy was so dismayed to see and hear his family turned into a howling mob that he went for a drive with a front door slam so hard it knocked one of Mom's favorite antiques, a glass figurine, off a shelf and it shattered.

So much for varsity spring training, and in a way alive with malice, Coach Embry told me that some fine outfielders and hitters were coming up through the grades, and because I was skipping my junior season, I had lost my place on the baseball team. I cornered Coach Morris in his office and said the rumors I backed out of football due to fear or laziness were just not true. I explained it all and reminded my favorite coach that Pete Silver had guaranteed my spot on the baseball team. "He didn't exactly promise," Coach Morris said. "And Coach Embry couldn't keep you on the team if he wanted to."

I stayed silent, breathing through my nose.

"See, coaches have this duty that gets to be a chore. Until we run out of uniforms, we let every kid come out for the Spikes. After we narrow down the list of the ones with a chance to make the varsity, we go through all their school records and look at their birth dates. These oil pipe towns have a history of scouting around and giving dads high-paying jobs on the rigs because their sons can play football. Nowadays if the schools and coaches get caught doing that, they forfeit every game that the boy is on the roster. I was talking you up to make the Antlers, so they told me to check your records. Turns out you were seven before you started school."

"I started when I was six and I didn't fail the first grade!" I blurted. "They just said I wasn't ready for school."

Startled by my outburst, he said, "It don't matter, son. You're eighteen years old now, and you'll be nineteen next year. Nineteen-year-olds can't play high school football in Texas. It's against the law."

I pointed that in the next football season I'd still be eighteen.

"That's not the way the works. I'm sorry. There's nothing I can do."

Once again, this place and its school system were making me out the *Retard.*

"Now I'm not saying this," he said, "but you might think of Oklahoma. You got any kin there?"

"Yeah."

"Where?"

"Ponca City. I've got an aunt and uncle there. He works for Conoco."

"Well, that's a fair-sized town. See what your parents think. I'd be glad to write those coaches a letter saying you'd be a good pick-up for them in two sports."

"I thought of that before. They'd never let me do it. Not to mention what Aunt Nell and Uncle Zip would say. They've just gotten my cousins out of the house."

He nodded sadly. "Well, then . . . "

"So that's it," I said.

"I'm afraid so."

"What about Carver?"

"Who?"

"George Washington Carver. The Jaguars."

He stared at me in amazement. "You'd go over there just to play football?"

"No. But I would to keep playing baseball."

"Are you out of your mind? The only white boy in the school? Are you trying to be some kind of agitator or something? Jackie Robinson in photo negative?"

He tried to stop a chuckle at his wit.

"I need to graduate from high school and don't want to do it here."

He got up, closed the door, and sat down again. "Well, it could be those colored schools aren't governed the same way. We talk to their coaches from time to time. Help them out with equipment, those kinds of things. I'll do this. I'll call that head coach over there"—he said it like Carver High was as far off as South Carolina—"and tell him the situation, that it's your idea, and see what he thinks. But I don't believe this is the right town or time to attempt such a thing. Have you talked to your folks about this?"

"Coach, it occurred to me two minutes ago."

I didn't say a word about it to my parents, but I lay awake that night thinking about it. When Coach Morris saw me coming in the gym the next day, he zinged a basketball that I caught with a thump in my belly. "I've got health class tests to grade and a basketball game to coach," he growled. "But I'll call him."

A week later he summoned me to his office, told me to sit, and closed the door. "I talked to Coach Sanders," he said. "Turns out there's no real law against nineteen-year-olds playing sports in public schools. It's a rule imposed by an outfit in Austin that's affiliated with the University of Texas. And colored schools like Carver aren't governed by it."

My heart leapt. The coach said, "I told him you could have been a linebacker for the Antlers. That people say you're a good outfielder and hitter in baseball. I didn't offer my opinion of your brains." He shook his head. "Coach Sanders was just as discombobulated as I've been. He said you'd have to make the football team in two-a-days, and he didn't know how the players would react to it. He was curious about your motive. I explained it to him the only way I could. He said he'd think about it and get back to me."

I waited, still hopeful.

"And he did. He thinks you're an interesting young fella. But he said, 'There'd just be too much heat, Coach.' That's what he said—his exact words—and it didn't have one thing to do with linebackers and outfielders. He wishes you well."

"Hey, Coach?" I said. *"Don Don!"*

The tone of it made him bristle. "You listen here—"

"Don't you think I could have been told before I went *through all this shit?*"

CHAPTER 8

ALI

Cassius always favored himself with the conviction he was star quality. Because he was. One day in 1960 a van had carried the Olympic boxing team to the Coliseum in Rome. Cassius wondered why they couldn't walk around inside. It didn't look like much could be broken and carried off. This was where they fed Christians to lions? He thought the stadium indeed looked very old and ramshackle, but he imagined bombing in the war had blasted off big chunks of it. The US Olympics program provided them an American lady to guide their tours of Rome's antiquities. Cassius thought she was nice enough but she addressed them like a schoolteacher, and this morning he would have rather slept in. He offered his opinion about the bombing of the Coliseum and surprised the woman.

"Oh, no, Cassius," she said. "The Allies never bombed ruins."

"Well, I was only three when that was over, but back home in Louisville we got a TV set and I watch shows about the war. If they didn't have ruins already, our bombers sure made them some."

His teammates laughed, and the Olympics lady smiled. This was not the first time she'd heard his good-natured provocations. This time she was prepared. "Cassius, you have such a Roman name," she said. "Your parents must have loved to read history! Just the names they gave you. Cassius was a senator and general and a leader of the plot against Julius Caesar." *Well, that don't say much for him,* Cassius thought.

She went on, "Marcellus was a general who won Rome's highest honor for killing the Gauls' leader and king in combat. They got out of their chariots and fought with swords."

Cassius always had good posture. It made him look taller than he was, six feet one at the time. He had a distinctive way of raising his chin when he begged to disagree or just wanted to spout off. "No, ma'am, my folks don't read nothing but the papers, especially when I win my fights, and that's not how I got my name. Daddy got his name from my grandpa, who got it from my great grandpa. They got the name from a white man in Kentucky. Cassius Marcellus Clay was a politician and plantation boss that freed slaves left to him by his daddy. The boy slaves also had that name, all of them. Mr. Clay was supposed to be the first abolitionist in Kentucky, but going back how far I don't know, *all* the boy slaves born on that plantation got that name."

"Why, Cassius," said the lady with a confused smile. "That's such a nice . . . "

He talked fast and didn't like to be interrupted. "Talk about names," he said, "you oughta hear the one hung on the guy I'm gonna whip up on tonight—Zignieu Pietrzykowski! People been coaching me how to say that for two days, case'n somebody wants to put me on TV or the radio. He's a Polack, a Pole."

"Well," she said, flustered. "Shall we move on?"

The other boxers on the team deferred to Cassius, though they also were the best America could send out in competition with the world. He wasn't even the biggest fighter on the team. The heavyweight had lost to a Czech and didn't win a medal. Most of them liked Cassius, and for those who didn't, no jealousy or pride let them try to match his force of personality, or his skill. He had been coaxed into boxing at age twelve by a white patrol cop named Joe Martin, who later got him on a Louisville TV show called "Tomorrow's Champions." Cassius had won 130 amateur fights and lost just one. And just two nights earlier, in the Olympic semifinals in Rome, he'd whipped the only boxer who'd ever beaten him, an Australian named Tony Madigan. Now it was the Pole's turn.

Pietrzykowski was a hard-hitting lefthander. You didn't see many of those back then. They were discounted for being awkward, which in boxing is another word for difficult.

Most coaches turned them around and made them learn to fight right-handed. Cassius usually controlled fights with his jab, but against the Pole he angled in right-hand leads that landed again and again. The Pole fought back in three-punch bursts that made Cassius retreat a step a few times, but it was no contest. Late in the third round, certain that the judges would award him a perfect 5 to 0 score, he brought out his shuffle of feet that didn't appear to touch the canvas. Already that was his signature and calling card.

Cassius's daddy, the elder Cassius, painted billboards for a living and played boogie-woogie piano. His momma was a cleaning lady. His daddy wound up in jail now and then for his reckless driving and marital rows. When Cassius won the Olympics and got tagged "the Louisville Lip," an English reporter described his daddy as "a hard-drinking, skirt-chasing dandy of a man." Offended by the newspaper story, Cassius said he inherited the ability to do shuffle from his daddy, the fanciest dancer in Louisville.

Back home, the same year he won the Olympics, Cassius didn't start his pro career with the usual seasoning of six- and eight-round fights. He won a ten-round decision and bloodied a thirty-year-old police chief from West Virginia. Big shots in Louisville wanted a piece of his action. The first proposal was vetoed by Cassius's daddy. Joe Martin had gotten Cassius started in the sport and gave him his first TV exposure, but his daddy didn't like cops in general, and Martin played a part of that group and planned to participate in his son's management and profit sharing. Martin had arrested the elder Cassius a few times, and he wasn't gentle with the handcuffs.

Another bunch of rich white businessmen made an offer that gave Cassius a $10,000 bonus and a starting income of $45,000 a year. They got Cassius the top trainer in the business, Angelo Dundee, with all training expenses covered when he was preparing for a fight, including houses in Miami for the fighter and trainer that would spare them Kentucky winters. In return the businessmen got fifty percent of everything Cassius might earn in boxing, entertainment, and promotions.

One of the men said it was like betting on the future of a yearling thoroughbred. The men shied away from calling themselves a syndicate, for that insinuated racketeers and the mob. They called themselves the Louisville Sponsoring Group. Cassius's manager of record had been a leading man on Broadway. Among the eleven who joined up were men who had money and power in horse breeding and racing, bourbon distilleries, the city's NBC and CBS affiliated TV stations, an Oklahoma oil company, a candy maker in Illinois, a Manhattan advertising agency, the manufacturer of Viceroy and Raleigh cigarettes, and Los Angeles big league sports franchises, baseball's Angels and football's Rams. The kid was an industry and was just nineteen.

A man who chose to keep his name out of it told a writer for *Sports Illustrated,* "Let me give you the official line. We are behind Cassius Clay to improve the breed of boxing, to do something nice for a deserving, well-behaved Louisville boy and, finally, to save him from the jaws of hoodlum jackals. I don't know who composed that—maybe the executive committee—but I think it's beautiful. I think it's fifty percent true and also fifty percent hokum. What I want to do, like a few others, is to make a bundle of money." Their business deal would dissolve down the way when Cassius refused to be drafted and changed his name and religion.

Cassius was nothing if not brash. When he had won just six pro fights he challenged a former world champion, Ingemar "Ingo" Johansson, to a televised bout for $100,000, winner take all. The backers in Louisville said they'd come up with the money. Ingo was then training for his third bout with Floyd Patterson, who had won the title back from the Swede. Ingo called his right "the Hammer of Thor," to the amusement of the American sporting press, but in the third round of their first fight, he led with a soft left hook, and then like a rattlesnake strike the right twisted and shot out from his shoulder and put Floyd flat on his back.

Floyd roused up, resting on his elbows, like someone rudely awakened in bed. He floundered and regained his feet and wandered toward a neutral corner, as if he thought he had scored the knockdown. From behind, for that's in the rules, Ingo clubbed him with a left hook and another right to the back of his head. Like a robot Floyd kept getting up, and Ingo started winging roundhouses and wild uppercuts. The ref let the champion fall seven times before he stopped it. His inaction seemed merciless and crazy.

Ingo was a handsome guy with a dimple in his chin and a great-looking Swedish girlfriend named Birgit. They shared hotel rooms without regard to American decorum and hypocrisy, and his looks and world title got him cast in a TV drama by Ernest Hemingway and a role in *All the Young Men,* a Korean war drama starring Sidney Poitier and Alan Ladd. Ingo sang on TV with Dinah Shore. He was an American celebrity.

A year later, though, after weathering another of those booming rights in the fourth round of their rematch, Floyd put Ingo down with a left hook in the fifth. It sent him under the ropes with his feet high in the air. Rising to a knee and staring at Floyd, he let the count go to nine. After a minute of clinching, Floyd vaulted through the air and dropped Ingo with another ferocious hook. While the ref counted, Floyd leaped along the ropes, yelling at the sportswriters who had humiliated him over the way he lost the first bout. When the count reached ten Floyd started over to Ingo, then jumped and knelt over him with clear alarm. One of Ingo's feet quivered, but for much too long it looked like he might be dead. At last a camera got through the shoving men and showed him breathing.

With Ingo's third title fight in three years on the line, Cassius started harassing the Swede. He taunted him with a bit of rhyme, *"If he woulda stayed in Sweden, he wouldn't have taken that beatin'."* Ingo said the $100,000 challenge was ridiculous, but the back-and-forth led to their wearing sparring helmets and putting on a three-round exhibition for about two hundred movers and shakers in the sport. Cassius danced, jabbed, threw a few combinations, talked to the ex-champion, and was so elusive slipping punches that Ingo couldn't lay a glove on him. Ingo was embarrassed and unhappy. Cassius said, "He told me the fight wouldn't draw three ticket holders, and I didn't have the ability to step in the ring with him. Then why don't he come on over here and knock me out and pick up a hundred thousand dollars cash?"

Ingo wasn't a great champion, nor was he a fluke and chump. In his home city in Sweden, he had gotten his first title fight due to a stunning first-round knockout of the heavyweights' top contender, Eddie Machen, a California ex-con that Floyd's trainer and management had been evading.

Unlike the first two bouts between Floyd and Ingo, the rubber match was a real fight. Midway through the first round Ingo knocked Floyd down with another of those booming rights and jumped over him and ran to a neutral corner. When Floyd got up, Ingo attacked wildly for a moment, then landed a left hook and another right and stepped away as Floyd tried to grab him to keep from going down. You could tell from the look on Ingo's face that he thought this one was going down like the one with Eddie Machen. But with seconds left in the round Floyd reached deep and floored Ingo with a short left hook. It was the wildest first round in heavyweight title fights since Jack Dempsey knocked down Argentina's Luis Firpo before getting blasted out of the ring in 1923.

Ingo looked a little overweight. On the stool in the fifth Ingo was gasping as his corner men worked to close a twice-opened cut over his right eye, but across the ring Floyd's left eye was almost swollen shut from taking all those rights. Ingo appeared to be winning the sixth, landing jabs, hooks, and rights. Floyd seemed to be taking a round off, but then as they were fighting out of a clinch Floyd landed two short clubbing rights, the second one landing on Ingo's forehead as he was going down. He tried to get up and fell back, then staggered to his feet just as the ref was counting him out. It was 1961's Fight of the Year.

Cassius didn't get to watch Ingo's third fight with Floyd. He was busy that night in his Las Vegas debut. The convention center had booked pro wrestling one night and a boxing card starring Cassius the next. The promoter of both events got Cassius on a radio show with Gorgeous George. He said he got chills when Gorgeous George said he would win his fight because he was "the prettiest fighter." He watched and cheered George's limp-wristed flamboyant style in his match, which drew a bigger crowd than Cassius's fight. The next night, while Ingo and Floyd got ready for their fight at Yankee Stadium, Cassius won a ten-round decision over a journeyman named Duke Sabedong. Afterward he told reporters, without acknowledging it was the wrestler's line, that he won because he was the prettiest fighter. Gorgeous George had given him another signature to go with his fast-feet shuffle.

Ingo went back to Sweden, regained his European title, but retired as a one-fight world champion with a record of 28 and 2. Sonny Liston put Ingo in boxing's rear-view mirror. So Liston became the next target of

Cassius's impudence. In the trade Cassius was disdained as a showboat and braggart, though a gifted one. Though he had beaten no contenders, prior to Patterson's first fight with Liston in the Comiskey ballpark in Chicago, Cassius was allowed to join the ritual introductions after Jack Dempsey, Joe Louis, and Rocky Marciano. Cassius stepped through the ropes last, wearing a stylish tan suit. He wished Floyd luck, started across the ring to Liston, then pulled up, flapped his hands in mock terror, and dived back through the ropes. He strode out shuddering between the officials and press row and the ringside seats.

The stunt was hilarious, though Floyd couldn't savor it, if he noticed at all. Two minutes into the first round he was dethroned by a left hook and one-punch knockout. When the count ended and Floyd's seconds had him back on his feet, Sonny hustled over to give him his regards. Sonny had taken up boxing in prison and had been run out of St. Louis by police who threatened to kill him, but he was a professional. He had prepared a short speech about how he meant to make his new hometown of Philadelphia proud of him, but when the plane landed no one came to welcome the new world champ. Not one person. He knew then he'd never find respect and redemption, no matter how many men he knocked out. One of those years *Esquire* put a red beanie associated with Santa's helpers aboard Sonny's baleful gaze and ran the photo on the cover of its Christmas issue.

Sonny moved on to Denver and again took out Floyd in the first round of their rematch. Of Cassius Clay, he quipped that if he fought the kid he ought to be charged with homicide. To justify his inflated ranking, Cassius took on Archie Moore, but the Mongoose's record was 185 wins, 22 losses, and 10 draws. Moore had turned pro seven years before Cassius was born. Cassius predicted he'd take him out in round four, and with three knockdowns he did that. He'd added a new trick, calling the rounds, to his repertoire.

When Cassius got his title fight, he had won just nineteen pro fights, and he'd struggled to win his last two. In the prior one the English hooker Henry Cooper, who had previously lost to Ingo, put him down hard and almost out. That was the first time Cassius ran out the line, "He hit me so hard he hurt my ancestors back in Africa." When his title shot against

Sonny was scheduled in Miami Beach, Cassius was just twenty-two but undaunted. One night on *The Jack Paar Show,* as Liberace played the piano, without tripping on a syllable he recited his poetic forecast of the fight.

Clay comes out to meet Liston and Liston starts to retreat
If Liston goes back an inch farther he'll end up in a ringside seat
Clay swings with a left, Clay swings with a right
Just look at young Cassius carry the fight
Liston keeps backing but there's not enough room
It's a matter of time before Clay lowers the boom
Then Clay lands with a right, what a beautiful swing
And the punch raises the Bear clear out of the ring
Liston still rising and the ref wears a frown
But he can't start counting until Sonny comes down
Now Liston disappears from view, the crowd is getting frantic
But our radar stations have picked him up somewhere over the Atlantic
Who on earth thought when they came to the fight
That they would witness the launching of a human satellite?

Since the Olympics in Rome, Cassius had sprouted two inches to six-three and weighed 210 pounds. He at least looked the part, but at the weigh-in on February 25, 1964, his yelling was so uncontrolled that the Florida boxing commissioner fined him $2,500 on the spot. Most observers thought it was a full-blown panic attack born of terror. Sonny's only response to the outburst was to hold up two fingers for the cameras, meaning two rounds. Sonny hardly looked scared but he did seem eager to get out of there. He had seen crazy men before, and he didn't like to be around them.

Considering its historic importance, it wasn't really a good fight. Cassius was a seven-to-one underdog. In the first round he showed off his hand speed with a combination that looked good and got a crowd roar, but the punches didn't land or harm Sonny. Cassius danced and circled and dodged and carried the fight to Sonny with his left jabs. Sonny spent the next few rounds trying to reach Cassius with jabs and the left hooks that devastated Floyd Patterson. Between the fourth and fifth round Cassius panicked, batting his eyes from an astringent that Sonny's men were accused of loading on his gloves. Cassius yelled at Angelo Dundee to cut off the gloves. The trainer shoved him out to mid-ring, and the bell rang before the ref realized the kid intended to quit the fight. Think of that one in the history books.

Sonny knew something was up. Whether his people caused it or not, boxers don't often get the opportunity to fight blind men. As Cassius dodged and tried to dance, Sonny leaped to the attack but he couldn't land the hooks upstairs. Cassius spent the last half of the round holding him off with his left arm held out like a football runner's stiff arm. And he got the stinging blur out of his eyes in the sixty-second break that followed. In the sixth he got off one good-looking combination, and then he landed an echoing right that for the first time sent Sonny in retreat. On the stool one of Sonny's seconds massaged his left shoulder but they appeared to pay more attention to a cut and sudden swelling of his left eye.

At that point one judge had it 58-56 for Sonny, the other for Cassius by the same score, and the referee had it 57-57—dead even, a draw on the scorecards. Sonny had as much chance as the kid to carry it off and win the fight. But the bell rang and Sonny stayed in boxers' oblivion, glaring from the stool.

Cassius jumped up and down and flung himself all over the ring. "I am the greatest! I am the greatest! I am the king!" Joe Louis, who was part of the telecast team, said he thought Cassius was winning the fight, but he accepted the explanations of a doctor and the ref that Sonny quit because he'd dislocated his left shoulder. "He was throwing and missing a lot of left hooks." But that was not the enduring public perception: Sonny Liston lost his nerve because of one tremendous straight right hand.

Howard Cosell chased Cassius and tried without success to get him to stop and share this moment with a television audience. Cassius lurched toward a corner and shouted, "Bring that man here! That man, bring him here!" A handsome and grinning black man in a suit and tie stepped through the ropes to congratulate his friend and admirer. "Sam Cooke," Cassius yelled, "the greatest rock and roll singer there is!"

CHAPTER 9

A festering boil of resentment, I cruised along in Darrell's Bel Air station wagon with my right wrist loose on the wheel and my left arm resting on the door, its window rolled down in an early spring day. I shot around a truck, gave the volume knob of the local pop station a twist, and sang along with "The Wanderer," my new favorite by Dion and the Belmonts.

Well, I'm the type of guy who will never settle down
Where pretty girls are, well, you know that I'm around
I kiss 'em and I love 'em 'cause to me they're all the same
I hug 'em and I squeeze 'em, they don't even know my name
They call me the Wanderer
Yeah, the Wanderer
I roam around, around, around

Virginia had picked up the trick of arching her eyebrow like Lauren Bacall. "That's twice," she said, "you've taken both hands off the steering wheel. You are not going to wreck our new car."

Your new car? It's six years old, and why aren't you driving it?

Virginia turned the radio off, which annoyed me even more, and resumed her monologue about Darrell's broken neck. "Major Drexler, who's a fine surgeon, calls the break a C-3 on the spinal column. Now,

C stands for cervical vertebrae, which ignorant persons think is related to a woman's uterus. Reason for their trashy snickers is that *cervix uteri* is Latin for 'neck of the uterus.'"

I started to say, "You been reading up on a lot of Latin, Virginia?" But she loped right on through my thought. "Darrell could have been paralyzed from the head down. Major Drexler calls that *quadra pleeja.* And praise the Lord they got to him in time."

"Well, why wouldn't they?" I said. "There were only a couple of flocks of airmen around him when he flew off the pole."

With a sniff and glare she went on, "And what Major Drexler did, once he had him on a stretcher in the hospital, was he took a sterilized pair of ice tongs—the kind you used to see people handling blocks of ice with. He had a little hammer and went *bop bop bop*, drove the points in his skull right over his ears. Then he hitched a wire through the handgrips, looped the wire through a pulley, and hung it to a weight of twenty-five pounds. Some doctors, Major Drexler says, believe you shouldn't employ traction for more than twenty-four, maybe forty-eight hours. But crush fractures, he says, demand *aggressive* therapy. In two or three months, Darrell will be good as new."

Just great. Good as new. In the rear-view mirror I looked at my sloping crewcut, down to the skin on my forehead from a height of two inches at the back. Cool look of the day at Deerinwater High. Now I drove a car with airman stamped all over the windows and bumpers, and with that haircut I could pass for one. I pulled up to the entry gate and stared with my wrist slung over the steering wheel as the MP looked in and Virginia flashed her friendliest smile. I wondered how long it would take for my hair to grow out.

Every day that spring I drove my sister back and forth to Allred Air Force Base. Daddy didn't give me a break on weekends; he didn't want any part of that either. My sulks and pouts brought with them a full ration of guilt. At last I went in the ward with Virginia. On the hospital bed Darrell was strapped in lying on his back, and the ice tongs in his skull didn't make the sight any less distressing.

He glanced but couldn't move his head. "How you doing, boxer?"

"I'm not one anymore. Listen, I'm sorry about all this."

"Shit happens." It was the first time I heard that expression.

"Thanks for bringing my little dumpling out to see me."

"It's nothing," I lied.

"You like my car?"

"You bet. It jumps right out there."

"Don't be drag-racing."

"Don't worry. It's automatic shift so even with that engine—"

"I meant, don't wind up like me."

"Oh. Well, I'm careful."

"Careful," Virginia sniffed.

Darrell's eyes flicked back to me. "Do me a favor?"

"If I can," I said. *You mean like another one?*

"Pray for me."

Knowing my bitterness, Daddy bought me two new bats and a fine glove endorsed by Stan Musial. When school ended, I returned to Roughneck Park and my precinct in right field, but our best players had moved on to other teams, and in any case pro scouts weren't going to be looking at players in a Deerinwater YMCA league. One night, Mom said she felt like getting out and watching the game, so she came along with Daddy and me. It was an error-filled shambles we lost by nine runs. Heading home I exploded and bounced off the door, throwing elbows. Daddy was so startled he bounced a front wheel off a curb. Mom whirled around and stared at me in amazement. "What's wrong with you?" she yelled.

"Just realized I'm never gonna . . ."

"Never *what?"*

I muttered, "Make it to the majors."

She flung her arms about. "Oh, well, that's worth running our car into a telephone pole!" We passed a streetlight and I saw Daddy's knuckles were pale from clenching the steering wheel. Mom said, "It was just a nothing game."

Exactly. A nothing game in a nowhere town.

That summer the refinery gave jobs to teenaged sons of its employees at two or three times the wages we could make anywhere unless we braved the oilfields. Daddy rewarded me for my sacrifice with a well-kept 1952 solid black Chevrolet coupe. With the money I made at the refinery, I got pleated Naugahyde seat covers and flashy spinner hubcaps. Daddy was incensed by my spendthrift ways. I took one of the McConnell sisters to the first school dance and came out to find the hubcaps stolen.

As the months wound on, Chuck, DeWayne, and I got serious about our underage drinking and became regulars at a downtown pool hall. We roamed the town's roads and drive-ins in Chuck's faster pink '57 Chevy Bel Air that his mom had bought him, once they sold the Cushman Eagle. It had just a two-barrel carburetor but we drag-raced it and won some. The looming end of many things in my life was playing havoc with my mind and mood. Now when we roamed around and I heard Dion and "The Wanderer" on the radio I doctored the lyrics, singing along.

They call me the squanderer
yeah, I'm a squanderer
I fool around, around, around

My folks let me to stay out till midnight on weekend nights, and I didn't push my luck on school nights. I'd be listening to KOMA in Oklahoma City, WLS in Chicago, or Wolfman Jack's border blaster routine out of Del Rio and Acuña, Mexico, when one of them said from the other end of the house, "Turn your radio off, Haid."

But one night I awoke to a ruckus of people yelling at each other. I looked at my clock and it said 1:16. My sister and brother-in-law were engaged in a full-blown marital fight, and by some logic they thought it proper to bring it over to my parents' house in the middle of the night. I covered my head with a pillow and listened, trying to make sense of it. Darrell was running around on Virginia, and the other married woman was . . . Susan Dingus.

I sat up. I couldn't have heard that right. The chaplain's wife was screwing *him?* For one thing Paul Dingus was a captain, and an enlisted man could get court martialed and wind up in the brig for banging an officer's wife. Darrell had once told me that himself. I thought it curious. It must have been weighing on his mind.

"I'll do anything I please," he yelled in our living room.

"With that whore," Virginia yelled back.

"I said," he snarled, "I'll do anything I goddamn well please."

"Get out!" Mom yelled. "Nobody takes the Lord's name in vain in my home!"

"Home, you call this dump a home? That did it, Virginia, get your coat. Before I hurt somebody."

Darrell had just insulted and threatened my parents. The next came from Mom, now her voice tearful. "Virginia, you're not going with him, are you?"

"Yes, Mother, I am," she said, also teary, and the front door slammed.

In my hearing there was never a mention of that disturbance. Maybe they talked about it when I was gone, but my folks were not the kind of people inclined to speak openly about conflict. And I was too wrapped up in myself and my disappointments. Another night I was two or three hours into my slumber when shouting once more jolted me awake.

This time there were five voices, and one belonged to Susan Dingus.

Darrell and Virginia had brought her over to our house, again robbed me of my sleep, and expected my folks to clean up their mess?

"Please stop this," cried the chaplain's wife.

Then some remarks I couldn't make out and a sound of a chair scraping and my dad saying, "Now you look here."

Then loud thumps on the floor and women's voices crying, *"No!"*

The door into my room opened, and I watched Daddy search for something in my closet. I turned on a lamp, got up, and saw blood spilling out of his mouth and running down his chin. He dug around in the closet until he found the long slender bat he wanted. I gently but firmly took it out of his hand and put it back with my Adirondacks and Louisville Sluggers. I was barefoot, wearing just a pair of pajama bottoms. A few seconds passed, then I bounded out in the living room.

"You come in here and hit my dad? All right, come on, let's do it. Out in the yard! I'm gonna put you in the hospital."

Darrell squatted and jerked one way then another, arms crossed like he'd learned in judo. He thought both of us were coming after him. I laughed and started to hammer the ooze out of him right there. With her bathrobe tied tight around her waist, Mom jumped in and with the heels of her hands backed me up. "Stop this! All of you, right this minute! This is not how this family behaves. We are not that kind of people. We are God-fearing people. And you"—she jabbed a finger at Darrell—"are not welcome here. Get out. One more word out of you, and I'm calling the police."

Mom shoved me back in my room, closed the door, and I got back in bed. The voices didn't go away, but they were no longer yelling. I turned over, punched up my pillow, and switched off the lamp. I wondered how much comfort Chaplain Dingus got now from that assurance in Psalms about no burden too great to bear. A redneck had made him a cuckold, and his wife was just another Runaround Sue.

Then the door opened and let in living room light. I raised and turned my head to see it was the chaplain's wife. Susan Dingus sat on the bed beside me and began to stroke my forehead and hair and rub her knuckles across my cheeks like my mother once had. "You're a good boy," she said. "You don't deserve this. Sometimes, it's hard for me to explain, people get caught up in things they think they can't help. Even when it's wrong. I hope it doesn't happen to you but it probably will. Some people call it sin. That almost kind of dignifies it. I don't believe in sin anymore. I don't think. To believe in sin, you have to believe the whole package. And I don't believe it anymore. I just know when I've been selfish and let myself get involved in doing people wrong. And I've wronged you. I am so sorry."

Susan Dingus went on talking that way and stroking my hair and cheek and forehead. She began to hum some tune I couldn't place. "I'd sing you a song to help you get back to sleep," she said, "but I'd be embarrassed. You sing so much better than I do."

I was thinking *I believe life just started to get strange.*

After that, Susan Dingus and the chaplain vanished from my life. I never saw or heard about them again. Darrell didn't get court-martialed, and he and Virginia patched it up for a while. He was transferred to Tinker Air Force Base in Oklahoma City. She mailed the family a letter on perfumed stationery. After Mom and Daddy read it, she put it back in the envelope and laid it on my dresser in front of my baseball trophies and the mirror.

Virginia wrote us that she was going to place membership and be restored in the faith at a congregation up there come Sunday, and she was pregnant. She signed off with a verse in Ephesians. "Get rid of all bitterness, rage, and anger, brawling and slander, along with every form of malice. Be kind and compassionate to one another, forgiving each other, just as Christ God forgave you."

On my bed I read it and pulled my pillow over my face, trying to call back the look and scent and touch of Susan Dingus. It was a warm spring day, a week before graduation. I thought I'd walk over to Chuck Mercer's place and see what he was up to. Chuck and his mom, a good-looking woman who managed a local grocery store, shared a small garage apartment that was a block from ours on Wilson Street. Daddy had traded in the Mercury for a white '57 Chevy station wagon. He was waxing it in the carport, and he called me back. "You know," he said, "you really ought to do something about that temper."

My temper? You were going to brain him with a fungo bat!

CHAPTER 10

I did a lot of growing up over the next two years. I had to. All the dry holes along the Texas-Oklahoma border convinced the Pioneer and Conoco companies to shut down their refineries in Deerinwater. At the same time my parents lost their home to a swindle at City Hall that condemned and tore down neighborhoods for a freeway that never got built. The swindlers were convicted of fraud but never saw a day in jail—the district judge reasoned they couldn't pay people back if they were in prison. Nobody got paid back a dime.

Daddy had to take a company transfer to Daingerfield, a little town in northeast Texas, at a much-reduced wage. But Mom was philosophical. They were just starting over, and she'd experienced it several times on her dad's cotton farms. Daddy at least had a job in Daingerfield, she would find one, and a congregation of our faith, as she still put it, was just two blocks away from the apartment they rented. She said, "You'll bring a nice shirt and dress pants and go to church with me when you come see us?"

"Of course," I said. In fact, she accepted her failure to keep me on the path of her religion. What could she do? She had given it her best, and I was her only loving son.

My fantasies of frat parties and University of Texas football games in Austin dissolved. I was ashamed of thinking that was so important. The city said I could stay in the house where I grew up as long as I paid the utilities and signed a document agreeing I could be evicted on two weeks' notice. For a while I didn't have to worry about rent. I got a commercial driver's license and caught on with two brothers who had a Purina feed store. I liked the job, which was full-time until classes began at our local college, Rolling Plains State. The brothers who owned the feed store also had a string of poultry farms scattered around the area. They sold eggs, not fryers, and I delivered cartons of eggs to grocery stores and cafés in town and a hundred-mile radius in north Texas and southern Oklahoma. Rotten eggs accumulated at the home store in a large bucket. I carried it down a slope and dumped the eggs in the Kiowa River. Our streams and stock tanks looked like red clay mud. They went down in a swirl and I assumed the gars and catfish were glad to get them.

I bought a German-made Hohner Marine Band harmonica key of C and amused myself sucking and blowing on it as I drove. With one of my paychecks one day I went to the music store downtown and on impulse paid five hundred dollars for a new F-style mandolin. The hard oak of the mandolin's headstock and neck were painted black, and that flowed into an oval of color described as Tobacco Sunburst. Financially it was a terribly reckless thing to do, but the instrument was so pretty I lifted it out of the case like a baby. I figured when I learned that, I'd take up guitar. I pored over the manual but got nowhere trying to play it. But it was a possession I cared about so much that for the first time I worried about burglars.

Driving those country roads, I hunted the radio for stations that offered something besides country music, preachers, and the price of hog shares in Omaha. It stayed very hot that summer, the poultry barns weren't air-conditioned, and a supervisor told me that hens were exploding in their cages. I drove along blowing my Hohner and singing along with Hank Ballard and the Midnighters. *It's chicken pop, poppin' time . . .*

Some days I drove a pickup and delivered sacks of feed to farms and ranches. My least favorite deliveries were to a hog farm. In the barns' dim light, the stench was a methane wall I walked through. The hogs turned their eyes on me like I was something they'd like to eat. At another stop I delivered sacks of horse feed to a cattle ranch. A ram had the run of the barn and corrals. The sheep was the ranch owner's pet and a hateful thing. It weighed about sixty pounds and would wait until I had one of the feed sacks on my shoulder and attack me from behind. It hit hard, and those horns hurt. I'd drop the sack, grab a scoop shovel, and counterattack, yelling and banging the ram's horns and backing it up. The day labor cowboys got a kick out of it when they were around. We were like Peter Sellers and his Japanese jujitsu stalker in the *Pink Panther* movies. We made a racket.

My parents paid for the modest tuition and books at the college. I didn't tell them about the mandolin. My grades were quite good the first semester, but as time went along, I put in more hours playing Ping-Pong in a church basement than going to class. I thought I was getting pretty good on the harmonica. In addition to sucking and blowing I'd learned I could make the notes staccato by dabbing the reeds with my tongue. But pretty good on that instrument means you pretty much sound like everybody else. One night I went in search of a record store on Shiloh Street I'd heard about. I was old enough to call myself grown, but the closest I'd gotten to the business end of Shiloh Street was the outfield and boxing gym in Roughneck Park. I parked in front of a big church that doubled as a funeral parlor and summoned what courage I had.

I asked an old man leaning against a light pole where I could find Big Joe John's Record Store. He nodded farther down the street and asked me if I had any change. I pulled out the money clip I carried like a big shot and gave him a couple of dollars. Jukebox music dominated by horn sections blared out of two bars I passed. Neon signs of the clubs cast the street in blue and pink. Across the street from where I walked, two girls in short skirts and high heels loitered out front of stairs that led up to one of the clubs.

One called, "You looking for me, white boy?"

The other said, "No, that boy got the hots for *me.*"

They shook their fannies at me and giggled.

A large black man appeared and rested a heavy hand on my shoulder. It scared me when I looked around. One of his front teeth was gold.

"Let them little bitches be," he said. He gestured down the street at a guy dressed in black with a wide-brimmed hat. "See that fella eying you? Hadn't been any years at all since he was a hot-shit running back for the Carver Jaguars. Called himself the 'Touchdown Machine.' All the good that done him. He's now a pimp. Manages those little bitches, and he'd rob you of all your money and stick a blade in you in a New York minute."

I returned the gaze of the muscled up black fellow. The man with the gold tooth said, "What brings you over here, son?"

"I was looking for a record store called Big Joe John's."

"Well, I'm Big Joe John. Closed it while I got myself something to eat. Come on, the store's down this way."

He unlocked a door and let me inside, and I told him about my Hohner harp and mandolin. I said I was looking for music I could learn from. In the course of a few visits Big Joe John turned me on to 45s of the blues harp play of Junior Wells, Gatemouth Brown, Peg Leg Sam, Studebaker John, Junior Wells, Jimmy Reed, and Little Walter Jacobs.

"Little Walter's 'Juke' is the only harmonica instrumental ever got to be a number-one hit," he said. "Tell you something else. A TV station in Denmark caught him playing 'Hound Dog' behind KoKo Taylor before anyone ever heard of Elvis Presley."

"I want to be a singer, not just a harmonica player. I want a band behind me."

"Well, go for it, youngster. Little Walter had his bands, and he could sing."

The big man didn't just take my money and send me home with records. He asked about my singing. I told him about being a song leader at church and that I liked Elvis and Fats Domino and the Everly Brothers, but nobody came close to Chuck Berry. "He does it all," I said. "Songwriting, singing, guitar playing, and when he's got a crowd in front of him, he's got the moves of an acrobat and he'd charm the stripes off a skunk."

The big man chuckled. "Yeah, that 'Sweet Little Sixteen' jive got him a money horse and he's rode it good. And he does have skill. But you got to be careful. That life often don't attract the best kind of people. Whatever you play and sing, you've got a natural advantage—that be the color of your skin. Don't take no offense. Elvis, Jerry Lee Lewis, and them types may think they had it rough coming up, but being black is something they want to *play like*. Color of their skin ain't no hurdle they had to get over."

He looked through his bins, pulled out five or six used 45s, and handed them to me. "Let me tell you about Jackie Wilson and Sam Cooke. You know them?" I nodded but it was clear I was uncertain. "Both of them got their starts singing church songs. Jackie was a Detroit kid in a rough part of town, but he got to singing gospel spending summers with grandfolks in Mississippi. He went to reform school and caught a bullet once that could have killed him. He'd made some girl mad. But he's luckier than Sam. 'Mr. Excitement,' they call him, and it ain't no lie. He's got better moves than Elvis or Chuck Berry. Check him out.

"Sam, now, we're grieving on him," Big Joe John went on. "He had his life made and just threw it away. Picked up an Asian girl at a restaurant and took her to a motel where she feared to go. The motel's night manager, a heavyset colored woman, yelled at him to get that girl off the premises and be on their way. Sam kicked the door in when she wouldn't open it and give him a key to a room. She had a pistol and shot three times and hit him once. 'Lady, you shot me,' was the last thing Sam said. Thirty-three years old, every song a hit, and he looked like a movie star. The godamighty *waste!*"

One of those nights I drove back over to Shiloh Street singing along with Sam Cooke's hit "Bring It on Home to Me" on the radio. I had the windows down and at a stoplight a car full of white girls heard my singing and cheered me. I found the record store closed, and the padlock on the door was not the one Big Joe John used. I saw that same old man down the street, still holding up that light pole. I asked him if he'd seen Big Joe John out making his rounds. "No," he said. "The big man passed."

"He what?"

"Happens to us all, sooner or later. He was helping himself to the mashed spuds at a fried chicken joint when he had the heart attack he couldn't rise up from. Man that big going down hard, he made a mess with his tray and the spuds. So they said. I don't know what'll come of his store. He didn't have no family, none he claimed."

He nodded at the church and funeral parlor. "People got up enough money to buy him a service, preacher and all. The singing was real nice. But the way that preacher carried on. Big Joe John was a pussy hound like any other natural man. The man had his fun."

During daylight I went back over to Shiloh's side streets and found the black folks' cemetery. It had one freshly dug grave. Some wilted flowers rested on it but there was no marker, just the exposed clay soil. Damn, I thought. That oval of red dirt is all that's left of my first black friend.

CHAPTER 11

While my brother-in-law was stationed at Oklahoma City, Virginia had given birth to a little girl they named Angelina, soon shortened to Angie. Then Darrell had been transferred to a new duty station near Fairbanks, Alaska, and Virginia and the baby moved back to Deerinwater. She wanted to move in our house with Angie. I let her have it, and DeWayne Holland and I rented a dump of an apartment over by the high school. DeWayne had gotten a good job at the railroad yard. His job was to ride the train to Amarillo and back. I don't know what he did during the ride. His schedule left me plenty of time to be alone and play my harmonica.

Checks from Mom and Virginia's dependent's allowance from the Air Force barely covered her living expenses. I wasn't indifferent to my niece. I just didn't want to have anything more to do with her dad. Virginia and I made an effort to hold the strings of our small family together. She had learned to drive, and Daddy bought her a '54 Buick that belched too much smoke to promise a long life. The headlights and grill made it look like the front end of a barracuda. Virginia would call me around midnight and ramble on with one-sided conversations.

I never said, "Virginia! Do you know what time it is?"

I know she was lonely. Her close friends had moved into marriages and kids and many of them no longer lived in our town. In the house where I grew up, they had just basic furniture and a TV that kept breaking its picture in diagonal lines.

She ragged me, "You need to be getting right with the Lord."

"Virginia, stop it. That business wore me out."

"Well, that was rude. Have it your way. All through eternity."

Another night while I was there the phone rang. While I played with Angie on the one rug now in the house, Virginia stayed on the phone with Darrell a long time.

She came back in the living room with a big smile and picked up Angie, kissing on her neck and making her giggle. "Your daddy's in a big place called the Santa Claus Store. The town outside the base is named North Pole, Alaska, and it's Christmas there all year round. Christmas street lights every night, and all the streetlight poles are painted red and white like peppermint candy. Maybe we'll go live with him. Won't that be fun?"

I said, "How often do you get to talk to him?"

"Once or twice a week."

"Does the Air Force let him call home free?"

"Not that I know of. He calls collect."

I thought about that for a second. "Mom and Daddy are paying for it?"

When I said something Virginia didn't like, she just acted like I hadn't said it. She swept up Angie and in momma baby talk she told the little girl how much her daddy loved and missed them. I walked out to my car squeezing my hands against my temples.

Virginia and Virginia's life improved when she gained a courtly suitor. She said they met at a church picnic. Oran Jones parted his hair down the middle and smelled of Wildroot Cream Oil and Old Spice. I didn't know if she and Darrell were separated or getting divorced and I didn't care—I liked Oran. He wore a cowboy hat and took it off as soon as he stepped inside a house or business. My sister said Oran wished he could have been out on his family's home place, growing hay and herding cows, but inheritance had divided the property between too many siblings. He lived in Deerinwater but was a boot maker and saddler in a little shop in Dry Creek, a short distance away.

Oran was the only veteran of the Second World War that I ever met who liked to talk about it. He was with Patton in the Battle of the Bulge, just a boy trying to stay alive and keep warm. Oran offered to build me a saddle, and I told him I didn't think I'd ever own a horse. Then he offered to make me a pair of elk-skin boots, and I took him up on that. He began to come over with a pretty Gibson acoustic guitar, and his playing impressed me. On some numbers he sang well in a soft country voice. He told me stories about singers and how they had affected him when he first heard them. Virginia had a stereo player, and he brought over scratchy old 78 records by Jimmie Rodgers and Bob Wills and the Texas Playboys.

I had been joining Oran with my harmonica, and one of those nights I brought over my mandolin. Oran was amazed that I owned such a beautiful thing and hadn't learned how to play it. I told him I'd tried. He plunked around on it and said, "No wonder. They didn't set it up right for you. Where'd you buy this?"

"From the music store downtown."

He snorted. "Figures. Them people make their money selling baby grand pianos."

He told me to let him know some night when he was coming to see Virginia, and I had time to stop by. He brought me a new set of strings and assortment of picks. After tuning it and watching me he said, "Tunes to start out with, you're not trying to pick many single notes with that right hand. You're strumming and developing a light touch. The real work is with your three strong fingers on your left hand. That's how you build the chords. There's a lot of music in that pretty little thing. And you got the long slender fingers a fella needs."

I started trying to play with him, and he was patient with me when I hit some snag or got it all wrong. One night I was staying with him fairly well when he sang some lines that made me lay the mandolin on my leg and listen.

"What's that, Oran?" I asked when he was done.

He smiled. "Old Woody Guthrie tune, 'Deportee.' You know about Woody?"

I guess I smirked. "Johnny Appleseed of folk music?"

Oran frowned. "Don't look down your nose at Woody Guthrie. He's the best songwriter the American working-man's ever had. Story behind that song. Los Gatos Canyon is out near Fresno, California. In the forties a plane went down there and killed everyone aboard, the flight crew and a couple of dozen migrant farm workers being sent back to Mexico. The authorities didn't even bother to bury 'em, much less try to identify 'em. Left 'em laying out like dry leaves to rot, way he put it in the song. One of his best."

Oran told me about Guthrie's adventures—roughnecks who lived in tents and shot heroin between tours on rigs in the Panhandle, and how he got himself to California during the Dust Bowl years hopping freights and playing saloons, and how he got in a fracas over Negroes' and Puerto Ricans' exclusion from New York City apartments owned by a man named Fred Trump. At first, I thought Guthrie's singing style was old-fashioned, corny. But soon the words got through to me. I was hardly the first of my generation to make the discovery. When Bob Dylan was starting out, I recoiled from his singing. I thought you had to work to sing that badly. Then a disk jockey on a college station out of Norman, Oklahoma, solved the mystery for me. Dylan started out trying to sing like Woody Guthrie.

Just months had gone by since I seethed when I had to drive my sister to Allred Field to see Darrell in its hospital. Now Oran told me that fine jazz musicians were stationed out there, that they played at the NCO club, and we ought to go some night. When we arrived, an airman at the door wanted to see my ID. Oran interjected that he was my dad and I was a music major at the college, writing a paper about jazz. The guy nodded and let us in. "Thanks, Pop," I said. Oran laughed and took off his hat.

The musicians played Glenn Miller-style swing and sometimes they riffed into bebop. I didn't care for it, didn't understand it. I told Oran it sounded tuneless to me—like the horn and piano players were making it up as they went along. "No, they've got some melody going there," said Oran.

"I can't hear it."

"Listen closer and you will. They *entwine* themselves around it. That's what jazz is to me anyway. Bob Wills and some others invented western swing by picking up on what Glenn Miller and Tommy Dorsey and Duke Ellington were doing with their big jazz bands."

There was a lot of cigarette smoke in the club, and we went outside to get some fresh air. Oran was the kind of guy who'd strike up a conversation with anybody. Some of the musicians were out there, and he walked up to them. Hanging around was a spicy odor that I realized was my first sniff of marijuana. Oran asked them what they thought of western swing. They shrugged and said it was okay. The trumpet player said, "Come back tomorrow night. We're supposed to have a special guest, Bob Wills. They say he put in some time here. "*Did* some time," said another. The airmen laughed.

Oran had told me Wills was famous in town for being a drunk private when Allred Field was an Army Air Corps post during the Second World War. One night out in the country a freight train came upon the crossing where his silver '38 Duesenberg sat and demolished it. A search ensued for his remains, since nobody else in that town ever had a Duesenberg. The searchers found him amid fallen horse apples of a bois d'arc tree. The lore had it that the army let him out of the service just to get rid of the problem.

The minute the horn player said that, I knew Oran and I would be back the next night. The same guys played their bebop the first set, but after the band break, Bob Wills came out and brought with him a mandolin. I thought he was just a fiddle player. "Watch him play that thing," Oran said. "Some day you'll be doing that." Wills may have washed out there as an army private, but he and the band of airmen played till two in the morning. At one point Wills alleged that Chuck Berry changed his hit "Ida Bell" just enough that he didn't have to give Wills any money when he wrote and recorded "Maybelline."

Virginia and Angie didn't make it to North Pole, Alaska. The Air Force suspended Darrell's family support when he went AWOL in Fairbanks. They caught him there trying to hire a bush pilot who'd take him where he could hunt and kill a grizzly. Virginia filed for divorce but she didn't want anybody at church to know. She had it in her mind that divorce was shameful and sinful. One night I told her exactly what I thought. "Oran's a good man. Anybody can see he loves you. Forget the age difference if that's what bothers you, or that he's already been married once, or that he has two kids in high school somewhere and they don't get along. Forget that. He'll be a better dad to Angie than Darrell ever would have been. Don't drive him off. To hell with what people in that church think." It was the last and best advice I ever gave her. Virginia married Oran a few months later, and though I drove up to Daingerfield to see my parents whenever I could, on family matters too often I tried to color myself gone.

CHAPTER 12

My class attendance and grades suffered further when I found myself in an honest-to-god garage band. I carried off egg cartons from work and we nailed them on the walls in the garage of a rent house owned by the bass player's parents. I know we ran off one pair of tenants. The only real musician among us was a guitar player called Little Mike Wilson. He'd been playing with his dad's western swing band since he was twelve years old, and he went on to have a solid career and could have gone higher with more luck and ambition. My harmonica won me the invitation to join the band, and it turned out I was the only one who could carry a tune. To my delight I was once more the song leader.

Little Mike knew what he could play and I found out what I could sing. I was a strong tenor but my voice faded when I tried to go too deep into baritone. We were a copy band racing to give those kids the sock hop covers of the radio hits they wanted. At first, we all dressed in Madras plaid shirts, blue jeans, white socks, and cordovan penny loafers. We called our band the Stolen Hubcaps. Then the doo-wop that had just about smothered rock and roll vanished. The Beatles landed in New York, followed by the Rolling Stones, the Animals, and the rest. We stopped getting haircuts so often and put our loafers away in favor of cowboy boots. We ditched our teenybopper band name and settled on another of my suggestions. Now we were a band with attitude. We were the Low Rent Collectors.

Word of us was getting around. Through Little Mike's connections we played a couple of fraternity dances at TCU in Fort Worth and another at SMU in Dallas. Billy the bass player's dad let us borrow his station wagon so we could pile in with our instruments and not have to buy gasoline for two cars. We played a couple of weddings. We were getting paid enough for the dances we played to keep our hopes alive. We hit our best stride one night playing for a dance for the KAs at Rolling Plains State. The KAs claimed a mandate to the Old South—Stars and Bars decorated the stage at every dance, and all the brothers dressed in phony Confederate uniforms for an annual wallow called the Old South Ball. I didn't care for frats but I didn't lump those KAs in with the rednecks that took on the so-called Lost Cause. They were just loud drunk kids.

We started our gig with our take on Dylan's "Just Like Tom Thumb's Blues." I loved singing that song. We kept going with covers of Buddy Holly's "Oh Boy" and Chuck Berry's "Promised Land."

> *Somebody help me get out of Louisiana*
> *Just help me get to Houston town*
> *There are people there who care a little about me*
> *And they won't let the poor boy down*

A crude fad called the Alligator had taken over frat dances. While the girls danced with themselves, the guys hit the floor, jerking their arms and legs like they were swimming. I laughed when I saw a girl kick her date on the top of his head. We offered "Deportee," my Woody Guthrie favorite, near the last.

A ruddy-cheeked guy with a good start on a beer gut barged up front and bellowed, "Hey, you assholes, that's a song about wetbacks!" Little Mike stepped up beside me and thrust the neck of his guitar like a rifle and bayonet. The drunk kid lurched back and had to swing his arms to keep from falling down. Some of the frat boys booed us but we won them and their dates back with the finale, our cover of the Stones' "It's All Over Now."

We loaded up our amps and mikes and instruments and went to the best of our apartments. We were enjoying the moment, getting drunk ourselves, when Little Mike held up his hands for quiet. "I love you guys," he said, "but I'm quitting the band."

A howl of protest and shock ensued. "I'm sorry," he said, "but some guys in Stillwater have a future, and they want me to join them. I gotta go where I gotta go."

"Stillwater, Oklahoma?" I yelled. "We've got a good thing going here! What about our future?"

"Six months ago, we were playing for whatever people put in tip jars. That's amateur hour, Haid. You look down your nose at Stillwater? At least they've got a real college there. Twice as many clubs and school dances, twice as many paying gigs."

We fell silent, stunned.

"It's not personal," Little Mike said. "You've got to learn to treat this like a business. Maybe we'll hook up again down the road, but I can't pass this up."

Without Little Mike we didn't have the nerve or confidence to keep going. Lenny the drummer got a draft notice, rode a bus to Dallas to take the physical, and passed it. Billy the bass player took a seventeen-year-old girl over to Oklahoma, where it was legal for a justice of the peace to marry them. He now had a full-time job at her dad's furniture store. My dreams were windblown scraps of paper on a pipe-town street.

Chuck had not done well at Texas Tech in Lubbock, a town like Deerinwater except for a much bigger college and the ghost of Buddy Holly. After three semesters he came home and joined the marines. He could have stayed put and never been drafted because his dad was killed in the Anzio landing in Italy during the Second World War, and Chuck was an only son. But he enlisted anyway. His mom couldn't talk him out of it. The night before he left, we moved on from the pool hall to a bar where we drank red draws—draft beer and tomato juice, the favored local concoction. The barmaid knew we weren't old enough to be drinking there, but it was too lousy a joint for the Liquor Control Board cops to fool with.

Chuck stared at the pink foam in his glass. "First week I was in Lubbock I saw sand blowing and drifting over the curbs like snow."

"That's reason enough to join the marines?"

He shrugged. "It's the only job offer I got in California."

"But four years?" It sounded like half a century to me.

DeWayne was challenging and betting on the pool table's game of eight-ball and losing two out of three. Chuck watched him and said, "If he starts a fight, I'm outa here."

"He's got sense sometimes," I said.

"God, I hate this town." Chuck slid his car keys and an envelope across the table.

"What's that?" I said.

"Your car and the title transfer. You'll need to buy insurance and get what you can for that old Chevy. One or two more breakdowns, it's gonna be in a junkyard."

"Chuck, I can't take this."

"Yeah you can, you don't have a vote. Drop me off at Mom's house tonight, and you can take me to the airport tomorrow if you want to."

I continued to protest. Chuck raised his glass of beer and tomato juice for another swallow, leaving pink foam on his upper lip. "Hey, I can still beat you up. I am still chairman of the local order of Righteous and Harmonious Fists. When I get back it'll be a ten-year-old car with a faded paint job, if you haven't blown the engine."

One night I drove over to Roughneck Park and found the GI Forum gym dark and closed. I called Mr. Guerrero and asked if the gym was still in operation. "I'd like to start training for the Gloves again," I told him. "It was locked up last night."

He said, "Well, it's open for guys that don't mind it being unheated in the winter and come in there on some kind of regular basis. The Gloves are still a while off. Are you serious this time?"

"Yes, Sir, I am."

I started going across town a couple of nights a week after I got off work, then it became three. Jesse Segura, a bantamweight who had reached the semifinals of the State tournament the year before, had gotten married and said he couldn't compete anymore, but he trained me more often than Mr. Guerrero did. Jesse said, "You're a baseball player, right?"

"Not anymore. I was."

"Think of it like a pitcher. To make it in the big leagues you've got to have at least three pitches—fastball, curve, and change-up or slider. You've got to master the basics. Same way in the fights." He moved in front of me, throwing punches that came close. "You've got a hard jab, good power in your right, and you're getting there with your right uppercut. I'd say lose the left uppercut; it's not coming to you. And you got to get more twist and hips into your hook. You can throw it straight behind your right like you been doing, and that's a hard punch, but it's not a hook. You throw it like you're slapping somebody, except instead of an open hand it lands with a fist. You've got most of the stuff, but like a pitcher you gotta learn to mix them up. You've got fast hands, for a white guy."

I laughed.

"Just telling you how it is, bro."

After a tournament in the little town of Vernon, Mr. Guerrero said, "Congratulations, *joven,* you just graduated from being a Novice."

"Yeah?"

"You could go on the rest of the season beating up farm boys, but Open fighters that win keep my gym open."

"You think I'm ready for that?"

"Yeah, but don't let it go to your head. I'm gonna get you better sparring partners and I want you to eat good and more. You're gonna be a light heavyweight. You're already filling out, and I don't want to get to the State tourney and have you struggling to make weight. I'll be surprised if you don't win our Regional. But State won't be no party."

I'd get up before dawn and run the dozen or so blocks to the college campus and an adjacent golf course. My route took me past the houses of rich people, and one morning a cop turned on his red and blue lights. "What are you running away from, bud?" he said.

"I'm not running away from anything, Sir." It irked me to have to address him that way. I hadn't done anything. "I'm training, doing roadwork. I'm a fighter."

"That right? What kind of fighter?"

"Light heavyweight. Just learning. I'm an amateur."

"You any good?"

"Some say."

"You got any identification?"

"Yeah. All right if I move my hands?"

The cop nodded, acting like he wasn't disposed to get out of the car. I produced my driver's license from a little pocket in the waistband of my sweats. He said, "You make the dogs bark."

"I'm not bothering anyone, Sir. Dogs, they gonna bark."

He handed my ID back. "All right, boxer. But I'd better not hear any breaking and entering complaints in this neighborhood. You got that?"

"You won't have any trouble with me."

The cop passed me often enough that in time he gestured good morning.

At the bank out near the college where I deposited my paychecks, I started talking to a girl named Ann. She was pretty and had short brown hair. When she smiled, she had a pleasing way of pursing her lips over teeth that protruded a bit. I had been aware of her early in high school but stopped seeing her in the halls, and I wondered if she'd moved away. She didn't wear a wedding ring now, and I started finding more reasons to go to the bank. I finally asked for her phone number, and she gave it to me.

Ann was a single mom. Back then that made her one of the town's bad girls. She had gotten pregnant when she was sixteen. Her little girl Josie was not quite two. A grandmother kept Josie during the days when Ann was working. Ann was doing what she was supposed to do—paying the rent on a duplex in a safe part of town and learning how to be a good mother on the fly. She had a chip on her shoulder about people who thought a mistake born of pleasure made her a whore. She said even some of her friends and especially their mothers treated her like that.

On one of our dates she told me she was filling in for a teller when the Rob and Roy Robbers hit the bank. "They wore masks like Zorro or the Lone Ranger. One of them said, 'I'm Rob and he's Roy.' Their guns looked real and it was scary, but they were polite and in and out so fast it was kind of exciting."

"I know Rob. That's not his real name."

"You do?"

"Yeah, he went to our church. When he and Roy, wasn't his name either, were arrested, that's how I got to be the song leader."

She said, "You're the most interesting boy I know."

Weeknights Josie was usually asleep in her room by the time I took a shower and got to their place. My dates with Ann largely consisted of lying on a sofa with her and listening to music. I knew Ray Charles for the great LP with his backup singers, the Raelettes. "Tell the Truth," "What'd I Say," "I Got a Woman," "The Night Time Is the Right Time." Then

Ann brought home his *Modern Sounds in Country and Western Music.* I didn't like the sugary string arrangements, but Ray Charles could make soul out of hillbilly! One night when we lay there, I sang along with him on "You Don't Know Me."

Ann cocked her head at me and grinned. "You're not bad. You can sing."

"Thanks. I grew up with it. Church songs, you know."

"You were in a band? Somebody at the bank . . ."

"Yeah. We called it the Low Rent Collectors. We broke up."

"You sang for *them?*"

I laughed. "Big deal. Fun while it lasted."

"I didn't get to see you! People talked about you guys. Why didn't you tell me?"

"It was over before we met. And I don't think it'll ever happen again."

She put her face in the crook of my shoulder and squirmed closer. "Doesn't matter, just sing to me."

I sang her one of Big Joe John's favorites, "Dark End of the Street." When I was through Ann was quiet for a minute, and then she said, "You know about Corby Ray."

"I've seen him around." Corby Ray was a good-looking doofus who stood six-four and liked to get drunk and fight. He was Josie's father. Ann didn't marry him and had sworn a peace bond against him. Still Corby Ray thought he had property rights to her.

She said, "He beat up the last guy who took me out."

"I'm not worried," I said. Which was not entirely true.

Ann was my first love, and she was worth the wait. One of those nights on her sofa we kissed and burrowed until I got the stone aches. I sighed and told her that. She was quiet and lay still in my arms for a moment, then said, "Well, let's fix it." She unbuckled my belt and started pulling loose the brads on the fly of my Levi's as I unbuttoned her shirt.

"We have to be quiet," she murmured.

We didn't get our clothes all the way off, and the sublime melding of us didn't last nearly as long as I wanted it to. But then I put my head back against the arm of the sofa, a happy young man. She said, "I've been wanting that, too. Was it your first time?"

I thought about it and told her the truth.

"Good," she said. "Means you'll always remember me."

"I can't imagine I'd forget."

CHAPTER 13

GEORGE

As a young man he pushed his eyebrows so hard together it seemed impossible for his face to break a smile. There was a boxing gym he could walk to. George would stroll in there indifferent to the workouts, steal something from every bag, and look the fighters in the face when he did it. Nobody called him out. He was that fearsome a presence. But his life didn't start out that way. He was just another little boy.

His mother, Nancy, was from Marshall, a small town in the state's northeast piney woods. She had married his stepfather, J. D. Foreman, after George was born. His birth father, Leroy Moorehead, lived in Marshall the rest of his life. Highway 59 down to Houston was a well-worn road for people seeking work, and Houston was where the Foremans ended up. Nancy Foreman was a hardworking woman prone to having babies, seven of them. J. D. would put in his hours at the Southern Pacific railroad yard and wobble home hours after he'd clocked out. When George and his siblings pulled some trick on him, he'd start to yank his belt out of his trousers. The effort careened him off balance, and he'd stagger off muttering down the hall and fall on the one bed in the house where children were forbidden, and their mother would send in the children to take off his shoes as he lay snoring. She worked as a fry cook in a succession of small cafés in the Fifth Ward, but two jobs were never enough. Not much railroad pay made it home.

The Foreman house sat unevenly on stone blocks, not a real foundation, in the southern half of the Fifth Ward, which had been cut in two by the construction of Interstate 10. George's world was bordered by the immense concrete swath of Interstate on the north and Buffalo Bayou and its flood plain of tangled woodlands and brambles on the south. The buildings downtown stuck up in sky that turned sunsets rouge with the smog. Though close in miles, to George they were just features of the horizon. No reason to be curious about them.

On schooldays he would walk east to Melva Street and eventually arrive at Bruce Elementary, which backed up against the cloverleaf of the Interstate and the Eastex Freeway, Highway 59. The growl and howl of the trucks, motorcycles, and ambulances melded with the shrieks of kids on the playground during recess and when school let out.

George's paper sack lunch might contain two slices of gummy white bread and a smear of Miracle Whip. Some days he'd eat the sandwich during the walk, and in the lunch room he'd tell members of his class that big kids had robbed his sack. Then he became one of those big kids shaking down children for *their* lunch sacks. At home he never had enough to eat. After work his mom would bring home a hamburger and slice it into precise narrow triangles for her children. She cooked them one real meal every Sunday, and that was more nurture than all the Baptist and Methodist churches in the Ward offered. Hunger turned George mean.

The house was three blocks from the intersection of Clinton Drive and Waco Street, notoriously the most dangerous part of the city. Juke joints, dice games, whores plying their trade in alleyways, their palms shoved against a wall to keep from having to wallow in mud. When calls came to white patrol cops of another late-night stabbing or shooting at Clinton and Waco, they let the victims bleed and get better or die. If an ambulance crew wanted to go in there, it was their decision. Good luck.

George roamed the streets with a disorganized gang of chums who called him Monkey. One night he and a couple of others mugged and robbed a white guy who'd downed too many drinks, took a wrong turn, and his car broke down in the Ward. They jumped him while he was looking under the hood. A woman who was tired of that mess saw it and called the cops. A man wearing pants and an undershirt stepped around his wife and yelled to the boys that she'd called them. Because the victim was white, three patrol cars responded with dome lights flashing as the man bled from his mouth and the boy muggers scattered. One of the cops looked for them on foot with a dog, a loud and growling German shepherd. George ducked under a house that sat on blocks like his own. There was barely enough room to squirm back under there, and he heard rustling behind him that he thought must be rats. He could smell himself, and he thought that dog was going to smell him, too.

One night his mom shrieked, "Boy, you got to gain control of yourself! You're gonna be the death of me." She wound up hospitalized with a nervous breakdown. A letter came to the house from her. He opened it and found a note and some dollar bills to pay for an older sister's graduation ring at Wheatley High School. He stole the money and bought himself a sweater, a hat, and a bottle of Thunderbird wine.

George never went to school another day or lived in his folks' house again. As a thief he had no talent but was not without ambition. He knew how a stolen car ring worked. The cars came out of Memphis, Beaumont, Port Arthur. Some guy with a sheaf of car titles and a stolen notary public stamp put the imprint on the papers, and the cars were off to bargain sales and new owners. George would have stolen one of the cars himself if he'd known what to do with it. Many years would pass before he possessed and drove a car.

It rained too much in Houston. The front yards of the new houses had grassy drainage ditches called bar ditches like ones out in the ranches and farmland where they were usually seen. Every yard had its mosquito-breeding swamp. He and his chums lived on the streets, but that didn't mean they slept in the bar ditches. The boys were squatters. There were plenty of abandoned roofs to sleep under. George didn't like eating out of garbage cans, and he couldn't rob somebody every time his stomach rumbled and he needed a meal. People who had a way out of the Ward were getting out as fast as they could.

George heard men jiving on the corners of Clinton and Waco about what Sonny Liston was going to do to this boy Cassius Clay, but that was about it. He wondered idly at times if his size and strength might have let him play football. He quit school before he could suit up and find out.

Sometimes it took a while for the city to turn off the electricity in the empty houses. In one that still had the power on, they had stolen an old television set with a rabbit-ears antenna. George hadn't had the opportunity to watch TV much, but he knew who Johnny Unitas and Jim Brown were. One night he saw a commercial on which the pro football stars talked up a government program called the Job Corps. Kids without educations, prospects, or breaks were going to be taught blue-collar trades at the government's expense.

The Houston police had begun to set up mini-cop stations in the Fifth and Third Wards and in Sunnyside Heights, trying to keep them from blowing sky high some hot August night. George was extra wary of police because he no longer had the cushion of juvenile laws, and too many cops knew who he was. He wanted to be a thief and hustler, but he was always getting caught or dropping what he stole when he ran. He approached the cop shop in the Fifth and remembered hearing somewhere it would be best if he removed his hat. A uniformed white cop took in the size of him and under the desk made a move like he was putting his hand on something. "Can I help you?" he said.

George told the cop what he'd seen on TV and asked if he knew how to run that program down. He never had any particular interest in having a job, but he figured if the government was training guys and putting them up in camps, it had to be feeding them, too.

The Job Corps first sent him to Grants Pass, Oregon, where they taught him carpentry. George thought it was boring; his mind wandered, and the hammer was always banging his thumb. Next they transferred him to a camp in Pleasanton, California, a pretty town out east of Oakland. The jobs were conservationist in nature—clearing shrubs in overgrown lots, picking up litter on roadsides—but they started him working on his GED high school equivalency certificate. The youths lived in dormitories with not enough personal room to suit George. A big white kid out of Walla Walla, Washington, thought himself a badass, and one night he talked back to George one time too many. George tore a door off its hinges and threw the kid through a window. The kid wasn't hurt too badly, though his confidence was shaken.

A short perky supervisor named Doc Broadus was called before the doctor who ran the camp. "It's federal property!" the camp director yelled. "Somebody's got to make a decision and make it fast. As far as I'm concerned, that boy belongs in a California penitentiary." He started to pick up a phone.

Doc was a former Air Force sergeant who stood five-feet-five. His grandfather had been a slave in North Carolina, and as a teenager Doc was a runner for a moonshiner. Boxing turned him around; he went to a camp and said Joe Louis called him aside and praised him. Doc claimed he won a hundred amateur fights, lost none, and never had a mark on him. He turned pro as a featherweight and won twenty-two in a row. His first loss must have been a bad experience for him, because he quit fighting after that and started training other fighters.

He told the doctor running the Job Corps camp that the big kid from Houston had potential. "All right, Doc," the supervisor said. "You like the boy so much, and he wants to fight, then you teach him how to do it the way that's legal."

Doc sat George down and made him listen. He concluded the kid just wanted someone to take an interest in him. The gym in the camp had a ring and the assortment of punching bags. He gave George a day and time to come in and they would get started. George didn't show up, and Doc went looking for him. He found George sitting on a stoop, looking forlorn. "What's wrong?" said Doc. "Why didn't you come?"

George dropped his head and shook it. "I don't have any shoes."

Doc got him tennis shoes that fit, and his training technique was not elaborate. "Stick and move, stick and move," he mostly schooled George in the ring. The stick was more effective than the move—George's natural gift was a left jab that one opponent said felt like the wrong end of a swinging telephone pole.

Doc entered him in the San Francisco Golden Gloves, and George won the Novice finals with a knockout. The director at Pleasanton was always talking about the CCC camps where boys built national parks and sent money home during the Depression. But there was a major difference. When the Job Corpsmen finished training, they were sent home to find work on their own. With more education George went back to Houston to seek a job and a gym. He couldn't find work that would let him train and run. The chums that called him Monkey lured him back to the streets.

Doc got permission from the director and wired him money for a bus ticket back to the camp in Pleasanton to work as an athletic instructor.

In the ring George wasn't an immediate sensation. His lost his first bout as an Open division fighter. Doc took him to Las Vegas for the Nevada Golden Gloves, and he won that tournament with all his opponents pounded to the canvas. But in the National Golden Gloves in Milwaukee, he lost in the finals to a more experienced fighter from Riverside, California, named Clay Hodges. He was six-four, weighed 210, and he fought George three times. He won each one with a decision. Hodges said that if you could get up after being flattened by George, he would lose heart when you stormed back at him.

Doc's understudy was an athletic work in progress. George's amateur record would only be 22 and 4. But he kept getting better. He won the California Golden Gloves and then in Dayton, Ohio, he won the national tournament of the Amateur Athletic Union, which qualified him for the US Olympic trials. As a measure of his progress, in Oakland that year Doc put him in the ring with a former heavyweight champion. He was discredited for the way he lost his title and failed to win it back, but in an explosive fifteen-year run, he had stopped Houston's toe-to-toe slugger, Cleveland "Big Cat" Williams, in the second and third rounds of their two bouts. He got rid of Zora Folley in the third, and Floyd Patterson in the first round both times they fought. Those were three of the top five heavyweights of that generation, and he was one of them. He never fought the fourth one, Johansson. No one thought the Swede would have had a chance.

George was eighteen, and his new mentor and sparring partner was Sonny Liston.

CHAPTER 14

Mr. Guerrero and Jesse Segura guided me through thirteen straight wins, and a referee stopped eight of them. The regional tournament was back in the Boys Club where I'd fought just weeks before. Due to the violence surrounding the prior year's tournament, the newspaper's publisher had grown wary of the Gloves. That year as I'd fought on through the tournaments and the Open division, the sports editor was directed to give the bouts little or no attention. It wounded me, for the only airman I'd tried to beat up was Tony Pereira. But a following in boxing is more about word of mouth than stories in a newspaper. Each fight I won in the Open division, the crowds got louder, and the motley bunch of street fighters trailing me out got larger. Penny ante stakes, but this year at least I was the town champ.

I trained hard for the State tournament in Fort Worth, which took place every year in a coliseum named for Will Rogers. Out front on the grounds was a statue of the famous humorist riding a horse and holding his hat down by his thigh. A tall column with no apparent function ascended from the hall in a style called Art Deco. I learned that from stopping to read historical markers during my jogs around the coliseum and barns of the Southwest Exposition and Fat Stock Show. The coliseum had nearly three thousand seats, and unless the weather was bad almost all of them were taken. The roaming bunch on the floor looked like they'd all been born with broken noses.

I fought seven rounds in four nights. The first fight was with a Latino kid who had won the San Antonio regional. He was slick and fast. He kept banging me with left hooks and right uppercuts. I think I got my nose broken in the first round. Mr. Guerrero and Jesse said I was lucky it didn't bleed like a backyard faucet and told me to pipe down the moaning or the ref might stop it, and I fought on through. Even so, I thought sure I'd lost and was startled when the judges' cards were collected and my hand was raised. If I had been that Mexican kid, I would have been pissed off big time. While we were still in the ring, I told him he'd won the fight. The bridge of my nose was puffy and both eyes turned black, which endeared me to the crowds as the refs stopped my battering of guys from Corpus Christi, Dallas, and El Paso. I looked like a raccoon.

The night of the finals Jesse and Mr. Guerrero were frantic when I showed up at the prep gym forty-five minutes before the first bouts began. "Where were you?" Mr. Guerrero said. "We thought you'd gone home or gotten rolled."

"Hey, I'm the one getting hit. I'm sore. Better to run it off than take Tylenols."

"Okay," Mr. Guerrero said. "But we've been looking for you all afternoon. You were supposed to be in your room resting."

I shrugged and started taking off my clothes. "My girlfriend got her mom to watch her little girl and she drove down. We went to a show."

"You what?"

"We saw a movie."

Mr. Guerrero cried, "Done all this, come all this way, biggest night of your life?"

"Relax," I said. "It was the most restful thing I could have done. It's all dark, cool and quiet, except for what's on the screen. One we saw today was *Dr. Strangelove.* Weird and funny. It's about America blowing up the world."

I listened to their worries about this black kid from Houston I had to fight in the finals. Kayron Coger had been fighting every night I fought, and his opponents hadn't lasted long. "This guy is going to be a world champion someday, or in the hunt. He's already got a nickname, 'Heat Wave.' He's stronger than you and just as fast, and he's got reach on you.

Plus he's left-handed, and you've never really had to deal with that. Keep moving left, away from his power, and don't let him cut off the ring. Bang him with your right, but keep it beside your jaw when you're not throwing it. That straight left hand can turn out your lights."

"And remember," Jesse said, "all his life he thinks he's had dirt kicked on him. He shows up angry."

"Because he's black?"

"Hell, yeah, because he's black!" Jesse said.

"He's going to try to get inside your head," said Mr. Guerrero. "So how are you gonna try to beat him?"

"What if I call him a nigger in the chairs?"

The looks on their faces made me burst out laughing. "You know I'd never do that. I'm the guy that tried to integrate George Washington Carver!"

"You did what?" they both said.

"Never mind," I said, laughing more. I shed my street clothes and started gearing up for what came next. "Well, I'm glad your girlfriend's got you loose," Mr. Guerrero said. "Let's get ready to fight."

I didn't tell them what else we'd been doing. Ann and I had gone to an early showing so we'd have most of the afternoon together. We went to the hotel where she'd booked a room. The weather was dreary and gray out, and she hadn't opened the curtains to her window outside. I was lying on the bed in my sock feet, hands clasped behind my head, a customary posture. I don't remember what I was talking about. She got up and went in the bathroom. On the way she flipped off the lights in the room. When she came back out, the light in the bathroom, she was as naked as the days we were born. A gift from heaven, if I still believed in that. She threw back the bed cover and slid between the sheets. I got busy joining her. This time there was nothing rushed. I don't know if she came or not. I was still new at this, but she sounded like she did. When we were done, I lay on my back, breathing hard. She looked at me and said, "Are you all right?"

"All right? Is that a serious question?"

She giggled and leaned on an elbow, the angle and slump of her breasts making me want to start all over again. She tickled my collarbone with a fingertip and said, "I hope you've got better wind tonight."

There you go. I had violated the taboo of fighters in the ring and guess I proved there's something to it. At the moment I didn't *care* what Kayron Coger did to me.

"All right," Mr. Guerrero said, after Jesse worked me out with the mitts and got me sweating. "Let's don't leave your fight in here. They're about ready for you to go out to the chairs. Remember, this guy's strong, and he'll throw an elbow, try to hit just low enough to get away with it. You gotta make him pay when he tries that. Establish your jab. Make him blink. Rip him with straight rights and the uppercut. You with me?"

"Yeah, let's get it done."

Coger didn't have much to say when we sat down in the folding chairs. He was tall and appeared skinny but every muscle on him looked like cordwood. "Where is this place you stay?" he said with no show of real interest.

"You mean where I live? Deerinwater's about a hundred miles north of here. Last big stop before you get to Oklahoma."

Coger rolled his head with a look of boredom. "Ain't ever been there."

"You haven't missed anything."

The welterweight finals ended with a decision, we moved to the next chairs. I said, just making conversation, "So you're from Houston. What high school did you go to?"

"High school? Boy, I shucked school two years ago. I'm turning pro soon as I win the Nationals."

"Oh. Well, good luck with that, assuming you beat me. But I'm not allowed to call you boy. Ain't that so?"

"You got that right. In a minute I be calling you bitch."

"Woo. I don't know if I'll be able to get up in the ring."

As soon as the middleweights were done and we stepped through the ropes, I started banging myself hard on the jaws. I had learned it triggered a flood of adrenaline and calmed me down. I bounced lightly, testing the canvas anew. Because all our bouts except my first one had not gone the three rounds to decisions, both the Fort Worth papers billed our light heavy finals as the night's main event.

Mr. Guerrero said the *Standard-Patriot* had finally given me my due on the sports pages, and a few dozen folks from Deerinwater would likely drive down to watch and pull for me. I knew the crowd would be mine, owing to prejudice, but I wouldn't hear them once we got started. I banged my jaws hard enough that Mr. Guerrero told me to steady myself.

"I'm okay," I told him.

All the finalists were afforded two ringside seats, and I claimed one for Ann. I knew where she was, but I kept my eyes away. I didn't want her to see me embarrassed or hurt. When the bell rang, Coger ignored my offer to touch gloves and drove me straight back. He was throwing wild ones at my head that I deflected with my arms and gloves. My jab started getting in well enough, then his left banged through and staggered me, but it landed high on the side of my head and didn't really hurt. Coger was snorting and grunting with each punch he threw. The noise irked me and got my blood racing. I fought my way inside his long arms and stayed there, whacking his ribs and trying to find jawbones with hooks and uppercuts. When he began to get the best of me, I threw both my arms over his shoulders and arms, squeezed his elbows against his ribs, and put my forehead against his neck so he couldn't butt me.

When the ref yelled at us to break, I drove right back at Coger. He tried shoving me to get his punching distance, but I was stronger than he thought and I stayed with him. "Get out of there!" I heard Mr. Guerrero yell. I was throwing too many punches this early in the fight. But so was Coger. I landed a straight right that jolted him. He made some more of his noises, then threw a flurry of punches that came from all angles. He was as good as they said. Two minutes into the round he nailed me twice with the left. The second one buckled my right knee, and I stumbled. The ref stepped between us, put his hands on my chest, and made me take an eight-count. He stuck his hand in front of my face, finishing the count. I was pissed because the eight-count was sure to cost me the first round.

When he waved us together Coger moved in planning to finish me, but I had been practicing something skipping rope. With my left foot I stepped hard on Coger's right shoe as he slid forward to let go of that left. He leaned away with a look of concern and dropped his gloves. My right flew out like it had a will of its own and caught him on the chin, and as he faltered, I clubbed him with a left hook and a better right uppercut, and I leaned over him as he toppled over and landed on his back. At that point I heard the crowd—first like a cough, then a roar.

The ref shoved me toward a neutral corner. He started the count then saw what shape Coger was in and waved his arms like a baseball ump calling a runner safe.

One of the Fort Worth papers ran a photo the next day of me leaning over Coger. I knew why they did that, but I wasn't taunting Coger. I couldn't believe it. Mr. Guerrero and Jesse came running. The ref broke up our party, grabbed my arm, and said, "You fouled him to land that punch. If I had any balls, I'd disqualify you, but I don't want to start a riot here."

I gave him a puzzled look of innocence, then looked down through the ropes and saw Ann in her blue dress. She was behind the judges' table now and jumping up and down with her hands clasped in front of the string of pearls I bought her. I savored that vision for a moment then went over to see if "Heat Wave" was all right. I owed Kayron Coger and Tony Pereira and the other guys I fought all kinds of favors. They changed me into someone else.

CHAPTER 15

With the delivery job, boxing, occasional jams with bands that weren't going anywhere, and my love affair with Ann, I was a busy young guy. If Mr. Guerrero could raise the money, he wanted to take me to the National Golden Gloves in Chicago. I longed to be exposed to a real city. Maybe I could volunteer for more hours at the feed store and take Ann with me. I was working up to asking Ann to marry me. She might have accepted. Then reality banged my door. No form to my life and prospects that didn't promise much what could I offer a young bank teller who had a small child to raise? Also I had finished the first three semesters at Rolling Plains State on scholastic probation, and now out of sheer stupidity I missed the deadline when I could have dropped all of my spring classes and hung on to my student draft deferment. I wasn't going to Canada or some creepy junior college that accepted boys like me just to cash our tuition checks. It would be over a year before I could regain my college student exemption. I was sure to get drafted. I guessed I'd just go.

Chuck came back from the marines bulked up and deeply tanned on his face and neck and hands. He and DeWayne and I went to a bar with a pool table and jukebox that yowled the kind of country music I hated. We were back in one of the same low-rent beer joints, and I'd never seen Chuck so low. He shook his head. "Soon as I get back to Pendleton

I'm gone to Vietnam. A goddamn grunt in a jungle war. What was I thinking?"

I didn't know what to say. Chuck went on, "In that world I'm once again Charles."

"What? You've always been Chuck."

"It's racial. The black guys call all white guys Chuck. 'Hey, Chuck.' And the dumb fucks don't even know Chuck Berry's in jail."

I laughed. "I think he's out now. I forget—what did old Chuck do?"

"Picked up a fourteen-year-old Apache girl in Juárez, took her to work as a hatcheck girl in a club in St. Louis, ran her off when he was done with her, and she took her story to a newspaper. They got him for crossing state lines for immoral purposes under the Mann Act, the 'White-Slave Traffic Act.' Like they did Jack Johnson one time. Not to excuse Chuck for underage honey hunts, but tell me, was that girl white?"

I nodded at the barmaid for another. "I'm just as screwed," I said. "I've got a girlfriend I'm crazy about, they're raising money to send me to the Golden Gloves Nationals, and this loud fast-talking black guy called me about turning pro. He told me not just anybody can knock out Kayron Coger. The guy said he worked for a promoter named Don King."

Chuck sat back and squinted. "You want to be a pro fighter?"

"No, hell no. I want to be a singer. A *recording artist.*" I said it bitterly and shook my head. "Doesn't matter what I want. I'll be drafted by the fall."

"You've got too much going on to let that happen."

"You got any suggestions?"

Chuck swallowed some red draw and said, "Join the marine reserves. If you can't get in, try the army reserves or national guard. Stay away from the navy, unless you want to spend two years walking around in a uniform that makes you look like a penguin."

I sat back with a snort. "You haven't been sounding real high on the marines."

Chuck tapped his fist on the table then turned the hand palm up. "What I did is what I did. I'll deal with it. But they'll let you in the reserves if you get on it before you get called to your draft physical. They'll take you for the boxing, that alone. Those recruiters used to never make their quotas. Now the reserves are popular. You can go out to California and be back home and in your life in six months. The reserves might get called up, but I doubt it. They're gonna fight that war with dumb volunteers like me and poor black and Mexican and hillbilly draftees whose moms and daddies don't have any pull with politicians. You'd have to go to weekend drills and summer camps, but that's nothing like being in the war. I wish it's what I'd done."

I took Chuck to the airport the next day and enlisted in the marine reserves two weeks later. The recruiter, a grizzled gunnery sergeant, read the *Standard-Patriot* sports page and knew about me. He shook my hand like he was trying to crush it and congratulated me for joining up with the best warriors in the world. Ann was none too pleased when I told her what I'd done. Mom and Daddy were scared. I told them not to worry, and over the next month I read all I could about Southern California. The marine base of Camp Pendleton was not far from cool beach towns that teemed with longhaired girls in bikinis, but I didn't say anything about that to Ann. Up the coast was LA, Hollywood—maybe my singing break was just up the way.

Mr. Guerrero shook his head and said, "The Nationals. The Nationals." I told him and Jesse that I'd miss the big tourney this year but I'd be back in ever better shape and pick up training again right away. Ann and Josie went with me to the airport. I held and kissed them and told them how much I loved them. That I'd be back in no time at all.

No time at all.

PART II THE GRINDER

CHAPTER 16

On that first plane ride in my life I looked down on the pastures choked with mesquite and thought, boy, you're going to make some mistakes in life, but this one's a doozy. Other youths and I changed planes in Dallas, and on the flight to San Diego the stewardesses were kind, knowing from the files in our hands what we were bound for. At the airport we were hustled into blue windowless buses and our captivity began.

After the shaving of heads, we were bald youths with wisps of toilet paper stuck on the nicks where shears had drawn blood. Our heads looked so pale. We endured the first night of screams and threats by drill instructors, then at sunrise with maybe an hour's sleep and the otherworldly cadence calls about us, the newest and lowest shuffled along in tennis shoes and yellow sweatshirts, ill-fitting caps that the marines called covers on our heads. My first breakfast was oatmeal without milk or sugar, and I had to get it all down.

Assigned to bunks in Quonset huts, we would wake up in utter black before dawn to a click, then scratching of a needle on a record. You had a few seconds of lying awake before "Reveille" blasted all over the post, and then we yanked on our utilities, boots, and cover and sprinted back and forth across an immense parade ground called the Grinder. My inner self wasn't attuned to strenuous activity first thing in the morning.

The DIs called us pukes and girls. One night I was called into the Quonset hut that housed the DIs' office. A scowling staff sergeant sat behind the desk, still wearing his Smokey Bear hat. The DI told me I had scored well on my intelligence tests and with that boxing title in my background, he could offer me a chance to ship over for four years as a regular marine and go to Officer Candidate School in Quantico, Virginia.

When I answered, the sergeant shot up behind his desk and bellowed, "Are you telling me you do not *want* to be an officer in the United States Marine Corps?"

"Yes sir, no sir, I don't, sir!"

The DI hurled me out of hut, skinning the heels of my hands when I hit the rough asphalt. I got up grinning because it was dark and he couldn't see. The marines inherited much of their language from their sister service, the navy. Your bunk was a rack. Your fatigues were called utilities. You didn't mop the floor, you swabbed the deck. Our platoon went through four different DIs in those first weeks. The only one I liked was Staff Sergeant Mulligan. He was a freckled redhead, wore glasses, and he was funny. One morning we were doing pushups on the Grinder when he said, "You girls missed a great *Mike Douglas Show* last night. The Rolling Stones were on, and you could tell he didn't like them."

As we heaved and pushed at the asphalt he went on, "Douglas was ragging them about all the barbers in England they're putting out of work. He called up three young girls. One of them was squealing, about to faint. After the girls went away Douglas asked them which one was the most popular with girls. A guitar player said that the singer, Jagger, was most popular with men. Douglas said, 'Well, you don't do anything for me.' Jagger said, 'You don't do anything for me either.'" Sergeant Mulligan danced around before us in his beige flannels and spit-shined shoes. He sang a few lines of "Not Fade Away," a Buddy Holly song the Stones covered, and pantomimed Jagger's moves with Maracas.

A few weeks passed, then with M-14s slung on our shoulders, we again boarded the windowless blue buses. They took us up the coast to Camp Pendleton and the Edson Range where we spent two weeks taking apart, cleaning, and getting used to firing the rifles. When we weren't handling the weapons and trying to stretch into difficult positions, we were goaded into long runs up and down golden-brown hills with brush that smelled like licorice. At two hundred, three hundred, and five hundred yards we fired standing, sitting, kneeling, and prone, at slow and rapid fire. A perfect score was 250. Sharpshooters were the middle rank, and the lowest qualifying score for marksmen was 190. We had by god better shoot at least as well as that shitbird marksman Lee Harvey Oswald. A young DI phrased it that way.

We slept in well-built tents that accommodated four of us. We shared the head with another recruit platoon. One morning long before dawn, we arrived to find some guys in the other platoon telling us that it was closed. They had just cleaned up the toilets and lavatories and swabbed the floor. They thought they could block us from what our insides compelled us to do. There was a lot of shoving and shouting, and a shorter but muscled-up black guy made a move at me. He walked into a good straight left, and it sent him stumbling back into his buddies' ranks. Guys in my platoon were slapping me on the back.

The fight didn't turn into a full-scale brawl, and the black guy came back over. I'd cut his eyebrow. He indicated we were all right with each other. Or I thought that's what he signaled. I didn't drop my hands but I relaxed and nodded. He turned his back—and then spun and sucker-punched me. The blow took me off my feet. Then the guy was on top of me, banging my head against the concrete. I could hear his platoon mates cheering him on, and none of mine fought through to pull him off.

"Please," I cried, "please stop."

This had happened between five and six o'clock in the morning. After breakfast chow, which I could barely choke down because my head hurt so much, a young DI led us out for a long run in the hills. I thought for sure I was going to fall out, but some way I didn't. At times I was woozy, seeing double. I'm sure I had a concussion.

I recognized the change in attitude of my fellow recruits at once. I was a walking sack of bad luck. Such a thing could happen to them at any time. That night we had mail call. The envelope sent an immediate flood of relief through one of the worst days of my life. Sitting on my bunk, I tore open the envelope with Ann's handwriting. I so badly needed this. Then I read, *"Dearest Haid, I'm so sorry to have to write this."*

Chuck Mercer had been killed in the war.

I crushed the letter in my hand, but then tried to smooth out the wrinkles and rips of the stationery. She had enclosed a clip of the short article and obituary that ran in the *Standard-Patriot.* It didn't say where or how he died, just that it was a combat mission of the marines. My thoughts raced to his mother, still a young woman, really, who had already buried two husbands and now her only child.

That day was the last practice drill at the rifle range. I got four Maggie's Drawers—red flags waved from the bunker meaning you had missed the big target altogether—and with the young DI screaming at me, my score was nowhere close to 190. He took me on a solo five-mile run, cursing me up the steepest hills. For the first time I wondered if I was capable of murder.

That night Sergeant Mulligan called me in. "Sit down, Shelton." He took off his glasses and cleaned them with a cloth. "I hear you had a meltdown today."

"Yes, sir."

"What's wrong with you?"

"Last night I got a letter that my best friend got killed in the war. He was marine infantry, only been in it a few weeks. He was nineteen."

Sergeant Mulligan let out a long sigh. "There's already been too many of those. Going to be a lot more. This hasn't been a day for proper grieving, has it?"

"No, sir."

"Who are you, Shelton?"

"I'm nobody, sir. A guy from Texas."

"No. You were a little different. Not making any noise about it, but you weren't going to be overwhelmed by this. DIs pick up on things. They offered you OCS and you turned them down. Smart call. You carried yourself well. Golden Gloves champ. Your civilian background got you some breaks, and you had attitude to go with it. That's good but also not so good. What we're expected to do is break every kid down, reduce him to a puddle, and then rebuild him into the kind we want—killers that follow orders and never leave a fellow marine down on a battlefield. I don't like that part of this job. But the Corps couldn't let you tear through here like you were God's gift to Guinevere. So you got taken down a notch today."

I wasn't educated enough to know who Guinevere was. I just thought it was a pretty name. Maybe Ann and I could name a daughter that if and when we got married.

The sergeant looked at his large freckled hands on the desk. "I'm sorry about your friend. I'm sorry because he was just starting out in life. I'm sorry for his family. You're a reserve but you'd better start thinking like a real marine, because that's what you're probably going to be. When you're in battle, you're going to see a friend die right beside you and all you can do is keep shooting and try to stay alive. That's reality, Shelton, and you'd better get hold of it. If you don't qualify tomorrow, you won't get out of here. You'll start over with a new platoon and do the whole thing over. And they'll treat you like you've already proven yourself a loser. You can aim and fire a rifle. It's not that hard."

The next morning, I got another Maggie's Drawers right off the bat standing at two hundred yards, and the young DI was once more screaming at me. But I rallied in the seated position, slow and rapid fire. "Good shooting!" Sergeant Mulligan said with a hand on my shoulder. "Now you're doing it." Something about him reminded me of my dad, and it wasn't just the red hair. By the time I got to five hundred yards I had made up for my poor start and could have fired sharpshooter. But those bull's eyes were a long way off, and my focus wandered. I wound up with the same qualification score as Lee Harvey Oswald. The sharpshooter and expert medals were pretty things on a dress uniform. The one of marksmen was a lead-colored square with a circle in the middle. It looked like a toilet seat.

We had been jacked with so much we were like primed explosives. One afternoon when we were in the showers and in the adjoining room of lavatories, a disliked black guy named McCombs got in a fight with a white guy who wasn't popular either. McCombs was light-skinned, his hips and butt were too big for his body, and he spoke and gestured in a way that seemed kind of girlish. It didn't seem logical that he tried to be such a badass. In the fight he got the other guy in a headlock and with his free hand started trying to shove his eyes into the faucets of a sink. The DIs had given one guy the platoon banner to carry when we marched; he had qualified as an expert on the rifle range, and he looked like a marine in a recruiting poster. The DIs' favorite cursed, stood over the fighters, and struck the first blow against McCombs. Then it was a school of sharks. I thought they were going to beat him to death. McCombs staggered blindly, raising his arms and crying out, and when he ran past me his face already looked like a cluster of red grapes.

He ran on to his Quonset hut and got from his trunk the bayonet we had been issued at the rifle range. I considered a guy named Henson our leader. From somewhere in the Midwest, he was handsome, stood about six-two, weighed close to two hundred pounds, had the photo of the best-looking girlfriend, and with somber loss read aloud to us in our hut the Dear John letter she sent him. Henson saw McCombs coming with the bayonet and laid him out in a bed of ice plants.

Tacked on our training was an extra week of mess duty. The chow hall work didn't give us any more rest but it gave our sore muscles and joints a chance to heal. That week we rolled out of our racks at four o'clock in the morning instead of five, and some spent their days up to their elbows in soapsuds and liver and onions. We didn't get back to our huts until after dark. We had been over-exercised to the point we were ravenous. One night as we marched back to the huts, I held back a laugh because so many of us had stuffed our utility jackets full of cereal packages. As the young DI sang his inept cadence, we raised a rustle and clatter of Sugar Frosted Flakes.

I had drawn a job that wasn't bad. As the platoons of recruits came through the chow lines carrying their canteen cups for milk or water, we handed them trays that looked like stainless steel. But they weighed enough that they felt like steel-coated lead. One crew passed on trays and utensils that had been washed and rinsed. We wiped and handed them out to the next platoons coming along.

One of those noontime chows a platoon came through that hadn't been in boot camp long. You could tell by their sunburns and utilities that hadn't faded from laundering. I was standing at the end of the table and joked, "This is a spoon and this is a fork. Use these. Don't eat with your hands."

A DI with a maroon birthmark on his right jaw and throat commanded that platoon, and he thought no one could jack with his pukes but him. He heard my lame jest, leaped to the table, and with the edge of a tray he whacked me as hard he could. It hit my adam's apple like a dull axe blade. I wobbled and thought I was going to faint as the hawk face loomed close and bellowed. I couldn't speak for a week, I hawked up clots of blood for a month, it hurt to swallow, and my voice came back in hoarse whispers. I told guys in my Quonset hut that I just had allergies. I didn't care to lose my voice for good, and I remembered that birthmark, I sure did.

CHAPTER 17

A few families came for the graduation from boot camp to see us in our new beige flannel uniforms. The recruit the DIs picked as our best got a set of dress blues and a PFC stripe. Sure enough, the guy who landed the first blow on McCombs won the dress blues and stripe of rank. He was a born leader, evidently. All the graduation really meant was that we were now snuffs, lowest of the low, but real marines at last.

The next day we were back into our boots and utilities and herded up on the windowless buses to Camp Pendleton for our month of basic infantry training. If the DIs knew about McCombs's beating and what he meant to do with that bayonet, they didn't let on. McCombs was smart enough not to want any more of Henson. But he decided we were going to have a go with each other. He must have thought after the shithouse fight that I was easy meat. He'd stand with his boots crossed and stare at me while tapping one cheek with an index finger. It was a strange kind of menace.

As we waited to put the San Diego Recruit Depot behind us, McCombs kept pushing through the mass of bodies toward me. Pressing me against the others without giving me a real shove. I yelled, "McCombs, leave me alone!" and hit him hard enough with a right that he reeled back into others who were jostled, and they shoved him aside. Sergeant

Mulligan saw it happen and barked at us to knock it off. When we were on the bus without windows McCombs stared at me as he came aboard. He was loudly promising to kill me until Henson snapped at him to shut the fuck up. Sergeant Mulligan, the redheaded DI who reminded me of my dad, came on the bus and looked us over, saying goodbye by making a speech. He came up the aisle a few steps, leaned toward me, and said quietly, "You're going to have to learn to hit a little harder. That or get yourself a club. Give my regards to Guinevere."

I never saw McCombs again after that bus ride, though I watched for him awhile. Over the next month we crawled on rocky ground until our shirts didn't have a button on them, and our knees and elbows were scabbed. We hugged the ground under soughing rounds from a machine gun. We got our lungs full of tear gas. We threw live grenades that would have killed us if we froze up. We were broken into squads, given maps and compasses, and told to find our ways back through the tawny hills. My bunch followed the clearly worn trails left by legions of other boots.

During those weeks I got a crumpled letter from Ann that read, "*Sweetheart, don't you ever leave me again.*" I didn't plan to. Free at last for two weeks, I joined a 105-millimeter howitzer battery at Camp Pendleton. I was in my flannels, headed home with thoughts of Ann's bare arms and legs on my mind when a grinning sergeant called out names that included mine and announced the leaves of all reserves were off. He said we were needed for three weeks in the field at Twenty-Nine Palms, a huge preserve in the Mojave Desert. She hung up in tears when I had to tell her I couldn't come home yet.

The first day in the desert I stepped under one of my squad's camouflage nets just as the howitzer went off, and I jumped back five feet. The old salts guffawed. They might have been two or three years older than I was. The Mojave would be interesting terrain if you experienced it in an air-conditioned truck with four-wheel drive. One afternoon found us in the company of a captain with a big moustache. He was friendlier than the others, and with a light kick he let us hear the rattlesnakes he kept in an ammo box under his rack. I thought he'd been out there too long. He pointed at a distant train, creeping darkly on the desert. "How far away do you think that is?" he asked.

"Eighteen miles," I ventured.

"Nope. Fifty."

"Sir, you can't see a train fifty miles away."

"You're not seeing the train. You're seeing its reflection."

They had us out there three weeks, sleeping in tents. When the war game ended, some fighter jets blew up a ridge with bombs and set it ablaze with napalm. "*Oorah!*" regulars yelled the Corps battle cry.

We were in the six-by trucks, in a good mood, heading back to garrison, when a sergeant yelled, "Reserves out!" He grinned as we were rounded up. "It's not over for you snuffs. You just became enemy guerillas. Fill up your canteens at the tank truck, rack your weapons, and sign for them—you'll get them back in Pendleton. Get ready for a hump."

I don't know how far we hiked through the desert, maybe eight or ten miles, stumbling down bone-dry arroyos cut deep by flash floods, tripping and muttering when it got dark. That sergeant delivered us to another one who told us to climb in another six-by, this one uncovered. The truck banged and pitched us for another hour. We arrived at a plot of open ground surrounded by a makeshift wire fence. The sergeant said, "A captain is going to be coming around trying to get information. You have been captured at a village called Tru Doc See. Don't tell him anything but your name, rank, and serial number. No matter how he threatens or what he does to you."

The night got chilly, and our beds were rocks and dirt. At some point, maybe 0200 as they say in the military, the captain appeared. He was a dark-skinned handsome guy who seemed young for that rank. One by one, we went forward to be interrogated. "What's your name, soldier?" he asked me, sounding bored.

"Haid Shelton, Sir." I added my rank and serial number and stood at attention.

"What are you doing out here?" he said.

"Beats me, sir. I was assigned to a howitzer battery at Camp Pendleton. I was on the way to the airport when a sergeant said my leave was canceled. We fired a bunch of rounds and blew up a bunch of rocks." I sneezed. "Excuse me, Sir. I have a cold."

He eyed me with more interest. "Anything else you'd like to say?"

"No, Sir. Except one night I think maybe I saw a UFO. First thought it was an illumination round, because the eight-inch guns were firing over our heads, but that light was different and shot off like a rocket, straight across the horizon."

The sergeant and the other snuffs stared at me with amazement. The captain and the driver of his Jeep left soon after that, and the sergeant just let it go. He wandered off to the truck for some sleep and a whiskey pint. I found a slope that was somewhat sandy. I lay back and pulled the bill of my cover over my face, hearing the stifled laughter. I didn't care how much trouble I'd gotten myself in. But the strangest thing, I never heard a word about it. Looking back, I see a hare-brained kid in a man's body, but I understand why I got away with so much. The regular marines were gearing up for war, and they didn't have time to square away reserves that were only going to be with them for eight weeks.

When we got back to Pendleton, garrison duty in Mainside's white-washed barracks wasn't bad. I only had eight weeks to go, so I decided to save the money for the leave's airfare and put it to better use when I got home. Ann didn't take that news well either, but I planned to surprise her. She hadn't had a vacation since going to work for the bank. I thought I'd take her to Puerto Vallarta or someplace like that. I got a routine promotion to private first class. I lived in the barrack where Don and Phil Everly had racked five years earlier. They feared getting drafted, and knowing what two years in the army had done to Elvis's career, they joined the marines as six-month reserves. They performed on *The Ed Sullivan Show* with boot camp haircuts, wearing dress blues.

I never thought I had a bad temper, despite that admonition of my dad. But one afternoon in the barrack I walked past another snuff who grumbled about something he couldn't find in his trunk. He said, "Have you got my wallet?"

I thought he'd asked if I'd seen it. Then I paused. "No. Why would I have it?"

"Well, you've got a reputation."

"You're calling me a *thief?*"

I reached the other kid at a run and hurled him over his rack with a loud bang against the lockers. Others moved in to separate us. He backed up wide-eyed, having learned not to make careless accusations. "Find your billfold?" I taunted him a couple of times.

Actually, I did steal on one occasion, but it was from the Corps, not anyone in particular. I hadn't had any alcohol since leaving Deerinwater, which made California bars all the more inviting. I drew watch one night. I walked around the barrack every hour, but my basic task was just to stay awake in the office in the unlikely event someone broke in and tried to steal our rifles. I was relaxing in an office chair when my eyes fell on a rubber-banded stack of pink cards. They were blank marine ID cards.

I thought of taking them all and selling them, but that was too big a risk. I looked around for a while and listened, hearing nothing. I moved over to a typewriter, rolled in one of the cards, and took a chance. I had been a good typist in a high school class, and quietly I clacked in a new ID with a birthdate in 1943. It would pass me as twenty-one years old—legal drinking age. I was eager to have some fun in the Golden Land.

The next night's liberty, I rode the bus into Oceanside with my flannel uniform shirt in a sack. At the bus depot I slipped in a stall with a coin-operated camera. I locked the door, put on the shirt, and took two or three headshots of myself. Back on base I glued one on the card, then the next liberty rode the bus back into town and found a copy shop that would laminate it. I was eager for some drinking.

The bars were on the main street of Oceanside, which is Marine Town on the West Coast. The Pacific was the first ocean I'd seen. I stuck a bare foot in the Pacific once and snatched it out, amazed at how cold it was. A couple of the joints had live music and go-go dancers, but I didn't notice the girls having any interest in taking drunk jarheads home with them. My favorite bar was small and dark, the AC frigid. It had a great jukebox, and every night a crowd gathered to watch a ritual. In a small tank behind the bar swam a perch-sized fish with an under-slung jaw. The piranha moved slowly, as if knowing this was as good a life as it was going to get. Every night at eight o'clock the barman dropped in a goldfish that sank and prepared to swim. Blink of your eyes and the goldfish was gone, maybe a tendril of blood hanging in the water.

Jarheads in civvies raised their glasses and yelled, "*Oorah!*"

One night I was standing beside the jukebox after the piranha had gulped its goldfish. My quarters brought up the Supremes' "Baby Love" and "House of the Rising Sun" by the Animals. I glanced away from the jukebox and noticed a man on a barstool who swung around to go take a leak. He had a red splotch on his right jaw. The birthmark.

The old salt came back and reclaimed the barstool others had kept for him, but it was evident he drank alone. He had a military crewcut and wore a short-sleeved pullover and khakis. He ordered another whiskey sour, and I sidled up to him. "How you doing, sarge?"

He gave me an annoyed look. "Not bad," he said.

"I don't mean to bother you. Did you used to be a drill instructor?"

"Sure did."

"San Diego?"

He sighed. "Yeah, Parris Island, too."

I noticed a bit of gray in the stubble over his ears and saw a wedding ring on his left hand. Neither spoke to me of mercy or restraint. "Do you remember me?" I said.

The old salt glared. "Should I? Were you one of mine?"

"No, I was in a platoon in the same company. You wouldn't have noticed me. But we'd hear the way you called cadence, and word went around you're some kind of legend."

"Well, maybe I am."

"Enjoy your drink, sir."

"You bet," the old salt muttered, turning his back on me. "Semper Fi."

I told some guys from my barrack that I might get a tattoo. On the sidewalks I turned my face and window-shopped when a pair of MPs strode by. About an hour later the old salt looked unsteady when he emerged from the piranha bar. I followed him to a small park facing the ice plants and beach where he'd parked his car, a dented Valiant with salt rust on the fenders. He stood by the driver's door and searched his pockets for his keys.

"Hey, sarge," I crooned, and when he turned, I let him have it with a right.

"Huh," he said, flung against the door.

"Just as I am," I sang, blasting him with a left. The sergeant swore and heaved himself off the car, trying to grab me by the balls, a favored way of marine fighting. I clipped him with an uppercut that dropped him to his hands and knees.

"I ain't got no money," he said.

"Who does?" I hooked him on the ear.

"What's your problem? What did I do?"

"You fucked with my dream."

The sarge was sobering up fast. "Your what?"

"My dream. My aspirations. My voice." I hit him again.

"Your dream? Your *voice?* You're crazy. You gonna kill me? Have a go at it. I'll kill you." He lunged but wasn't fast enough. I put him down again, grabbed the back of his collar, twisted it tight, and dog-walked him through ice plants to the sand and waves.

"Drown you in the surf, that'll work, but first I'm gonna baptize you. Cleanse you of your sins, 'cause I know there must be a multitude of 'em laying heavy on your soul, but never you mind. Just prepare to meet your Maker. You know, hope for the best."

The preachers had always raised their right hands, but I didn't want to lose control of the chokehold I had made of his shirt collar, so I raised my left hand. "Hear me now. It goes like this. 'In the name of the Father, the Son, and the Holy Ghost . . .'"

That's when the Oceanside patrol cops turned on the lights.

I don't know why I thought I was going to get away with it. I didn't know I was going to do it at all. The talk of drowning him was just talk. I was going to leave him in the ice plants and vanish in the darkness, an unknown assailant. If I missed the last bus to the base, I'd just make the hike, tell the MPs at the gate I'd gotten too drunk, and there would be an ass chewing for violating curfew but nothing else.

At least that was how I reframed the moment for the major assigned to argue my defense. I knew I was sunk when the prosecutor, another major, put the old salt on the stand and got him talking about a select club of veterans called "the Chosin Few."

It went like this. In November 1950, when I was six years old, a UN force led by American soldiers and marines thought they would reach the Yalu River, the border between North Korea and China, and deliver on General Douglas MacArthur's promise to have the Korean War won by Christmas. The colonel and judge of my court martial leaned toward Gunnery Sergeant Geoffrey Edwards, who was thirty-four the night I assaulted him in Oceanside, as the prosecutor led him through the battle at the Frozen Chosin Reservoir.

"How cold was it, sergeant?"

"Thirty-five below zero, sir. Constant blizzard. Medics thawed morphine capsules in their mouths so they could inject it. The oil in our M-1s froze up and they wouldn't reload."

The colonel rubbed his palms together as he listened. "You were under the command of Colonel Chesty Puller?"

"Yes, sir. Proud to have been."

Ye gods, they had me up against the marine saint Chesty Puller, the most decorated marine of them all. The prosecutor said, "What did Colonel Puller say about your unit's situation when he learned the Red Chinese had come across the Yalu River with twenty-two divisions?"

"I didn't hear it personally, but we were told he said, 'We've been looking for the enemy for some time. We've finally found him. We're surrounded. That simplifies things.'" Ho ho ho. My defense attorney said not a word in this give-and-take.

The prosecutor said, "You were awarded a Silver Cross for valor in defending high ground against Chinese wave assaults as you and other marines fought your way out of there."

"Yes, sir," the gunny sergeant said. "I'm wearing it on my uniform."

"I see that. How old were you then?"

"Nineteen."

"All right. Let's talk about the night of 16 October 1966 in Oceanside, California. What happened to you as you were headed home?"

The old salt pointed an index finger at me. "That *puke* jumped me from behind. I'd have stuck his head in the sand and stood him feet up like a commie battle flag if the local police hadn't come along."

"Did you know this PFC, the defendant?"

"No, sir. Never saw him before in my life."

"Are you certain?"

"Yes, sir."

He passed the witness to my defense attorney. I knew the deal was done when my guy said he had no questions. "All right, sergeant," said the colonel. "You're dismissed."

"Aye aye, sir," said the birthmark, and he walked past me, glaring. My hands were clasped on the table before me. I laid a middle finger over the knuckles of the left one and let him see it. If the colonel had seen that he would have put me in shackles.

In my defense the major put just one witness on the stand. Staff Sergeant Ronald Mulligan gazed at me with sadness. The DI said he remembered me well, and that he recalled me choking at chow on two occasions and that I had trouble speaking for a while, but I couldn't or wouldn't tell him what was wrong.

"Do you remember the dates of those incidents?" the prosecutor asked.

"No, sir. It was sometime last summer."

"Did he ask for medical attention or file a complaint against Sergeant Edwards?"

"No, sir. I knew something was wrong with him. I should have made him go to the doctor assigned to us."

After the guilty verdict, the bird colonel said if I had been convicted of the same crime under California jurisdiction, I would have been looking at fifteen years and a $15,000 fine. I was busted to private and sentenced to four years in a marine brig, after which I would either finish out a four-year enlistment as a regular marine or receive a dishonorable discharge. The colonel said the Uniform Code of Military Justice was giving me a break. Well, horseshit. Back home it would have been just a misdemeanor. I would have been writing my name with the smuggled Crayon like those thugs that beat up the airmen. But it brought to mind the apostle Paul's advice to Christians to leave vengeance to the Lord. It was not an act of real good sense.

CHAPTER 18

If you've survived one day of busting rocks, they don't get much different or any better. Fifteen months into the hell of my own making, when Colonel Bullick offered me his devil's bargain, it wasn't a hard call for me to make. I don't care how good or big fighters are, they don't spar every day, and on days they do, they rest a minute between rounds.

That first morning the corporal in charge of photocopy drove a Jeep through an underpass of Interstate 5 that let us into the sand dunes of the Pacific. No buildings were in sight. When he stopped the Jeep, he tossed his cover in the driver's seat, and I left mine as well. "So which one is it?" I asked as we took off running.

"Huh?"

"Ken or Kenny?"

He grinned. "You can call me Kenny, but I'll make you pay for it."

In the murk ahead I made out two columns of running marines. Kenny saw them, too, and veered up into the soft sand. A thick-necked man wearing a utility cap ran beside them. In the roar of the surf we could make out his calls of cadence. They were all thick-necked and muscled up. They jogged in perfect step. "Who are they?" I asked.

"Force Recon."

"Oh." Force Recon was the Corps' equivalent of the Army's Green Berets and Navy SEALs. Marines regarded them with a frightened kind of awe. If Kenny was afraid of them, I knew I was.

"That sarge would jump our asses for not wearing covers on our heads," he said. He looked over with another grin and said, *"Haid."*

After they were gone, I said, "You mind if we get back down in the hard sand?"

As we ran he breathed deeply and shook out his long arms. "I love ocean and the beach," he said.

"I'm used to air that's a little drier."

He swung around and jogged backwards, exercising his hamstrings. "Sarge tells me you're an outlaw."

"People who think that, they got the say."

"What did you do to wind up in the brig?"

"Beat up a drill instructor in Oceanside."

Kenny barked a laugh, swung back around, and jogged forward. "Every swinging dick in the Corps would like to have done that."

"I don't recommend it."

We geared up and sparred four rounds that afternoon. I was in tremendous shape from the rock pile but I hadn't had a glove on in nearly two years. I had never been in with anyone who hit anywhere near that hard, and he didn't let up. He had an unusual style. He had a little head movement but for defense he mostly relied on a right glove that he kept high beside his head and moved around in front of his face. He picked off punches with it well. He carried his left low across his body, and this habit made his jab shoot upward; it landed hard. I tried to slip his punches and wasn't quick enough. I had better luck deflecting them with my forearms and gloves, and I was good at gliding and circling to my left. But that was into the power of his right, and he was good at cutting off the ring. My arms and shoulders were going to be sore all the time from the pounding they took. I was glad I had that sparring helmet. He seemed to hit me everywhere except the top of my head.

When the sergeant announced we were done Kenny gave me a nod and said, "Good workout. You got some skill."

"Thanks. So do you."

I held the ropes so he could step through first. When he was gone, I flopped on the ring apron. Sarge unlaced my gloves and yanked them off.

I pulled off my headgear and he tossed me a towel. "You did all right in there," he said. "Surprised me. What do you think?"

I looked for the incessant bell and said, "You ever turn that thing off?"

"When I go to the house. Sometimes I forget. I was asking about my fighter."

"He is one. You know that."

"Can you push him? Help him?"

"Hell if I know. It's in my interest to stay in the ring with him."

When we weren't sparring, hitting the bags, or taking turns slugging a truck tire with a sledgehammer—Kenny looked impressed and surprised, I didn't fill him in about the rock pile—in the ring I wielded gloves that resembled the mitts of baseball catchers, except they had no webbing between the forefinger and thumb. I started getting the hang of it after a few sessions. I called *one* for his lefts and *two* for his rights, singly but more often in combinations. There are only six punches in boxing, though Kenny had seven. It's simple that way. But I had to match or exceed his speed to make it worthwhile. Sometimes I stepped away shaking my wrist in pain. Other times Kenny's punches knocked a mitt loose and sent it flying out of the ring.

He worked me out, too, which I appreciated. My favorite routine was when he propped his shoulder against a flattened black medicine ball with a circular tan-colored inset that denoted the target. "That's it," Kenny said as I banged away. "Back me up." Then he took his turn. One day he blasted me clear through the ropes. Sarge came running, but Kenny and I were laughing. As Sarge predicted, we began to enjoy each other's company. It made me feel better about myself. My past relations with black men were a mixed bag at best.

Kenny worked just as hard on defense. Some drills my job was to throw punches fast and hard enough they would have hurt if they landed. He parried with both hands and forearms. Or he used the crossed-arms defense perfected by Archie Moore as I banged away.

"I don't like you doing that," Sarge yelled.

"I don't care," Kenny said through his mouthpiece.

"It's not international style. In the amateurs it's going to get you beat."

"Purpose of the game, Sarge, is to hit and not get hit."

One afternoon after we'd sparred six rounds and Kenny had gone to the shower and wherever he spent the nights, I asked Sarge, "Is anything wrong with his legs?"

"What do you mean? He's pretty spry in there, cutting off the ring. He was a football and track star in high school. Set records running the hurdles."

"He drags his right foot. I've never seen anyone do that. Like he had childhood polio or something."

Sarge snorted. "Just his way. I spoke to him about it, but it comes natural to him. He said it gives him power and keeps him from getting squared off against the other guys. Shows them just an angle, he says."

Late another afternoon Kenny and I were lounging in the gym, sitting on the ring apron. "How'd you get into boxing?" he said.

"The Society of Righteous and Harmonious Fists."

He laughed and said, "The what?"

"Oh, in high school my best friend got sent off to military school for half the year and came back talking about the Boxers Rebellion in China. The rebels wanted to chase out all the foreigners, and they loved killing Christians, especially missionaries. An international force went to put the rebellion down. Britain, France, Italy, and America did most of the fighting. You'd think it wouldn't be hard for all those to chase off militia taking orders from an empress dowager, but about four hundred marines wound up under siege in Peking, trying to defend a weak spot in the city's wall and keep the foreign legations from being overrun. You don't read anything about that in the marines' Little Red Book."

Kenny studied me and said, "You're a warehouse of information."

I shrugged. "When my friend got back from military school and three of us entered the Golden Gloves, we decided we were the Society's secret chapter. All three of us got beat the first night."

"You the only one that kept going?"

"Yeah."

What was your record over there in Texas?"

"Seventeen and one."

"Well, hell, I'm just twenty-one and two."

"You're not doing four years in the brig."

He whistled. "You must have really hurt that DI."

"No. I just got caught."

CHAPTER 19

Our talk meandered into our personal lives. He told me about his Aunt Mary, who raised him as much as his parents did, and every morning gave him a breakfast of Cheerios, milk, and bananas. "Aunt Mary lost her three children during the Spanish flu epidemic that happened at the end of the First World War, and in the course of that she found out her husband, who'd been drafted in the all-black regiment, was gassed to death in the Argonne Forest. She never thought of ever getting married again." He chuckled, remembering. "On her front and back doors she put up this sign. *If you're a lone grown man that ain't kin you got no purpose in this house.* Aunt Mary was big and loud, and she didn't put up with no nonsense, except from me."

I volunteered that I was in love back home with Ann, a divorced young mother. If I ever got out of this mess, I'd try to make it up to her and marry her. I'd help raise Josie, and maybe we'd have another child or two. And I'd move us far from Deerinwater. I told him, "Most of Texas is as overrated as longhorns on a cow."

He grinned and said, "Jacksonville's not a bad place. A farm on the outskirts used to be a safe place of the Underground Railroad, slaves trying to escape into the free states. There are still pockets of Klan around there, too. But I never felt that in the town."

"Because you were an all-state football player."

He shrugged. "I dispute that, but it didn't hurt. I got offers from Ohio State, Nebraska, Oklahoma, Michigan, Wisconsin, Illinois, Iowa, and San Jose State."

"What did you play?"

"Defensive end is what got me all-state. I was tall and big and fast, and I was a good tackler. Dropped back to linebacker and picked off passes now and then. But I liked running the ball better. My favorite coach told me I could be the next Jim Brown."

"Why weren't you?" I said.

My impudence drew a sniff. He sighed and stretched his shoulders and arms by pulling on a ring rope. "It started while I was in high school. I had this girlfriend named Glory that I was crazy about. Good kind of crazy when we were steaming up Pop's old Ford. Jealous crazy, the way she talked to other guys in the hall, putting her hand on their arms, snuggling up close to them for a second. Glory was a year behind me in school, and I didn't want to let her get away. She's why I didn't sign with any of those big schools. Northeast Missouri State was just two hours away on a bus. That way I wouldn't lose her.

"The summer before I went over to Kirksville, damn if I didn't see her going past our house in a car with another guy, sitting real close to him. I jumped in Pop's Ford, banged off a parked car two or three blocks later, kept going, and cut them off. The kid let me get out, watched me come, then gunned it and flipped me off the windshield and the hood."

"You're lucky he didn't run over and kill you."

"Yeah. I couldn't do anything about it at the time. I never went to the doctor, because I didn't want any more grief from Pop, who was mad as hell about his car. I told him somebody must have run into it while I had it parked. And I didn't know if they'd let me keep my scholarship if I missed all the first year with a non-football injury."

"You played a season with a broken collarbone?"

"Getting dumber all the time. I played on the freshman team and we practiced against the varsity. The collarbone break was right up against the shoulder joint and didn't heal right. I thought I played pretty well, considering, but it bothered me enough that I always tried to hit with my right shoulder, so you miss a lot of blocks and tackles. Grab a lot of air and turf. The coaches got on me, thinking I wasn't trying, because I came with this big reputation, and I didn't live up to it. First time I'd ever had a coach decide he didn't like me.

"On the other hand, forget Glory. There were plenty of good-looking girls on that campus. I was gone by mid-season the second year. Girls and football and grades all rolled into one sour dumpling. I told off the head coach and stormed off. By the time I reached the field house one part of my brain was telling me to go back out there and apologize and tell the man what was wrong with my shoulder. But I was too pissed off and proud. I cleared out of the dorm and caught the bus back to Jacksonville that night.

"So I was back living at home. Because of who I was, men would come up to me on the street, talk football a minute, then offer me a job. I never followed up. I was going around with this girl named Carina who'd been just a friend in school. Then one night we were making out and she put her hand between my legs and got a handful of my jeans, and we started being more than just friends. An older sister of hers was renting a house and didn't mind if we took one of the bedrooms and closed the door. It went on for weeks.

"At home Pop didn't exactly kick me out but he read me the riot act. He told me I had to get back in school or get a job or join the service, or I was out. Get a job. My loneliest fear was that I was going to get stuck in Jacksonville the rest of my life, and I was already doing it to myself."

"I knew all-state guys in Deerinwater. It was hard for them to deal with things when they found out they're just another guy."

He glanced without moving his head. "Thanks for your opinion. More weeks passed. Pop got madder and madder, so I talked to Coach Al and he told me to join the marines. So I did. Then Aunt Mary died, I couldn't stand missing her funeral, and the recruiter arranged a three-month postponement of my reporting. Back at Carina's sister's house, I showed up one night with a package of rubbers. Carina told me to throw those things away. She wanted to feel me and me to feel her. Said she knew her rhythms, when to shove me away."

"Ever heard of birth control pills?"

"At the time, no, I hadn't. You want to hear this story or not?"

"Go ahead. Please."

"This was up to October in 1964. One of the TV stations in Springfield carried the Liston-Clay fight, the first one, before he announced himself Muhammad Ali. I was with Carina, and we were watching the fight. I thought Liston was gonna kill him. But right away Clay was doing pretty damn good. But then he started blinking his eyes and stumbling around like he'd gone blind. Carina picked that moment to tell me she was pregnant. She sprung that on me right when Liston didn't come out for the seventh round.

"I said, 'You're what?' She said, 'You got ears. You heard me.'"

"I was stunned. One part of me staring at that craziness in a boxing ring. The other part knew one thing for certain. I didn't want no child of mine called a bastard. No way my mom could hide from it in that small town with little boy me hanging on her hip. Account of my family history, I said, 'All right, I love you. Let's get married.' She laughed in my face. She beat her hands on her legs she thought it was so funny. *'Marry* you! Are you out of your mind? Boy, you don't have a thought in your head. You ain't got a bowl to pour milk in. You gonna be off in the marines anyway.'"

"Ouch," I said. "Did you love her?"

"I don't know, but in those circumstances it's what you say."

"She had the baby?"

"Sure. Carina's a smart girl. She married a cousin of mine named Keith, and they named my son Gilbert. I was about to get out of boot camp when she wrote me, 'Keith say he don't have nothing against you but he don't think it be good for you to come back around here confusing our boy about who his daddy is.'"

The silence was interrupted by Sarge's bell. Kenny said, "What's your MOS?"

"Artillery."

"They teach you how to do that? Drop rounds on targets miles away?"

"They taught me to lug howitzer shells that weigh twenty pounds apiece."

Kenny nodded and started unlacing his ring shoes. "They sent me to Pensacola to learn how to operate radios in the field. The Morse code and wireless history stuff was interesting, but they made it clear I was going to be with platoons of grunts. What had I got myself into? Big black guy carrying a radio against a green jungle background—who the Viet Cong gonna shoot first?"

"How'd the boxing come in?"

"I was waiting for the orders to ship out when I found out Camp Lejeune had a football team. Half a season of that, I got into it with this captain that thought he was a hot-shot running back. I ploughed him under one day when they had him on defense, and he jumped up and called me a nigger. The coach was trying to calm me down. I told him off, threw my helmet half the length of the field, and stomped off. Luckily an old fellow we called Pappy recruited me to the boxing team. I hadn't known him much time at all when he got killed in a freak accident. Sitting on a bus stop bench when some guy lost control of his car and crushed him against a rock wall.

"Even without a real trainer I was doing pretty good. Name in the papers, knocking people out, and I won the North Carolina Golden Gloves. But I had no guarantees. And I fell for this nineteen-year-old named Jeanette. At first, I thought it was a good omen that the town nearest the base was called Jacksonville. But Jeanette's dad had a bar just outside the base. I thought I was going to get my ass shot off *before* they sent me across the pond, because I got her pregnant, too, and she already had a little boy named Tommy."

"Jesus, Kenny. How old were you then?"

"Twenty."

Twenty years old with two sons by different mothers and maybe a stepson in the bargain. Besides boxing gloves and shoes, I had nothing in common with this man.

"I did the right thing and married Jeanette," he reflected. "She's gorgeous, and I was in love for real this time." Another sigh. "Thought she was, too."

Some mornings we ran up and down firebreaks in the hills of brush that smelled like licorice, past junked landing crafts with rope nets for training in case another war dialed back Guadalcanal and Iwo Jima. Sarge had told me Kenny was raising a little boy by himself. A day or so later, when we were walking back from our uphill run, I asked him how that came about. He gave me a sideward glance. "The way it works, you get a girl hot and bothered and you spurt some juice in her, and it feels good to both of you, and sometimes a tadpole starts growing and looking for a way out."

"Jerk. I meant your particular tadpole."

"Life was going along pretty good. Me still living in the barracks, Jeanette still at home with her parents and Tommy. She wasn't showing yet and she hadn't told her folks. Then I got orders out to Pendleton. Better than Vietnam, but making PFC money, how could I support Jeanette and the baby? I got her to move in with my parents back home. She didn't take to it at all. Hardly ever came out of my old room, except to eat. They got on each other's nerves. She liked Jacksonville fine, only it was the one in North Carolina. But our boy was born big and healthy, and we named him Kenneth Howard. Kenny Junior."

"Did she come out here with you?"

"Not for long. Jeanette was missing her Tommy bad. When Kenny Junior started getting his milk from a bottle, she told me to bring him on out here and get us situated, and she'd be along in a few weeks. I tried to do right by my marriage, but *six months* is what went by. Sarge was glad to get me, and I love it out here. The sun and noise of the birds and surf. Black girls, Mexican girls, Japanese, Korean. Make eye contact and catch a smile. I couldn't help myself. When Jeanette finally arrived, she saw me leaning in a little too close talking to a girl in a car one time. Then she found a pair of panties under the bed. All the reason she needed to leave and divorce me. She's not a bad girl. She just didn't want me. She's Kenny Junior's mother. I hope they'll work that out some day."

"What do your girlfriends think about you having a little boy?"

He grinned. "Drives off some, but it fascinates more of them. My scoring percentage went up."

"How do you go about raising a baby?"

He looked at me like it was another dumb question. I guess it was.

"You get good at changing diapers. You put milk in a bottle and stir in nutrient powders supposed to be good for him and walk him around at night when he's fussy and crying. You sing him lullabies. How's he gonna know it's a song by the Four Tops? *Sugar pie, honey bunch, you know that I love you . . .* It's worked out, thanks to a babysitting service the marines have. Boxing got me all these breaks. I got no right to complain."

As we neared the Quonset huts below, we had a mild argument about boxing. I asked him what he thought of Ali. He shrugged. "Master showboat. Or he was."

"But don't you like the way he fights?"

He shrugged. "He gets away with it."

"He took apart Sonny Liston."

Another shrug. "Famous phantom punch, the second fight."

"No way, I've seen the stop-action film clips of that. Liston's thrown a left jab, and he's over-extended, all his weight on his left foot. The next frame he's flat on his back."

"They can edit film, you know. Ali is boxing's Gorgeous George."

"Well, they say the man could rassle. Boxing's show business, Kenny. Ali understands that. Otherwise people will say fighters, we're all just hooligans."

I realized I said *we.* He ignored that and said, "It's hard to showboat and grandstand much when all the fights last three rounds."

"Are the name change and the draft the reasons you don't like him?"

"I didn't say I don't like him. I don't know him. But I admire the way he did that with the draft. I remember seeing him on TV coming down steps of some courthouse, and a young white guy got in his face. Crewcut college boy type, like you say you were. Ali said, 'Why don't I just fight *you?* All you white boys running off to London and Canada.' I'd like to fight Ali, is all. It's a shame he's losing all that money."

CHAPTER 20

Another day we didn't work out because Sarge had impacted wisdom teeth pulled. It involved a lot of jerking and bruising, and the navy dentist decided to keep him at Mainside overnight. I was walking between Quonset huts when Kenny pulled up beside me in the Jeep and told me to get in. He tore up the dirt fire lanes of the hills with more than his usual enthusiasm. He negotiated curves with wheels spinning and downshifted to brake, banging the gearbox. I hung on and hoped he didn't flip the thing on top of us.

"Did they give you this thing?"

He grinned and eased off the accelerator. "I can't take it off base. But I take it home at night, and I'm free to use it as long as I pay for the gas."

"Where's home?" I said. I'd never known where he went after he left the gym.

"Base housing now, Camp San Onofre. Kenny Junior and I have a little duplex, and there's a kindergarten and day care place for him. Living on base has cut into my love life, but it's not bad. I'm doing what I'm supposed to be doing right now."

We came over a hill and the ocean and a small settlement lay before us.

"Where are we?" I said.

"San Onofre Beach. North end of the base. They rent those cabins cheap and I've used them a few times to have girlfriends in for the night. Some neighbors have a couple of teenagers who don't mind babysitting Kenny Junior. I pay them all I can."

He drove past the cabins and parked in front of a bar. It felt strange going inside with him. I hadn't seen one since the night of the piranha and the old salt with the birthmark. We were the only customers in the early afternoon. The bartender was a young marine. "Hey, champ," he greeted Kenny. "What'll you have, fellas?"

Kenny ordered a Rainier and I asked for an Olympia.

"You got an ID?" the bartender asked me.

"No. We're on base so I didn't think I'd need it." In fact, I had no identification. They had taken away my marine ID and Texas driver's license when they pulled me out of custody in Oceanside.

Kenny said, "You're twenty-one, aren't you?"

"Twenty-three now, matter of fact."

"He's okay," Kenny said. "He works for me."

Kenny paid for the beers, and we carried them out on a small deck. This beach looked pebbled, unlike the dunes where we ran in the mornings. The taste of beer was harsher than I remembered, but it was mighty fine.

Then Kenny startled me: "Have you thought about taking off?"

"From here? Not really. I wouldn't know which way to go."

Camp Pendleton is vast. It's ten times the size of Manhattan Island, and has a coastline of seventeen miles. Kenny pulled sheets of paper out of his hip pocket and unfolded them on the table before us. "I move a lot of paper in our copy shop," he said, "and I read some of it." I saw that the papers detailed kinds of discharges from the military.

"When they sentenced you," he said, "did you get any documentation?"

"Not that I remember. The CO just told me what the sentence was, gave me a lecture, and back to jail I went."

"He just *said* you could get a dishonorable discharge after you get out of the brig."

"I guess. I was pretty dazed at the time." I gave him a questioning look.

"According to this, the only crimes that can get somebody a dishonorable discharge are desertion, sedition, sexual assault, murder, and manslaughter. You done any of any of those things?"

"Not that I recall."

He stretched his mouth at my sarcasm. "Then the worst you can get is a bad conduct discharge."

I revolved the beer can in my hands. "What difference does it make?"

"Plenty. Tack a dishonorable discharge on top of your assault conviction, and you'd be lucky to get a job in an Orange Julius stand. They're not just trying to break you. They want to punish you the rest of your life."

I looked at him and listened.

"I could get you some civilian clothes," he said, "and run you over to a place near here, give you some money, and you could wait until dark and hike on out. Catch a bus in San Clemente. But you've got that haircut and the tan on your hands and face and neck. They wanted to make it so bad for you that you had to run, that you'd go AWOL. That's what they *want* you to do. That way they can tack on desertion."

My silence was filled with all the things exploding in my mind.

"It's up to you," Kenny said. "But if you decide to do it, you'd better start thinking about how to be a real criminal. A guy's got to eat."

Talking like this made my head hurt, and I changed the subject. "Can I give you some advice? Boxing, not personal."

"Sure. Go ahead."

"They don't call Archie Moore the Mongoose because he looks like one. If his style of defense works for you, and you get hit and need to clear your head, use it."

"I mean to."

"Another thing. Sarge keeps bitching at you to straighten up your right. Forget that, your straight right is fine. But he's got you thinking about it, trying to correct yourself. I used to be a baseball player. It's like you see a fastball coming, and you know you can get around on it, but you're thinking about what the coach said, trying to doctor your swing. You're just an instant slow. That's what Sarge is doing to you. You've got a great jab, a world-class right uppercut and left hook, a good straight right, and this other one. It's not a roundhouse, like Sarge says. It's an *over*-the-house right hand. Don't get talked out of that punch. You see a way to use it, let it fly."

"Why, thank you, Haid." He grinned and said, "You really like this stuff, don't you? You'd like to be the one going to international tournaments and maybe turning pro."

"No way. I know the difference between good and not good enough."

One week I had nothing to do but keep the gym swept out, watch over the jarheads that came to work out, and tell them Sarge didn't want any sparring until he got back. My dodge with Kenny and Sarge would soon be ending, one way or another. They had their sights on the 1968 Olympics in Mexico City.

Kenny had a good chance, but it was by no means guaranteed. In international amateur boxing there was much buzz about the Cubans. Castro had banned all professional athletics in his revolution, and a veteran trainer from the Soviet Union had taken over the boxing program of its vassal state. Their top heavyweight now was named José Cabrera. The best Cuban heavyweight would be the one that succeeded him, Teófilo Stevenson, but Cabrera was said to be a bruiser.

A year out from the Olympics, two heavyweights dominated amateur boxing conversation in California. One was Kenny, who had been working his way up through the military and international tournaments. He may have had the edge at that point because in addition to his North Carolina Golden Gloves and All-Marine Corps titles, while at Pendleton he won the US trials for the Pan American Games.

The other California heavyweight that Sarge talked about was George Foreman. He had come out of a Job Corps camp up by San Francisco and Oakland. He clubbed his opponents to the canvas in the finals of the California Golden Gloves and the Nevada Golden Gloves, but he was outpointed in the finals of the National Golden Gloves in Milwaukee.

Kenny passed up the 1967 Pan Am Games in Winnipeg because he'd developed tendinitis in one of his shoulders. In his absence a New York fighter named Forrest Ward beat the Cuban José Cabrera in the finals. Sarge and Kenny meant to overcome that and ensure his invitation to the Olympic trials by beating Ward in the national tournament of the AAU, which tried to maintain its hold on which boxers wound up in the Olympics. Since Kenny had won the Pan Am Games two years earlier, Sarge figured he couldn't be denied if he won the AAU's tournament.

Kenny stopped three opponents, and in the finals, he won a decision over Forrest Ward. They came back to our boxing camp elated. Sarge said we'd continue training but at a lighter pace. A complicating factor in the mix was the end date of Kenny's four-year enlistment. It would come up before the Olympic trials. Officers, ranking sergeants in the re-up department, and Sarge were trying to get him to reenlist for four more and keep going on that route to the Olympics. He was in a position to bargain, so they sweetened the offer with two years in the regular marines and two years in the reserves.

Then one morning I came to the gym to meet Kenny for our run and Sarge growled, "He won't be coming in today." The change in atmosphere was like the methane wall in those hog barns where I dumped sacks of feed in my prior life. After a couple of hours of that I went in Sarge's office and asked what was wrong.

"We got screwed," he said. "This Ward kid has New York money behind him, and his backers want him to have a leg up turning pro. After he lost to Kenny, they got busy behind the scenes. The AAU threw out the decision and said they're sending Ward to the Olympic trials. First excuse, they said that Ward's win over the Cuban at the Pan Am Games will carry more weight with judges at the Olympics. Their next excuse was Kenny's style is not amateur enough. I told him, I told him. You've heard me tell him."

Boxing's dark underside existed even in the amateurs. When I saw Kenny the next day I said, "This is terrible. Can they do that?"

"Seems they can," he said. "After all I've done for the marines, you'd think they could stand down some chickenshit outfit like the AAU. They had to break their own rules to do this."

"There's no way to appeal?"

"Nope, as if there'd be time for it," he said. "Even Sarge is acting weird. Have you noticed he turned off the bell?"

"What are you going to do?"

"Take my discharge. All my trust in these assholes is gone. The Marine Corps can't stand down some chickenshit organization like the AAU?"

"Then what? Turn pro?"

He let out a desolate sigh. "I don't see how. That takes money, unless you care to live in a cave and eat snakes. I've got a high school education and a boy to raise. I told you Pop's a dispatcher for the police department in Jacksonville. When I was home on leave one time the chief told me when I got out, he'd like to make me the town's first black patrolman. Said it could lead to me being a detective. I guess I ought to go home and accept his offer. I figure my folks would help with Kenny." He shook his head. "Token nigger cop."

It shook me to hear him say that. "You can't just quit. You're too good at it."

"What choice do I have? I've gone as high as they're gonna let me go."

I sat on the ring apron beside him and put my head in my hands. "Ah, you needed somebody better than me. If you'd knocked out Ward, they couldn't have done this."

He gave me a sharp look. "What?"

"So close to something so important, you needed somebody bigger and better than me to work with you. Somebody that pushed you more. I've been doing just enough here to look out for myself. Trying to keep from going back to the brig."

"Forget that, you've pushed me plenty. Made me speed up and improve my combinations and defense. None of this is your fault." His tone went from bitter to reflective. "Oh, there's something in what you say. Most of the guys they ran in here were sluggers. I could stay in shape sparring them, but they weren't challenging me. But yeah, there were days when I lightened up because I didn't think you could take it. Because I liked you."

He glanced my way and said, "Now don't give me that wounded look. You know what I mean. It doesn't matter. We're both a couple of losers."

"You're not," I said, trying to cheer him up.

Kenny's plight and despair gave me much to think about, none of it good. I walked back to my hut and found a soiled envelope on the blanket of my rack. Ann had mailed the letter months earlier. Her handwriting sent a bolt of joy through me, until

> *My dear Haid, It makes me cry to write this. You haven't answered my letters in so many months I can't remember. I hate that you joined that thing and left me. You told me it would just be six months! I was lonely, confused, and I thought I knew you, but I don't. I have to move on with my life. I have to think of Josie, not just myself. I met a man who works at another bank in town. He's kind and gentle, I know he loves me, and he's very good with Josie. He's asked me to marry him, and I've told him I will. He has a new job that will be moving us to Oklahoma City. I hope you're well and safe and happy, wherever you are. Remember me. Ann*

I lay with a pillow over my face. I didn't want anybody to walk in and see me crying. What a fool I'd been to think it might still work out for us.

I went back to the gym and geared up. Sarge said he wanted a light sparring session this afternoon. He'd turned the bell back on, and I went into my leftward glide. Kenny had a bored look on his face as he stalked me. His left arm swung lower and lower. It looked like he was helping somebody saw a log. I drove inside his reach, in the pocket as fighters say, and cut loose on him. I aimed for his headgear, but my right landed flush on his nose. Knowing I was in for it now, I threw punches with all the speed I had. He made a grab for the ropes and fell on his hip.

"Whoa!" Sarge yelled. "Time!"

Kenny threw him a glare and shook his head. "Man seems to want a fight."

He got up, stared at me a moment, and came at me in a fury. I was trying to fend off his blows and flee when I experienced a flash of black, which sounds like a contradiction, but that's what a knockout is. It's a black hole of the organism, a little *blip* of coma, then the organs decide collectively they aren't yet willing to die.

I was on my back and first felt like I'd been taking a nice nap, but then pain in my right ear and jaw let me know it had been a left hook. I never saw it.

Sergeant and Kenny kneeled on the canvas beside me as I came back to myself. Kenny's helmet and gloves were off. "You scared us, brother," he said. "Didn't like the way you were breathing. For about thirty seconds you were making noise like a freight train. Brought to mind that expression 'death rattle.'"

"Shut up, Kenny," said Sarge. "Goddamn it. We've got a hurt man here." He muttered, "And now I've got to find you another one."

I sat up and pushed Kenny's hands away. "Wipe your nose," I told him. "You're bleeding on my sweats."

He shoved me and I fell back like Jack Johnson dropping to the canvas after beating up Jess Willard twenty-five rounds in Havana. Taking that dive was the only way he could get the feds off his back. He made his point by putting his forearm over his eyes to block the afternoon sun.

"I'm sorry," Kenny said. "I didn't mean to hit you that hard."

Yeah, you did. That's how it works. If you land a punch like that, one that knocks somebody unconscious, the thrill of it electrifies your bones and inhabits your whole being. But when the other fighter's brain bleeds and swells up and it takes him into a real coma, one he's not apt to find his way back from, that's the regret you'll never get rid of, the rest of your life. For about thirty seconds there I was Billy Conn having his way with Joe Louis. Then I slipped far enough into that netherworld of darkness to know I was done with it. The world of violence had brought me nothing but grief. Peace, you all.

CHAPTER 21

The marines had me out of there so fast I barely had time to tell Kenny and Sarge goodbye. I could tell Sarge was emotional about it, but he just shook my hand and wished me luck. Kenny and I scribbled our hometown addresses on the backs of some other people's business cards and got tangled up in awkwardness, trying to embrace. We were too used to clinching. He said, "If you ever get to Jacksonville you'll never have to pay a traffic ticket."

After I was frisked and buzzed back through the gate of the brig a corporal walked me to Colonel Bullick's office without the routine of calling cadence. The colonel returned our salutes, the corporal went away, and he told me to stand easy and rocked back in his chair.

"How'd it go?"

"A concussion and sore jaw. Sir."

"Concussion. Did a doctor tell you that?"

"No sir, I didn't see one. But your champ put me out cold. Two nights ago it felt like I had a railroad spike driven in my skull. It's better now."

"How was he?"

"As a fighter? As good as they say. I liked him. We got to be friends."

"You've done all right here. About as well as any man could."

"Thank you, Sir."

"I'm not complimenting you. You're still a sorry-ass bonehead marine."

He spoke then like he was talking to himself. "I could run this outlaw depot till doomsday and never get a general's star. My wife wants me to get out while we're still young. It's up or out anyway. I want to be the one that makes the decision."

"Sir, if I could say—"

"What?" he growled. "Say it. Do it now."

"Just that you've treated me fairly, sir. And I, well, I wish you well."

He blew wind through his lips in a silent laugh. "Boy, does that warm my heart. Stand at ease, Shelton. I didn't tell you not to."

I relaxed and clasped my hands behind me.

"Some other officers and I've been looking at your case. We think it should have been brought up in your court martial that the gunny sergeant was no angel himself. He had a police record, and you didn't. He's a drunk. He's been in jail for beating his wife, and he's been written up three times for abusing recruits."

I tried to *tell them* he's an asshole.

"I can't see the sense of putting you back on the rock pile. I don't know if you got to read newspapers or watch much television at the boxing camp, but there's quite a war on now. They need bodies, and not the kind coming home in boxes covered with the Stars and Stripes. The Marine Corps wants to let you out of here three days from now. They'll give you time to make out a will, and help if you want it. You'll draw new utilities and boots, and they're going to put you on a big airplane for a long flight. When it lands, you're going to join an infantry unit, draw a weapon and the rest of your equipment, and you're going to fight for your country and the values we hold dear while defending South Vietnam against the communists. You are being given still another chance, Private. Don't blow it."

I said, "Sir, my training was in artillery."

I kept making him laugh. "That's not an offer, Private. It's called an order."

The grunts called the enemy Charlie, Charlies, slopes, gooners, gooks, North gooks, South gooks, VC gooks, and Nagoolians, that last one because so many of them are named Nguyen. They actually pronounce it more like *nwin.* I used that one because it didn't sound quite so foul. I can't remember anyone ever referring to them as Vietnamese.

Da Nang is on a coast of the Pacific Ocean. This heat was dank, suffocating, and the air smelled like latrines, mud, and jet fuel. I got the message right away that all my bad-boy attitude would accomplish here was to send me and others home in body bags. A corporal briefed me on my arrival. *"We own the days. Charlie owns the night."*

In the interest of my survival, I was as scrupulous a rookie as they come. Nights when I wasn't terrified standing watch outside the razor wire, I spent the idle time in our tent field stripping and cleaning my M-16, doing it for speed. M-14s had been standard issue weapons when I took my detour to the brig. With plastic replacing the wooden stocks, the M-16s were lighter, and so were their .22 caliber bullets, which meant we could carry more loaded magazines. I heard that some of the wounds imposed by M-16s were so ghastly the photos were classified. They were alleged to be more accurate than the M-14s when fired automatic, but they had a reputation as "sand traps." They jammed if they weren't kept clean.

A Kit Carson scout named Ahn and I hung together because everybody else was suspicious of us. Unless they were coming back for a second tour, almost all the marines who came off the transports to Da Nang were PFCs or lance corporals. My private's rank meant I'd been in trouble, and these guys didn't want or need any more trouble in their lives. Several grunts in our company had been relieved and airlifted out of the siege of Khe Sanh. Anh spoke English well enough that he had to have had some schooling. Most marines despised the Kit Carson scouts. They were Viet Cong who crossed over and were getting paid better, some said, than the sergeants. How could traitors to their own cause be trusted?

If we didn't get hit and flown out right away, we acquired nicknames. Mine was "High Noon." On patrols outside the perimeter of Da Nang I reminded some guy in the company of the nervous way Gary Cooper walked in that old western. One day word came that our company was moving out. With our packs and weapons, we boarded six-by trucks and rode for two hours on a buckled pot-holed highway that skirted the coast and a long lake. Our convoy drew no fire. About two hundred of us were the first to arrive. Phu Bai was a navy staging area and supply base built for the Marine Corps, Army, and Air Force. Anh told me to look around and draw my own conclusions. The Phu Bai base was less than five miles from the South China Sea, but it was almost undefended. We might as well have been out by our lonesome in the bush.

Anh interpreted for our platoon when we were sent out through villages on daytime patrols, and for the company captain, he was a spy who could dress like a peasant or laborer and bring back eyewitness recon without tipping off his past friends, the VC. To us it appeared he came and went as he chose, just informing our sergeant and lieutenant he had orders to go. One night in our camp when Anh was off on one of his missions, I asked the others, "What's the deal about Kit Carson?" Our lieutenant sat with us smoking a pipe. Behind his back grunts sneered that he'd been to *grad school.* "Carson always had a bunch of Ute scouts with him," he said. "Mean mountain Indians. They helped him drive a herd of sheep to San Francisco one time. They must have been a big hit there." Another night I asked Anh why the village dogs around us barked all the time every night. He laughed and said VC would walk at night in enemy-held villages just to make the dogs bark. That way, when they came in force, the dog noise would have lulled people to think everything was normal.

Anh and I racked beside each other in a crib at Phu Bai. He hadn't given me any reason not to trust him, and I came to know why he switched sides. Before we set out on a night patrol, I saw him make quick jerky movements with his right arm and elbow. At first I thought he was signaling someone we were coming. Then I realized he had crossed himself. He was Catholic. He'd turned on the communist Nagoolians because they made war on people of his faith.

Seven miles away, Hue was his people's shrine city. Song Huong, the Perfume River, wound through the onetime imperial capital of Hue, dividing the ancient city from the new one. The broad river's name came from its upstream passage through orchards of fruit trees that dropped sweet-smelling flowers in the flow. For a few weeks the water smelled like those blossoms. According to Buddhist tradition, the city originated with a lotus flower that bloomed from a mud puddle.

North of the Perfume River lay the old city and the Citadel, a diamond-shaped four-square-mile fortress. Surrounded by moats, the Purple Forbidden City had walls ten feet thick that rose up to twenty-five feet in height. The Perfume River flowed past the southeast walls of the Citadel and on past the Imperial Palace, where the royal family had lived from the 1820s until the end of World War II. The last two decades of the dynasty a prince named Nguyen ruled as the Emperor of Annam and renamed the country Vietnam. When the Allies let the French try to reclaim their colonial empire, the prince abdicated and lived the rest of his life in France.

The communists and their fathers and grandfathers had been at war for thirty-seven straight years against one occupier or another, and their legends told of centuries more. After the battle of Dien Bien Phu drove out the French, Anh told me that Buddhist monks dominated Hue's political life, and they held both sides of the civil war in contempt.

As 1967 turned into 1968 a dense fog enveloped the valley. Sound became a muffled echo chamber. The warring Vietnamese armies had always observed a cease fire for celebrations of Tet Nguyen Dan, the "Feast of the First Morning." January 31 began their New Year. As usual, soldiers in the South Vietnamese Army signed out on leaves and went home to celebrate with their families. The meaning of Tet holiday was a mystery to us, but it gave us a chance to rest and get resupplied.

Anh left our billets in Phu Bai in peasant rags and sandals one night and came back two nights later. He told me there should have been fireworks and people out with helium-filled balloons and paper racket-makers in the streets. He said he'd seen a small column of men moving in South Vietnamese uniforms, but they wore the rubber-soled sandals of his former VC comrades, not boots. All the stores, bars, and restaurants ought to have been doing much business, but shutters were pulled down. Even the whorehouse was closed.

CHAPTER 22

At three thirty that morning a signal flare lit up the fog over the city, and a small group of saboteurs cut the telephone lines to headquarters of a general in command of a South Vietnamese infantry division. Dozens of sappers were killed after they got through one gate and killed the guards. They carried rocket-propelled grenades and wore South Vietnamese uniforms. Faulty logistics got most of them rounded up and killed, but fourteen battalions of Viet Cong and North Vietnamese Army soon poured into the city. The VC and NVA did not perceive a difference between them, as we did. There was no separate chain of command. The enemy Nagoolian brass told the soldiers that the opportunity for so grand a victory came along only every thousand years. Some North Vietnamese soldiers wore dress uniforms into battle.

But the Nagoolians suffered war fog, too. They fired mortar shells that clunked as duds because they forgot to remove the shipping labels. They had anti-aircraft in place and ready for South Vietnamese and US Navy and marine jets, but they didn't know how to take on helicopter gunships. Soldiers sprawled on the ground in grotesque postures, hoping they looked dead. Gunners riddled them where they lay. But by eight o'clock that morning a large blue-and-red flag with the yellow VC star flew above the Citadel. An American recon officer in a low-flying plane saw VC flags in villages all around the city. NVA soldiers walked openly in most parts of the old city and called out hundreds of people's names on bullhorns. They had been identified as "cruel tyrants and reactionary elements." Among the ones executed were an American agricultural assistance worker, two French priests, three German doctors teaching at a medical school, and a Vietnamese priest who had a photo of Ho Chi Minh on his wall. The communists shot a janitor and his two-year-old daughter and five-year-old son and left their bodies lying in a street.

About the time the big VC flag went up over the Citadel, we were ordered back in the trucks. Two were mounted with .50-caliber machine guns, but the sides of the beds and the tailgates that we crouched beside were not armored, and the lean-tos and thatched huts of the suburb villages were hornets' nests of shooters. When someone saw a muzzle flash and we heard the rounds sough past we popped up and unloaded on their approximate location while the driver weaved side to side. If a round took out a tire we were mincemeat. Four marines were hit in my truck before we made three miles.

Bounded by the Perfume River, a tributary, and a canal, the newer and smaller part of the city was called the Triangle. It contained prosperous neighborhoods, province headquarters, the city's main hospital, a prison, and a prestigious university where Ho Chi Minh had once been a student. Ten minutes after that first signal flare went off, the enemy artillery had attacked those neighborhoods with howitzers, heavy mortars, and spinning and tumbling 122-millimeter rockets that terrorized the civilians. They were inaccurate but were six feet long and carried fourteen-pound warheads—it didn't matter where they landed. The civilians of Hue had never experienced weapons like that.

Our battle for Hue was just getting started. South Vietnamese and US Army units took the lead in the fight to recapture the Citadel and the old city. Our orders were to drive the Nagoolians out of the Triangle and protect the bridges that could support the weight of our tanks and other armored weapons. Our immediate mission was to rescue a compound called the Military Assistance Command Vietnam near a university. Inside were a small South Vietnamese Army detachment and about a hundred American soldiers and marines.

We were in line of sight of fortifications that had been dug in the walls of the Citadel by the Japanese. The communists used gargoyles as shields for their recoilless rifles, which made them hard for us to spot, and no help was coming to us from air cover. The high command had decreed that the Purple Forbidden City could not be attacked because of its historic and religious significance. And a vast cemetery lay between the besieged command center and us. The Nagoolians had dug bunkers around the gravestones. Guys who could hot-wire cars were taking our wounded back to Phu Bai in commandeered civilian vehicles.

Late that afternoon the weather cleared enough that a helicopter could reach us. At dusk Anh and I were on the detail of those grabbing, dragging, and heaving the body bags. The number of them reached a point where the pilot said he couldn't get off the ground with any more. Anh had his rifle propped on his pack. He shed his uniform shirt, dug C-rations, some loaded magazines, and a rain slicker out of his pack, and set them on the ground beside me. They were gifts. I understood that we probably wouldn't be seeing each other again.

He pointed off to the west and said he came from a Catholic village over by the Phu Cam Canal. He said the communists had taken the village and made its cathedral a command center. They made men, women, and children line up on all sides of the church to shield them from incoming fire, and the interrogations, accusations, and executions had begun. He said some of his people killed enough communists to take their weapons and fight back. Ahn's explanation of his desertion was simple. "I go help."

Just then there was a sound like *tuhhh* and a sniper round pitched him over on his side. The round blew off his skull cap as neatly as a church key pops the cap of a beer bottle. Blood belched out of his head like it was a fire hose, and his legs and arms jerked and twitched until he was still. Moments later, our platoon sergeant, a black guy called Raynard, stood over me and said, "You bury him. You're the one that liked him."

When I was done with my trenching tool, I grabbed him by his boots and twisted his legs until his corpse rolled in the shallow grave. When I had him covered with soil, I took his magazines and jammed the barrel of his M-16 in the ground beside the grave. "Godspeed," I said. At least it hadn't been hard digging. Sand traps.

CHAPTER 22

Our artillery and helicopter gunships kept enemy heads ducking, but by the fifth day we had advanced just half a mile into the Triangle. "Sweet baby Jesus," I said that night to a kid named Lanzarotta. My hands were shaking so badly I couldn't get into my C-rations. "They're lighting us up."

Lanzarotta said, "You're doing all right."

"How do you know?"

"I'm the commander in chief. Here, let me help you with that can."

The next afternoon snipers thought to be in a three-story building and a heavy machine gun emplacement in another graveyard had us pinned down behind a wall and stand of cactus. Blasts of the incoming fire filled our mouths with concrete grit.

Sergeant Raynard was trying to hear on the field radio. "All right," he yelled. "Buckle up and hear up. Second squad lay out cover fire on automatic. When I count and yell 'Ten,' all the rest of us go. Our objective is that next wall across the street."

We laid out the cover fire, and when Raynard yelled the number Lanzarotta jumped up and ran fifty yards across the street then hit the dirt behind the low wall. He stared back in horror on seeing he was the only one out there.

"What happened?" screamed Raynard. "Why didn't you go?"

"Why didn't you?" somebody yelled back.

I cursed on seeing Lanzarotta roll over on his side. He'd already been hit. With Anh gone, Lanzarotta was the closest thing I had to a friend in this outfit. I counted three, then with the rifle in my right hand and my left clamped on top of my helmet, I jumped out and started running as fast and low to the ground as I could. I tripped just before I got there, and collision with the rifle's sight chipped off part of my right front tooth. Another guy tried to follow me and was dead before he made fifteen yards. The fire coming through that first wall and bank of cactus had been like a cocktail party. I crawled to Lanzarotta and saw that he was hit just under his ribs. "Corpsman!" I yelled through the gunfire, looking back toward the navy medic. He raised his hands in a gesture that said, *As soon as I possibly can.*

Lanzarotta looked at the blood on his hands and shirt. "Oh, man," he moaned, "this is the Empire State Building of pain. This is King fucking Kong."

"You from New York?" I said.

"No. South Philly."

"I gotta go look at something, pal. I'll be right back." Lanzarotta grabbed hold of my hand. "Hang on," I told him. "You're going to be okay."

"How do you know?"

"I'm the commander in chief."

The wall had a hole in it you could have driven a Jeep through. I peeked around and saw the machine gun flashes just before a concrete block fell on my helmet. I shrugged out of my pack and shrapnel vest so I could throw better and gripped one of my Mike 26s. The grenade was egg-shaped and weighed a pound. The spoon on top was a spring-loaded device that once squeezed and released, you had about five seconds to get rid of it. I lurched up and with a howl made the throw of my life.

Most guys could throw one of those things forty or fifty yards. Guys behind me told me my heave carried at least sixty, and it bounced and went off in the laps of the three Nagoolians with the machine guns. It felt like I'd torn something in my shoulder. That night I rolled over my left side, getting weight off the sore one. I pulled Anh's poncho over mine and tried to get an hour or two of sleep. Lanzarotta didn't make it to the aid stations at Phu Bai. He'd lost too much blood.

Two days later I crouched behind the remains of an ambulance on the campus of Hue University. I was watching for movement in a bullet-riddled three-story building where at least one sniper was holed up. Next to the building was a street corner sign that read *oú* LÉ-LÓI. I was humming "Louie Louie" when Sergeant Raynard broke the bad news.

"All right, High Noon. The captain's pretty sure the gook's on the third floor now, and he's in there by himself. He keeps moving between classrooms and windows, and he's giving us too much trouble. You're the man so brave, you're going up to get rid of that sniper. The captain agrees. We think you're the one with luck."

How about blowing up the damn building with artillery? How about blasting tear gas grenades through every window of every floor that faced us? I knew it would do no good to say those things. On reaching the ground floor I shed every piece of equipment that might make any noise, including my flak jacket and helmet. The abandoned university building looked like the professors and students had fled when the first shell came in, leaving exotic chalk writing on the blackboards and a mess of discarded papers on the floors. I glanced at one and it could have been calculus or teachings of the Buddha. I found the stairwell, lay on my back, cradled my M-16 and a frag grenade on my chest and stomach, and very slowly began to creep up the stairs. I would move one or two steps up, shove with my boots, and climb in a way that made no noise.

When I reached the third floor, I was glad to find the door of the stair well blown off. I peeked over the top step and could see the length of the hall. I counted to three then heaved the grenade bouncing and skittering down the hall, but I didn't trigger the spoon. A couple of seconds later the sniper burst out of a classroom, planning to kill as he was being killed. He looked younger than me. His gaze fixed on the grenade then up for the round-eye who threw it. My rifle wasn't on automatic but I was scared out of my wits and I gave him several rounds in the chest. The sounds of the M-16 that reached my ears were not explosive but *tink tink tink tinks* of the firing pin striking and the shells ejecting. The Nagoolian kid's hair flew up like someone electrocuted in a comic book, and blood flew out of his wounds in the shape of a cone. As he sailed back to the wall, he lost both of his rubber-soled sandals. He died as he was born, in his bare feet.

CHAPTER 23

I can't say how many lives I took over there. With all the automatic fire it wasn't that kind of war. Much of the time I was firing back at muzzle flashes. I made a habit of shooting at anyone wearing a helmet decorated with twigs and foliage. To my knowledge I never fired on women or children. The abundance of poisonous snakes scared the bejesus out of me. Around rice paddies we were apt to walk up on a cobra. They were smaller than the ones found elsewhere in Asia, but they fed, defended, and expressed themselves the same way. One day I was walking point when one rose in front of me. I leaped back, the next grunts caught up, and the cobra didn't seem disposed to go on its way in search of its next rat.

"Ask the louie what to do," I said. We didn't know if the village we approached was pacified or VC. Our new second lieutenant came up and said, "Will it just go away?"

"Maybe you can persuade it. Shoo."

"You're the closest," he said. "Can you hit it?"

"Yeah."

"What did you shoot on the rifle range?"

"I was a goddamn marksman. Do you want it gone or not?"

"*Somebody* kill that thing!" Sergeant Raynard hissed.

I shouldered M-16 and moved the muzzle from side to side. The cobra's head moved right and left with the flash guard and sight. It was quick and deadly but it was stupid or it wouldn't be a snake. It lined up precisely with whatever threatened it. The cobra's head flew away and the report echoed across the rice paddies and valley.

"Good shot," said the louie with a light clap of his hand on my shoulder.

"Oswald's luck," I said.

No less terrifying were the patrols through elephant grass and bamboo. Except for the points of tail, the scales of the red-tailed pit vipers were bright green, perfect camouflage. I'd be trying to watch my step and stay on the trace of a footpath when all at once there would be a roar of guns and bullets snapping the air.

When I got hit, I had crouched beside the abutment of a concrete bridge. I saw the tracer. If it's coming from a distance you can see it in the time it takes to blink your eyes, but there's not enough time to duck. Death is coming after you and there's nothing you can do but see how it goes.

The round exploded the concrete block where I had stooped, resting my hand on it for balance. Rebar in the bridge answered with a deafening *whang.* At first I couldn't see from all the grit in my eyes. I had a terrifying presage of life without sight, as blind as that old great-grandfather who would sit with my sister and me on our parents' porch swing and regale us with hymns and cowboy songs. When I could finally see it, I assumed I'd lost my left hand. Our corpsman hit me with morphine, and soon I was on a chopper's dust-up.

A navy surgeon at Da Nang told me that if the whole round had gone through my hand I would have lost it, and maybe my arm. My hand was torn up by metal fragments and concrete grit. He said he cleaned it up as well as he could to prevent infection and used "nails" to repair the metacarpals of my middle two fingers, but he couldn't fix the tendons, and nerves locked in scar tissue sent jags of pain all the way up to my jaw. I regained strength and movement only in my thumb and middle and ring fingers, but after six weeks I had to quit fantasizing about a nurse because I could hold an M-16. I rejoined my unit. Toward the end I spent my week of R&R drinking beer and watching surfers from under a beach cabaña in New South Wales, Australia. The Aussies liked Yanks, as they called us, and bought us beer. They had their own force fighting on our side in Vietnam. I fantasized about disappearing in the Blue Mountains to the west.

That war was lost during the first dark hours of Tet, when VC blew a hole in a wall of the US embassy compound in Saigon and the voice of an army sentry blared from a radio: "They're coming in! They're coming in! Help me!" His last words. The battle for Hue lasted thirty-one days and was the longest and costliest of the war. A hundred forty thousand civilians had lived in the city when the battle began. When it ended 116,000 of them were homeless. The brass later claimed that the enemy executed 4,856 civilians and buried them in mass graves outside Hue. How they came up with that exact count I can't say.

I didn't have one thing against the young men and women, my peers, who turned the tide of opinion against the war. I had as much reason to hate it as they did. I was thrown in the fight because I was a criminal. But I surprised myself. I rose to the occasion, though it was a sorry one indeed.

The official tour of duty in Vietnam was twelve months, but marines pulled thirteen because the first troops had gone across the Pacific in navy ships. At the end of my time I bought two changes of civilian clothes and a pair of shoes at the commissary in Da Nang. When I was back in the States there was no sensation of being set free. Other marines wandered off into the rest of their lives, but I had to report to Camp Pendleton. The marines had issued me a new military ID and let me take out my combat pay in cash before I got on the plane. I rented a hostel room and poked around Oakland until the jet lag was over.

Downstate, I found Pendleton's Mainside almost deserted. The First Division was in the war zone or in Okinawa preparing to mount up with the Third. A master sergeant put me up in an empty barrack, gave me directions to the nearest chow hall in operation, and told me if I left the base, I was AWOL and could be charged with desertion. I'd heard that before. He said my status was being reviewed. He came back one day and handed me an envelope relating acts of human kindness. The letters revealed that Colonel Bullick and the red-haired drill instructor, Staff Sergeant Mulligan, had convinced the commanding officer of my court martial that an escrow of my private's pay for the months in the brig and boxing camp would be held for me if I made it back. I had spent little over there except on my R&R and bags of smoke. I had a nest egg of eight thousand dollars.

I found a television set in the deserted barrack. One day I turned it on and got the opening ceremony of the Mexico City Olympics. My thoughts of Kenny Norton had grown occasional during my year at war. But memories assailed me when I watched the finals in boxing. In a jolly way an announcer said the three-round heavyweight bout was being called the "Cold War Clash." The Soviet Union's Jonas Chepulis was ten years older than George Foreman, but the Russian didn't have a chance. He tried to fight but he couldn't find a way around that left jab. The referee made the Russian take an eight-count midway through the first round, and blood poured from his nose and mouth by the bell. The ref stopped it in the second while the Russian was still on his feet.

With a pleasant and shy expression George walked around the ring with his right arm raised and a little American flag in his taped hand. The two sprinters who bowed their heads on the medals stand and raised black gloved fists during the playing of "The Star-Spangled Banner" were reviled in the States, but the press lionized George for his patriotism, knowing nothing of his background in Houston. If Kenny was now a small-town cop in Illinois, I hoped he wasn't watching. He would have had to beat George in the Olympic trials, which would have been a chore, but he shouldn't have been cheated of his shot at trying. I could only imagine how seeing that would have hurt.

I had been awarded a Purple Heart and promoted two ranks to lance corporal. I was nominated for a Bronze Star for my grenade throw and killing the sniper in the university building in Hue, but the marines wouldn't have let that go through if I had fought like Chesty Puller. The master sergeant sent for me the third time we met. His offer at first left me speechless. Then I told him that neither a corporal's stripe nor all the horny women on earth would get me to sign up for another combat tour. So they cut me loose OTH—other than honorable discharge. Which meant I might or might not receive any veterans' benefits. I didn't care. I had taken my crack at contesting the United States military. With a duffle on my shoulder, I caught the bus out of Pendleton wearing sandals, jeans, love beads affixed to my dog tags, and a T-shirt with an image of Jane Fonda nude in *Barbarella.*

PART III TWO BUBBLES OFF PLUMB

CHAPTER 24

I prowled Laguna Beach and Newport Beach striking up conversations with girls who smelled of patchouli oil and wore shifts when they had on anything more than a loose shirt and bikinis, but I got nowhere with them, and I could make no sense of mammoth LA. Big Sur entranced me, but I couldn't afford it and moved on. In San Francisco I found the bloom of the flower children spent; now there were panhandling junkies, and there was something else—an air of menace that I didn't expect to find there. I didn't think it was just the police. I was trying to conserve my money, didn't want to pay for a long cab ride, and I didn't want to see the Golden Gate from a bus. So I caught the ferry to Sausalito. Near the dock I checked into a small two-story hotel that was half a century old and in much need of renovation. From the guys who worked shifts at the desk I learned it had once been a whorehouse whose madam preferred the more elegant label, bordello.

During Prohibition, they said, the whiskey and rum boats would dock between midnight and dawn, and the cargo would be wheeled into the basement pending further distribution. The mob ran things there in those days, and a boss called "Jimmy the Hat" kept a suite for his use of select whores on the second floor. Later an author and B-list movie star, Sterling Hayden, lived in the hotel and presided over a salon of musicians, actors, writers, and ne'er-do-well hipsters. I knew Hayden as the actor who played the cigar-chomping maniac general Jack J. Ripper in *Dr. Strangelove,* the movie Ann and I saw the afternoon before the Kayron Coger fight in Fort Worth. I wondered if that memory had anything to do with who I was now. I guess that disorientation happens to all ex-convicts and shooters in a war. I was twenty-five years old and had managed to be both.

I didn't want to bother the other guests and tenants, though they were few in number, and I worked on my harmonica chops in the little park between the hotel and ferry landing. There were two drinking fountains in the park, one dedicated to Sally, the celebrated madam who became an elected city council member and then mayor, the short one dedicated to her dog Leland. For people coming off the ferry, I got where I'd blow alternating verses on my harp and then sing ones like Hank Williams's "So Lonesome I Could Cry" and "Cold Cold Heart" and Otis Redding's "I've Been Loving You Too Long" and "Dreams to Remember." I didn't try to do too much with my harmonica. I needed to buy and learn some other ones tuned to different keys. I was testing my voice, seeing how much I had left to work with. I didn't put out a pencil box or mayonnaise jar because that would have made me feel like a panhandler. I'd seen enough of those across the bay.

I hadn't held a real-world job since delivering crates of eggs and sacks of feed for the Purina store in Deerinwater. I couldn't apply for anything like that here because I didn't have a driver's license. The marines took away my Texas license and any other IDs when the Oceanside cops turned me over to the MPs. They didn't even issue me a service ID when I got to Oakland. I was too proud to wash dishes in a restaurant. I was constantly recounting my sleeve of cash, which I kept in a safe that the hotel provided. I allowed myself only a breakfast of coffee and a pastry, and for dinner I often got by with bread and soup.

Near the hotel I found a bar with a deck out where I sat and watched seals raise their heads out of the water. I thought they looked like brown bleach bottles. I drank beer because it was cheaper than the whiskey I wanted. One sunlit afternoon I was perched on a stool watching the seals and sailboats when a young blonde woman in a brightly colored short dress came in, took another stool to my left down the bar, and ordered a drink. She was slender and tall. I nodded and she responded with a world-class smile. We glanced and flirted for a few moments, then I got my courage up and asked if I could join her.

She smiled and said, "Sure, come on."

I introduced myself and she said, "My name's Clarinda." She extended an arm with several bracelets and shook my hand. Her fingernails were painted sunset orange.

"What a pretty name," I said.

"Thank you."

I'd been wondering if she might be some kind of high-priced hooker—why else would she hit on me? But I saw something in her that was both empowering and addictive. Her vaguely freckled skin was so fine and fair that when I said or did something that gave her pleasure, rose-colored blushes appeared on her cheeks and around her eyes. As we talked, I thought I heard a trace of accent from somewhere in the Southwest, but she was very much a California girl. Our small talk led us into where we came from. When I told her about my origins in Deerinwater, she said that when she escaped Fort Worth to go to college at San Jose State, she swore she was never going back to Texas, and so far, she hadn't.

"I don't blame you," I said. Just to keep the conversation going, I said, "I had a good time in Fort Worth once. You know that odd building that out front has a statue of Will Rogers on a horse?"

"Yeah. They have a big rodeo there every year. The whole building smells like a cattle and horse barn."

"Well, I don't know how they roll out a floor and make it stable, but they do. I had a fight there every night Wednesday through Saturday one time, and I won a state Golden Gloves title. If you grow up in Deerinwater you have kind of a soft spot for Fort Worth."

She looked at me with curiosity. "You're a boxer?" she said.

"No. Gym rat at best. Doing it in real competition, it was just that one winter and spring of amateur tournaments in my hometown and other places. Lots of cities in the state have tournaments and the winners get to go to Fort Worth. They were three-round fights, all of us amateurs. I was twenty."

She wriggled off her barstool, propped her hands on the bar, and gazed toward the city. When she did that, her skirt had come up for a moment, and I saw cream-colored thighs with the same faint freckles. She put her hand on my shoulder briefly, as if for balance. The breeze was moving her hair around her face. "My father," she said, "who's dead now, was a college professor in Fort Worth and was on the board of the zoo."

"Really. What did he teach?"

She smiled and looked back to me. "If he was talking to a stranger, he'd say his specialty was 'Wildlife science.' Most people got nervous if he said, 'Herpetology.'"

I had to think for a second, then said, "Snakes?"

She nodded. "Among colleagues he'd laugh and say, 'I'm just a jolly old herper.'"

"What kind of snakes?"

"All kinds, I think, but he was an authority on poisonous snakes of the Sub-Sahara. Two times when he got grants, he took us to Kenya on his field trips."

"Sounds like dynamite vacations."

"Oh, they were. He was careless about his own safety but very careful with Mom and me. He didn't keep them around or anything."

"What kind of poisonous snakes?"

"His favorites were gaboon vipers and boomslangs."

I laughed at the names. She climbed back on the stool, and with her right hand she touched my left one. For a moment her eyes stayed on the scars. "Deadly, deadly," she said gaily. "Except for cobras, the gaboons have the longest fangs of any venomous snakes. The boomslangs are tree snakes, though they come down to hunt. The male boomslangs are a beautiful bright green."

She sipped her drink and said, "What happened to your hand?"

"A bullet or shrapnel went through it. The surgeon did the best he could."

"In the war?"

"Yeah." I felt my face redden. I was sitting, after all, across a small bay across from a city known for its peace marches. "Don't hold it against me. I didn't volunteer."

"I wouldn't."

I put my elbows on the bar and touched fingers and thumbs together. "I used to pray, 'Please, Lord, let my hands be alike.'" Then I tightened the right one into a claw.

She laughed and gave me a slight bump with her shoulder. I asked what her drink in a tall glass was. "Dark and stormy," she answered.

"Say again?"

"The drink's name, dark and stormy. Two jiggers of rum, a squeeze of lime, and then fill the glass with ginger beer. You want a taste?" I did, and liked it. When the waitress came back by, I asked for one. She ordered another and asked if I liked calamari.

"Sure," I said, though I'd never had it. She squeezed lemon on the breaded squid when they arrived. "At the moment," I said, pointing past her, "where I'm really from is that hotel." I talked about Jimmy the Hat, the madam mayor Sally and her dog Leland, and Sterling Hayden, who played Jack J. Ripper in *Dr. Strangelove*.

"Almost everyone here has heard those stories. They're one of the reasons I like it here so much. They cheer me up." We watched a ferry. She said, "Did you sing today?"

"Yeah, a little while. It gets me outdoors. I like the little park. I leave my windows open because a day-care center brings kids over in the mornings. Nothing better than waking up to children laughing and singing."

"I stopped and listened to you one day. You don't remember."

"If I'd seen you I would." Once more I brought the color to her cheeks.

"Quite a few people stopped. I liked your voice and harmonica."

"Thank you."

We ate the calamari and got drunk enough to slump against each other's shoulders.

"Know why I came here?" she said. "I'd heard you sing down there, and one time when I was with someone else, I saw you here by yourself. I came hoping you'd be here."

"I don't know what to say. Except I'm amazed and glad."

The sun had set far enough that the buildings across the bay now looked steely. Clarinda said, "Are you up for a three-block hike?"

"Yeah, if it's with you."

As we climbed a winding lane she said, "Were you in the army?"

"No, the marines."

"Are you in good condition?"

"Decent, I guess. Why?"

"I'm in this situation and need strong help. If you got paid well and worked day and night for a couple of days and then got to see something wonderful, close up, would you be interested?"

It didn't take me long to say, "Probably."

Her apartment was sleek and clean, no dirty dishes in the kitchen sink. The walls were decorated with framed rock and roll posters. Hendrix, the Doors, Cream. She got out a small glass pipe and we smoked hash oil. I'm not sure how much time passed. She told me about a free concert headlined by the Rolling Stones that was supposed to have taken place in Golden Gate Park. City Hall in San Francisco had issued a permit but the mayor and council got nervous. They withdrew the permit with the excuse that the 49ers were playing the Bears that day, and traffic would be too much of a problem.

"These people I work for found an ideal spot, an auto racetrack up the coast called Sears Point. But the track's owned by a film and TV production company, and word got out that the concert's going to be made into a documentary. Greed got the best of the Sears Point guys, and Mick Jagger refused to negotiate. He said a free concert with their name on it had to be free in all things. The Sears Point deal fell apart, and another site's been offered at no cost, out by Livermore. They said it's another race track, but it looks like the start on an auto graveyard. It has to be cleaned up fast, too fast, and I don't really know if it's possible. Except it has to be. If you're up for it, you'll be paid well."

I started to ask how much but didn't. "What's your role in this thing?"

"I'm a publicist. Except when I'm overruled. Then I'm just like you. The help."

"I'd have to buy some work gloves and boots. Sausalito doesn't seem like the kind of place that would have a lot of hardware stores."

"We'll pick some up on the way." The smoke and booze had brought our hips and legs in contact in the sagging sofa. She turned to me and kissed me, not a long one, but it was a kiss. I hadn't enjoyed one since the last time I saw Ann. "I don't think you ought to walk down the hill to the hotel," she said, "and I shouldn't drive you."

I waited. She gave me a friendly shove and stood. "If I let you sleep here, will you just sleep? I picked you up because I wanted you to pick me up, but I'm really not that kind of girl. We'll work hard together and then we'll see."

I undressed to my shorts, got under the covers of her large bed, and asked my pecker to behave. She came out of the bathroom wearing a filmy short nightgown, thin enough in the light behind her I could see under it she only wore panties. She turned off the light and when she crawled in bed it didn't take long for my hands to find their way to her. She gripped my wrists and firmly moved my hands away. "No, please, not yet. It's not you, it's me. I have complications." I assumed that meant a boyfriend. "Besides we're too drunk and stoned. If we did, I'd want to recall it."

Having laid out the rules, she squirmed her bottom against me and wrapped my arms around her. "Night," she said, and I bet it wasn't four minutes before the change in her breathing told me she was asleep. Nothing ventured, nothing gained. I had just signed on to the labor crew of Altamont.

CHAPTER 25

We were both hungover but she got us up and moving anyway. She made us a thermos of black coffee, got a couple of croissants out of the refrigerator, and in a sleek red car she picked up a freeway and we circled around the bay toward Oakland. "What kind of car is this?" I said.

"A Saab," she replied, shifting gears. I had to tell her I'd left all but beer money at the bordello hotel when I went to the bar to watch the ferries and seals. She nodded, stopped at a store in Oakland, and bought me my clothes, boots, and gloves. I had to assume she had more resources than just her dad's pension as a professor. On out the Interstate we passed the town of Pleasanton. She was right about the festival site. You'd think they'd want something flat if it was going to be a speedway, but it sloped at least a ten-degree angle and narrowed down to a shallow ravine, where hippie carpenters were nailing and bolting the stage together. After I'd laced on the boots, pulled on a sweatshirt, and downed another cup of coffee in the Saab, Clarinda came back and delivered me to a guy who handed me a clipboard and waiver sheet to sign. I'd get twenty bucks an hour, a good wage back then. I signed the sheet and handed him the clipboard.

He said, "Ex-marine, huh. Get your ass to work."

"You don't have to spread that around," I teased Clarinda. My haircut was short but no longer military; I'd made a point of not seeking barber shears during the weeks they had me parked at Pendleton. The acreage looked like a mass grave of Corvairs, the rear-engine GM disaster that made Ralph Nader famous. They had a busy fleet of large Bobcats and dump trucks but a moronic shortage of wheelbarrows. I found that I really disliked the noise of helicopters now. I helped pull tangles of wire, disconnected bumpers, mounds of tires all sizes, unrecognizable metal junk, and partly scavenged wrecked cars into piles that the Bobcats could hoist to the dump trucks. I was sweat-soaked by noon, though the December air was cool. In California it was the season of rain. I wondered if some front might scoot in and turn their festival into a mud pie, as it happened at Woodstock five months earlier. I was wrestling a truck tire when one of the hippies yelled, "You're not my boss!"

I snapped, "Just get out of the way, let me do it."

Clarinda happened to be nearby, carrying a walkie-talkie with her briefcase slung over her shoulder. "He *is* your boss!" she told him. "If he asks you to help, help him."

"Bitch," the hippie muttered.

By late morning most seemed to accept me as just another stoop laborer. There were a lot of glass shards, scorpions galore, and some guy was bitten on the finger by a rattlesnake. It had been resting inside a length of pipe he lifted on one end. Clarinda sped him off to an emergency room in Livermore, and when she returned without him, she found me, handed me a sub sandwich and can of Coke, and told me she'd rented us a motel room.

Even with the remains of the hangover I was in better condition for the heavy lifting and dragging than most of the guys I worked with. The film crew was erecting mobile poles and klieg and flood lights for their own purposes and so we'd able to work into the night. When we quit, it was one o'clock in the morning. The motel room in Livermore was standard, cheap, and featureless except for mass-produced art on the walls. It did have a small cooler, and Clarinda had gotten us a bottle of white wine. After we showered, we sat on the bed cover with the wine and slices of a wretched pizza. She wore the short nightgown she had on at the apartment the night before.

She wanted to talk about music. I talked about my regard for Eric Burdon and the Animals, Sam and Dave, and Wilson Pickett's cover of "Hey

Jude." Her taste ran to Joe Cocker and Delaney & Bonnie & Friends. She talked about people who had told her about their foibles and snafus at the Atlanta and Atlantic City festivals that preceded Woodstock. "We're going to be part of Woodstock West," she said. We were tired enough that sharing a bottle of wine gave us a definite buzz.

I was wondering if now might be the time to help her shed that nightie when she started in about the war. After a year, My Lai and the company of army grunts continued to dominate the news. I knew My Lai was an Americanism. The soldiers had roamed through a cluster of villages with separate names in the rampage. "They were supposed to be the cavalry," I said. "Not the Comanches." But her semi-intoxication and passion made her an expert. Without warning she turned on me. "How could you?"

"I didn't have a choice."

"Bullshit. Guys were going to Canada, convincing the draft shrinks they were queer, taking acid to make their blood pressure spike at their physicals."

"When they put me on that plane over there I was under arrest. You don't know what you're talking about." I turned away from her and plumped up my pillow.

"I'm sorry," she said after a while.

It turned out there were three days of work day and night, not the couple she'd mentioned. The last night they had a closing celebration of sorts. The people running the show all had the air of rich hippies. Three guys handed out beers, paid us in ten and twenty-dollar bills, and said the ones who had been asked to come back should arrive by daybreak. The others could line up and get passes for the concert, and they were free to sleep on the ground. I looked at Clarinda, who nodded that I was still on the payroll. Back at the motel, we laid out her briefcases, my work boots, and what we were going to wear the next morning, and stuffed the rest back in the bags she'd brought.

We showered then, and once more in my shorts I slipped under the covers. Clarinda was a rangy girl, and when she came out of the bathroom after toweling her hair somewhat dry, she started to get under the covers with me, thought of something she'd forgotten, and when she stepped out of bed I caught a glimpse that she no longer wore the panties under her thin nightgown. Her love hair was redder than the blonde ones on her head. True, she said she'd under-packed and she was washing them out by hand in the bathroom. But for Christ sake, it had been three and a half years since I'd been with any woman. True love though Ann was, she didn't measure up to Clarinda in her looks and languorous way of moving. I was frozen, afraid to make my move.

She said the only thing she missed about Texas was part of a ranch she inherited near a little cowboy town called Meridian. She missed her registered paint horses Quincy and Blowhard. She said she liked horses because they were big panicky things that could kill you without meaning to, but the same horse would give you a nose nudge of affection. She had put her head on my shoulder as she talked about the smooth lope of Quincy and the cranky humor of Blowhard. She noticed I wasn't saying as much, and she raised her head.

"Something wrong?"

"No. Just tired."

"Have you got your harmonica?"

"Yeah."

"Want to sing me a song?"

I looked about and said, "I don't think so."

"You only sing in parks?"

I sort of laughed. "I don't do it in motel room that looks like this and pretend I'm opening for the Rolling Stones."

She sat up, locked her arms around her bare shins, then pulled the sheets over them. "You are mad at me."

All I had to do was raise my hand, turn it over, and cup her young breast.

"You frustrate me," I said. "I just don't understand."

She rested her chin on her arms and was quiet for a few seconds. "You don't know how much pressure I'm under. It's not a measure of how much I like you. Do you think we'd be here like this if you were just some guy? The work and pressure doesn't make me horny, that's all. Some women may relieve it that way. I can't."

"Okay. I get that. And the boyfriend."

"What boyfriend?"

"You said you had one."

With a knuckle she pushed my chin up. "Please hang in with me. I need you tomorrow. All this work's been worth it. It's going to be a fabulous time. You'll see."

"What am I gonna do tomorrow? What's my job?"

For the second time she kissed me. "You're my bodyguard."

It's hard to describe a crowd of three hundred thousand. What came to my mind was the Grinder at the boot camp in San Diego. I thought this crowd would have more than filled that up, maybe doubled it, and they never seemed to stop coming in. Clarinda was all business now, dashing around, taking orders from slightly older men and women and trying to keep the reporters and photographers happy. But when she thought I'd pulled away, she reached for my hand or arm. The stage that had gone up in three days felt solid underfoot. Massive piles of amps and speakers sat on each end of it. On the ground people nearest us were spread out on blankets, releasing helium-filled balloons, sailing Frisbees, and getting loaded. One road had been graded into the site, and a few New York City cops had been hired to keep the road clear for the cars and trucks of the movie crew and three EMS units that I could see.

"That's all those cops are gonna do?" I said. "Who's the security?"

"Please stay close," was all she said.

Guys wearing sleeveless black leather jackets were sitting on top of the speakers and spreading across the front of the stage. The jackets were colors of Hell's Angels from San Francisco and Oakland. "Are they the security?" I asked her.

She shook her pretty head. "They're getting free beer to make sure nothing happens to the sound and lighting systems. Their leader said, 'We ain't no cops.'"

I decided to just roll with it, take care of myself and her, and enjoy myself. The first band, Santana, had just finished when a helicopter delivered Mick Jagger and his entourage. Surrounded by reporters and photographers, Clarinda pressed toward the craft, and I jostled and stayed with her. Jagger had on jeans, a black T-shirt, and a velvet fringed jacket for the night's chill. I was surprised by how small he was, and how old he looked—he was just a year older than me. He had barely gotten his feet solid on the ground when a young guy yelled, "I hate you," and slugged him. Jagger looked, well, shocked.

I got to the guy first and grabbed him in an armlock, then others were shoving and punching at him. One hit my shoulder. "What do we do with this guy?" I yelled.

"Have him arrested," one of Clarinda's colleagues yelled.

"Arrested by who?"

"No, no, no," said Jagger. "Let him go." The side of his face was flushed where he'd taken the blow. Escorts moved him and his entourage off to the trailers assigned to them. The puncher was cussing, spitting, and trying to bite me. I got a firmer grip around his neck and walked him fifty yards before I turned him loose and shoved him to the ground. It had brought back in an unpleasant way my treatment of the old salt with the birthmark. "If I see you up here close again," I told him, "you're not gonna like the outcome. You're lucky you didn't get hurt back there."

I made my way back to Clarinda, who was pleading with reporters to overlook and forget what they'd just seen. Radio stations were reporting live out there, and lots of people were yelling at her. The Jefferson Airplane started their set. Gracie Slick was singing when a fight started offstage, then tumbled onstage, then offstage again. She was saying, "Easy, easy," when the Airplane's guitar player jumped offstage and tried to break up the fight. Bad move. An Angel wearing a raccoon-skin hat laid him out for a full two minutes. Clarinda was yelling at the Angel, calling him Mule. I tried to pull her away, and she threw an elbow at me. At last the Airplane's guitar player was helped to his feet. Mule told Clarinda and a couple of her superiors that he wanted to apologize. I sighed and trailed after them. Mule told the guitar player, "Hey, man, no hard feelings."

The guitar player said, "Fuck *you!*"

Bad move. The Angel laid him out again. Another helicopter arrived carrying the Grateful Dead. Santana's drummer told Jerry Garcia what had just occurred. Garcia blanched, yelled at the pilot to give him a hand, climbed back on the chopper, and the Dead pulled out of the show.

The concert proceeded with lively sets and long stalls. The Angels were hanging out on the stacks of speakers and amps drinking the beer they'd been promised, but there were some "prospect" Angels trying to prove their worth out in the crowd with sawed-off pool cues weighted with lead cores. Hippies were going down like they'd been shot. The Angels around the stage said they had no control over those guys. People in the crowd fought back, hurling full cans of beer at the ones with the pool cues.

Some guy handed me a joint and after several hits he told me it was loaded with opium. Great. The Flying Burrito Brothers were dicking around with a country sound I didn't care for. Clarinda looked like she was occupied and taking care of herself. I decided to go out and look around. I stayed on the road, stopping to chat with the New York City cops. One mentioned that some hippie had gone swimming and drowned in an irrigation ditch. The last one I spoke with looked out and said, "If I had gasoline to pour on 'em, I'd strike the match."

Then at a short distance I saw a driver of a black sedan run over some kid, front wheels and back, tumbling him over and over, and then kept going, leaving him for dead. Snap of the fingers, I was back in the soup.

One of those days when we'd gained the upper hand in Triangle, I saw a carload of marines joyriding a black Mercedes taken from a civilian. Kalashnikov tracers were sparking off the car. My squad and a tank crew had gone out in search of an American Mennonite who was supposed to be trapped in the Triangle. Wary of snipers as we jogged and walked with the tank, we weren't sure what house we looked for. The tank commander's map wasn't much help. It was supposed to be across the street from a Catholic cathedral. We finally found the church, and one of our guys spotted a sniper in the belfry. The tank's turret swung around, the big gun boomed, the sniper was no more, and neither was the belfry.

On the street an old woman ducked out of a doorway, waved her arms, and jumped back inside. In answer to our shouts the Mennonite stepped out wearing suspenders, a flat-brimmed hat, and a beard grown from only his chin and jaws. I hustled him to the tank and told him to get down. He refused. The tank commander, a captain, yelled, "What were you doing in there?"

"Hiding!" the man yelled.

"Are there VC?"

"Yes, of course!"

"They better move out that old woman," said the captain, preparing to send us in.

"No, wait," the Mennonite yelled. "You can't do that. They're not armed. It's just their beliefs, their politics—they're not soldiers. They were the ones hiding me!"

The captain looked at me and said, "Is this a great war or what."

The man was distraught and I had to struggle with him. "Sir, you're safe with us if you'll just calm down." As he jabbered, I followed the point of his hand to a scene that at first I could make no sense of. Curs were fighting with skinny hogs over some prize.

"My wife," the man sobbed. "That's the body of my wife."

I fired a burst of automatic that killed some of the scavengers and sent the others running. The enemy Nagoolians had killed the Mennonite's wife and then, like Jezebel in the Old Testament, they threw her out to be eaten by dogs.

Clarinda's bosses decided to hurry it up and just try to get the thing over with. But when Crosby, Stills, Nash & Young finished, the Stones couldn't start because Bill Wyman had gone shopping in San Francisco, and they had no way of getting in touch with him. The crowd had nothing to do for two hours but get more wasted on booze and high on smoke and acid. The day passed from afternoon to dusk. The Angels were spread out front. Others sat on the piles of speakers, banging their heels like they was bored. It was fully dark by the time the Stones got onstage. The Angels looked at Jagger like they wanted to throw him to the mob. They started "Sympathy for the Devil," and Jagger was singing and dancing when he just stopped and stared, like he couldn't believe his eyes, whatever was out there.

"Who's fighting? Who's fighting and what for are we fighting? We don't want to fight. Come *awwnn.*"

When the Angels did something especially violent, there was a collective *woooo,* and the crowd pressed back into each other. I had weathered the flashback and opium smoke enough to find and rejoin Clarinda at the rear of the stage. I thought the Stones were terrific. They had been in the studio finishing *Sticky Fingers,* which became my favorite. Jagger was finishing "Under My Thumb" when the Angels threw a black kid in a green jacket and top hat away from the stage. Hunter Meredith was only eighteen, but he was out of his head on speed and PCP. His white girlfriend was screaming and trying to hold him back, but he pulled a gun, rushed the stage, and fired two shots. Clarinda had been walking forward when I saw the muzzle flashes and heard the shots. I ducked and tried to yank her away. "Take your *hands off me,*" she snapped, unsure what was going on. An Angel named Alan knocked the kid's gun hand away and stabbed him in the back. In the documentary, *Gimme Shelter,* an

EMS guy tried to console the girl—she kept saying her boyfriend wasn't breathing. He said that Hunter was stabbed twice in the back and once in the eye. I saw Angels stomping on him when he was down. A jury would acquit Alan the Angel on grounds of self-defense.

When the Stones were done, the lighting and film crew started killing the kliegs over the stage and the crowd. They were trying to make them go away. I tried to find Clarinda and tell her why I'd handled her so roughly. When I found her she had one blue-jeaned thigh wrapped around that of the Flying Burrito Brother's bass player, I think it may have been. He had his hands on her ass, and she was kissing him with a great deal more energy than she had expended on me. I just took a seat on the ground. Then a helicopter was landing, and I stood up and tried to shield my eyes from the dust and grit. Clarinda saw me then and she rushed over to me and put her car keys in my hand. Her briefcase was slung over her shoulder.

"I'll meet you in Sausalito," she said. "Tomorrow at your hotel, I'll come get the car. I'm sorry it's been so chaotic. I think I might love you." Then she ran with the bass player, or whatever he was, and from behind he helped her up in the helicopter. She blew me kisses, I swear to god, then in the swirl of dust the aircraft lifted and she was gone. When I found the Saab, I got her bags out of the trunk. I separated her clothes from mine and dumped her jeans and panties and shirts and especially that nightgown on the ground.

CHAPTER 26

I had to go but had nowhere to go to. So I wound up back in Deerinwater. I found a run-down duplex near what was now an almost deserted downtown. The Kress's variety store where I got in the fight with that boy at the bus stop was boarded up, as were many of the storefronts. Once there were three movie theaters on its three main streets; now there were none. The population hadn't diminished much since the oil played out. It gradually relocated into newer subdivisions flung out amid shopping centers out to the west. Per capita income slipped a notch or two or three. There was no animus toward Allred Field anymore. Lyndon Johnson and Sam Rayburn in their congressional primes had awarded Air Force bases to almost every Texas town of any size. Despite the war in Vietnam most of those towns lost them in the Pentagon's move of checkers on their global chessboard. When I was in Australia on my R&R I drank beer one night with a fighter pilot who said he'd soon be going home. When I told him where I was from, he said he was from Amarillo, a similar town two hundred miles higher on the plains. "Amarillo had a base," he said. "Now it's gone, but SAC keeps the runways and control tower maintained. Those long flat runways were made for B-52s."

Deerinwater was fortunate to keep Allred Field as a job training base, a big one. Endless airmen still routed through. Now Deerinwater sang a different tune about them and the base. With the refineries closed and the gas flares no longer lighting up the mesquite thickets at night, Allred Field provided the best civilian jobs and supply contracts now.

DeWayne Holland was married to an Osage girl and living in Guthrie, Oklahoma. He had left my pink '57 Bel Air with Chuck Mercer's mom. It was hard talking to her again but I'm glad I did. She gave me the keys with a snapshot of Chuck and a parting kiss on my cheek. She was crying when I walked out to the car.

George Washington Carver had been closed, and I heard the infusion of black talent had revived the fortunes of the Antler football teams. But the eastside slum along Shiloh Street was as segregated as it ever was. The railroad yards lying between downtown and Shiloh Street were packed now with freight cars that moved seldom if at all, blocking off each of the three direct crossing points into the eastside. You'd have to circle around in the country out toward Dry Creek to get into it. I discovered that one day when I thought I'd go see if anyone had put up a grave marker for Big Joe John.

When the freight cars moved enough to let me slip through, across the railroad yards I found Roughneck Park in ruins. Night scavengers had gotten off with most of the fence wire, and the lumber of the stands lay in rotting piles. The stadium supports of oilfield pipe lay in rusted tangles. The clubhouse was still intact, though. I found Mr. Guerrero still teaching kids boxing for the GI Forum. It was good seeing him again and hearing him brag on me as the town's last state champ, but my heart wasn't in the workouts, and I doubted banging on the bags was good for my hand.

The distance between Virginia and me had never stopped growing. I was fond of my niece Angie and her stepfather Oran, but they had moved out to Dry Creek and I doubted I'd see much of them. I had asked Oran to keep my mandolin when I left for my six months in the marines. Life's surprises. Oran told me he took it out of the case sometimes and played it just to keep it in tune for that day when the good Lord let me make it home. I found it was impossible for me to play—the fingers on my left hand just wouldn't do what they had to do. The hand seized up in cramps every time I tried. One night while drunk and sitting on the grimy linoleum floor I smashed the neck and body and broke them in two. I banged the remains into splinters and buzzing coils of strings. Then sat with my back to a door as tears poured off my cheeks and jaws.

I got a job manning a cash register in a Zip-In convenience store, making change for people who came in for packs of cigarettes, candy bars, packages of Fritos, six-packs of beer. I awaited some shift when a guy like Joey Carrigan would come in and stick a gun in my face. A few people asked me if I was the guy who used to be a local boxer. I said, "Yeah, that was me," and pushed them their change.

The break came by way of Little Mike Wilson. He was still up in Stillwater, but he was married and had a little boy now. He scuffled for session work in Tulsa and helped make commercials for Oklahoma City TV. He'd come back to town to see his parents and gaped on seeing me behind the cash register. Thanks to Mike I caught on with an ambitious group called the Shenanigans. They hadn't recorded any more than demos but were playing clubs in Oklahoma and Dallas and spoke of a cool psychedelic club in Austin called the Vulcan Gas Company. Mike's recommendation and favor got me on as the harmonica player, and I kept having to trade shifts and call in sick at the store. When the manager started yelling like he really was my superior I gave him back his keys. Until I put a jarhead stare on him, he threatened to cancel my last paycheck because I hadn't given him two weeks' notice. If I didn't give music a real try, I never would find out.

The Shenanigans' bandleader was a fair guitar player and a piss-poor singer. A few numbers of our gigs he let me sing out front. I was paying close attention to the vocal style of the Band's drummer and sometime mandolin player Levon Helm. We had a gig one night in a dive called the Quanah & Geronimo in Lawton, fifty miles across the Red from Deerinwater. They were mirror images in lots of ways. Southern Oklahoma largely missed out on the oil, but it had the Wichita reservation that was ceded to the Choctaws after the Trail of Tears and then ceded once more to the Comanches and Kiowas. The Apaches put there never stopped being classified as prisoners of war. Fort Sill was built to keep the last firebrands of the hostile tribes on the reservation, and white ranchers got rich or richer leasing bargain grazing rights to a bunchgrass prairie called the Big Pasture. The last Oklahoma land rush opened the prairie to settlers who promptly plowed the prairie under, which killed it and gave birth to Lawton.

A club there called the Quanah & Geronimo honored the last Comanche and Apache war chiefs who spent their later years on sprawling

Fort Sill. It was always packed with drunk Indians and drunk soldiers from Fort Sill. The night the Shenanigans played there I sang The Band's "Up on Cripple Creek," and what was there not to like about that?

A drunkard's dream if I ever did see one . . .

A roar went up when I sang that line, and the noise got louder each time I sang it, three more times. When my time to sing came around again I started another of my Levon Helm and Robbie Robertson favorites, "The Night They Drove Old Dixie Down." Some of the soldiers sang along, but soon the Yankees and Johnny Rebs were bellowing insults and the bar fight was on. The Indians joined in, it seemed, just for the opportunity. With a ragged segue and splice our leader made a three-minute song into a merger with "Let's Spend the Night Together." I backed off from the fray but carried the mike with me. Even with an M-16 in my hands I had never felt such power.

Leon Russell was entertained by the brawl but he hadn't overcome childhood polio by exposing his body to unnecessary risks. When the fight erupted, he moved back behind the bar and the station of the bouncers, who weren't eager to wade out in that either. Leon had been a maestro studio piano player in the LA talent pool of session players called the Wrecking Crew, who shared their name with a movie starring Dean Martin and the subsequent Manson Gang victim Sharon Tate. Leon recorded behind Frank Sinatra, Sam Cooke, the Stones, and many others. He broke out on his own by writing "Delta Lady" and "A Song for You" for Rita Coolidge. Then he recruited a well-paid band and stole the show from Joe Cocker in the movie companion of Cocker's album *Mad Dogs and Englishmen.* With his long gray hair and beard and matching gray top hat, for a time he was full-blown rock and roll star.

He founded Shelter Records with an English partner, and they hyped it as the American equivalent of the Beatles' Apple label. Along with a place in the hills outside LA Leon kept a home in Tulsa and motored down to Lawton now and then because he was born there. He liked the vibe of the Quanah & Geronimo because it was named in honor of the Comanche and Apache war chiefs who saw statehood and the twentieth century arrive on reservations soon consumed by the farmers and Fort Sill. Leon blew off the Shenanigans, but after a few days of hearing me sing and play the harmonica, he signed me to a contract with his new label.

He put me up in one of the little houses in walking distance from a big stone building he transformed into the Church Studio. Built during the First World War for a congregation called the Grace Episcopal Methodist Church, it was a two-story structure that had a pimpled look because it was built with sandstone and river rocks. He worked me hard for six months in the Tulsa studio. I was so green I knew that Leon thought of me as a long-shot prospect, like an outfielder in the rookie league. But the studio band on my first record consisted of Leon on piano, the Comanche-Kiowa lead guitarist Jesse Ed Davis, the bass player Carl Radle, and the drummer Jim Keltner. One session when I showed up at the studio, behind the keyboard sat a guy with long blond hair and a hard look in his eyes. Greg Allman. A grizzled little guy walked in with a guitar case one day and introduced himself as J.J. Cale. A couple of them died young, but they were rock and roll legends all.

Jesse Ed took a particular interest in me because of my limitations. He saw my hand and asked me how it happened. "In the war," I said. "I saw it coming."

He answered like an Indian. "You mean a vision?"

"No, I mean I saw it coming. It was a tracer round. It hit a concrete bridge where I had stooped and rested my hand. The round missed my head by about a foot."

Jesse Ed nodded. "Now on, I'm calling you Bad Hand."

"Over there they called me High Noon. Only nickname I ever had."

He explained. "Both my peoples, Comanche and Kiowa, were finished off as warriors by a horse soldier officer named Ranald Mackenzie. He fought for the North in the Civil War and had more bullet holes in him than a highway sign. He had a hand that looked worse than yours, according to them old warriors that fought him and his cavalry, lots of them freed slaves. They called him Bad Hand and Chief No Fingers."

My ignorance of his peoples' histories embarrassed me. I knew the last battles of that plains war played out along the Red River, where I grew up. Jesse Ed shrugged it off and said, "Your hand still hurt?"

"Not all the time. The worst is when I wake up at night and it's cramped."

I told him if I was going to be lead singer of a band I ought to be able to play guitar, at least a little. Jesse Ed agreed it was helpful, but observed a lot of singers had done without it. Frank Sinatra, for instance. Jesse Ed tried to get me started playing slide or bottleneck guitar, like him and two of my heroes, Elmore James and Ry Cooder, but eventually he decided my hindrance and frustration would never let me learn the instrument. He didn't have time to waste on me. I was stung.

One night when we were smoking some choice weed Jesse Ed said, "You ever heard zydeco?"

"Yeah, Cajun music. I like to listen to it. I didn't grow up with it."

"They're not the same," he said. "Cajuns are French folk that got run out of Nova Scotia by the English when America was just a few colonies and a lot of wilderness occupied by Indians. They came to Louisiana and hooked up back in the swamps with Creole blacks out of New Orleans and Haiti. Accordions, banjos, they call it swamp pop. Dance music. They do something called the Mamou jitterbug."

I smiled at the name. "So what's zydeco? It's got accordions."

"Difference is the blues. They can be south Louisiana Creoles, too, but they're also north Louisiana prairie blacks. They're descended from slaves and there ain't hardly any Haitians. They dress up cowboy and sing English as much as French. Zydeco came out of Port Arthur, Beaumont, Lake Charles, swampy places like that. The first hit zydeco song, "Paper in My Shoe," came out of a guy called Boozoo Chaviz when you and me were little boys. The song's about people so poor they have holes in their shoes."

"Okay," I said. "I've heard it then. Clifton Chenier."

"That's right. Ever seen him and his band play?"

"No. Why?"

"Something just came to mind."

The next time I saw him he handed me a box wrapped in brown paper and package tape. "Open it," he said. I pulled out an instrument called a *frattoir* in French. It was thin, flexible, silver-colored metal marked "The Snake. Key of Z Rubboards Made by Tee Don."

"It's a vest," he said. "Clifton Chenier invented it because he wanted an instrument his brother Cleveland could learn to play. See the shoulder straps? You put it on like an apron. Here, let me fix you up."

"You're giving me this? How much did it cost?"

"Not much. Look at the materials."

"What am I going to do with it?"

He handed me spoons. "You play it."

I strummed the spoons and laughed with pleasure. "Like I'm playing my ribs!"

I took to playing it at once, but I was clumsy enough with my left hand that I kept fumbling the spoon. On a visit to see my folks, I found that Mom had been sewing, and I asked her if I could talk her out of a couple of her thimbles. She said, "Of course," but seemed to think it curious. With them on the strongest fingers I could manage and make a strong *tock tocking* that worked off the rhythm of my good hand and spoon. I thought of it one day when we were riffing on Eddie Floyd's "Knock On Wood."

I was getting an education in musicianship, the life. I take back all the snide things I used to say about Oklahoma. Those guys threw a rope to a nearly drowning man.

CHAPTER 27

I was twenty-eight when I changed my last name. I tried to convince my parents I had nothing against the name on my birth certificate. It was just show business, I told them. I had a career in music that might be taking off, and I wanted something with a little more pop and sizzle. They didn't understand, but what could they do but try to believe me? I'd worried them sick for a good part of a decade. They knew about my year in Vietnam; I wrote them then, but they knew none of the rest. I never wanted them to know the real story of the lost years in my life.

The name change occurred to me on a pretty day when I was driving past Sawtooth Peak in my favorite part of Texas, the Davis Mountains of Big Bend, stoned out of my gourd with a girl called Del Rio who wore cut-off jeans and a white T-shirt. She had a bare foot propped on the dashboard of my newly purchased '68 Olds emerald green Cutlass convertible. The expanse of desert, high prairie, and stark mountain ranges is called West of the Pecos, and it occurred to me that this was what I was after—way out yonder, beyond the pale.

Haid *Pecos,* I thought. That's who I'll be.

Del Rio was a wild child. The wind flung her honey-colored hair all around and she was enjoying it. Comely nipples poked through her thin cotton T-shirt. She had been living in the pretty little town of Fort

Davis for some months but had decided to move back to Austin. "I love the country out here," she yelled out of the blue, above the convertible's wind, "but the people are about two bubbles off plumb."

I laughed and asked her to say that again, and when she did, it brought back the spirit level that carpenters use. Joey Carrigan's dad had given one to all the boys in our congregation when we graduated from high school. The spirit is clear alcohol put in a glass or plastic tube in a way that creates a moving bubble. Lines on the tube are marked at intervals that correspond with the length of the bubble. The bubble rests between two lines at the center when the level is horizontal. Tilted to angles, the bubble moves down to rest between other pairs of lines. Brother Carrigan, as we called the deacon and dad of Joey the armed robber at our church, didn't buy us cheap ones out of a run-down hardware store, either. It came in a varnished wood case with a neatly folded little essay on the building tool's invention by the French royal librarian of Louis XIV. He must have had some time on his hands. Leon shrugged when I told him about my name change but laughed when I said I wanted to call the record *Two Bubbles Off Plumb.* "It's kind of funny even if you don't get the joke," he said. "But where's the song that goes with it?"

I was shy about my songwriting. I didn't think it was any good because the lead egotist of the Shenanigans had assured me it wasn't. Leon told me, though, that if I was going to get a foothold in the music business and especially do it on his label, I had to write some good songs of my own. "You can't just be a damn catalogue of all the songs and singers you admire. Unless you want to hit fifty playing Holiday Inn wedding parties in a copy band." He wanted at least half the songs to be originals. Part of my problem was logistics. Composing songs would have been a lot easier for me if I'd been able to play chords on a guitar or plink along on a piano in search of a tune. The words came to me first, then I'd start hearing a trace of melody for them in my mind, and pick it up on my harmonica, the newborn lyrics changing in my brain all the time.

And then came the awkwardness of singing it acapella and then playing it on my harmonica for real musicians who thought in terms of keys and bridges and arrangement—the collaboration process that made the song possible if it was going to be played by a band. Every time I ventured a new song, I felt like I was going to an audition naked. But knowing how much rode on it, I holed up in Tulsa with my Hohner, two fifths of Jack Daniel's, and a bag of Thai sticks. My start on the title track began:

Screen door slams open
And through it you come
Like you don't own nothing
Of all the harm you've done
Hot-wired your daddy's Caddy
You're the one knows how
You might be a scorpion
Might be a saint
Why can't I just say
Aw baby I cain't?

You've got the sticks
I'm just the drum
We're two bubbles off plumb

Rattlers and cobras they're courteous
They rise up and say beware
But here we're making love in the bluestem
Watched through a halo of gnats
By a pink-nosed Charolais cow
You're my ration of guaranteed hurt
You're the reason God made Eve
Wanted to see how that might work

You've got the sticks
I'm just the drum
We're two bubbles off plumb

When I got back to Austin I knew I needed to tend to business. Leon let me know I couldn't expect him to carry me the rest of my career. Others on the Shelter label included Phoebe Snow, Tom Petty and his first band Mudcrutch, the great bluesman Freddie King, and a wry young singer and songwriter, Willis Alan Ramsey. *Two Bubbles Off Plumb* came out, and because it was on Shelter and the names of those sidemen appeared on the liner notes, it got a fair amount of play on FM stations. The reviewer for

Crawdaddy wrote that maybe this was what Texas music was supposed to sound like. Never mind that Leon and most of the sidemen were from Oklahoma. I don't think it was a compliment.

Jesse Ed had told me that any decent singer can attract a good band. The trick, he said, is keeping them. As well as musicians had treated me in Tulsa, I didn't like the place enough to stay there. I moved to Austin before the record came out, and at the risk of being unrealistic I wanted two lead guitar players on the order of the Stones and Eric Clapton's studio band of Americans, Derek and the Dominos. I tried to get Little Mike Wilson to join us, but he had a wife and a small child now, he was trying to do right by them, scuffling and about ready to give it up. But doing me another favor, Little Mike sent me the first hire.

Johnny Stafford was from Victoria, a town down near the coast that like Deerinwater had a lot of oil money. Johnny was tall and looked like the actor Jimmy Stewart—he was the one who took home the babes with the backstage passes. He brought in a strong-fingered bass player, Shack Brown, who was from Lamesa, a woebegone little town in the Texas Panhandle. Shack had the unkempt hair and haphazardly trimmed beard that in another time might have cast him as a Dust Bowl refugee.

Shack and Johnny brought in Jake Bloom, the other lead guitarist, who had grown up in a little town near Abilene named Stamford. Since the 1930s it had claimed to host the country's first rodeo with prize money in which all contestants were working cowboys, not pros. Jake swore he once rode a bull almost to the buzzer in that arena, and he wanted to land us a gig at Stamford's Cowboy Reunion. We assured him we'd get the shit kicked out of us if we ever played there. Jake was a good singer, and he was a better and more prolific songwriter than I was. And he was a smartass, which I liked. "The problem with your virgin harmonica," he said, "is it made you think every song has to be in key of C." He kept us loose with songs like "Daddy Was a Killer," about a daughter of Jerry Lee Lewis. For business purposes, Jake and I were a songwriting team sharing the rights to the material. Jake was also hard to match onstage. In addition to his guitars he had an antique instrument called a Serpent. He said it got its name from its S-shape and leather-covered tube. The brass mouthpiece resembled those of trumpets, but the tubes had holes for finger play like those in woodwinds. He said it eased out of symphonic orchestras about 1850. I thought it looked like a water moccasin digesting somebody's poodle. I didn't strap on my *frattoir* throughout the shows, and Jake only brought out the Serpent for part of a set, but our playing off each other helped build the band's live gig reputation.

We went through a few drummers before we settled on Howie Fletcher, who was steady and seldom let his mind wander off the beat. But Shack and Jake were the rhythm guys I counted on. They had the ear and spoke up when a drummer got disinterested or distracted. Next we gained a keyboard player named Lester Small. He told us we were Baptists, not Presbyterians, because we favored piano over organ.

We put the word out for a horn player who could play both the clarinet and tenor sax, which brought us a guy from Piedras Negras named Ramón Guillermo. Ramón could also play a flute with the breathy sound of South American Indians, and he showed up one day with a button accordion and showed how well he could play that. Ramón was an illegal when we found him, but Leon was able to get him a visa. Every time he had to go to Mexico and get it renewed, though, we didn't know if this time we wouldn't get him back. Ramón was full of surprises. One day he hauled into our squalid rehearsal a set of vibes, the tuned metal bars of which he played like a xylophone.

We were on a roll. We could jump from conjunto to zydeco in seconds, with plenty of nods granted to gospel and country, but the core of our sound was blues-anchored rock and roll. On Johnny's suggestion we named ourselves Haid Pecos and the Rip Chords. If we could hold it together—afford to hold it together—we were a hot and versatile seven-piece band. Austin was alive with good music venues, small and large. The one with the biggest reputation and longest life was Armadillo World Headquarters. It was a big onetime armory where national guard vehicles once got repaired and young Elvis once played. They had a great sound system, they sold just beer and wine, and the worn carpet smelled like mildewed beer. When you walked in you were greeted by a large painting of Freddie King blasting out of the chest of an armadillo. The artist was Jim Franklin, who was Austin's answer to Salvador Dali. The string of star performers at the Armadillo soon included Van Morrison, the Pointer Sisters, and Bruce Springsteen. I thought my debut on the Shelter label might persuade people who booked the Armadillo that our band could sell tickets and beer. But the invitation didn't come for a long time.

Maybe it was because we became the de facto house band of a rival. In Deerinwater I had a friend named Bronson who owned a little bar called the Dark Horse. I found the bar closed and learned Bronson had moved on to Austin, and we caught up with each other again. With some pals he had made good money with a record store chain, and when they sold the chain, he partnered in a sprawling joint called Possum Kingdom Opry House. The name honored a popular lake south of Deerinwater that was carved by canyon lands of the Brazos River. They scored a lease of what had once been an upscale motel complex a few blocks south of the river. The Possum Kingdom Opry House had a small room for the singer-songwriters and their fans and a big one for the hell raisers and dancers. Both had full bars and gallons of milk punch backstage for the musicians, groupies, and guests.

Bronson got his money out of the Opry House before the investment turned into mounds of cocaine going up too many noses. State taxes went unpaid, and there went our steady Austin gig, but it was fun while it lasted. One night, knowing my regard for the man, Bronson got us to open for Jackie Wilson. Big Joe John had schooled me so well on the man and his voice I thought I almost knew him. In Detroit he learned to sing from hearing his mom in a church choir, and he caught on with a group called the Dominoes when he was sixteen. Wilson's breakout hit as a solo artist was "Lonely Teardrops." All at once he moved in a crowd that included La Vern Baker, Clyde McPhatter, and Wilson Pickett.

He was no altar boy. He claimed he started getting drunk when he was nine. He dropped out of school when he was fifteen and wound up in jail several times. He fancied himself a Golden Gloves fighter with pro potential. His mom said boxing was how he got his pretty nose smashed, and maybe he ought to stick to singing. He performed in suits that he got dirty sliding on stage as if into a stolen base, standup mike still in hand. His stagecraft was sheer abandon. He showed off dance moves that reminded me more of Muhammad Ali than Chuck Berry. Roll of the head and shoulders like bobbing and weaving then finish off a spin by flinging out his hand in a quick left jab. I thought, Why, I can do that.

We closed out our set that night with what we called our peckerwood twang on my favorite of Jackie's hits, "(Your Love Keeps Lifting Me) Higher and Higher." For the backup singers in his version Ramón rolled in strong with his clarinet. Before Jackie and his band went on, he said,

"Much obliged. I like the way you do my song." Then he ladled milk punch in each of our cups. I know my hand was shaking because I spilled some on his shoe.

Not long after that, Leon's British partner wound up with the Shelter label in a split-up and settlement. Leon said we shouldn't wait on him starting a new label, and anyway it would be a better fit if we recorded for an indie label in North Carolina called Cow House Creek. He had that all worked out before he told us. It was just business, and we liked the people at Cow House Creek. But it hurt that he did it in such an impersonal way. Due to the friendship he struck up with Willie Nelson, Leon became a fixture in Austin for a while. When I saw him, he'd stop to talk but his eyes were always moving past me.

Willie was Austin's big-name immigrant. Just from writing "Crazy" and "Night Life" in his Nashville days, he could have lived well without ever picking up his battered guitar. He handed out joints like other people offered beers and cups of coffee, and the dope he smoked was so powerful I couldn't carry on a coherent conversation with him. His baritone ranged far south of my tenor, and the only song of Willie's I recorded was "It's Not Supposed to Be That Way." But I learned much from watching him and hearing his discipline in phrasing. He enunciated. The best song will never find an audience if people can't understand the singer.

The Rip Chords generally got what they wanted. Our original songs and covers tended to have long bridges and end with a few minutes of instrumental arrangement. I borrowed material and style from Jackie Wilson, Chuck Berry, Levon Helm, Rick Danko, Al Green, Sting, and Bobby Whitlock. I was an interpreter more than a songwriter. I was an equal opportunity thief of style and material, though I did my best to get songwriters paid for anything of theirs I recorded. I learned a lot from several singers who grew up on the Texas plains that sprouted me. Terry Allen, Joe Ely, Jimmie Dale Gilmore, and Butch Hancock all came out of Lubbock. Another singer I envied, Delbert McClinton, started out singing Lefty Frizzell songs on the loudspeaker of a bread delivery truck in Lubbock, but he found his own voice and gift for lyrics when his folks moved him to Fort Worth. At twenty-two, he blew an unforgettable harmonica lead solo on "Hey Baby," by one-hit wonder Bruce Channel. On a tour of England, a band that opened for them called themselves the Beatles. He said the story that he taught John Lennon how to play the harmonica was exaggerated. I wondered how he could sing with such power night after night without blowing out his voice. I came to think it was because he knew how to let his voice rest throughout his songs. He *breathed* his music. In and out, pacing himself.

Sometimes I'd be captivated by just a phrase or fragment. Driving down the interstate in a frightful thunderstorm: *See how the lightning makes cracks in your air, Tearing the clouds then closing the tear*—Terry Allen. *Come on and let it out, baby, stir it up and mix it in, two parts religion about three parts sin*—Jimmy LaFave. Jimmy had worked with Little Mike Williams in Stillwater before he migrated down to Austin with his red dirt folk rock. I was older than Jimmy, but we became friends. He had such a gift for love songs. They won him a stalker, though, which gave me pause. Was he a better singer than I was? Of course he was. They all were. When I was home alone, I liked to sing along with Linda Ronstadt.

Pipe Town Blues didn't fare as well as *Bubbles* had. My favorite on the album was our cover of the Stones' "Sweet Virginia." My sister caught me on the phone late one night and gave me an angry earful, thinking I'd recorded the song to insult her. "Virginia," I said. "Have you listened to the damn song? The line that goes *Yes, I got the desert in my toenail?* What could that possibly have to do with you?"

A reviewer gibed, "Señor Pecos is trying too hard to be Mick Jagger." Well, touché. At the time our band was in the running to front the Stones on one of their US tours. We had hired a business manager, and he sniped that we were way back in the running, after getting our hopes up. We fired his ass over that. We had a conceit that we were a *national* rock and roll band. Live and learn.

CHAPTER 28

I suppose it was just time. A woman came along who didn't seem to promise another horse wreck. The first time I saw Sabine she was talking into a coin-operated phone on the wall of a 7-Eleven. It was warm that night, the skirt of Sabine's dress was short, and she kept pulling up a strap that slipped off one shoulder. Her hair was down below her shoulder blades. From my car I could see she was unhappy with the other person on the line. She hung up with such force that the plastic receiver shattered in her hand.

"Young woman," I called from my Olds convertible. "I saw that, and I work for the telephone company."

"Fuck off," she replied. First words she said to me.

I turned on all the charm I could in the short time I had. "Come on, look at me. That was a joke, a bad one, I admit. Please, tell me your name. Just tell me your name." I kept talking in that breathless way, and she finally said her name was Sabine. She wouldn't give me her phone number, so I handed her one of the new cards that I'd had printed up for the band. I said I'd like for us to get off to a better start if she would just call me. She put the card in her bra, boarded a Vespa scooter, pulled on her helmet, and with her skirt riding high she rode away with maybe a touch of smile. And damned if she didn't call.

Sabine told me she hung up and smashed the phone like that in the course of an argument with her ex-husband, who had joint custody of their child. She was thirty-two, three years older than me. She was a lawyer employed at a lower level by the state attorney general. Her hair was black with strands of premature gray. The silver and black strands were so fine no tailor could have matched it in silk. She had huge brown eyes that sometimes seemed like they might leap out from under her eyebrows. She had round cheeks and a small mouth that had a merry tilt when she laughed. But when she was distracted or peeved, she had a habit of twitching her mouth sideways and chewing the inside of her cheek.

She told me with an edge to her tone that her name was really Sabiñe, which had three syllables. She said her parents descended from French Basques who came out west in America to find what work they could. "In their language the expression *amerikak agin* means to get rich. The men usually started out as sheepherders. With luck they might own a small hotel and restaurant someday. A lot of them went back to the old country when they made their little pile. Papa and Mama were second generation native-born citizens. He was an engineer and mid-level executive with US Magnesium. They mine salt from the shores of the Great Salt Lake. He and Mama were killed in a plane crash when I was fourteen, and one of my grandmothers raised me. I was Sabiñe until I graduated from Utah State. The University of Texas had the best law school I could get into. I didn't know a soul when I got to Austin. Eventually I gave up and just started being Sabine. Like my parents named me after a muddy river that borders Texas and Louisiana."

"I'll call you Sabiñe," I offered.

She smiled and shook her head. "It's all right. Easier to become Sabine. It's a nice name. The Texans won."

"I bet the river was named by Spanish Basques who pronounced it right."

She cocked her head, drawing my attention to her eyebrows. "What do you know about the Basques?"

"Not much. *The Sun Also Rises.* The running of the bulls in Pamplona. And some music that I like a lot and don't understand a word of it. I seek out a lot of stuff that's not British or Canadian or American. We try to work some of it into our band. There's some first-rate folk rock coming out of there. Moody blues, but not like that band. I can't understand a word they're singing."

Sabine laughed. "Grandma wanted all of us to have Basque as our first language. Mama and Papa wanted none of that; from the cradle on, we should be English speakers. So when they were killed and Grandma took on raising me, she muttered to herself and tried to teach me Basque but it was impossible."

"Is your grandmother still with us?"

"No, she died the same year I had Emily."

I think in Sabine's mind that conversation made me not just another dick trying to get lucky some night. Sabine cherished her motor scooter but also had an MG two-seater for going to work, buying groceries, and taking Emily where they needed to go. I told her that Vespa in pickup traffic was going to get her hurt and scarred, if not killed. Sabine's little girl was eight, and forever stung by being orphaned, Sabine protected her with near ferocity. I didn't see Emily for the first couple of months—in the joint custody arrangement she was always with her dad, Russ Million, a sometime lawyer. I don't know if Sabine calculated it like that in letting me in her house and bedroom. We were tussling on her sofa one night when she pulled the hair away from her eyes and said, "I don't know about this."

"If you want me to, I'll go."

It's a tired line but it got us off the sofa. In the bedroom she took off her clothes then folded and put them on a chair as methodically as dinner napkins. I wondered if any other woman did that. She shaved her legs and under her arms but making love to her was a wonderland of hair. One long black strand curled out of the nipple of her right pear-shaped breast. When she was aroused her fluids gushed out of her like a flood, and when she came she gulped hard and made quiet cries. She made love as naturally as other people tie their shoes.

Our affair deserved the word love, but Sabine and I had issues. One of Austin's oddities is a three-story, windowed, red-tiled roof building with floor space about the size of a bathroom big enough to have a hot tub. The handsome little building was put up decades ago so that firemen could practice scaling and rappelling a sheer wall. It hadn't been used for that or anything else in a long time, but it's a minor landmark and dissent would arise if the city ever tried to tear it down.

The so-called Firemen's Tower sat on First Street and to the rear was handsome parkland that sloped across running trails to the shores of dammed-up Colorado River that was then called Town Lake. Sabine's department in the attorney general's office was in a building three blocks from the lake. She liked to get out of the office during lunch hours, and she didn't enjoy grabbing a bite and window-shopping downtown. After our first nights in bed but early in our courtship, she proposed that I join her at the Firemen's Tower one day for a picnic lunch.

I put down the top of the Olds because it was such a pretty day, drove downtown, and found her sitting just below it. She had gone to a fair amount of trouble. Spread on the park grass was a blanket, a basket of food wrapped in a plaid cloth, a baguette of French bread, a bottle of red wine, and two wine glasses, one of them used. "Hi, you," I said, sitting down. I leaned over to kiss her, but she turned her head and I got her cheek.

"What?" I said.

"You're an hour late. I wear panty hose to work and they're hot. I have to get back to work. There's a meeting."

"I'm not late. I set the alarm."

"No, you didn't. Or you slept through it."

"I'm not late!"

She showed me her watch, which read 2:05.

I blinked my eyes in confusion until finally I groaned, *"Ohhhh.* Daylight Savings started yesterday. I forgot to reset the clocks."

She gave her mouth one quick stretch of disdain. "Is that the best you can do?"

I was being paid back for all that boyhood lying. This time it was true!

I coaxed and cajoled and told her I'd swear on a Bible if I had one.

"I thought you'd stood me up," she said. "I cried a little and . . . "

"You cried?" I said. "Over me?" I was stunned.

"I love you," I said. "I'd never stand you up." It was the first time I'd told I told her that. I'd been wondering if it might be true.

"Do you really mean that?" she said.

I helped myself to a glass of the wine. "Yeah," I said, gaining confidence. "I do."

With a quiet laugh then she kissed me.

"I'm just absent-minded," I said. "I'm not irresponsible."

I'm glad I didn't say what else came to mind. Musicians keep musician's hours.

What did she expect?

CHAPTER 29

Sabine had been in law school in Austin and worked at the capitol for Russ when he was in the House of Representatives. She said they had an affair, though not while she was on his payroll. Halfway through law school she got pregnant with Emily. Sabine laid out a semester to have the baby, but she was more committed to the law profession than Russ was. He had some family money in his hometown of Cuero, and when she was being generous, she said he had been an excellent stay-at-home dad. Their marriage lasted six years.

Russ had quit politics when he saw the rightward lurch coming in Texas, and he occasionally sang and played guitar, chords only, in a folk trio he and two friends called the Meanders. The woman in the trio had a big strong voice. They played at campouts more often than in bars, and when they appeared in beer joints, I don't think they even set out a tip jar, much less charged a cover. They were amateurs dedicated to the entertainment of their friends. Russ started to get work as a character actor when movie productions came to town. He was a handsome and charismatic guy. I think family money must have allowed him to enjoy such a bohemian way of life. He still belonged to the bar and took a few court-appointed cases sent his way from friends who were now local judges, but his income was erratic and not geared to monthly child support, a source of friction between him and Sabine.

One night I peeked in the dark bedroom, and Emily was sprawled out in that total bliss of small children asleep. Later that spring I doctored her knees when she was skateboarding and a concrete ramp pitched her. I'm certain the tenderness of my doctoring helped win the child over. She never got on another skateboard, I know that. From those moments on, she was part of the package for me, as Josie had been with Ann.

The attorney general who employed Sabine ran for governor and lost in a primary. He moved on to private practice, so she and two other women started a law firm specializing in civil mediation. Some of their clients were walk-ins, but at the start most came from judges and lawyers that knew them as assistant AGs and had reason not to want an issue taken to trial. She worked long hours and her practice entailed considerable travel. It was convenient to her that Russ "just bummed around the house," as she put it, chewing on the inside of her mouth. In fact he was catching on as a character actor in movies made in Texas. Apart from getting her firm on solid footing, Sabine's passion in the law was keeping government out of people's bedrooms and decriminalizing abortions. She said an important case called *Roe v. Wade* was then working its way up appellate courts to the Supremes.

"You mean the singers?" I quipped. "I'd lick the feet of Diana Ross."

Sabine had a sense of humor but my wisecrack drew an irritated glance. Her profession bestowed on her titles like Special Master and Ad Litem. Often her cases involved divorcing parents who were trying to avoid or press custody battles over children. I could tell much of that was dispiriting work. I wasn't always as interested in it as I should have been.

I was just going along in our affair, true to my nature, when Sabine started twisting her mouth one night and startled me with a burst of temper. "If this isn't going anywhere, I want to end it now." The next day she called me at my rent house and said she was sorry, that she was stressed out over a collision of difficult cases, but I got the message. The first time I proposed, we were on the bridge over the Rio Grande gorge outside Taos, New Mexico.

"You hear about the party years," she said, "but I'm a practical and sensible person. You live from one gig and contract deal to the next ones. I like music. I like your music. If I could get away from my work I wouldn't mind going with you to Amsterdam or Oslo or one of those places where the fad for your kind of music keeps your band afloat—"

"It's not just a fad," I put in.

"Whatever. I like the way you sing. But I'm not your groupie."

I looked at rapids so far down in the gorge dug by the river that it looked like a frail white ribbon. I started trotting toward the cars and blanket displays of silver and turquoise on sale at the west end of the bridge; there was an unfenced ledge you could reach if you worked at it.

"Where are you going?" she yelled at me.

I walked backward and called, "Thought I might just as well jump, you condescending bitch!" I crossed my hands over my heart then flopped on my back on the concrete, arms flung out wide. A tourist stood over me and took my picture.

We nearly drowned the night she agreed to it. We were at a dinner party in Austin with two of her friends, and there was lots of wine and talk; we barely noticed when a storm came up. At some point we realized it was raining so hard that water poured down the chimney into their fireplace. The intensity of the rain reminded me of the monsoons in Vietnam. I could barely see to drive, but we made it to the house she rented on a street called Possum Trot from a generous appellate judge, and at last she said, "All right. I love you. And I'll marry you." The next morning, we learned the cloudburst had set off a flash flood down a creek that left businesses downtown chest-deep in water and swept away and killed half a dozen people. I had almost driven us right into it. I spent the next weeks trying to convince her that practical and sensible people did not believe in bad omens.

A veterinarian married us. He had been pastor of an Episcopal church but got run off because he opened the doors of his congregation to blacks and Hispanics. So he went to Texas A&M for the necessary schooling and got the state's license to doctor animals.

To lessen the strain on us, intense enough from the start, we decided not to invite my parents and my sister and her family. We would make those travels and introductions later. The wedding took place on the hillside lawn of two of Sabine's friends on a warm fall night. An almost-full moon rose above the winding riverine lakes that flow through the hills and Austin. I had thought it would be strange to favor one of the Rip

Chords over the others, so I rounded up all of them as groomsmen and got my high school friend DeWayne Holland to come down from Oklahoma as my best man. He was divorced from the Osage girl and stayed drunk throughout the weekend; it was the last time I saw him. Some things you just let go.

Sabine had a number of good-looking bridesmaids, and Emily and several other little girls dispensed flowers. Maybe a couple of hundred people came to the outdoor affair, and the band had insisted on playing after the deed was done. Jake Bloom was hot to make an impression with his singing, I had already noted. Bride and groom and our close friends and several little girls assembled in front of the veterinarian cleric, and Emily came forward with the rings. I was thinking: *Never gonna work, never gonna work,* she's too much woman for me. Then I noticed that the veterinarian, Emily, my bride, and everyone else stared at me. There had been a pregnant pause as I had stopped hearing what was being said.

The vet repeated the vow, I rallied strong of voice, kissed my wife, and hurrahs were raised. Afterward our pastor swirled a glass of whiskey in his hand and remarked to me, "I once spent several months in Barcelona. The Catalans have this saying. When there's a pause like that and the flow of talk stops, they say, 'An angel passed.'" He smiled and patted me on the shoulder. "An angel passed. Then it came back and blessed you."

Our happiest time together came in the second year. To our surprise Sabine thought she was pregnant. She took birth control pills and made that as much her morning routine as brushing her teeth, but we were giddy about it. Two of Sabine's friends had a big birthday party that Sunday for their son on the grounds of their restored Victorian home. There were so many little kids squealing and running around it seemed like a grade school playground. Russ picked up Emily at the party, and after sipping a few mimosas Sabine and I slipped away and went for a long drive on a fine spring day.

We drove out east of the city where there were remnant patches of native Indian grass and big and little bluestem. Sabine and Russ had lived out there for a year when they were married, and she knew all the farm-to-market roads and old church cemeteries where the land had never been broken by plows and the native grasses still flourished. And there was a wealth of spring wildflowers—bluebonnets and orange-pink Indian paintbrush and the gold and maroon Mexican hats. We sat among them and tossed out names for this little boy or girl we were going to bring to life. We drank wine, handing the bottle back and forth. A few hundred yards from us was a rickety little stadium where the Hutto Hippos played their games. She said, "Would you still love me if I cut my hair?"

"I'm not sure," I joked, fingering strands of her hair and letting them slide through. "How come you ask?"

She raised her hands and pulled her hair toward the nape of her neck. "My ears stick out." I sang two lines from a Van Morrison favorite. *Making love in the green grass behind the stadium* . . . And among the tombstones with great care we did just that. Afterward as we lay beside each other she said, "We're so *good*. Let's don't ever let go of this moment, this one right now."

But in the week that followed, our doubts began. Sabine was thirty-three, well within childbearing age, but when the time came to take a leave from her law practice, could my music career keep us afloat? Neither of us had any wish to end the pregnancy. As it happened, nature took the decision out of our hands. The guys and I were playing a gig in Fort Worth when I got back to my hotel room and found the message light blinking on the phone. She said, "Call me," and though it was two in the morning, I did. She had miscarried. She shared some hurtful thoughts about my not being there, and then said she was sorry and started crying. I gave her as much comfort as I could. Then we turned off the lights in different cities and different beds. As we did too often in the years to come.

PART IV MUHAMMAD ALI'S JAW

CHAPTER 30

Ever since I took that hook from Kenny Norton, my right jaw hinge has crackled when I move it certain ways. It often happened when I sang, though it seemed only I could hear it. The mikes in studios never picked it up. It might have been commercial if they had—like one of those African languages that make popping sounds.

When the band and I were in town, I started working out again at Richard Lord's Boxing Gym. A young woman who was a physical therapist and regular at the gym showed me a better way of wrapping my hands, and I got where I wasn't so tentative with my left hand. Richard's dad Doug Lord had trained and managed a black Dallas fighter, Curtis Cokes, who held the world title and dominated the welterweights between 1966 and 1969.

Richard Lord had grown up in boxing. He started fighting in the Golden Gloves as soon as he could lift a pair of gloves and aspired to go to the Olympics. That didn't happen, and he turned pro as a featherweight. He won eighteen fights against a loss and a draw, stopped fifteen of his opponents, and gained a lower-rung top ten ranking. But he couldn't see a title shot coming, so he retired and got a degree from the University of Texas. Austin had never been much of a boxing town, but Richard's dusty little gym changed that. He brought back the city's Golden Gloves tournaments, which had lapsed out of existence. Early mornings and midafternoons brought out men and women of all ages, and often children brought out by their moms to Richard's gentleness and trust. The hallmark of Richard's fighters was conditioning. Every Sunday morning, he would gather the serious fighters in his gym and they'd sprint up the ramps of the University of Texas's double-deck football stadium. Though the gym emphasized its amateurs, some of the young fighters turned pro, and two claimed multiple world titles—my young friends Jesus Chavez and Anissa Zamarron.

But those crowd pleasers would emerge years later. Richard had started promoting boxing cards in the downtown Rock Music Hall. The first one featuring young women was a fundraiser for rape victims. He and workout regulars would tear the best of his two rings down, transport it across town, and assemble it again. The "Brawls in the Hall" were vintage Austin—rock and roll married to boxing. One of the autographed posters on the dust-caked walls recalled the time David Bowie got himself in shape for one of his international tours by hiring Richard as a trainer.

Nobody talked much shop at the gym, and I was just one of the older guys who came in for the workout, but Richard thought he remembered seeing me win my state Golden Gloves title in Fort Worth. He looked back through the records and established that my last name back then was Shelton. "Why'd you change it?" he said one day.

"Oh, you know, music business. There's lots of that."

"You want to sing the National Anthem on this card we got coming up?"

"No way. The high notes are too high and the low ones are too low. You can make a fool of yourself, singing that."

For all I knew Kenny Norton was now a small-town cop in Illinois. Before I left the boxing camp at Pendleton, he had scrawled the Jacksonville, Illinois, address and phone number on the back of a card and told me to stay in touch. I failed to do that, and six years had raced by. In Richard's office one day I was thumbing through a tattered 1970 issue of a boxing magazine. It contained an article about an American heavyweight who had won his first sixteen, stopping all but one, and had been Joe Frazier's sparring partner. Then a Venezuelan who was outweighed by twenty pounds and had a record of twelve wins and three losses knocked him out in Los Angeles. A photo with the piece had Kenny toppling head first toward the canvas. I knew what a crushing moment that had to have been for him. I found the card and wrote him.

> *Kenny, you may barely remember me and the months in 1967 when we worked out with each other. I'm glad to know you figured out a way to get through the lean times of the game and pursue your dream. I just now read about you losing a pro fight for the first time. I hope you haven't gotten down on yourself, and that you're battling on. I hope you never lose again. You're a good man and a great fighter. How is your little boy? Haid*

I added that my last name was now Pecos and enclosed cassettes of *Two Bubbles Off Plumb* and *Pipe Town Blues.* I doubted I'd ever hear back. Sabine and I bought a small house down the street from her rental on Possum Trot, a neighborhood populated by artists and dope-dealing hippies, well-heeled young professionals, plenty of children, and enough old people to add to its character. A creek ran through its urban forest. In my studio, a remodeled two-car garage, one afternoon the phone rang and Kenny was on the line. I was so surprised I stammered.

"A singer!" he laughed. "You can't sing any better than you could fight."

"Easy now. I'm sensitive. And nobody's knocking me out."

"You mean since I did? Nah, listen, that's good stuff—I hear some blues and soul in there. You got a lot of nerve covering Percy's 'Dark End of the Street.'"

"Not his version," I said of Percy Sledge. "I think more of the first hit made of it. Mississippi preacher's son named James Carr."

"Oh. I stand corrected. What's with the name change?"

"Music biz. You know."

"Yeah. So fill me in. What else you been up to all this time?"

"A year in Vietnam, right after I last saw you. Then some weeks in California, but I was running out of money, and didn't know what else to do, so I went back to my hometown in Texas. Bad idea, I thought at the time, and it was at first. But I caught a break in Oklahoma that got me the first of those albums. I've got a band with me now that's not the one on the solo record, but they're good, we're getting plenty of work, and we've got more albums in the works. I'm married now. I live in Austin."

The humor in his voice changed tone. "All that brig time and they still sent you across the pond? Are you all right?"

"A Purple Heart and a bunged-up hand, but I'm okay. How about you? How's your son? He still with you?"

"Oh yeah, just me and him, way it's always been. He's in grade school now in LA. Doing fine."

Kenny left a pause, or as the Episcopalian veterinarian said, an angel passed.

"I appreciate that letter you sent me," he said. "Right after you left, I let them know I wanted my discharge. They didn't like it but they couldn't turn me down. I was about to head home to the Jacksonville police department, like I told you. I thought my folks could help raise Kenny Junior, the way Aunt Mary helped them raise me. But Pop said, 'If I help you now, you'll never stop asking. You got to work through this on your own.'"

"Wow."

"Yeah. Tough old bird. But Pop was right. A ref in the amateurs named Bob Biron had seen me fight and kept tabs on me. He was successful enough in business that he bought a piece of the Padres baseball team. He and some other guys turned me pro. They started me off at a hundred dollars a round."

"How'd it go?"

"My first three fights were in San Diego. I love the town, but if you're going to be a fighter you've got to go where the fighters are. In southern California that's LA, not San Diego. My trainer steered me to the Hoover Street Gym, down by the Harbor Freeway. It's crummy looking on the outside, but it's great inside. All kinds of talent come through there. 'Bossman' Jones. 'Scrap Iron' Johnson. One day I was in the gym and a Trinidad steel band made the scene and started setting up. Then all this commotion and here came Archie Moore and an entourage. Hands taped, robe slung on his shoulders, ready to go. Long as you paid your dues, there was no shortage of people who'd give you serious work."

"Where do you live?"

"South LA, close to the gym. It's sorry little apartment, but I'm lucky to have some neighbors who take good care of Kenny the hours I can't, and I help them with their rent. In those days I'd get up at four in the morning, run five miles, then get Kenny Junior up and fed and to school, and then I'd head out for a job on the assembly line of a Ford plant. I aligned the frames to make the seats fit. That's heavy work. Then back to the gym for two or three hours. I was trying to do all those things and afraid I wasn't doing any of them right. If my car broke down it was a disaster. Many's the time hot dogs and Wonder Bread and milk were all the food we had in the house. I added on some guilt because I'd make my workouts drag on, knowing the neighbors wouldn't let Kenny Junior go without supper."

"You were Joe Frazier's sparring partner?"

"Eventually."

"Was that your big break?"

"Yeah, but it wasn't the first one, even the second one. Right after my move my first trainer left to handle somebody in Germany, and Eddie Futch picked me up. Amazing guy. He played on a basketball team that a year later changed its name to the Harlem Globetrotters. He was an amateur stablemate of Joe Louis but had a heart murmur and couldn't turn pro. He worked as a hotel waiter, on road construction gangs, in a sheet metal plant, finally scored a job at the post office. Always looking for that someone special to walk in the gym. Joe Frazier was *Eddie*'s big break. Joe let him quit pitching mail and train fighters full-time." He chuckled. "Eddie's a master psychologist. I'd stopped everybody I fought until I got my ass kicked by that Venezuelan. It was no joy waking up the next morning. When I dragged in the gym and opened my locker, Eddie had taped on a newspaper picture of me headed for the canvas. He said, 'Damn, Norton, that photographer done got your best side in that picture. You going to listen to me now, Sugar Britches?'"

"Has he changed your style?"

"No, he works with it, makes it better. I was making three hundred bucks a round now, but Bob Biron and my other backers in San Diego started doubting I had a winner's attitude, so they hooked me up with a psychologist and hypnotist. Know what they used to call hypnotists? Mesmerists. He gave me a book called *Think and Grow Rich* by a man named Napoleon Hill. Ever heard of it?"

"No."

"It's been a bestseller since the thirties. Hill got his ideas from Andrew Carnegie and these free thinkers, people like Mary Baker Eddy and the Christian Science folk. They believed optimism is the cure of evil, and all disease is mental in origin, so with correct thinking you can heal just about anything."

"So if I gave enough thought to this crackle in my jaw you gave me . . ."

"What's that?"

"Never mind. Kenny, what's all that got to do with boxing?"

"Well, when I read that book and my psychologist hypnotized me, things began to come together. I was able to quit the Ford plant. Eddie put me in working with Joe Frazier, and I sparred with him off and on the next five years. Joe paid me five hundred a week, and I earned every nickel."

"How'd you do?"

"First time, I'd made the mistake of going out drinking the night before. I thought he was going to kill me. Next time it turned into a six-round war. He's a hard sucker to hit, I'll tell you that. Best head movement I've seen, and he's got a hook you don't see until you're on the floor from it. How he put down your pretty boy Muhammad Ali."

"He's not my *boy,* Kenny. I admire them both. Frazier won that fight fair and square. Would you fight him?"

"I'd hate to, because he's too good a friend. But yeah, I'd fight him if the money was right. He'd say the same thing."

His voice changed again. "Haid, I got to ask you something."

"Shoot."

"Why did you cut loose on me that day at Pendleton?"

"Dear John letter, pure and simple. First love dies hard."

"Oh. I was afraid it was something I said or did."

"No way. You were the only friend I had." I wanted to steer the talk away from all the trouble I was in at the time. "So you're still in the hunt?"

"Damn straight. I'm twenty-nine and one and I'm training for a fight with Ali."

"You're kidding."

"Why you say that? You think I'm not good enough?"

"No, no," I hastened. "I've just been doing my thing, not following boxing much. Good for you. Where is this fight? When?"

"San Diego. March thirty-first. Come on out. I'll comp you good tickets. Bring your wife."

When we hung up, I looked at the band's bookings and saw nothing that couldn't be rescheduled the last night of March, 1973. I told Sabine what I meant to do, and she was invited. "Really?" she said. "Let's go."

I was astonished. "You've told me you hate boxing."

"Not if it's Muhammad Ali. Brady took me to a closed circuit TV in a big hall in Houston the first fight after Ali's layoff over the draft. All these black chicks in knockout clothes. Singing, dancing, and it was just a big TV screen, but they were all styled up anyway. It was a hoot. I loved it."

Women. They're a constant surprise.

CHAPTER 31

I lied to Kenny when I said I hadn't kept up with the fights. I just hadn't dug deep enough in the pile to find him. Ali's refusal to be drafted cost him three years of his prime and millions of dollars. When he fought Jerry Quarry in his first fight after the layoff and stopped him with a cut in the third round, he still had a five-year federal prison sentence hanging over his head. He was out on bond pending his appeals, and was able to fight again only because the Georgia Boxing Commission broke ranks with the other states and granted him a license. Five months later, Ali took the first loss in his career to Joe Frazier, a decision punctuated by a fifteenth-round knockdown. But his victims since then included the rugged Canadian champion George Chuvalo, the ex-heavyweight champ Floyd Patterson, the dominant light heavyweight champ Bob Foster, and Jerry Quarry twice. Ali's record stood at 41 and 1 and he'd stopped twenty-nine opponents. He didn't seem to have lost anything at all.

The 5-1 betting odds against Kenny were jeered as obscenely generous. Though all the authorities had him ranked in the top ten, *Sports Illustrated* dismissed him as "Ken Somebody." Howard Cosell called it "the worst mismatch in boxing history—a disgrace." Those weren't the kinds of reviews I'd want for my next album.

But Sabine and I found Kenny chipper and composed. His camp was at a run-down resort called the Massacre Canyon Inn in the San Jacinto

Valley. He looked good in his light workout when we arrived. Most of the emphasis was on speed and footwork, cutting off the ring. There were less than ten people in the gym. The only difference I could see in Kenny was a well-trimmed mustache. He was working with a muscled-up black guy who stayed right with him. They weren't hitting hard, this close to the fight. They were moving so fast that at times I couldn't tell which one was Kenny, except he dragged the right foot.

After ditching his sparring helmet, gloves, and hand wraps he greeted us warmly. "Mrs. Pecos," he said with a smile. "I'm pleased to meet you."

"Sabine, please," she said merrily, shaking his hand. "I bet there aren't fifteen people on earth besides Haid who are named Pecos. I didn't find out his family name is Shelton until his mother had engraved it on a Bible she gave me. I forget sometimes and call him Pecos Bill."

Sabine's smart mouth and wisecracks were among the reasons I loved her, but that seemed to rattle Kenny. He called over the other heavyweight and introduced him as Mike Weaver. Mike was shy and about as handsome as his boss. "May not look it," Kenny said, "but Haid was one of the best sparring partners I had in the amateurs."

Weaver smiled, said hello, but didn't offer to shake hands. His hands were still in wraps, and he didn't want to get his sweat on ours. Kenny's trainer Eddie Futch also came over to meet us. Kenny bragged on me again. Sabine was giving me looks like she didn't know me at all. After Kenny showered, he took us riding in a Jeep. "Like the old days, huh?"

"Your driving's more sensible now," I said.

The canyon near Riverside was bounded by steep rock cliffs and had a spring-fed creek with a twelve-foot waterfall. Kenny said, "Some hot springs near here used to be a health resort."

"Why's it called Massacre Canyon?" I said.

From the back seat, Sabine leaned forward to listen. "There was an Indian tribe called Temecula that lived here and they got most of their food from seeds they called *chia*. It's a native kind of salvia." He glanced back at Sabine, whose hair was being blown all around in the wind. "You know those flowers?"

"Yes, a nice red. I've grown them."

He nodded. "One year they had a drought, and the crop was weak. The Temeculas caught a tribe called Ivahs poaching their part of the canyon, and they had a daylong fight to the death. Over flower seeds."

Kenny had asked us to stick around and join him on the patio behind his cabin for dinner. There was a small table and three chairs, plates, steak knives, some battered forks, glasses for water, and a bottle of red wine. He drank iced tea. The sunset was gold on the cliffs and violet where the shade crept up.

"It's pretty here," Sabine said.

"Hot in the summer," Kenny said. "So Sabine, tell me about you."

"I'm a partner in a small law firm in Austin. We mediate, settle disputes."

He smiled. "Boxers could use you in the fight with promoters."

Their chat went on in an awkward way until they learned that Emily and Kenny Junior were both seven years old. Then they had something in common. "I admire single dads so much," she said. "Your son must be very proud of you."

"I hope. We're making it up as we go along. If I'm religious about anything, it's keeping him out of boxing."

The camp cook uncorked the wine for us and brought us grilled steaks, roasted sliced potatoes, and a salad of lettuce, green onions, and wedges of orange and avocado. Kenny said his iced tea was called *oolong* and was good for his enzymes. I rolled my eyes and he laughed. He raised his glass to us, we ticked it with ours, and he knifed into his steak. "It's really gonna be my third dance with Ali. When he was in his draft limbo, he went around the country looking for guys good enough to spar. He didn't want to lose his skills. Eddie got us together at Hoover Street. He told me, 'You know the drill from working with Joe. Just be smart. Work with him and try to learn something. But if it gets rough in there, take care of yourself.' We were in the corner one round and Ali had me bent over and tied up, and he started whipping me around, side to side. I used to be a football player, you recall. I hefted him up like I was making a tackle and slung him clear across the ring. Ali said, 'Okay, boy, I'm through playing with you.' We got going pretty good that day. Next day Ali came back making noise. '*I want Norton,* where's that Norton?' Eddie told me, 'Keep your clothes on, Kenny.'

"Ali said, 'Ain't he going to work today?' Eddie said, 'No way.' Ali said, 'Why not?' Eddie said, 'Because yesterday you came in looking for a workout. Today you came in looking for a fight. When this guy fights you, he's going to get paid and paid well.'"

Kenny went on that Ali had called and offered a fight when he got licensed again if they would take a $25,000 purse. "Eddie told him, 'Not a chance.' Eddie knew I wasn't ready yet. And he's the boss."

He chewed for a moment, swallowed, and touched his napkin to his mouth.

"Life's funny, till one day it's not. In 1970, Sonny Liston was living in Vegas and knew about me. He needed dough and was looking for some young hotshot he could use to rev up new attention. He was talking to Eddie all that spring and start of summer. Then the Venezuelan knocked me out, and it was back to the drawing board. I could have been Sonny Liston's last fight. End of that December he was an overdose stinking up his house in Vegas. His wife was away when he died."

Sabine blinked her eyes and looked at her plate.

"How much will you get for fighting Ali?" I asked.

"Haid," Sabine said. She thought it was rude.

"I don't mind," he said. "For fifty thousand I'd fight the Russian army. I like Ali okay. When he fought Bob Foster at Lake Tahoe, my fight with Henry Clark closed out the night. It was my first time on TV. Ali was too big for Foster, but Bob gave him his first cut and made him pay attention. I stopped Henry in the ninth, showered, and joined the party. Ali was wearing sunglasses to cover his cut and bruised eye. A couple of girls started drifting my way, and he got loud and put on a show. 'You're next, Norton. I want *you!*'"

Sabine said, "It's hard for me to imagine fighters being friendly."

"He was just fooling around. Hell, I owe the man. He made this happen, the same way he made Joe Frazier two million. Joe was champ but he'd never seen that kind of money. Ali's a nonstop promotion machine. I've won twenty-nine fights, lost one, and stopped twenty-five of them. Henry Clark was my biggest payday. Eight thousand bucks."

I asked Kenny what he thought of Howard Cosell, who would be calling the fight on ABC. He shrugged. "He's a cheerleader for Ali. Let him and the rest say what they want. I'm in the best shape of my life. My psychologist has got my mind right. Before I was overconfident. Now I'm just confident."

"So you've got nothing personal against Ali," I said.

"Nah. It's a golden opportunity. But it'll be personal if I get to fight Foreman."

"Why? He just did what he was supposed to do. If he could."

In Jamaica in January 1973, Foreman had dribbled Frazier like a basketball, knocked him down six times in two rounds to become the new undefeated heavyweight champ. "It's what he did afterward," Kenny said. "He claimed Joe Frazier quit. Joe was too busy bouncing off the canvas to think *Quit.* It's not right to insult a man like that."

Kenny was rankled that the buzz in the sporting press was not about his fight with Ali. Instead it was all about, When would Ali fight Foreman? Kenny cut off another piece of steak. "There's something about George that nobody outside boxing picks up on. How come he never fights in the States anymore? Joe had to go to Jamaica to fight him, and Joe was the champion, for god sakes. Why weren't they in Vegas or Madison Square Garden? There's a story going around that George crossed some mob associates of Liston, and they told him they'd kill him if he ever fought on American soil again."

CHAPTER 32

Sabine wondered what kind of world I'd brought her into. But at the hotel in La Jolla the night of the fight, she dressed up in style—a filmy green dress, her favorite pearls and earrings, and high heels she seldom wore. She had on an anklet I'd never seen before. "Like it?" she said, raising her foot. "I got it just for this." In San Diego as we approached the arena in our rent car, I watched the prowling groups of young sailors and marines. When we got to our seats I was too excited to pay much attention to the undercard fights. I worried that the blood and spit buckets would turn off Sabine before the real show began. I told her that Foreman was now the undefeated world champ, but Ali had to be on cloud nine because the Supreme Court had just thrown out his conviction and certified him as a conscientious objector to the Vietnam War. It was a bigger triumph for him than twice stopping Sonny Liston.

Sabine listened to me keenly, but her bright eyes fastened on young black women with big Afros and skin-tight dresses. The experts at ringside might be sure this would be an easy warm-up fight for Ali, but I couldn't have been much more tense and excited if I'd been about to get in the ring myself.

They were fighting twelve rounds, not fifteen, because only a vacant North American title was at stake. But any fight was a big fight when one of them was Muhammad Ali. In the dressing room, Kenny told me later, Eddie Futch was reminding him that Ali's jab established command in his fights, but when he threw it, he let his right glove drift away from his head. How would Kenny know the jab was coming? *"Watch his pecs,"* Kenny said. When the muscles of Ali's shoulders and sternum contracted his pectorals, the jab was coming. Futch stressed to Kenny to be patient, to cut off Ali's dancing and force him into a corner. He couldn't just head hunt. Ali was a master at slipping punches with the quickness of his eyes and head. Then he'd come off the ropes counter-punching, and those combinations could put you down and out. Bang away at the body, force Ali to lean forward, and then go after his head.

Joe Frazier was in the dressing room. "Don't listen to Ali," he told Kenny. "He'll play mind games, you know. Just take care of business and make him fight your fight."

There were shouts and a round of applause as Frazier came down the aisle to ringside. He waved off Cosell and any others in the press and took a chair about ten yards from us. Kenny came in wearing a dark blue robe. The crowd noise was a sound of anticipation, not endorsement. Though Kenny had gotten his professional start in San Diego, the show tonight was all about Ali. With an entourage of at least thirty trailing him, Ali was greeted with a huge roar as he slipped through the ropes and skipped around the ring wearing a plush white robe glittering with rhinestones that proclaimed him "The People's Choice." Elvis had given Ali the robe in Vegas after he beat Joe Bugner, a Hungarian who'd escaped the Soviets and was the British Commonwealth champion. As Ali danced and Kenny jogged around the ring, Sabine yelled in my ear, "Ali's so cute! They both are."

Ali was thirty-one now and looked a little soft around the middle at 221. At 210 Kenny looked just like he had when I knew him six years earlier, hard and sculpted, but he was five months shy of thirty—make or break time in his career. They were the same height, and Kenny had just as much reach. When they met with the ref Ali was mouthing off. Kenny kept his head down and moved his shoulders slightly. At the bell Ali came out dancing and throwing jabs and straight rights in combination. When his punches landed, they thumped and some sounded explosive. Unimpressed but careful, Kenny moved as he always had, with his right glove moving, his left held low. It struck me that Ali danced left and right with equal ease. We heard Ali's cheerleader Bundini Brown yell near the end of the first round, "This sucker ain't got no heart! You the king!"

I was torn in my loyalties, though Kenny was my friend and Ali wouldn't have known me from somebody digging food out of a Dumpster. The first big crowd noise came in the second when Kenny jerked Ali's head back with a left hook lead and then twice pounded hard at his midsection. But I'd never seen anything like Ali's hand speed in a fighter so big. Kenny was patient but intense, staying with him, landing his own jabs. When the bell rang he gave a little hop and tapped Ali on his shoulder as he headed toward the stool.

With a show of contempt, Ali stood with his back to Kenny, arms on the ropes as he listened to his trainer Angelo Dundee, his fight doctor Ferdie Pacheco, and the jabbering Bundini. Another man rinsed Ali's mouthpiece and squirted him swallows of water.

Ali had predicted he'd take him out in three and he came out like he meant to do it. He was frowning, up on his toes, and he got a crowd roar with a popping right-hand lead and a swift left hook. Kenny's jabs popped loudly, too. The crowd began to get behind him when he cornered Ali in the fourth. After taking some loud shots off his arms and hips, Ali draped himself over Kenny to tie him up. Kenny picked him up and set him down on the second rope, and the crowd roared happily.

In the sixth Cosell yelled, *"Ohhh!"* when Kenny landed a big overhand right, the fight's best punch so far. At the end of the seventh he wobbled Ali again with a left-right combination. Kenny jolted him again in the ninth with a smooth right behind a jab, a left hook lead, and another of those overhand rights. We heard Kenny taunt Ali once when they were over by the ropes where we sat. "You're nothing!"

Joe Frazier was on his feet and yelling at Kenny, "Body punches, body punches!"

Ali had his best round in the eleventh, counterpunching off the ropes and letting go his first real blaze of combinations. Kenny looked unhurt but he covered up with the crossed-arms defense perfected by Archie Moore. Between rounds Ali gasped for wind and held onto the ropes in the corner. They touched gloves at center ring as the last round began. Twelve thousand people on their feet and screaming. A jab from Kenny rocked Ali back a step. Kenny landed body hooks with both hands, and with a minute left he unleashed a succession of overhand rights. Even through the bellowing crowd we heard one pop like a gunshot. It flung Ali's head far around, and only a grab of the ropes kept him from going down.

The ringside judges split in giving a one-round advantage to each fighter, but the ref didn't think it was close. He scored it 7 rounds for Kenny, 4 for Ali, one round even. It was one of the biggest upsets in boxing history.

In the mayhem after the decision Cosell yelled, "Kenny, you made me look silly."

"That's okay, Howard. You always look silly."

Cosell fought through the mass of bodies toward Ali's corner, where Bundini growled, "The champ can't talk."

We didn't stick around for the post-fight press conference or try to go to Kenny's party. Sabine was in no mood for it. Silent most of the way back to La Jolla, at last she said, "It's savage. I'll never watch another one."

"You wouldn't mind if Ali had done that to Kenny."

"Oh, shut up."

In the days that followed, the fighters' teams had their turns spinning the outcome. Ali's trainer Angelo Dundee claimed his fighter's jaw had been broken in the first round, and the boxing commission's doctor knew it. Later Dundee declared it was an uppercut that happened in the second round. One of Ali's corner men named Wali Muhammad had worked for Sugar Ray Robinson and had been a bodyguard of Malcolm X. In the corner he carried the ice and water and spit bucket. "I was taking out the mouthpiece and there was more and more blood in it."

Kenny told a broadcaster after the final bell that he didn't know Ali's jaw was broken. The surgeon who wired the jaw shut in a ninety-minute operation said, "It was a very bad break. The bone that was broken had three or four jagged edges. The edges kept poking into his mouth. He had so much pain during the fight that he's totally exhausted now."

Eddie Futch wasn't buying it. "Nobody knows for sure when Ken broke Ali's jaw. But with all the shots he took, if his jaw had been broken that early, it would have been shattered by the time it went twelve rounds. I think Ali's jaw was broken in the eleventh with one very good right uppercut that Ken threw when he caught Ali on the ropes."

When it happened didn't matter. Kenny's life was transformed. Johnny Carson invited him on his *Tonight* show and introduced him as the man who was able to shut Muhammad Ali up. Kenny's moneymen in San

Diego bragged to sportswriters that Kenny had broken other heavyweights' jaws in his eleventh and twenty-second bouts. His first product endorsement was of a ball of hard candy on a sucker stick called a Jawbreaker.

I caught up with Kenny by phone a few days after the fight. I told him I thought he might have broken the jaw with the right that flung Ali's head around in the last round.

"I don't know. I just thought I'd knocked him out when I landed that one. But the sucker didn't go down. As soon as Ali lost, his people started spreading this hokum: Why, the superhuman wonder that he could hold up and go the distance with a broken jaw. Bullshit. I'll say this for him, though. The talk about him being out of shape was baloney. I hit him plenty in the body, and it was like busting my hands on sacks of cement."

"I guess your son's all excited."

"Actually he's upset. As soon as the check cleared, I moved us into a nicer and safer apartment in another part of LA. Kenny Junior didn't want to leave the school he went to. He'll get over it, make new friends."

Then Kenny laughed and said, "Ali's a piece of work. After the fight and his surgery, I went up to the hospital to see him. His mouth was wired shut. First thing he said was, 'I want to fight you again, Norton.' I said, 'You got it, champ.' We shook hands on the bargain and he said, 'Pull up a seat. Visit awhile. Now that you beat me and the world knows who you are, there are gonna be temptations. Be careful about going through your money too fast, and all the women who'll be coming your way. People gonna come outa the woodwork, and you got to know who's your friend and who just wants something out of you.'

"As I got up to leave, in this wired-shut motor-mouth mumble he said, 'Now, just because we had this nice talk, don't think I'm gonna sit here and take being the loser. That referee robbed me, robbed the whole world. I'm gonna have to teach you a lesson when we get back in the ring, and let me tell you, it ain't gonna be pretty.' On the elevator I was laughing so hard that people stared. Only Muhammad Ali can lift your spirits when you go see him at a hospital you put him in."

CHAPTER 33

After Ali's jaw healed, he wanted a quick turnaround on a rematch. He had to establish himself again, and he didn't want to wait for a year to do it. Ali's losing for the first time to Frazier stung, but this outcome was a financial disaster. So the parties agreed for a rematch in six months. Kenny called me from his training camp a few weeks before the fight and asked if Sabine and I wanted to come out to Ingleside for the rematch, which came off six months after the upset. I told him I'd have to see. True to her word, Sabine wanted no part of it. I mulled it over but decided against it. Our money at home was tight, and the band needed the gigs we had lined up. I liked watching fights on closed-circuit TV as they aired back then. A few hundred or thousand folks stared at a big grainy screen and cheered their favorites, sitting side by side. The crowds got into it yelling, almost like really being at the fights. I went to the telecast with Jake Spoon, my friend and songwriting collaborator in the band, and Sabine's ex-husband Russ Million. She didn't object to my growing friendship with Russ. She just thought it was weird.

For us it was boys' night out. We went to a capitol area joint called the Texas Chili Parlor and claimed a table in a back corner. I told them that earlier that week I had seen a news clip from the time when Ali refused to step out of line when his name was called to be drafted. "He said, 'My conscience won't let me shoot my brother. Some darker people for some poor pieces of mud. For big peaceful America, and shoot them for what? They never called me nigger. They never lynched me. Killed my mother and father. Shoot them for what? How can I shoot them poor people? Just take me to jail.'"

Jake groaned. "Give me a break. Malcolm X and his Black Muslim friends put those words in his mouth."

"You've got your dates wrong. Malcolm X was already dead."

"All right, he stole it from *Soul on Ice.* Listen, I remember the stuff about Ali and the draft. He'd been given a draft exemption because he failed an intelligence test. Then they changed the rules on that, so he decided he had a conscience."

"Have it any way you want," I said, "but just by his force of personality the uproar over the name change and the draft evaporated. Vets I know will never forgive Jane Fonda but they don't have anything against Ali. He's as big as the Beatles. Bigger than the Stones."

"That does it," said Russ. "I'm for Norton."

I said, "Actually, so am I."

"Huh?" Jake said. "You've been making out Ali as Allah's next of kin." He swallowed some of his margarita. "I don't know why we're paying good money to see this thing. Let's say they go the distance again. They'll fight thirty-six minutes and have eleven one-minute breathers. High school football players are out there nearly an hour. Playing linebacker and guard like I did in Stamford, banging helmets and pads, that's a real contact sport."

"Did you make all-state in Stamford?"

"No. Why?"

"Kenny was all-state on defense and broke records running track in Illinois."

"How come you know so much about this guy?" said Russ.

"I was his sparring partner for a while in the marines."

"Bullshit," said Jake. "Why you?"

"He beat up all the others. I was in the brig, and they saw I won a state Golden Gloves title. So I drew the black bean."

"You won Golden Gloves in Texas?" said Russ.

"Sure did, for the team in Deerinwater. By the last night I *was* the team."

I had let my mouth run off, but I could see they both now viewed me in a different light. "You didn't know that because I'm a drunkard but not a braggart."

"So how'd you do with him?" said Jake, still skeptical.

"One day he turned out my lights. What do you think? Drink up, let's go."

As soon as Ali's jaw healed, he had no reason to put off their second bout. Ali's purse was $275,000; Kenny got $200,000. That was chump change to Ali. The lawyer Bob Arum, an aspiring promoter, had been negotiating for a ten-million-dollar package of fights against Foreman and Frazier. In San Diego Arum had watched those millions slip away round after round. Ali claimed he had never trained more than three weeks for Sonny Liston or Joe Frazier and none for Kenny. For this one he holed up in Deer Lake, Pennsylvania, for fourteen weeks of torture by a Cuban trainer. He was out running before dawn, and when he wasn't sparring or banging the bags, he was outside chopping wood. The mail brought him a taunt.

> *The butterfly has lost his wings. The bee has lost its sting. You are through, you loud-mouthed braggart. Your mouth has been shut up for all time. It's a great day for America. You're finished!*

He taped that fan mail in his locker at his training camp so he'd have to see it every day. He didn't pipe down in the press. "What happened is Muhammad Ali ate a lot of ice cream and cake, and he didn't do his running, he didn't punch the heavy bag. And still he almost won. If he hadn't been clowning around with his mouth open and got himself hit with an uppercut, he would have beaten Norton the first time. I took a nobody and created a monster. I put him on *The Dating Game.* I gave him glory. Now I have to punish him bad."

Ali never again wore the rhinestone-studded "People's Choice" robe that Elvis gave him. He looked sleek again, down nine pounds to 212. Kenny came in at 205. Ali had planted the bug in sportswriters' ears that the weight indicated Kenny had trained himself "a little too fine." Again they were fighting twelve rounds for the North American title. Ali got a big affectionate roar as he skipped around snapping punches. Kenny jogged about and ignored Ali. At the introductions, cheers for Kenny were mixed with boos.

When Jake and Russ and I got to the convention center, they had insisted I take the middle seat, since I was now the expert. In no time they informed some black guys in front of us, Ali fans, that I used to spar with Norton. They looked me over and one said, "Bullshit. You're not big enough to be in the ring with that guy."

"Don't listen to these guys," I said. "They'll make up anything."

Kenny stared at the canvas as the ref repeated directions at center ring. Ali smiled faintly but had nothing to say. They didn't bump gloves before going to their corners.

At the bell Ali bounded out with a fast right off a fast jab, but neither landed. He tried it again, and this right popped, getting a cry from the crowd, but Kenny had taken it on his shoulder. Ali had said he was going to dance this time, and he was more fluid on his feet. Kenny stalked him patiently. At one point, Ali lunged as if charging in to be done with it, a feint. Kenny leaped back in mockery, smiling.

When the bell rang Kenny raised a glove to Ali, who refused his stool and rested the minute between rounds with his back to Kenny. The broadcasters for the closed-circuit telecast were two Southern California pros, Bob Sheridan and Bud Furillo. Sheridan said, "Ali's attitude toward Norton is one of complete scorn." They expected it would go well for Ali, and they talked about Kenny's skinny legs and unusual habit of dragging his right foot.

"Yeah, yeah," I told my friends. "They ought to be looking at the chest and shoulders. Kenny's got just as much power, and he's not afraid of Ali."

When the bell rang for the second round Ali performed a bit of his shuffle dance, getting a roar from the crowd. Kenny began to have some success cutting off the ring. Ali tied him up in a corner, they grappled for a few seconds, then Kenny picked him up and set him down on the second rope, as he had in his first fight. Furillo laughed, "No knockdowns yet, but we've had a sit-down."

In the third Ali scored with a jab, a right-hand lead, and another jab followed by an uppercut that jerked Kenny's head back. Ali appeared to be coasting in the fourth until Kenny cornered him just before the bell and landed one of those looping over-the-top rights. It was the hardest and loudest punch of the fight so far, and Kenny shouted at Ali as they headed for their corners.

"That was one hell of a right hand!" yelled Furillo.

For the first time Ali took his stool.

The fight began to turn with that punch, but Eddie Futch was lecturing Kenny that he had given away the first four rounds, trying to bob and weave like Frazier. He was not good at it, and it gave Ali target practice for those jabs. Kenny returned to his usual defense; he kept his left low and caught punches with the right when Ali was away and moving, but he got both hands up when Ali put combinations together. Ali raised a welt under Kenny's eye, but the thumps on Kenny's body reminded me of those eight-inch cannons firing over our howitzers at Twenty-Nine Palms.

"Are those jabs hurting Norton?" Russ asked.

"Sure. They're getting through and scoring points. But look at Ali's feet. A lot of time when he lands those jabs he's in midair."

A minute into the sixth round Sheridan exclaimed, "I don't know why, but the world heavyweight champion George Foreman is leaving!"

"Isn't that amazing?" said Furillo. "I think he must not like fights that go longer than two rounds."

When Ali nailed Kenny with a right, Furillo said, "Ali just landed his best punch of the fight and it didn't faze Norton." They battled in toe-to-toe fury the last thirty seconds of the round, with our crowd at the arena and in our hall standing and howling. Sheridan yelled, "Come back, George Foreman, you're missing a great fight!"

In the seventh Kenny banged away at Ali's midsection and forced him into a corner and landed an uppercut that sent Ali reeling. Kenny bore in with more body blows, then a straight right and a left hook and another uppercut. "Ali's hurt!" yelled Sheridan. Ali wobbled along the ropes but maneuvered out into the center ring, where he landed multiple rights behind the jabs. Kenny forged through them and landed an uppercut and another overhand right, the heaviest punch of the fight so far.

Amid the roar of the crowd I yelled at my friends, "Ali's got no defense for those! They're falling out of the sky on him." But in the eighth round Ali came out blazing. Furillo said, "Ali just threw four hooks before you could call them, and he landed two of them." Then Kenny landed another right and a hook that made Ali again grab the rope to steady himself. At the end of a furious ninth the live crowd gave them a standing ovation. So did ours in the Austin concert hall half the continent away. Sheridan yelled, "Fight of the year!"

The Ali fan turned to me and said, "You really sparred with Norton?"

"Yeah, but he was still an amateur, and I didn't last very long."

"How would you fight Ali?"

"Not with a bazooka. Too big, too fast."

The guy nodded and turned back toward the screen.

In the eleventh Kenny barged out and threw a wild hook meant to end the fight, but connected with only air. He was tired and losing accuracy, but Ali had no more dance in his legs either. In the last minute, Kenny drove him into a corner of the ropes with a picture-perfect uppercut. But Ali escaped and landed his biggest punch of the fight, a straight right that threw Kenny's head backward. "What Ali may have lost," Furillo said, "is the ability to finish a fight."

"Well, he almost did," said Sheridan. "Look at Eddie Futch. He's giving Norton smelling salts." When the last round began, the fighters raised gloves and touched them. Ali got off two left-right combinations, but Kenny bored after him, talking to him again. Ali seemed to think he had to win the last round. In the closing seconds he landed a four-punch combination. When the bell rang Kenny threw an arm around Ali's shoulders, and they staggered as they tried to catch their breaths.

When Ali got back to his corner, he threw an annoyed punch at Bundini, who threw a punch at someone who had come up on the ring apron. It was either a photographer or the promoter Bob Arum—I couldn't tell because Bundini's aim was so far off. Ali's ego had demanded a dominant win, and he hadn't delivered. Head down, looking unhappy, he rested with his arms on the ropes, awaiting a call that he knew might not go his way.

The judges both scored it six rounds to five with one round even, differing on who had the one-round advantage—it would be another split decision. Kenny threw his head back when the ref's scoring of 7 to 5 gave it to Ali.

The fighters embraced again in the ring after the decision. Furillo caught up with Kenny and said the fight had just enhanced his stature. Kenny said, "Thank you for the compliment." Furillo asked if Ali ever had him in trouble.

"Yes," Kenny said, "I got hurt once in the eleventh round with a right hand. I, uh, didn't move my head like I was supposed to." If I ever heard a one-sentence description of defending yourself in boxing, that was it.

In his corner when Kenny was gone, Ali got busy combing his hair out with a rake. He reached across some shoulders and pantomimed bopping Howard Cosell on his toupee. People in the Austin hall had not rushed out, as they often did at the end of a fight. We hung on like we were hoping for more drama. To the crowd of reporters Ali said, "There's no way I could have won that fight if I hadn't been in such good condition. Ken Norton's a threat to the title, whether it's mine or somebody else's. Not only that, he's the best in the world, next to myself."

When I got home long after midnight, Emily was asleep in her room with her gray tabby Daisy curled up beside her. Sabine raised her head drowsily. "Who won?"

"Kenny lost but it was another split decision. Great fight. Great time."

"I'm so glad," she said, and burrowed back into her pillow.

I crooned the Cream lyric *I'm so glad I'm glad I'm glad.* As I pursued her, she laughed and decided sleep could wait.

CHAPTER 34

I liked to think I had a guiding principle: I was never going to see an old fool in the mirror. When I first noticed the blonde woman, she was standing behind me at the counter of a liquor store. There was a mirror on the wall, and both of us were in it. In the mirror behind the bar, I saw that her hair was long and she wore a small cross at her throat. I bought my Bushmills and when I turned around, she was still there.

She said, "Hello, Haid."

Good god. "Clarinda."

She wore a pair of jeans that were threadbare at the knees and a pair of boots. She raised the heels off the floor slightly and kissed me on the cheek, then stepped back and considered me like she'd won a prize. "You're a singer now. Big name in town."

"Not very big. What brings you here?"

"I live in Austin now. I've been hoping to run into you. I was too shy to call."

My face was burning up with surprise. Apart from the clothes, there was something different about her. She was older, of course; we both were. She looked wonderful, but there was something tetchy about her pale blue eyes.

We stepped out of the way of other customers coming out of the store. I glanced at the headlights and taillights moving on Manor Road. "How long have you been here?"

"Not quite a year." She also looked at the traffic. "Are you busy? Have to be somewhere now?"

My curiosity was fighting a battle with trepidation. I said, "No. You told me you were never coming back to Texas."

"Austin's not Fort Worth."

"No. But it's getting a little big for its britches."

"You and your band don't play here much, do you?"

"We can't afford most of the venues now. And they can't afford us. Better bands than us are playing for free."

"I doubt that. I've heard your records. I'm proud of you."

"Thank you."

I was thinking boyfriend, husband, surely. I glanced to see if she wore a ring.

"Listen," Clarinda said, "if you really do have a few minutes, I have a little rent house a few blocks from here. Why don't we take what you've got there and I've got here, and let's get into them and catch up."

That's how it started. She picked me up in a liquor store.

When we got to her small well-furnished house, more or less a cottage, she got me a glass and ice for my whiskey and uncorked her wine. "Do you and your band ever play for private occasions?" she asked, standing in the kitchen. I was looking at her jeans and the way she rounded out the pockets.

"We don't rule it out."

"Outdoor venue if the money is right?"

"As long as the weather cooperates. I don't like the idea of being electrocuted." And I had learned not to make booking decisions without consulting the band.

She led me to a sofa and said, "Let me tell you what I have in mind."

As she talked, I guessed though didn't say that she and her partners had felt the need to get out of California. Clarinda hadn't been one of the high rollers in the Altamont debacle, but I surmised that her profile had been high enough that she thought it might be good to move on.

She and some majority investors had bought a run-down horse track out east of Austin with the conviction they could make it the next Churchill Downs. The times I'd seen the track, it had gap-toothed fencing and a dirt oval of a little more than a mile. A few trainers exercised young or thoroughbreds there, but it was one of several quarter horse brush tracks in central Texas. Trainers started their two-year-old colts and fillies on the brush tracks to see if they could run well enough to take them to the summer season at Ruidoso, New Mexico, and its big money showcase, the All-American Futurity. Racing quarter horses weren't the agile little workers bred from mustangs in cowboy lore. They were bulked-up thoroughbreds without the long fragile legs. They were sprinters, quarter milers. Watching them was like hot rods in a drag race.

I had gone out to the track a couple of times when it was under the prior ownership. The grandstand might have seated five hundred people. The county sheriff positioned himself at the rail and the betting transpired, all of it in cash. I didn't know how they knew what horses to bet on, but it looked like they had a good time.

Clarinda said the track was being used for dirt bike racing when they first saw it. They shut down the quarter horse operation, which caused some grumbling, she said, some of it heated. Some trainers thought they were entitled to use that track. Clarinda and her colleagues were certain Texas was primed to legalize pari-mutuel gambling, and with that would come the investors, the major construction, and big-time thoroughbred racing in the orbit of the state's coolest city. They replaced the fences, plowed up the infield, planted a kind of grass that could hold up under the summer heat, installed whirlpools that helped the sore or injured legs of the horses, negotiated with a nearby small town to give them a break on the water bill, and soon stabled a hundred horses out there. They thought the endeavor was going to make them richer than the principal investors already were.

Clarinda and I carried on that night like we were talking business, the possibility of it anyway. I drank a fair amount of my whiskey and she had three or four glasses of wine. She reminded me about her love of horses that we'd talked about one of those nights in the Livermore motel. She said they wanted live music to be part of this operation. "You guys would be a good house band."

"Sounds like fun but I can't say. I'm just one of seven."

"No. The other guy sings some, and he's good, but it's your band. A girl can tell."

The conversation lulled a moment, then she sunk deeper in the sofa, uncrossed her legs, and put her boot and calf across my thigh. "Why did you treat me like that?" she said.

"Like what?" I was surprised it suddenly got so personal. She made a face and I said, "Oh, there's lots of water under that bridge. I could ask the same question."

"Here's the kind of guy I bet you are. Something doesn't go the way you want some night, and a woman in the morning wakes up to find you gone."

Her reading of me stung. "Couple of times I plead guilty. It's not a mark of good character. But if it's gone bad enough that you're not going to sleep at all, it gets worse if you just lie there." Since she'd made the first move, I lightly put my hand on her knee. "Here's the kind of girl you are. Or were. You torment a guy three nights sleeping in the same bed with him and then tell him you love him. Next thing he knows, he sees you wrapped around somebody's bass player and off in the chopper you go."

"I'm not proud of that either. Are you going to kiss me or not?" Half an hour later, when we were naked under her sheets, my principles and vows strewn like sand in a whirlwind, she said, "I see you're married now. I guess that doesn't matter anymore."

"That's a song by Buddy Holly."

"Was that a grudge fuck?"

"Not for me. But if it was, maybe there's something to be said for them."

She laughed and squirmed back over on top of me.

It went on for five or six weeks, I guess. I asked Sabine's ex Russ about the newcomers' reading of the horse racing politics in Texas. He said, "Eventually they'll get what they want, but this is still the Bible Belt. Every other year the legislature convenes a session, and every morning of it a long prayer is read by preachers who are generally hard-shell Bible thumpers. I wouldn't bet money on those preachers being out-lobbied soon."

The Rip Chords and I never played out there. I never brought it up to them. She was hot for us to open one time for the Grateful Dead, and though I knew they were supposed to be the grandest thing since hash oil, I'd heard better harmony at the church on Keeler Street. Besides, I was guilt-riven and dancing way too near the flame. Easing my anxiety some, the assignations moved to a onetime ranch house that came with the horse track. The problem was you never knew what doper was going to wander into the bedroom.

One warm winter afternoon we watched injured horses swimming in pools they'd built with the help of a price break on the water they bought from an outlying small town. They treaded water for a set number of minutes, with a rope to their halter tied tight enough that they couldn't try to climb out. Then in the stalls we were feeding other horses when I pressed her against a wall, the feed bucket hit the ground, and we had another go of it in one of the vacant stalls. A sorrel in an adjoining one bumped the boards with his hip and snorted in an apparent sign of interest.

Afterward I lay with my jaw propped on one hand and elbow and with the other hand perked her small pink nipple erect again.

"Why do you wear your wedding ring on that hand?" she said.

I waved my left hand away from my jaw and reminded her of its condition.

She nodded. "I just think doing that to me with that particular hand is rude."

"Sorry," I said, and moved my hand away.

She caught and guided it back. "I didn't say stop. I can live with rude."

I changed the subject. "What's Altamont like now? The place."

"It's all wind farms now. The Audubon Society is upset because the turbines kill hawks and eagles." She sat up, picked some straw from her hair, and with a fingernail traced the shrapnel scars on my lower back, knowing it gave me chills. She held her shirt against her chest. "Jerry Garcia," she said, "was a driving force behind Altamont. The Dead split as soon as they saw what was happening, and then he went off in goofball philosophy mode when he was back in the city. He said, 'It was the music that generated it. I think the music knew. It was known in the music.' That helps, Jerry, thanks."

She switched gears with a jolt. "Do you love me?"

I didn't know what I was doing in that horse stall. Well, that's a lie. But it was occurring to me I'd been smitten by blondes like this ever since that night my bedroom door opened and sitting on the bed petting my face was the chaplain's wife Susan Dingus.

"Your silence says it all," she said.

"Clarinda. Honey. Listen, if things had just gone a little different between us—"

"You son of a bitch, don't ever call me 'honey.' Let's go get a drink."

She got to her feet and brushed hay off her jeans. She put on her blouse and as we walked to the house, the way she took my hand seemed almost fond.

Clarinda was making our whiskeys when the ex-Angel walked in. She filled her glass two-thirds full and added only a splash of water. The Angel went by the nickname Teardrop. He had followed them out from his Oakland chapter, I heard. He had a pitted face and a grimy ponytail, wore a battered straw cowboy with a snake-skin band, and was about the size of Kenny Norton, though not that firm around the middle. On rougher ends of the Austin music scene I had heard him called "the pistol whipper."

"Teardrop, you know Haid, don't you?" she said, setting our whiskeys on the table.

He helped himself to a chair. "Sure. Seen him around. Watched him sing once. Howdy do." I raised my glass to him, smiled, and sipped without reply.

"Haid went to war in Vietnam," she said. "Has the scars to prove it. He must have killed lots of people."

I should have just gone on. I should have known not to come in this house.

Teardrop pushed his hat brim back. "Got your clocks cleaned, didn't you?"

"About fifty thousand have got worse than that. So far."

"You wouldn't know it but I pray a lot. I pray for their souls."

"I'm sure they're grateful."

"You got one of them black gimme caps that the vets wear?"

"Nope. You got one of them jackets that bikers call colors?"

"You're kind of a smartass, aren't you?"

I glanced at Clarinda, who smiled and downed a mouthful of drink. "I was talking to you," Teardrop said. "Why you looking at her?"

"She's nice to look at."

He chuckled. "Yeah, she is that. She is."

Clarinda said, "Haid doesn't like to talk about Vietnam."

"Maybe he's ashamed of it. That right, Sinatra?"

"Teardrop, my mother grew up on tenant cotton farms."

"Did she? Bless your momma's heart. She still with us?"

Clarinda cocked her head and studied me, losing the smile along the way.

"Yeah, she is," I said, "thanks for asking. She had three brothers, two sisters. Her favorite brother was Uncle Monty, who married her best friend, now my Aunt Blanche. Uncle Monty was a working cowboy all his life. Roped at little rodeos while he was young, doctored cattle, drove the pickup and trailer to auctions. Got where his face looked like elephant hide. Asking you to supper he'd say, 'We're having cow.' His favorite hat was a sweat-stained dirty old black beaver skin Stetson. He kept another one in a box for funerals and such, but I never saw him go outside without the beat-up black one."

"Haid's being quaint," Clarinda said.

"No, there's a point here," I said. "I'll try to talk faster. When Uncle Monty came inside for any reason, he always hung his hat on a rack beside the front door. My cousin Donnie got grown enough to be ornery, and he came in one night and sat down at the table with his hat on. Uncle Monty slapped him out of his chair. That was something you just didn't do. There's a sheriff out in Presidio County who's been in office a long time. When he's in a café and he sees a guy with a hat on, he walks over and thumps the brim, flips it off."

Teardrop stroked his chin with a forefinger and thumb. "You gonna thump mine?"

"Nope. I just thought I'd give you a tip about hat comportment. You may have been a bang-up Hell's Angel, but on a cowboy's ass you're not a smear of screwworm dope."

"Excuse me," he said. "It makes my hip ache, sitting on this."

He put a pistol on the table. It didn't seem to alarm Clarinda.

"Relax," he said. "Didn't mean to scare you. We're just talking here."

The table had a glass top cut to size. Teardrop got out a vial of cocaine. He dumped out a large mound of it beside the gun, then reached in his jeans and came out with a knife. It was the kind that warehouse workers use to cut through packaging, but the blade jumped out with a loud click like a switchblade. He chopped the coke and arranged six lines. Then he reached over and stirred my whiskey and ice with the blade. "I'm the one," he said, "that decides where I wear my hat."

Teardrop wiped the blade dry on his jeans, left the knife open, and laid it beside the gun. "Sweet thing," he said, "get us straws." Clarinda got up as ordered. She returned, sat back down, and pushed oversized plastic straws forward.

Teardrop gestured for me to go ahead. I chose a straw, stood up, and leaned over the table. I said, "Thing is, Teardrop, I'm not afraid of you. Or your gun. Or that box-cutter. I don't dig your chili." With the straw I blew most of the coke in his lap.

"Stay put, Teardrop, stay right there," Clarinda snapped. "And you, white trash, tenant farmer, get off this land."

"Sounds like a plan," I said. I didn't back out of the room, but I was ready to whirl around if I heard a chair scrape.

She followed me. "That's the last favor I'm doing for you."

"Oh, you've been doing me favors?"

"I hate you. I have for a while."

I looked at her and sighed.

"Clarinda, quit. We just made love. I'm sorry if I hurt you."

CHAPTER 35

After I got home, Sabine came in from her law office and kissed me, then said, "Woo, you smell like a feedlot. You need a shower."

"Oh, sorry. I was out in the country with some guys that have horses and we went for a ride. I'll be sore in the morning."

The lie wasn't bad, given how rattled I was. What got into me? What got into me the past several weeks? It was a Friday, the band was off the road, the next day Emily was spending the night with a friend, and Sabine and I had no social obligations. I stretched out on the sofa and turned on the TV. Later I'd grill us stuffed pork chops for dinner.

In boxing Kenny and Foreman had turned the starring duet of Ali and Frazier into a foursome. Ali's loss to Kenny had taken the money off the table for a huge bout with Foreman now. So Ali took a rematch with Frazier in Madison Square Garden in January 1974. Though the promoters billed it "Super Fight II," their reputations and records were sullied by their losses, and it didn't generate the hype of the first bout. Ali would hurt Frazier once in the second round, clinch him 133 times, and win a unanimous decision that wasn't close. The more entertaining face-off occurred that Saturday after my incident at the quarter horse track. Sabine was doing laundry when I saw that the fighters were going to appear together on Howard Cosell's program *Wide World of Sports.* I watched it for a while then called, "Hey, babe, come here. There's something on that you'll like."

She walked in and said, "What?"

"It's Muhammad Ali."

"I don't want to watch a fight, Haid."

"They're not fighting. They're talking."

"Well, it looks like somebody's fighting."

The heads of the heavyweights appeared in egg-shaped bubbles against a backdrop of black and white footage of their first bout. I explained what was going on as Cosell was saying off camera, "The start of round ten—"

"Who's the other one?" said Sabine, sitting down.

I sighed. "Frazier. Joe Frazier."

She nodded, having heard the name. Ali rhapsodized, "A billion people waiting to watch. Those promoters deserve a hand, accumulating a billion people. Which is more than the Super Bowl, the Rose Bowl, the Kentucky Derby—"

"All right, all right," said Cosell. "Let's get back to—"

"And the World Series!" Ali pressed on. "The best America could produce. Two black brothers." Sabine giggled and put her foot on my thigh.

"I want to get back to the fight," Cosell said. "What were you feeling at this point?" he asked Ali.

"I'm not gonna remember," Ali grumbled. "My hips were sore. My legs were sore. The referee didn't say nothing. I got hit ninety-nine times—"

Frazier grinned in his bubble. "You had to go to the hospital."

"I went there for ten minutes. You went for a month. Now be quiet."

After the first fight Frazier had been hospitalized for three weeks with high blood pressure and a kidney infection. Still grinning, he said, "I was resting."

"How come you bringing up the hospital?" Ali said. "I didn't bring up nothing about hospital. That just shows how dumb you are."

"Watch this," Cosell said, trying to steer them back to the tenth round of the first fight. "What was happening there, Joe?"

"I really don't know," said Frazier. "I'm trying to listen to this speech."

"That's embarrassing," Ali said, frowning. "Nobody goes to the hospital to rest. That's just ignorant."

Sabine laughed again. "He's amazing."

Frazier didn't think so. The bubble on the right showed the lower half of him leaving the chair. The camera view switched to a studio scene with the tenth round unfolding on a big screen behind them. Frazier wore light-colored bell-bottoms, a long-sleeved shirt of the same color, and a large gold watch. Dressed in similar fashion but without the bell-bottoms, Ali looked up at him from his chair with his long legs extended. To one side Cosell sat in a chair with his legs crossed. "Why you think I'm ignorant?" demanded Frazier.

A figure came on camera with his back turned. It was Ali's brother Rahman. "Sit down, Joe," he said, trying to be a peacemaker.

An older black man also came on the screen and took hold of Frazier's left arm. Frazier threw off the fellow's hand and glared at Ali's brother. "You want in on this, too?"

Ali came out of his chair and grabbed Frazier in an inexpert headlock. *"Quit, Joe!"* he cried as they went to the carpet. The background film played on.

Cosell said, "Well, we're having a scene here, as you can see, and it's hard to tell if this is for real or clowning. This kind of thing has been going on all along, in terms of promotion. This time it appears to be real, because Joe Frazier is really angry."

"It's a small riot," Sabine said.

"Between black brothers," I said.

"Grown men."

"You want in on this, too?"

She laughed and punched me on the shoulder.

The scene gained seven, eight, nine men, all of them black. One wore a camel overcoat, for it was cold in New York. Cosell again: "It's an ugly scene, and I think it's unfortunate that it happened. A classic fight between two extraordinary athletes—"

A young white man with well-trimmed long hair joined the group, grinning no doubt about the ratings. Cosell said, "I think Ali is probably clowning, but there is no question in my mind that Frazier is not. They were both on the floor, Joe's watch came off, and we're really sorry. We'll be back in just a moment." Off camera Ali yelled at Frazier to be on time for their next appointment. Frazier bellowed, "*You* be on time!" The New York State Athletic Commission fined them each five thousand bucks. I thought they deserved a bonus.

Afterward I napped with Emily's tabby cat Daisy on my stomach. I jerked awake and Daisy jumped to the floor when Sabine came in the living room yelling. She was holding the pair of jeans and shirt I had worn home from my last romp with Clarinda. Sabine brought them close to her face and in fury shoved them in mine. "Smell them!" she yelled at me.

Though I couldn't be certain, I figured that Latino kid the first fight in the state Golden Gloves reconfigured my nose with a deviated septum. I couldn't smell much of anything but Sabine sure could. She shoved the Levi's close enough to my face that I smelled Clarinda's perfume mixed with odors of hay and horse manure. "If you're going to lie to me," Sabine fumed, "at least give it some thought. Don't insult my intelligence."

The fool in the mirror.

CHAPTER 36

Emily's presence helped tamp down the outbursts of fury, but it was a day-to-day proposition. I was too ashamed of myself to attempt the alleged tried-and-true of consistent denial. I admitted there had been someone else but I wouldn't tell Sabine who she was. I tried to explain it was over with, that it was a short and stupid thing to do, and I was glad to be rid of that woman. That only made Sabine angrier and she started casting about for suspects aloud—mutual friends, singers in Austin, even associates in her legal profession.

"Trust me now if you never do again," I said. "Believe me, you do not want to know. How much sorrier can I be? What can I do to make it right?"

"Fuck off," she said.

"Got it. That was the very first thing you said to me."

Our stubbornness dug the hole deeper. Despite the way it ended with Clarinda, I had mixed emotions. She and I had a prior emotional history. For the minute or two before she took off with the bass player at Altamont, maybe she *meant* it when she said she loved me. Nobody had said anything anywhere close to that to me in over three years.

My refusal to give Sabine a name stoked more fuel in her anger and hurt. At least she went to her office during the weekdays. Sometimes she had overnights for court dates in other towns, and I frantically tried to line up new gigs for the band. Emily had to know things weren't right at home, but her mother and I carried on forced civility when she was with us. When Emily went to Russ's house in the joint custody arrangement, Sabine's unforgiveness meter cranked up again as soon as the little girl was gone. As we settled into a kind of truce Sabine and I slept in the same bed, but for a long time that was all.

The Texas legislature met in sessions every other year, starting in January. Russ told me that the preachers who read the morning prayers in no time out-lobbied the Altamont expats and established that legal betting on horse racing in Texas was not going to get out of the commerce committee, not this legislative session. Clarinda was one of the first to pull the plug of fantasy that the little brush track outside Austin would one day rival the big rich tracks in other states. She moved to Telluride, or so I heard from a favorite bartender, and I hoped it was true. I know I was tired of being the household asshole.

Despite the discord at home, things weren't going badly for the band. I got a call from Cow House Creek's new distributor, who lived in LA, and he said he'd gotten us a Friday night gig at the Troubadour in West Hollywood. A Los Angeles County sheriff had once arrested Lenny Bruce for obscenity there for saying the word "schmuck" onstage. In recent months bouncers had tossed John Lennon and Harry Nilsson for heckling the Smothers Brothers. The distributor showed up with a pretty girl on his arm, expecting to hear our gratitude, which he did. He was a prick, but he was our prick. The Troubadour was tall cotton for us.

The crowd filled the room by the time we started the second set. Running through the best of *Bubbles* and *Pipe Town Blues* and our favorite covers, I was in good voice, and the band was tight and firing on all cylinders, to my ear. I had called Kenny and told him we were coming his way. I hadn't seen him since the fight in San Diego, but we talked on the phone several times. He always asked about Sabine. I said we were fine, fine.

Because Ali had taken the rematch with Frazier, Kenny had gotten the title shot against George Foreman. It would come off one year since Kenny had broken Ali's jaw and given their lives new directions. I read in the sports pages that at the press conference when the fight was announced, Foreman refused to shake Kenny's hand. He was stone-faced about the booing and stood his ground. "There's no way I'm going to be laughing and shaking Ken Norton's hand right now."

The Foreman-Norton promotion was Don King's first piece of a heavyweight title fight.

Kenny wound up a week of training in Massacre Canyon and came to the Troubadour for the last half of our show. I saw him when he came in. He wore a hat with the brim pulled down, not wanting much recognition or chat with strangers. He stood by the bar and some men came up to pay him his due. Some women eyed him and looked intrigued.

I'd learned from watching Willie Nelson that medleys are fine if they work. We ended the encore with my favorite broken-hearted love song, the Band's "And It Makes No Difference." Johnny bridged that well into Hank Williams's "Cold Cold Heart," and then we made a rock and roll production of the Everly Brothers' "Bye Bye Love." I sang high and Jake sang low in the harmony, I did a percussion solo on my *frattoir,* and Jake weaved around the stage and out through the crowd with his amplified Serpent. The uproar that kept going when we were backstage let us know we had passed our Hollywood audition.

After our gig was over, the rest of the band roamed off with the distributor and the blonde to a party, he said, at the house of some actor. Kenny drove me to a quiet bar where I downed a double Bushmills fast and he sipped club soda and lime. "Is it like this for you after a fight?" I said. "Hard to come down?"

"Sure, every time. No matter who it is. You get hangovers from adrenaline." He was quiet a moment then said, "Hey, you guys are good. Surprised me, I have to say, and don't take that wrong. I wished I'd swung by home and brought Jackie."

I thanked him and said, "How's your training going?"

He winced and shook his head. He hadn't taken off the hat. "Not so good."

"What's up?"

"Something happened while I was training for the second Ali fight. This guy named Bobby is the matchmaker at Madison Square Garden. He's been trying to get me to fight Jerry Quarry up there. Sure, if the money's right, I'd love to bust up Quarry."

"Why's that? Bust him up."

"Oh, he goes around saying he knocked me out one time when our trainers had us together sparring in LA."

I grinned. "Did he?"

"I didn't say he's not any good. So this guy from the Garden got me to go over to Vegas with him and watch Quarry take out a ham-and-egger. Then I couldn't shake the guy. He came back to camp with me. One night he came banging on my door. He said Joe Frazier's manager Yank Durham, who was just fifty-two, was on life support because he'd had a bad stroke. And Yank didn't make it. He must have known something wasn't right, because he got my trainer Eddie Futch—you met him—to swear to take on Joe's management if something happened to him. Eddie of course said he would. After my fight with Ali, Eddie said he was going to move his base of operations from LA to Philly because that's where Joe lives and does most of his training. I didn't have a problem with that. Joe Frazier's my friend. I sparred with him in Philly and I like the town. But Bob Biron manages finances for me now, and he decided Eddie had a conflict of interest. And he took Ali's bait that Eddie over-trained me for the second fight. I got off too slow and then got robbed is what happened, but so what. George Foreman's the guy in front of me now."

"Big one, too."

"Yeah. They pressured me into letting Eddie go, and a sportswriter gets wind of it. He calls Eddie, who says, 'After five years of guiding Norton's career and bringing him to the threshold of the world title, I've been informed that my services are no longer needed. If it weren't so tragic, I could think of it as somewhat amusing. I do find the thing most ironic, to have come this far with Norton, and then be told that I am no longer of importance.'

"'To the threshold.' 'Weren't so tragic.' Put a sports page hack in front of him and he turns into Shakespeare. Instead of just saying no comment, I told the guy, 'I hope this can be resolved. I'd feel bad, because Eddie and I've been through a lot together, and it wouldn't seem right if he's not in my corner when I win the title. But Bob's always done right by me, too, and I'll have to go along with what he says." Kenny paused. "Then something made me say, 'Bob is my great white father. He's the manager of my boxing career and my personal finances. I never have to worry about Bob giving me the shuffle.'"

"Ouch," I said. Uncle Tom.

"Yeah, you don't have to say it. So Eddie fires back, 'I'm disappointed in Ken because I've had fighters that I expected less of, who did more. But if he goes along with them, I don't have a leg to stand on. Ken is not the type of individual you can turn loose to just anybody and everybody. There's so much you have to know about him and his personality. He's a very strong-minded individual, and you have to have complete control over him to get results.' *Control* of me? That pisses me off, but I've let this long friendship turn into a feud."

"It's a shame," I agreed. "But you've got another trainer, don't you?"

"Well, sure. He's a veteran LA guy named Bill Slayton. Trained Quarry that time I sparred him. Bill's an LA guy, ex-high school football star. We got some things in common. He offered to train me for two weeks, and if I didn't want to continue, I didn't owe him anything. Fair enough. His style and Eddie's are different, but he's a pro. And I've got to have someone training me."

"I'd think they'd be lining up for the chance."

"I don't know, Haid. I just know I made a mistake. Next thing I read is an article about Slayton saying I don't have many close friends. He says, 'Kenny's a Leo, you know. Leos don't get too close to people.' A *Leo?* I've got George Foreman across the ring from me, and my trainer's talking California woo-woo."

CHAPTER 37

One afternoon a couple of weeks later, I was heading out with the band to do a sound check for our gig at Gruene Hall, a place on the Guadalupe River between Austin and San Antonio, outside the town of New Braunfels. It drew large and rowdy crowds, but that dance hall was built for cotton farmers trying to survive the boll weevil plague. Getting the sound right at Gruene Hall took longer than playing the gig. The phone rang, and a fuzzy connection gave me Kenny on the line. He said, "I'm in South America and the situation's crazy. I need your help, pal."

"Help? What do you mean?"

"You're supposed to say, 'Sure. I'll do anything.' This place is crawling with gun-toting goons, and they're putting out all kinds of threats and rumors on the street. They say they're gonna kidnap and ransom Americans down here for the fight, especially family of the fighters. All the American fighters on the card, if they can get hold of us. They think Foreman and me are the answer to their prayers."

"Well, that's awful, Kenny. Make them promote it somewhere else."

"Come on, man. You know better than that. And you don't back out of a world title fight. You might never get another one. Mike Weaver, my sparring partner you met, couldn't come because he's got a big fight in San Diego with Rodney Bobick, Duane's little brother. And my money guys are businessmen. Ain't no dirt under their fingernails."

"Is Foreman getting threats, too?"

"How would I know? I'm not going to have any contact with *the champ,"* he said bitterly, "until the weigh-in and the fight. It's chaos, man. You know that guy Jose Luis Garcia that knocked me out? The Venezuelan. At the gym where I was training, he kept getting past the security and yelling insults. The papers and TV ate that up. And the threats got so bad they moved me out of my hotel to this place outside town that doesn't even have a ring. I work out on tumbling mats. It's like a military compound, razor wire and all. Heavy bags are chained outside to trees. Look like bodies been lynched."

That set me back. "Aren't the Venezuelans providing security?"

"Well, they say. These guys are walking around in black shirts and carrying Uzis. Most don't know any English and I don't know Spanish. The ones who do speak English tell me not to trust the others—they might be the kidnappers."

"What's Don King say? He sounds like a street guy to me."

"I guess he is. Killed two people. Did time for stomping a guy to death over money. King's got goons with him, but I think they'll shoo like flies if anything rough happens. When I told him my worries, he proposed this ex-marine Leon Spinks who won the light heavyweight Gold in the Montreal Olympics."

"Proposed him to protect you?"

"Yeah. That and sparring. But I hear he's a goofball."

"What do you want me to do?"

"I want you to call out the marines! And you're the only one I trust."

"Are you crazy?"

"I'm not concerned about myself," he said. "And it wasn't hard to convince Jackie not to come here. But my parents aren't gonna stay away. After I started to get anywhere in boxing they've always come. Pop enjoys the fights, even the one I lost to Ali. Mom comes with him but she won't watch them, not even on TV. She sits in the hotel room and worries and waits till it's over."

"Tell your parents they can't come and get your head back in the fight!"

"They're coming down here, period. They've never been out of the States before. Neither have I."

"So you want me . . . "

"I want you to meet them at the airport in Chicago and just make things easier."

I was quiet for a few seconds. "You're asking me to be their *bodyguard?*"

"Well, yeah. Just look out for them. You know."

"I don't know! Do I remember you saying your dad's an amputee?"

"Partial, at the knee. He's got a prosthesis and walks with a cane. He's a cop! He gets around pretty good."

"This is crazy," I said again.

The long pause on Kenny's end didn't sound like angels passing. "Maybe so. Or just desperate. Haid, listen, I wouldn't ask you if I wasn't in real need."

"How much time are you talking about in Venezuela?"

"About a week. Just come down with them, look out for them wherever they go, and make sure they're on the plane out when it's over."

"Look, I don't speak Spanish either. And I don't know if I could manage it. Sabine and I are actually going through a difficult period, and I don't know what might be up with the band on those dates. We're working overtime now, taking any gig that's offered."

After another long sigh he pressed ahead. "This is another two-hundred-thousand-dollar fight for me. Most of what I got from the second Ali fight is still in the bank. I can make it worth your while. It won't cost you anything. I'll pay you well, and just let me know how much it would take to cover your band having a short, paid vacation. It's for my peace of mind. This is no way to get ready for a title fight with George Foreman."

"It sounds like I'd need a gun."

"I'll have one waiting for you at the airport."

"Listen, when I was a kid, I had a brother-in-law that tried to make me learn to shoot a thirty-eight. The only other pistol I've ever fired was that forty-five they put in our hands in infantry basic. I couldn't hit anything with either one. I don't own a gun. I don't like the things. I left that business in Vietnam."

"You won't have to use it but you'll need to have it, just in case. Buy one, go to a firing range, get used to it. Just tell me what kind you want, and I'll have King put his goons on it. The gun will be waiting for you in Caracas."

"I can't legally buy a gun in the United States."

That set him back. "How come?"

"I've got a conviction for aggravated assault."

"But that was just . . . "

"Yeah, just a military court martial. It's the same thing. If I try to buy one and they pick up my name change and alarms go off in the data bank, I'm in a heap of trouble I don't need. I'm a happily married man. Trying to be."

"Well, I don't want to mess with that," he said, and then offered another idea. "You ever been to a gun show?"

"No."

"Lots of them in Texas. You can buy a gun there no questions asked."

"So I'd be a felon with a *stolen* gun?"

"No, hear me out. Just don't buy at the table of a licensed dealer, because they run a background check. Pay attention to whoever you might be buying from. Half of 'em are doctors, business executives, professors. Law abiding gun nuts. But wait till the show's almost over, then show up." He took in the length of my silence and tried again. "I don't own a gun either. I've never kept one around the house. Kenny Junior's got no more sense than I had. Boy kids think they're toys. I'm a prizefighter, that's all I am."

"How do you know about gun shows?"

"I go to things out of curiosity. They have them in Nevada. When I fought in Lake Tahoe that time on Ali's card with Bob Foster, I went to one and hung out there a couple of days just to see what they're like." He went on, "Here's an idea. Did anybody ever give you one of those Marine Corps coins?"

"Yeah."

"Do you still have it?"

"I might."

"You know what to do with it?"

"No, Kenny, I don't!"

"Hey, don't get mad. I've never been mad at you."

I laughed and tried to make my jaw click so he could hear it.

"Okay, that once, but you started it. Here's what you do. Find that coin if you can. The way it works, you go in a bar and take a stool beside some guy. You put down the coin, and if he's an ex-marine he slaps his coin down, and he's obliged to buy you a drink."

"You want me to try that at a gun show."

"The worst that could happen is the guy thinks you're a nutcase."

"I'm willing to bet some ex-jarheads work for the federal gun cops."

"Okay, Haid. I get your drift. I understand. I just thought I'd ask."

He sounded so disconsolate I said, "Kenny, I'll see if it's possible. Get me the dates and how I can stay in right-away touch with you. But one thing I can't and won't do."

"What's that?"

"I'll be goddamned if I'm gonna sit in a hotel room with your mother while you fight George Foreman. I'd have to have a choice seat right beside your dad."

"Okay, that's fair. I'll tell King he's got to handle it the night of the fight, and if anything happens to her, I'll kill him. He understands the language."

CHAPTER 38

All hell broke loose at home when I told Sabine I was going to Venezuela for several days to work a prizefight. "Huh?" she said. "What kind of work?"

"Oh, Kenny doesn't have confidence in the publicists the promoters have hired." In telling of lies I might as well heave one far downfield. We made Emily cry from all the yelling, and I carried a pillow and quilt back to the living room sofa for more nights.

The band members didn't take the news much better, even though they were going to get paid all right for doing nothing. I went to a big outdoor gear store that looked like an aircraft hangar. The first thing the gun salesmen told me was they had a special on AR-15s. I said I had used their relatives the M-16s and didn't much care for them. "Vietnam?" the salesman said. My shrug let me in the club. I cut through their pitches of shotguns and deer rifles and said I might be interested in a reliable trouble-free handgun. They showed me Glocks, Rugers, Sig Sauers, and a Heckler & Koch small cannon called Flat Dark Earth. They pushed nine-millimeters hard. One guy said, "Let's say you're going overseas, security contracting or something like that, they're all you'll see. And it's the only ammo you'll find."

I noticed that small cameras on the walls recorded my every twitch. The salesmen pressured me to handle them, fall in love with holding one, but I declined. I wasn't about to leave fingerprints. I left them with the impression I was just another jerk-off to be forgotten by nightfall.

After one of our gigs a day or so later I was driving the band's old Mercedes van on the loop around San Antonio and was first struck by a billboard that was all white except for the large black message, *THINK GOD.* I'm glad it got my attention because the next one had a map of Texas turned backward and offered a gun show two days later.

It was the creepiest slice of humanity I'd seen in a while. One table offered an array of past issues of *Soldier of Fortune* and T-shirts of a guy in camos and boots with an oversized pistol in one hand and a hunting knife in the other and a chaw of bloody flesh between his teeth. T-shirts were going fast that read *"Come and Take'Em, Sucker."*

The glass-enclosed US Marine coins were about the size of a silver dollar, but much thicker and heavier. On the faces of them were the eagle, globe, and anchor symbol of the Corps. The damn thing worked! An ex-colonel gave me a "Semper Fi price" of three hundred bucks for a Brazilian-made .38 special with a two-inch barrel and magazine clips that held five rounds.

I walked out of there with the gun, two boxes of bullets, and a holster made in El Paso that, he said, was the favorite of John Wayne. I made him put them in a sack. At one of the firing ranges that cluttered Austin's outskirts, I fired and reloaded and fired until I was out of shells and comfortable with the recoil, if not the man-shaped outline on the target. I smuggled the gun inside the house when Sabine was at her office and Emily was at school. I stuck it far back on the top shelf of my closet after wrapping it in a patchwork quilt my late Granny Nichols made from my little boy shirts.

I walked through the mob at Chicago's O'Hare airport looking out windows at the sky. Weather maps on the TV monitors suggested we might not be going anywhere, and if we did, it could be a rough ride. Carrying my bag of clothes strapped on my shoulder, I found the American gate to Miami and points beyond in Latin America. I had gotten my hair cut and dressed in jeans and boots and a wool sport coat over my shirt. My bartender friend told me if you were young and big enough, that look got you taken down there for some kind of gringo badass. I wanted a drink but it was too early in the day. From my bag I pulled out a cardboard square on which I had written *Mr. & Mrs. NORTON*. I found a pillar to lean against and held up the sign.

After a while I watched an airport cart coming, its driver beeping at travelers to make way. Kenny's dad and mom were dressed for cold because they had driven up from Jacksonville and left their car on a long-term parking lot. They looked tired. I hustled over and introduced myself. John Norton was short and thick of shoulders and waist. He wore a fedora with the brims rolled up like my dad's when he went out to his shifts at the refinery. The hat touched me. He waved off my offer of assistance and when he was solid on his feet, he stuck out his hand. "Pleased to meet you, Mr. Pecos." Every time somebody said that, I was reminded what a dumb idea that was.

John Norton's handshake was strong but he wasn't a knuckle bruiser. I was at least six inches taller, and Kenny was two inches taller than me. I wondered what it would be like to have a son with an eight-inch height advantage. Ruth sat with her purse in her lap and wore a hat and winter coat. She had thickened with age but I could see what a beauty she would have been when she and that boy in Jacksonville created a son when she was fifteen. She allowed me to help her off the cart and take her carry-on bag and also called me Mr. Pecos. "Please. I'm Haid. Just Haid."

She looked up at me and smiled.

"That works," Mr. Norton said. "You're Haid, I'm John, and this is Ruth."

"Here's our gate," I said. "The board says our flight will be leaving on time. But I don't know about the weather out there."

"The front's gonna pass," John said. "We drove through the worst of it."

John acted like he didn't want or need my help, so I took my place in the boarding groups when they went ahead with the disabled passengers and families with infants. We had three seats together. When I arrived beside them and stowed my bag they had shed their coats but had their hats in their laps.

"Anything else you want me to put up here?"

John lifted his hat and grinned. "No, it's beat up enough as it is."

I took off my coat, rolled it up, put it up with the bags, and took my seat. "So you and Kenny knew each other in the service," said Ruth.

"Yes, ma'am, for a while. He was about to get out when we met."

"No sirs or ma'ams either," said John. He was a feisty man with short gray hair and a thin line of mustache touching his upper lip. He buckled his seat belt like he was getting ready to fly the plane. He said, "You were his sparring partner."

"For a while."

"You don't look big enough."

I grinned. "You're the four hundredth person to say that. I got to it first."

"Kenny says you're a famous singer now," said Ruth.

"He's known to exaggerate."

John chuckled. "The tales he came up with when he was a boy."

Airborne, the plane rocked and dipped with the turbulence for a few minutes, then we were up and out of it in sunshine. When two stewardesses passed beside us with their tray of drinks I asked for a ginger ale. Ruth just wanted a glass of water, and John asked for coffee black. I took the cup from the stewardess and handed it across Ruth. She noted my left hand and said, "Kenny told us you were in the war. We're glad Kenny didn't have to go."

"So am I."

"We're proud of Kenny," said John. "Whole town is. He enlisted and served his country and did what they ordered. But we got a new police chief who was in that war. When he took the job and was making rounds, I remarked that Kenny didn't have to go. He said, 'For me it was an honor.' Okay, son of a bitch. I was just making conversation."

She frowned at his language and said, "He was the most cantankerous boy I ever seen. Trying to ride a three-hundred-pound sow like it was a rodeo bull."

"Yeah," John said, "and riding his bicycle beside a freight train and trying to jump up on the ladder of a moving box car. Could have killed him, and it sure made a tangled mess of that bicycle when it fell under the wheels and got dragged."

"You're the one bought him another," said Ruth.

"We both spoiled him. Sports was how he got command of his energy."

"Third grade," she said, "he came in with a bunch of blue ribbons he won in the Junior Olympics, never seen him so proud."

"Maybe when he beat Muhammad Ali," said John.

She shook her head. "Boxing, I never expected that. I watched the football but didn't enjoy it. I liked to watch him run track. The coach used to enter him in eight events."

John said, "I never understood why he was such a bust in college football. Team he played on as a senior won the state championship, and he was all-state. He was the best high school athlete our little town had ever seen."

I smiled. "You don't know about the collarbone?"

"What collarbone?"

"Oh, maybe I shouldn't say."

"Well, now you got to."

"He told me he was crazy about a girlfriend, and one night at your house he saw a car go by with her sitting close to the driver. He said he jumped in your car, banged it off another car parked along some curb, and chased them into a cul-de-sac. Her new boyfriend waited until Kenny was on foot, then gunned his car. Kenny wasn't sure if he broke his collarbone bouncing off the windshield or hitting the pavement. He was embarrassed to go to a doctor but it should have been a season-ending injury. He tried to play hurt and couldn't."

John sighed and shook his head. "Brains are wasted on a kid. I sure remember the fender on our car. Every explanation he offered was a lie. I never got the truth out of him. I looked for the other car and its owner but never found it."

"Now, John," she teased him, "how hard did you look?"

"Well, damn right that was expensive. I thought his busting out of that college was just over chasing girls and being too lazy to make his grades. Kenny got scholarship offers from big schools. He had everything but discipline. I guess he needed the marines."

"Not in that war, he didn't."

John considered that and nodded. "I hope it didn't make you bitter. Back home we'd see young men come back from it and they were all busted up inside. Get on drugs, acquire themselves a record. Just can't get their lives together."

Ruth changed the subject. "Haid, tell me about your wife."

"Her name's Sabine. She's an attorney. She mediates civil disputes that the judges and opposing parties don't want to go to trial. She's the responsible one."

"Do you have children?"

"A stepdaughter named Emily. She's about to turn eight."

"So is Kenny Junior, our grandson."

"It's a good age." I smiled. "She's a lot of fun."

"Life," she said, looking at the hat in her lap. "You know John here is a very good father to Kenny, but he's not the biological one."

John turned his head away and stared at the piles of cloud. They were bumping us around some. "Kenny got his size from a boy who didn't want to have anything to do with him," she said. "They saw each other and knew who the other one was, but that was it."

"Why you bringing that up?" John said.

"John, you and I've been married twenty-seven years. So hush, you got no reason to be jealous."

John again looked away.

"That man's passed on," she said. "Died too young. He was in a car driven by a drunk man trying to beat a train to a crossing and didn't make it."

"Probably running from the law," grumbled John.

"I said hush."

She asked me, "Did Kenny tell you what his birth daddy's name was?"

"If he did, I forget."

"George. That boy's name was George."

CHAPTER 39

The Nortons were shocked on being greeted in the Caracas airport by uniformed soldiers with AK-47s slung on their shoulders. The stone-faced customs agents went through every article of our luggage and finally waved us on. When we emerged in the noisy and bustling lobby three American black guys were holding a sign for Mr. and Mrs. Norton. At my nod they moved to greet us. They all wore sunshades, though our arrival was deep into the night. They said they worked for Mr. Don King and they would take us to a nice hotel where we had reservations. The air outside was smoky and damp and rank. One of them trotted off to get the van. Another touched my arm and motioned me aside. He handed me a cloth bag and I felt a semi-automatic pistol and about a dozen loose rounds. "I asked for a revolver," I said, glancing at a soldier who eyed us.

"Well, that's not what you got," King's man said. "It's a better gun anyhow. That Beretta Pico has six .380 caliber rounds in the magazine. Have you ever shot one?"

"No."

"All you have to do is pull the trigger and a new round's chambered and ready to go. It don't ever jam but it's got a lot of recoil. You'd have to be ready for that. It packs a lot of powder and scares the shit out of people when it goes off."

"All right," I said. "Thank you and Mr. King and the fellas."

"You're welcome."

The driver pulled the van in traffic behind a smoking bus that listed to the left. The billboards in Spanish jolted me alert. I could almost smell the Nortons' anxiety. The Lidotel Centro Lido was a swanky place, but the man who spoke English at the hotel's desk said we had no reservations, doing nothing for the travel-worn nerves of the couple I was sworn to help. I stayed after him until the reservations came up on his computer. He apologized and told the Nortons they would have a suite. "Oh, we don't need all that," said Ruth. John gave her an irritated look. He had come down here to enjoy himself.

The man said it was hotel policy to hold our passports until we checked out. I brought out the gringo bad-ass frown. "No," I said. "The rooms are already paid for. I'll give you a credit card number that will cover any meals or incidentals." My bluff worked, at least on this guy. "Is my room on the same floor?"

"Yes. Also a suite." He bowed and said, *"Bienvenidos a Caracas."*

On the elevator Ruth told me, "We're so tired."

"A long flight," I agreed. When the Nortons and their luggage were in their room I said, "This is an impressive place and I'm sure it's safe. But just call room service tonight. And let me know when you do. Let's see what the restaurants are like in the morning." As I turned to leave, their phone rang. Ruth picked it up and said, "Oh, son, it's so good to hear your voice."

I went for a walk the next morning. Downtown Caracas was filled with high-rises and plazas and parks, but when I looked between the buildings my insides convulsed. The slum hovels were packed close together, some painted red, some aqua, with roofs of metal scavenged somewhere. The population of about twelve million mostly lived on those slopes. My bartender friend in Austin also told me Caracas had the worst murder rate on earth.

Kenny had convinced his moneymen from California that the threats and menace were genuine enough that they pulled him out of his hotel and installed his quarters at an exercise spa and resort framed by razor wire and patrolled by armed sentries. A van brought Kenny to the hotel the second night. I met him in the lobby. He was accompanied by a driver who spoke passable English and wore a black shirt that on back read in white *Vigilantes de Seguridad.* Kenny wore a hooded sweat jacket, and we had dinner brought up to their suite. I couldn't tell which of his concerns made him so edgy. John wanted to go out to his camp and watch workouts but Kenny told him it was too intense now.

"Not tomorrow, Pop. But we'll do it while you're here." I walked out with Kenny and the bruiser. Kenny kept a nervous eye all around.

"You doing all right?" I asked.

"Yeah, I'm in shape. Wish we could get it over with tomorrow."

"If your folks can't come out there, what am I going to do with them?"

"Take them shopping. To a museum. Simón Bolívar, the George Washington of South America, is buried here. They might like it. Just don't go out after it gets dark."

"So they're gonna be bored and pissed off at me."

"Pop spends his days now taking calls and sending out cops. The job requires patience. He doesn't get too upset about things. Just make sure he and Mom don't leave the hotel without you. I'll bring them out to the camp a time or two. They don't have to leave their big fine room until Pop comes to the weigh-in and fight. Tell them to lock the door and watch American television."

"Okay."

"Thanks for this, pal. I owe you."

Kenny came one evening when the Nortons said they were tired and going to bed early. He and I went downstairs to a coffee shop. The *Vigilante* set up his watch from a table across the room. Kenny looked at his latte with suspicion, like it might be poison. "Do you want me to taste it first?" I said.

"Sorry. I just generally don't like it down here." At first he didn't say much about the fight, then: "The press writes about Foreman like he's this monster who walks in like Frankenstein and just starts throwing roundhouse haymakers. Joe came right at him but not for long—you couldn't tell anything from that, except the power. I've been watching the films. George fought George Chuvalo in Madison Square Garden when he was coming up. He was moving damn good and putting together combinations. Chuvalo was too proud of never being knocked down. George worked him into a corner and the guy didn't have the sense to take a knee. Stood there taking punch after punch. The ref acted like he was *afraid* to get between them. Chuvalo's corner had to stop it. I know how to fight him, though. I'm more at peace in my mind than he is. And I'm on a mission, on account of how he treated Joe."

While I was in Caracas both fighters made themselves available to *Sports Illustrated.* Kenny told the writer Tex Maule, "He's like a Mack truck. He's far more physical than Ali was. With Ali it was a chess game. But Foreman is not as fast as I am, physically or mentally. My conception is that he'll come out swinging, and I'll move away from him and he won't be able to think as fast as I do. I've been thinking about this fight, what I'll do if I get hit, how I'll react, so it will be instinctive, and I won't have to think."

Maule passed that on to George, who said, "He better do all his thinking now. When he gets in the ring, he ain't gonna have time to think. He don't know what I'm going to do, but he can pretty well guess. Wherever he goes, there's gonna be George Foreman right in his face. Somebody got to pay for all that nice weight I lost. I like to eat. I'm prettier slim but I'm happier fat. If I can ever afford it, I'm gonna eat all I want and I'm gonna be very fat. He's gonna have to pay for making me stay slim."

One night a driver set out to take the Nortons and me to have dinner with Kenny at his camp. The driver passed out of the central city, followed a big highway at great speed, and then turned off on a road that wound up into the foothills. It grew narrower and more crooked, with less and less traffic. We were in woodlands with streetlights almost non-existent when the driver stopped, threw open his door, killed the headlights, and took off running. The last I saw of him were those white letters *Vigilantes de Seguridad* on his shirt.

"Oh, fuck," I said.

"What's this?" John said.

"Pardon my language, Mrs. Norton."

"You think I ain't heard that?" she said.

I looked over in hopes the driver had forgotten and left the keys in the ignition, but he hadn't. With the Beretta in hand I opened my door and stepped out. I heard John start to slide open the door on the other side of the van from me.

"John, please," I said. "Stay in the car."

"I'm a grown man, son. I'm a police officer."

Yeah, a cop that leans hard on the cane he walks with.

"We've got company. Look there," said John, pointing. "And there."

I counted seven shadowy figures—one more than I had rounds in the magazine.

"John, get back in the van and lock the doors. I'm gonna scare these guys off."

"How you gonna do that?" he said. I showed him the gun.

"You any good with it?"

"I hope we don't have to find out."

"*Ruth,"* he said sharply. "Lock all the doors. Leave them locked until we're done with these fellas."

Circling through the headlight beams, they closed in cursing us in Spanish. I supposed they were cursing; they didn't sound friendly. The leader responded by letting me see *his* gun. One beside him showed a machete. Others let me see baseball bats. If they started circling again the leader would walk out of my range of vision.

Moving to the front seat, Ruth called, "Haid, who are these men?"

"They're low-life mean people, ma'am."

"Don't do anything crazy. Give them what they want."

"They're not here to rob us. They're kidnappers. They want you."

John's voice found a higher register. "When are you gonna shoot?"

"Soon, I guess."

"Whoa," said John. He pointed up the street at the approach of five more men. They were black, speaking English, and one of them was huge. He wore sweat pants, athletic shoes, and a black hoodie. The others dressed like him except for one. That man was much shorter, thick-bodied, had bushy gray sideburns, and his hat looked like the ones Russians wear in winter weather. "Are you Americans?" I called.

"Yo," one replied.

"Your car break down?" asked the one with the hat. "You need help?"

"Sir," said John, "are you the great Archie Moore?"

"I am," he said with a tone of pleased surprise. "Who are you?"

I spoke fast. "I'm a friend of Ken Norton. These people are his parents. Kenny asked me to come down here and keep them safe. I'm not doing a very good job of it."

The huge man looked at the thugs for a few seconds, pulled his hood back off his head, and started toward us. "Careful, champ," said John. "These punks are armed."

George Foreman said, "Bodyguard, how come you're a friend of Ken Norton?"

"I was his sparring partner for a little while in the marines."

"Kind of puny-looking for that. Maybe lower that gun? They do go off."

"Right," I said. I did that but eyed the Venezuelans and kept my finger on the trigger. The thugs had fallen silent and now stood still, looking apprehensive.

George said, "What happened to your driver?"

"He stopped and took off. He's in on this. The delivery man."

"In on what?"

"They're kidnappers. They want to grab Mr. and Mrs. Norton and hold them for ransom. I expect they'd just kill me."

"Would they now," the big man said. He leaned forward so he could see Ruth, through the open driver's door.

"Ma'am, you're Ken Norton's mother?"

"Yes, I am, and I'm proud of him, Mr. Foreman. We call him Kenny."

"Well, you should be proud. I wish my mother could come to my fights. She's not feeling too well back in Houston."

Foreman considered the Venezuelan who fidgeted. He was still the leader but uncertainty now figured in his stance. The champ introduced himself, and another one added Spanish. *"Jorge grande. El campeón del mundo . . . fuerte peso pesado."*

"You, bad guy," George said. "Why you want to hate on these people?"

George's man translated him with each sentence and pause.

"I used to lay up drunk with the likes of you," said George. "You're not gonna shoot me, and that other one's not gonna cut me with that sword. God walks with me all the time. If you hurt me, you'll be dead men. Your country will kill you. All of you. Chase you down like rabbits. Stand you up against a wall after doing terrible things first. Count on it." He raised his hand at them. "You get on back where you came from. Before I lay hands on you. I don't speak your tongue but you hear what I say."

The thugs didn't wait for the translation to start moving back. Then sounds of running, and in the darkness, they were gone. George came over to John and offered his hand. "Mr. Norton, I know what you're feeling for your son and what you feel about me. That's just the way it's got to be. But thank you for calling me champ. Makes me feel respected, coming from you." George looked at me. "Bodyguard, where you headed?"

"Mister and Mrs. Norton were going to have dinner and spend the evening with Kenny. Somebody trusted or paid off that driver. I don't know where the training camp is."

He nodded. "Well, you hang on to that gun. I'm going to leave two of these men with you, including one that speaks Spanish. My camp's just up the way. Fortunate we walked up on you. I'll find out where Ken's camp is and send a driver that can get these folks where they need to be, seeing their son. And he'll get you and them back where you stay."

He leaned over so he could see Ruth again. "You have a good evening, ma'am. I'm pleased to meet you."

George and the others moved off in the night. I was so full of adrenaline I felt afloat. "Man that size," John said with wonder. "He's got the very softest hand."

CHAPTER 40

At the weigh-in both men shed their robes and stood in their underwear. They were the same height, and Kenny had bulked up to 214. George still outweighed him ten pounds. While this ritual went on, officials of the regime seized and held equipment necessary for the closed circuit telecast until the day of the fight. At midday a co-promoter named Hank Schwartz, who was providing the telecast to two hundred locations in the States and venues in sixty-nine other countries, called a press conference and sounded harried. The coliseum manager had handed Schwartz a note that on government stationery and in uneven English stated that some taxes would have to be paid. But the manager assured Schwartz he had personally taken care of the matter. Hoping that was the case, Schwartz stammered that he had signed Foreman and Ali to fight for the title in six months in the central African county of Zaire.

Schwartz apologized to Kenny's furious San Diego moneymen, saying the deal had been leaked to the press and he had to try to gain control of the story. The leak came from Don King, who wanted all promotion rights to a Foreman-Ali fight. He had thrown a major wrench into his own title fight debut. What if George lost to Kenny? It would be safer if this fight with a fraction of payout didn't happen at all.

The day of the fight, rumors swirled. That morning, as reported by *Sports Illustrated*'s Tex Maule, George limped out of the hotel, supported under his left shoulder by a member of his entourage, headed to a hospital for an x-ray and examination of his right knee. An hour later, he limped out favoring his left knee. The doc in George's entourage explained that he brought the champ back into fighting shape with a shot of cortisone and Novocain late that afternoon. "I didn't get no shot," George said. "I hate needles."

George's trainer Dick Sadler said his concern about the ref was a matter of competence, not integrity. Foreman's camp wanted the Seattle ref that had overseen his destruction of Frazier in Jamaica; the Caracas officials said they had already assigned a Venezuelan ref. George said, "I don't care if three little old ladies judge the fight." Late in the afternoon the Venezuelan officials gave in and agreed to let the ref from Seattle call the fight.

I gave a great deal of thought to George Foreman that week. How could I not? He walked out of that night and likely saved my life. The night of the fight the Nortons dined early in their room. Too nervous to be hungry, I sat on the bed in my suite and weighed the question of taking the gun. If I wound up frisked for any reason, the police or military would be certain I meant to shoot one of the fighters or a Venezuelan dignitary, and I didn't want to see the inside of a Caracas jail. Still I thought of those thugs who closed in after the driver ran off. I had to take the gun.

Before we left, I had a talk with the two large black men that King assigned to chairs in front of the Nortons' suite. One said, "This is the only door into his momma's suite. Batman couldn't fly this high and through the window at her because there's no ledge and besides we've got a man with a rifle and scope watching from the same floor across the street, in case Batman tries. She'll be fine."

Our driver and a burly escort took John and me to ringside seats behind the table and chairs of the telecast team, which included Muhammad Ali. A horde of policemen wore white helmets and there was a complement of the *Vigilantes de Seguridad.* I took in the arena and had seen bigger crowds at a high school football game. John's ringside seats placed us right behind the American broadcast team. The announcer was Bob Sheridan, who had called the second Ali-Norton fight with humor and flair. Wearing a brown suit, white shirt, and orange tie, Ali had flown down to provide color commentary. We leaned forward and eavesdropped. Ali declared, "I see Ken Norton winning by a late knockout or for sure a decision. I'm saying that because he gave me trouble twice."

"Here's Norton coming in now," said Sheridan.

Arriving first because he was the challenger, Kenny looked great. He was wearing white shoes that reached halfway up his calves, a dark blue robe with a white cloth belt, and a white towel wrapped around his neck and head.

"You can do it, Kenny!" Ali yelled. Kenny sat on his stool and stretched his arms along the ropes. He nodded at the encouraging stream of advice from Ali.

Ali predicted a Norton win on grounds the man had gone twenty-four rounds with him. World title fights then were scheduled for fifteen rounds, until a South Korean got killed in one. Kenny's fights with Ali had been twelve-rounders because all that was at stake on paper was just a North American title. "I was in shape the second fight and still barely won," Ali said. "This man George Foreman fought Joe Frazier when Joe was out of shape. Hit him with a hard punch, had him on queer street, knocked him down six times, and *still* couldn't keep him down. Fought a nobody, José Roman, and couldn't keep him down either." In fact George had stopped Roman two minutes into the first round.

John looked at me and laughed. "Queer street? You all talk like that?"

I grinned. "Not me, and I've never heard Kenny say that."

Ali continued to run his mouth. "George hasn't had no action the last year and a half, and this man Ken Norton boxes. As fast as I am, as accurate as I am, I still had trouble with him. I'm saying if he boxes like he fought me, keeps his distance, hard-swinging, wild-punching George Foreman . . . just see if I'm not right. If George doesn't luck out and knock him out early, Ken Norton will be the new world champion."

Sheridan said, "I don't know if you believe what you said there, but it sounds like you believe it."

"That's right. That's right. It's no fake. It's on record. I got film of it, and he was rough. Foreman is in for some trouble tonight. I was getting on George because he hadn't been fighting nobody. But I'm giving him credit now. He's fighting the best man in the division, next to myself."

We were in for a long wait. Kenny sat on his stool with his arms and taped hands stretched along the ropes and kept nodding at Ali's persistent coaching. A man came up behind us yelling in Spanish at Kenny. George dragged things out because he was the heavyweight champion, and he was not to be hurried. "I think George might be coming in now," said Sheridan.

George stepped through the ropes with sweat gleaming on his face. He moved around with an expression of going about business. He bounced up and down a few times, showing no sign of pain in his knees, and jogged around the ring wearing a robe of scarlet satin, "The Fighting Corpsman" sewn on the back in white.

"Fighting Corpsman?" said John. "What's that about?"

"He joined the Job Corps. One of LBJ's Great Society programs. He was training for some trade when a supervisor got him to take up boxing. I guess George is a loyal guy."

"I'm scared but excited for my son," John said. "I was the same way the times he fought Ali."

"He did all right in both," I tried to reassure him.

As the two fighters jogged, Archie Moore again wore the shiny flat hat with no brim. He followed George around with last-minute suggestions. Several more minutes passed before the fighters took off their robes. Sheridan said, "I've heard people talk about Norton not having a good jab."

"Oh, he's got a good jab," Ali said. "He was just fighting the fastest man in the history of *all* fights. When you're fighting the fastest man in the history of boxing, you don't hit him with a jab all the time."

The time came to call in the celebrities. Joe Louis strolled across the ring, getting a big hand from the Venezuelan crowd and a warm reception from Kenny. Next came the Argentine heavyweight Oscar Bonavena, who wore a garish green sport coat with a darker green shirt and a black and white tie. When he fought Ali, he couldn't get inside Ali's reach so he ducked and winged haymakers at the body. Ali danced and threw combinations with contempt, but Bonavena slugged with Ali before going down three times in the fifteenth round, which automatically ended the fight. The only legitimate contender he'd beaten was George Chuvalo. That didn't stop him now from taking off his jacket, handing it to a flunky, and leaning over the ropes to insult Ali. He pawed at Ali like a cat batting at a ball of string.

I could see Ali smiling. Twice he pointed his finger at Bonavena. Then he changed his tune and came to his feet making a commotion. Sheridan told him to sit down—this was a world title fight they had to call. Ali took his chair and with the camera on him looked unhappy. "Well, I knocked him out once in the fifteenth round. The fight was kinda close and he says if I hadn't knocked him out, he'd have won. I don't know—he just makes me lose my cool. Standing over me like that, me of all people."

The national anthems went on forever. As was his custom, Kenny stared at his feet at mid-ring when they went out to hear the referee's instructions. George didn't exactly glare. He just stared. Sheridan asked Ali what they were feeling now.

"Oh, right now you're a little nervous, shaky in the knees," Ali said. "But after the bell rings, you come out like it's just another day in the gymnasium." Ali talked so fast that his thoughts banged off each other like bumper cars. He blurted, "George Foreman and I've just been offered five million apiece by the government of Zaire, which used to be the Belgian Congo. If Foreman wins this fight, which I don't expect, I'll be fighting him next."

John looked at me and said, "They offered him that fight when this one hasn't started yet?" That's boxing, I thought but didn't say.

Kenny and George bumped gloves after hearing out the ref. Kenny came out in his usual stance, left glove low and the right beside his jaw and in front of his chin. George used a defensive style I'd never seen before. He advanced with both gloves high, palms open toward Kenny. He was much quicker with them than I thought he'd be. He had excellent hand-eye coordination. If the punches were coming at his head, he caught most of them in the palms of his gloves. If they were aimed for his body, he bumped them away with his gloves or forearms. When the fighting came in close and he didn't see an opening he wanted, he gave Kenny a hard shove.

"Uh oh," I said.

"What?" said John, alarmed by me.

"Nothing," I said. "I thought I saw something in the crowd but it was just a woman putting on lipstick. Threw up a glint of light." That was quicker-witted than most of the lies I told. I wondered if Kenny could fight running or backing up.

George whacked him in the ribs a few times and landed some jabs. One knocked Kenny back a couple of steps. Kenny tried a couple of those overhand rights that had worked so well with Ali, but they didn't land. Ali was yelling. "Box him, Kenny, box him!"

With a minute left Kenny landed two good punches, a left hook off a jab. In my experience that was the hardest combination to master with any speed and power. Kenny scored another good jab just before the bell. As the bell rang George landed a left hook on Kenny's sternum just over his heart. For an instant Kenny jerked forward. But then he gave a little hop at the bell and thrust the mouthpiece partway out and walked smartly, as he often did at a round's end. Sheridan asked Ali how it looked to him.

"It's just like I thought," Ali said. "Norton boxing, Foreman throwing those hard punches but not landing, trying to take him out early, like he did Joe Frazier. Kenny Norton's a great fighter. Any man who can go twenty-four rounds with me has gotta be great. Foreman's still a good amateur. He's not gonna destroy Norton because I couldn't do it. I'm proud of Ken Norton, he's showing the world he's great."

As Ali stood and continued yelling instructions to Kenny, he sat on the stool and lowered his head as if to shut him and everything else out. "Norton looks like he's trying to concentrate," said Sheridan. "He believes in the power of positive thinking. He won an award for positive thinking from the Napoleon Hill Foundation."

Kenny later told me about his real mindset. "We began to trade jabs when he landed a jackhammer to my face. He pursued me with wild bombs until the bell ended round one. Even though I knew Foreman's strategy was to come straight for me, his ferocity scared the living daylights out of me. I had just experienced three minutes of sheer terror."

At the start of the second round Kenny landed three good jabs and a hook upstairs that made George yank back his head and frown. Then I had to swallow a yelp. In trying to keep moving and yield canvas, Kenny was squaring off his stance. The right foot that gave him the strength to drive forward while punching wasn't in its usual position, and he wasn't showing George the angle that made his body easier to protect. George landed a right uppercut so hard I saw one of Kenny's white shoes ascend from the canvas.

Kenny circled away in a crouch. He didn't cover up with the crossed-arms defense of Archie Moore. He had always been so good with that. I wondered if he abandoned it because Archie was in George's corner. Did Kenny think that jinxed it? Superstition rides a big horse in a boxing match. Or had the uppercut blown his fuses?

George bore in with a clubbing right and then another right uppercut that would have floored Kenny if it hadn't seated him on the second rope. The ref made Kenny take an eight-count. He nodded gamely and prepared for more battle.

The champ was on Kenny at once with a straight left that sent him sailing back into the ropes. The ref started to make Kenny take another eight-count but changed his mind and waved them together. Foreman landed a right lead this time and then two brutal right uppercuts and a left hook as Kenny was going down. He landed with an alarming thump of his head. He struggled up and managed to get his right glove over the top rope.

"He's in queersville, he doesn't know where he is!" yelled Sheridan. "Count's at five, six—I don't know if he's going to make it!" Kenny got to his feet and wobbled along the ropes toward his corner. "This might be the end of it!" Sheridan yelled. George had sidled out of the neutral corner and was in arm's reach of throwing more of those punches. "It is!" As a white towel fluttered in the ring, the ref waved at the corner men to come help their man.

I slumped in the chair and put my elbows on my knees and my head in my hands.

John muttered, "Queersville."

"I'm sorry, John."

"I have to go see if he's all right."

I couldn't let him do that now, for the bedlam in the ring spilled in all directions. Don King leaped about with his outlandish Afro and a look of absolute glee. His show was on the road to an African city named Kinshasa. Ali vanished without saying anything more. George pressed past the bodies with arms raised to the crowd. He reached over the ropes and raised a small boy over his head, then set him down again. I wondered if the boy was his son, or just a Venezuelan who had wriggled in close. Sheridan couldn't get to either fighter. Kenny pulled the hood of his robe over his head and started out, offering no comment.

George grew annoyed at all the shoving and pockets being picked, and the white-helmeted cops formed a cordon and led him out. John and I had been told to stay put until our escorts came. I said, "Hold on, John. They'll get you there."

"The goddamn thing about it is I'm not surprised."

I put my hand on his shoulder. "He'll be in the hunt as long as he wants to be."

"At what cost?" he said.

No escorts came for us. I had to force our way through the crowd to the gatekeepers of Kenny's dressing room. I didn't go inside with his dad. So much for the power of positive thinking, I thought. I got John safely back to the hotel and then both parents to the airport the next morning. Ruth didn't want to talk about the fight or how the news had been broken to her. "Bless you," she said, putting her hand on my face, then the airlines agent signaled them aboard a van that took them across the tarmac, and they were off to Miami.

At the hotel I went out on the street, found a trash container outside another hotel, and got rid of the gun and ammo in a paper sack. Many hours later I walked out of the Austin airport and saw Sabine and the car. She kissed me with a twist of feeling that had been missing for a while. "I'm sorry your friend lost but I'm glad you went. A little space was good for both of us. Sometime you've got to take me to Caracas."

"They say Quito and Cartagena are nicer," I said as she pulled the car away.

I didn't learn till later that insult had been added to injury. Both fighters were stopped at the airport and told they couldn't leave Venezuela unless they posted bonds to ensure the national government got 18 percent of their purses. The US ambassador tried to intervene, but the office of the new president was firm. Kenny had to hunker down five more days while his money men negotiated, and it cost his purse $36,000. It took George eleven days and $126,000 to get home and see his mom.

When the postman brought my issue of *Sports Illustrated* I read that George said after the fight, "I was in certain places before he was. I knew where he wanted to go and I went there first. It's like magic when I lay my hand on these guys. I know Norton isn't hurt at all, because I went over to his corner and heard him saying, 'What happened? What happened?'" The photo that lived on after the fight had George bending over Kenny, his left hand swept around in that last hook. Kenny was in the air at a thirty-degree angle, looking as stiff as a show room mannequin, his arms and gloves raised like he might have been trying to catch a basketball. The magazine's cruel headline was *"Buenas Noches, Señor."*

Sabine saw what I was reading and that I tossed the magazine aside.

She said, "Who *is* George Foreman?"

"Beats me. But God help Muhammad Ali."

CHAPTER 41

You had to go back to the 1936 Olympics in Berlin, when America's sprinter Jesse Owens won four gold medals and left Hitler's gunsels grumbling that blacks weren't really humans, to find a sporting event as feverish as "The Rumble in the Jungle" in October 1974 in Kinshasa, Zaire. Muhammad Ali hyped it into more than a boxing match. "This fight is for the freedom, justice, and equality of the black man in America so that I may take my title and my fame and go out and uplift little black people in the ghettos. Black people is catching hell, black people that entertainers won't speak for—I have to lead the way. God has made me bigger than all the entertainers in the world. Now it's my job to whoop this man, get my title, so I can use it to uplift the black man in America." Ali pledged to retire at thirty-two when he won back the crown.

Of the fight, Ali brayed that he was fearless. He explained his thinking to the British TV interviewer David Frost. "No problem. No problem," he began. "This will be the biggest upset since I beat Sonny Liston. And I think it's befitting that I go out of boxing just like I came in, defeating a big monster, a hard puncher, that nobody could destroy. I'm the underdog—if he hits me, I'm in trouble like it was with Sonny Liston. But I came back and shook the world when I got Liston, and it's been ten years. I'm meeting another big strong monster who's knocking out everybody. Sonny Liston knocked out Floyd Patterson twice, and I was supposed to fall, too. But he didn't knock me out, because he could hit hard, but he couldn't find *nothing to hit."* Ali also said tasteless things in his self-promotion—among them, that natives of Zaire were going to boil George in a pot.

The problem with Ali's view of himself was that Foreman was no less an American black man. He had a record of 40 and 0, had taken out Joe Frazier and Kenny Norton, the only pros that had beaten Ali, and neither fight lasted into the third round. And he had a mindset as dark as his skin. "I remember one time I was trying to court a girl in Houston," he would say, "and I told her I was gonna be a boxer. And she said, 'I seen Muhammad Ali the other day on the street. He was acting like, I'm beautiful, look at me.' I never dated that girl again, I got so upset."

A year after his triumph at the 1968 Mexico City Olympics, George turned pro with a six-rounder in Madison Square Garden. He stopped it in three against a target of an opponent who had won only five of eleven fights. The most notable thing that happened to him in New York was seeing Ali on the street in Manhattan. "He was just wearing trousers and a long-sleeved shirt, cruising along." He thought in envy, Man, he *is* beautiful. George fought eleven more opponents in the next six months. The most notable opponent was Chuck Wepner, the big New Jersey liquor salesman who had then won nineteen of twenty-five. George's punches opened a gaping cut over Wepner's eyebrow, the blood streaming and splattering like water from a broken pipe. The ref waved his arms and stopped it. Wepner was on his way to being cast among the heavyweights as "the Bleeder of Bayonne."

George's twelfth fight took place in Miami Beach. "Ali was out of business because he refused the draft," he said. "I knew a fair amount about that because he did it in Houston. After that, everybody turned on him. Everyone. Nobody wanted to be in his presence. He was dropped. He still made himself available. He went around the country, loved being in the media, but nobody even wanted him on television. I was in the Miami gym one day with a TV crew there for an interview. Ali came in, and they just shut down. Turned off the cameras and went away until he was gone. He had a briefcase, and he said, 'Sit down, George. I'm gonna show what you got to have if you're gonna be the world heavyweight champion.' I sat down and looked at the briefcase, thinking it had to be full of gold or something. He opened it up, and it was a telephone. He said, 'This is a miracle, George. It's called a mobile telephone. It doesn't have to be connected to any of them poles and lines.'"

That summer and fall in Zaire, Ali would be doing his roadwork outside Kinshasa and people ran after him yelling, "Ali, *bomaye!"* Ali, kill him! George didn't go out of his way to endear himself to people who had come halfway around the world to see the bout. Norman Mailer, who wrote a book about it called *The Fight,* greeted George and offered a handshake, which the champion declined. He explained he couldn't shake hands at the moment because his hands were in his pockets.

But the hype had to narrow to the fight itself. Ali and George scheduled a few back-to-back workouts in a Kinshasa gym, and press reports came back to the States that when George was pounding the heavy bag it sounded like he was going to bring down the walls and roof. On hearing that, coming down a corridor, Ali fell uncharacteristically quiet.

"I knew he was a phenomenon," George said. "I also knew I'd beaten Joe Frazier and Kenny Norton easily. They were the only people that had beaten Ali. I thought this was gonna be the easiest five million dollars I'd ever pick up. I was *certain* I was gonna knock him out. I had no respect for him as a boxer, none at all."

Yet nothing in Zaire went the way George expected. Aware of Ali's antics to fire up the native throng, George went for strolls with his German shepherd on a leash. He was trying to develop some affinity with the folks. Nobody told him that breed of dog was a reminder of the brutal rule of the Belgians. Then George suffered a cut over his eye while sparring, and it was serious enough that the fight had to be postponed six weeks. Don King talked Howard Cosell and other reporters into embargoing the news for a day so musicians wouldn't start bailing out of a concert in the stadium where the fight would take place.

The South African trumpet player Hugh Masekela and a partner showcased salsa's Celia Cruz, Zaire's rumba singer Tabu Ley Rochereau, South Africa's Miriam Makeba, and the American blues and soul standouts Bill Withers and B.B. King. A barker warmed up the crowd for "the man who will make your liver quiver, the man who will make your bladder splatter, this man will *freeeeze* your knees, if you will, let's all welcome the godfather of soul, Soul Brother Number One—James Brown!" The singer ran on wearing extravagant bell bottoms, a shirt showing off his back and chest, and a pearl-studded choker collar, and he jumped into a split.

The writers' publishers didn't want to pay for bringing them home and then sending them back. They wound up bored and stuck, and the long wait in Kinshasa turned into a circus. George Plimpton had been assigned lead coverage for *Sports Illustrated.* In one of his first-person sports writing stunts, Plimpton had spilled a river of blood from his nose down his chest in a sparring match with an apologetic Archie Moore. Now the Mongoose was in George's corner. Plimpton reported Moore's claim that Ali's loudmouth act was "time-worn, an act as thin as a Baltimore pimp's patent leather shoes." Plimpton picked up a rumor that Ali had consulted a pygmy *féticheur* that the Ruler for Life Mobuto used for charms and jinxes. Ali's cheerleader Bundini Brown was indignant. "What is you talking 'bout? They ain't *room* for more than one witch doctor when that witch doctor is Bundini!"

The title fight came off in a soccer stadium with political prisoners locked in dungeons beneath it. The stadium had a capacity of fifty thousand people, but about eighty thousand packed in the stands. Ali scored the more telling punches in the first round, but not all of them, and on the stool afterward he looked wide-eyed and frightened. Then in inspiration he turned and started pumping his gloved right hand up and down, raising cries of "Ali, *bomaye!*" Getting the crowd roaring the chant helped Ali weather his psychological crisis, but Foreman was too seasoned to be swayed by that.

In the second round Ali went to the ropes, leaning back with hands high and arms clamped in a protective shield. His trainer Angelo Dundee screamed at him in panic. Ali later explained his strategy. "I didn't really plan what happened that night. When a fighter gets in the ring, he has to adjust according to the conditions he faces. Against George, the ring was slow. Dancing all night, my legs would have got tired. And George was following me too close, cutting off the ring. In the first round I used more energy staying away from him than he used chasing me. Between rounds, I decided to do what I did in training when I got tired."

George tried to short-circuit Ali's nervous system by hitting him on the neck. "I didn't think too much of him as a man. Then in Zaire I got in the ring with him, the fight began, he hit me a few times, but I beat him up for three rounds. I hit him hard in the third, and he looked at me like, 'I'm not gonna take this.' Then the bell rang, and he looked at me as if to say, "I *made* it!" I knew I was in trouble. The water had just gotten deep."

Whatever George tried, he soon appeared to be exhausted, and his banging at the raised arms and gloves of Ali looked like they were thrown in slow motion. His hooks flew wide, and he seemed to forget the right uppercuts that destroyed Frazier and Norton. "About the sixth or seventh round he started whispering, 'That the best you got, George?' Scary thing to hear, because it was all I had! Now I'm thinking, *This ain't what it was supposed to be.*"

"The girl with the slightly trembling hands!" George Plimpton yelled at Norman Mailer. "She's *got* to him! The succubus!" But Plimpton's theory of a female demon who spread curses by making love to a man didn't turn the fight in favor of Ali. He did it by himself. In the eighth round Ali spun off the ropes with a combination and then a lead right hand that put George down.

Plimpton wrote that on the rubdown table after the fight George had ice packs on his face to limit the swelling. The dethroned champ said, "Where's my dog?" He put his hand on the head of the German shepherd Dago, who wagged his tail. George counted backward from one hundred to one and then called out the names of everyone in his entourage. "The Ping-Pong games," he reflected. "All those games. With this fight I have found serenity in myself. I felt secure until my corner men jumped in the ring. I was not tired. I truly felt like I was in control of the fight. It was a privilege to fight in my ancestors' land. We have built a bridge that will never be broken again."

CHAPTER 42

VIRGINIE

All over the world, a billion people were supposed to have watched the fight between those two Americans on television, but a thousand miles away from Kinshasa, the bout was just a rumor in the Virunga Mountains. The spelling of Virginie's name was French because it had come with Belgian priests and nuns. The Nalula family also spoke Portuguese and Swahili and a tribal dialect, Ibembe. Virginie arrived on earth in a kraal called Mujoga in Nord-Kivu, a province of Zaire. Mobuto, the Ruler for Life, later changed his mind and gave the country another name, the Democratic Republic of Congo. Along with the milk, touch, and scent of her mother, Virginie first became aware of things of beauty—the reds and golds of long fabrics worn by women who came back in the village balancing loads of firewood on their heads, and the lush green of the savannah and haloes of smoke on the summit of Nyiragongo. One day she would associate the circles of smoke with the rings of Saturn.

There was no center of town in Mujoga kraal. It was a scattering of small farmsteads connected by tribe, mostly. Their eggs and most of their meat came from guinea fowl. Virginie's father Mwykiza milked the female goats and occasionally dug a pit and roasted a kid goat or crippled calf. Her mother Sifa gardened manioc for its starch and cocoyam for the edible leaves and root, but their staple was *kwave*, casaba melon fruit cooked in banana leaves. Virginie heard the roar of lions at night, and when she heard the trumpeting of the roving elephant herds, she knew they would wreck trees, and in the fields, they tossed their casaba melons like tennis balls.

Three sprawling wilderness and wildlife preserves were divided by the boundaries of Zaire, Rwanda, and Uganda. Mwykiza was then a ranger in Zaire's Virunga Mountains National Park. Of the bamboo groves and dense jungle near the summit, Mwykiza told her about rare golden monkeys, whose thick coat was just as often red or auburn. They dashed about chattering and turning somersaults, jesters of the rain forest. Up there, too, were silverback gorillas, and Virginie remembered seeing one, a baby carried on the hip of a white man who waited on a Goma ferry dock of Lake Kivu. Her father wished he was still a park ranger, and he courteously scolded the white man. He said he was rescuing the infant gorilla, not stealing it. Poachers had shot its parents and butchered them where they lay. Hidden by its mother, the gorilla would have been choice bush meat. The baby gorilla on the white man's hip wore a strange garment Virginie came to know as diapers.

Virginie's father had been forced to give up the prestige and pay of being a park ranger because armed gangs of rebels and poachers set up camps on Nyiragongo, and from their outposts they raided Congolese army camps and terrorized cattle and goat herders and their families on its plateaus. In the fighting that caused Mobuto to disband the rangers and close the park, making it lawless, Mwykiza came back with bloodstains on his machete and wouldn't talk about it. He feared the consequences if anyone knew, even his wife.

Lives of children are prefigured by events that occurred long before they were conceived. Virginie's destiny arose from a half-mythical wilderness and the reign of a lavishly bearded king of Belgium called Leopold the Second. Unable to convince his parliament to join the battle for colonies in Africa, Leopold proclaimed a personal fiefdom called the Congo Free State in 1885. After twenty-three years of chaos, brutality, and untaxed private riches, the Belgian parliament finally declared it a colony called the Belgian Congo.

That didn't mean Leopold gave up his claim to the Congo's 905,000 square miles of jungle, savanna, and mountains. He didn't give up his dream inspired by the Welsh explorer Sir Henry Morton Stanley. He named the capital Leopoldville, the future Kinshasa, in honor of himself. Divided by one of the world's great rivers, the Congo then offered about all that one could want to exploit from a conquered land—gold, diamonds, copper, cobalt, zinc, uranium, plantations of rubber trees, ivory tusks of elephants. The Belgian king set up a "colonial trinity" of rule by private companies, Catholic priests, and strong-armed military. Leopold's outlook toward people native in that sprawling land never varied from a speech he made when he was agitating in Europe on behalf of his proposed colony.

> Teach the niggers to forget their heroes and to adore only ours. Never present a chair to a black that comes to visit you. Don't give him more than one cigarette. Never invite him for dinner even if he gives you a chicken every time you arrive at his house. . . .Your action will be directed essentially to the younger ones, for they won't revolt when the recommendation of a priest is contradictory to the parents' teachings. The children have to learn to obey what the missionary recommends, the father of their souls. You must singularly insist on their total submission and obedience, avoid developing the spirits in the schools, teach students to read and not to reason; evangelize the niggers so that they stay forever in submission to the white colonialists, so they never revolt against the restraints they are undergoing. Recite every day: "Happy are those who are weeping because the kingdom of God is for them."

The number of Congolese murdered under Leopold's watch was estimated at ten million. The old tyrant's death, Hitler's effortless conquest of Belgium, and the collapse of European colonial empires around the world brought self-rule to the Congo in 1960. Five years later a lieutenant general, Mobuto Sese Seko, gained power by leading a coup and executing the new nation's communist first prime minister, Patrice Lumumba. In revolt Simbas, or "lions" in Swahili, seized vast territory in the eastern Congo and declared a secessionist state called the People's Republic of Congo.

Three hundred warriors armed with nothing but spears and bows and arrows followed a witch doctor into the streets of the city then called

Stanleyville, in honor of the Welsh explorer. Though outnumbered five to one, the Simbas sent the army of Mobuto's regime running with their weapons thrown aside. The worst Simbas were *jeunesse,* gangs of street youths who took pleasure in dismembering and disemboweling Congolese accused of consorting with Europeans. In Stanleyville, later renamed Kisangi, the Simbas took hostage about two thousand American and Belgian consular officials, missionaries, businessmen, and their families. They forced nuns into hard labor in the fields they captured.

On the other side of the fray, *les affreux,* or "dreadful ones," were white mercenaries led by "Mad Mike" Hoare, a former British army major and safari guide. Hoare was ethnic Irish and branded his recruits the "Wild Geese" in honor of Irish mercenaries who fought in European wars for three centuries. Mobuto didn't like relying on white mercenaries, but his army was hopeless. In one battle, outnumbered Wild Geese led by a South African lieutenant watched Mobuto's army escorts break and run, and the Simbas and their witch doctor marched at them with no cover and total confidence. "They have no fear of death," said the lieutenant. "We just walked slowly up the hill, firing as we went. It was like a shooting gallery." The Simba rebels were shocked that the witch doctor's magic hadn't turned the bullets to water; there must have been some mix-up in cooking the porridge. Still they kept coming. If you can't see what imperils you, a certain logic holds that it doesn't exist. Only when the witch doctor went down did the Simba rebels run for their lives.

The Congolese soldiers reemerged from the bush and commenced a traditional massacre of vengeance called *ratissage.* Ignoring that, Hoare's commandos planned a three-pronged attack to rescue the diplomats and missionaries with support from Belgian paratroopers. Simba radio in Kisangi, the renamed Stanleyville, railed at the warriors of the breakaway state: *"Sharpen your knives! Sharpen your machetes! If the paras drop from the sky, kill the foreigners. Do not wait for orders."* The Wild Geese overran the city, freed the hostages, and then looted all the liquor stored in the hotels. Hoare shrugged at the frenzy he'd set loose and the bloodshed in the streets. Most of his Geese were Rhodesians and South Africans, though one German commando had been a Wehrmacht captain. He wore an Iron Cross with a swastika and allowed his troops to decorate their Jeeps with shields and heads of rebels they killed. One Goose shot a camp cook when he found a monkey's hand in his soup.

CHAPTER 42

For all its natural beauty the earth itself could be the killer. Nyiragongo was southernmost in a range of eight volcanic peaks that Congolese had once called Mufumbiro, "mountains that cook." The two volcanoes that were still active stood close together in Zaire's now theoretical national park. Mujoga rested on a plateau of Nyiragongo, whose summit contained a crater enclosing a lake of molten lava. Virginie was old enough to remember the day that two sides of the mountain cracked like an eggshell, and the lake emptied within an hour. The most fluid lava stream on earth raced down the mountain at about sixty miles an hour. The stream ran six feet deep and four soccer fields across. The intense heat caused kraals nearest the flow to pop aflame like matches being struck.

The kraal of Virginie's family was spared, but there could be no staying put. The mountain rumbled and shook and sent their livestock running. Virginie was then an only child. Taking turns holding her, her parents fled the mountain on foot. Whole villages and their occupants were consumed by the river of fire. At the foot of the mountain the provincial capital of Nord-Kivu, Goma, was a rag-tag string of squat shelters along the shore of vast Lake Kivu. The lava crossed the airport's runway, burned up the small district of markets and shops, blew up a petrol station, and with a great hiss of steam dug a new gouge in the lakebed of volcanic rock. Thousands of people fled across the border into the nearby Rwandan town of Gisenyi. Vents within the stream's path released pants of sulfur, and in those cracks, relief agency workers in helicopters could see the lava's glowing threats to erupt again. People ran across lava that was still hot, trying to reach families on the western shore of Goma.

Why would Virginie's family go back up such a dangerous mountain, with the lava lake already filling up again? Because camps for the displaced persons of Goma and Gisenyi were intolerable. Water treatment plants and lines were ruined, and from a thin layer of topsoil above the volcanic bedrock, heavy rains fed contaminants from latrines and cemeteries into the lake water, which came to the camps untreated in buckets, animal bladders, and rusty tanks hauled by the few available trucks. Cholera and dysentery took out old ones and children first. And from long ago, tales had been passed down that when Kivu, one of the Great Lakes of Africa, was roiled by earthquake or invasions of lava it belched from its depths bubbles of poisonous air. Science explained the phenomenon as methane and carbon dioxide, but in Swahili, *mazukos* were the "evil winds" that suffocated people.

Virginie's father took up the life of a herder again, and he restocked their herd of cattle and goats. Like everyone else, Mwykiza claimed his animals from memory and eyesight, not brands, which led to disputes, bitterness, and violence with tribal kin. They came back up the slopes of Nyiragongo and reclaimed Mujoga because herding cattle and goats, growing a large garden, and taking water from clear-running springs and creeks was how they knew to stay alive. They came back for the shades of pink and red the lava reflected on night skies, cloudy or clear. And because they believed the spirits of their ancestors dwelled in that lake of fire.

CHAPTER 43

Six months had passed since Kenny's nightmare in Caracas, and I hadn't heard from him. I tried to call him a few times, and when he didn't call me back it wounded me, considering how badly it might have gone for me and his parents down there, but he had to heal in his own way. I knew he'd skidded to fifth in the rankings and he made himself get back in the ring just three months after the loss to George. He took a ten-round fight in the Seattle hometown of Boone "Boom Boom" Kirkman, a great white hope until Foreman got hold of him. By the seventh round Kenny had Kirkman face down on the canvas, bleeding. He got up and staggered to his corner; the ref wouldn't let him come out for more.

Later I read that Don King was trying to promote a fight with Kenny against the Argentine Oscar Bonavena. But I was busy in my own life, trying to get myself and the band to the next level of income, if not celebrity, and repair the damage I'd done to my marriage. Kenny finally called me. It was awkward at first, with chat about obligations and prospects and the challenges of being a dad and a stepdad, then he asked, "How are you and Sabine?"

"Some ups and downs. The usual. How are you and Jackie?"

"Great," he enthused. "We just got married."

"I'm glad to hear that, Kenny," I said. "Congratulations. Both of you."

That let us ease more gracefully into his boxing. I remembered Bonavena handing his garish green sport coat to a flunky in Caracas and pawing across the ropes at Ali. I said, "You could handle him, couldn't you?"

"Of course I could. But that fight won't happen. Some fight hacks tried to make Bonavena into a terror but he's through. He knows it. Besides, I just turned down a quarter-million-dollar fight against Jerry Quarry."

"What? You told me you want to fight him. Bust him up."

"Yeah, but he can wait. Some people liked the way I look on camera and cast me in a movie."

"You're acting?'

"Why not? The money's good and my trainer and money people told me I was as good as ever against Kirkman. While I'm doing this I'll stay in shape, have some fun, and I'll be back in the hunt when the film's wrapped."

Film wraps. They already had him talking the talk.

"What's it about?" I said.

"Can't tell you. Terms of my contract, I can't say a word about the script. It's adapted from a novel that sold four and a half million copies in the fifties and was made into a play in New York."

Kenny stayed out of boxing nine months while taking acting lessons and trying to apply them on the set. Meanwhile King announced in his persistent way that he would promote a double bill with Kenny against Bonavena and Ali against the Bleeder Chuck Wepner. As Kenny predicted, Oscar pulled out two weeks before the fight, saying he had a liver infection. It pissed off Kenny because he had been training hard for the chore. That's what he thought of Oscar in the ring, a chore.

In Honolulu, Jerry Quarry had just won a decision over Scrap Iron Johnson. Trying to hold the card together, King begged him to take a fight against Kenny in Madison Square Garden. It didn't take much begging because Quarry was in shape, he needed the money, and he didn't like Kenny. With the movie in post-production, Kenny took the fight because if he won he was back in title contention. A few weeks before the bout, Kenny called again. He told me his trainer Bill Slayton thought he needed more work before he took on Quarry. In March 1975, Slayton arranged a warm-up fight against Rico Brooks at an Oklahoma City Red Carpet Inn.

Kenny asked, "Do you know the town?"

"A little. It's not a movie lot in Hollywood."

"Hey, don't get started. I get enough of that from the sports page hacks in New York. They love Quarry because he's Irish."

"You ever heard of Bat Masterson?" I said.

"Old West gunfighter? Wasn't there a TV series? Why?"

"When he was a kid, he was a skinner for buffalo hunters, a filthy job that almost got him killed by Comanches. He was a trigger-happy lawman and big-time gambler in Kansas, Colorado, and Arizona. Then one day he realized he had no more Old West to shoot up. He went to New York, became a pal of Teddy Roosevelt, and was the top boxing writer in America for forty years. John L. Sullivan, Gentleman Jim Corbett, Jack Dempsey, he knew them all. He hated Jack Johnson and coined the term 'great white hope.'"

Kenny laughed. "All right. Thanks for that. I'll try to use it."

"You're welcome."

"How far is it from Austin to Oklahoma City?"

"About four hundred miles."

"Why don't you come up and see me take care of Brooks, and then go on with me to New York and the Garden? I could use a smart boxing writer working with me. You know, turn out press releases with some spark in them. The publicist that King's got working the fight is hopeless. I can make it worth your while. It'll be fun."

The moment he said that, I toyed with the idea of trying to find Ann in Oklahoma City. On second thought, a terrible idea. "What's this guy's record?"

He chuckled. "Ten wins, twenty-one losses, and two draws."

"Kenny, you've got no shame."

"Oh, Slayton likes him. Says he upset a contender one time. Haid, I'd really like for you to do this. I shouldn't have been quiet all this time. I'd like to see you."

I made the drive up the interstate to Oklahoma City, which has the sprawl and freeways of Los Angeles but none of its charm. Kenny wasn't staying in the hotel where he'd be fighting. I checked in his hotel across a freeway from the Cowboy Hall of Fame museum. The hotel's lobby was gussied up with mounted longhorn heads, rodeo photos galore, bales of hay, and coils of lariat. A country band, the kind I called hat acts, was setting up to play. In my room I called Kenny, who said, "See you in the bar downstairs in fifteen minutes?"

The bar was dark and muffled enough that the twang of a George Strait imitator didn't hound us. Kenny looked great and was growing back the mustache he had to shave for the movie. He asked the waitress for a glass of soda with a twist of lime. I had a double shot of Bushmills on ice. It had been a harried drive. For a moment he moved the glass of soda around in his big hands. "Haid, Pop didn't tell me until two weeks ago about those kidnappers in Caracas."

"Oh."

"Yeah. You've been thinking I'm an ungrateful jerk. I mean you could have told me, but it's my business to find out things like that. I'm sorry. It's no way to treat a friend."

"Well, there was the fight, and you got hijacked and extorted by the president of Venezuela. Not many people have that on their resumés."

His smile was wistful. "This movie thing has been good for me. Critics may say it stinks, but it kind of took my mind off Caracas. I still lie awake at night playing the fight over and over, what I remember of it. What could I have done different? Ali beat him. Why couldn't I?" I sipped some whiskey, saddened by his drift.

"At first I was sky high on adrenaline," he said. "I went out jabbing, then I got him with a right uppercut and got a big noise from the crowd. But it was like hitting an eighteen-wheeler. In the corner Slayton told me everything was going to plan. Why, both rounds were nightmares. I sort of recall getting up and trying to make it to my corner, but Bill threw the towel and came through the ropes and grabbed me." He sighed and said, "Now I'm back on hunger street. If it hadn't been for the movie, I think I would have retired."

"What's up with your psychologist?"

He smiled. "I talk to him. He asks if I want him to hypnotize me. I tell him, 'Not yet. I'm afraid you'll put me back in that fight, and I'll never get out.'"

"Kenny, George rescued your parents and me in Caracas. I'd be dead, and God knows what would have happened to them."

"I know that. I'll thank him some day. Right now, I just want him out of my life, out of my mind. Power to the fucker. He knocked me out."

"Would you fight him again?"

"Ah, nobody would pay to see it. My business is prizefights, and the fights dictate the prizes. Another fight with Ali is what I've got a real shot at. It's all I want. With Ali you can remind yourself that boxing is a sport. But it's not a game. It's no goddamn game."

I signaled to the waitress that I wanted another drink.

"What do you say about coming to New York?" he said. "Quarry is a huge fight for me. We'd have some fun. My parents ask about you. They'd like to see you. And I'm getting hammered in the press up there. They call Quarry the 'Bellflower Bomber.' Carry on like he came right off the boat, like he's one of those Irish kids driving the tourist carriages in Central Park. Bullshit. He grew up in Bakersfield. Think about it, will you? I need a *white guy* taking up for me."

The bout against Rico Brooks was the third time I'd seen Kenny fight in person.

For knocking off some of Kenny's ring rust, Brooks got paid $3,500. Overnight guests of the Red Lion Inn eyed our small motley crowd with curiosity. Maybe five hundred fight fans and lowlifes gathered in the hall where a borrowed ring had been set up. A wedding party went on meanwhile, and a rock and roll cover band of Peter Frampton vein reverberated through the walls as the fighters climbed in the ring.

At 224 Kenny was bigger than I'd seen him, but he always looked sleek and muscled up. Brooks carried a slight gut at 214. When the bell rang, Brooks tried to glide and dance but got his feet tangled and stumbled. Kenny stalked him, slapping away a few punches flung his way. Halfway through the first round Kenny landed a jab followed by straight right and looked flabbergasted when Brooks went down and stayed down.

Slayton hurried over to see how Rico was. Brooks asked him, "How'd I do?"

"Aw, man," said Slayton, "I thought you might be hurt."

"He hit me pretty good but I coulda gotten up."

How'd he do? *Howdy Doody* could have done as well as that.

CHAPTER 44

Sabine wanted nothing to do with that, or me I supposed, though she loved New York. I flew alone and at the suggestion of Johnny Stafford checked in a hotel called the Mayflower. From the West Side it offered a grand view of Central Park. The Mayflower's clientele had been taken over by musicians and ad agency and movie business types, but not celebrities. The morning after I arrived, I was on the sidewalk looking up at the hotel's handsome blond lines and tall windows. A doorman who was hailing taxis for guests saw me craning my neck and said, "In the '29 market crash, bodies flew out of there."

I said, "Did you work here then?"

He smiled, stepped around me, and raised his hand at another cab.

I loved being on New York streets but I had a bit of a chip on my shoulder about the place. My small imprint on American music had been ignored here. When I had the boost of association with Leon Russell and his Shelter label, the *Village Voice* assigned a freelancer to write a feature about me and *Two Bubbles Off Plumb.* He apologized and claimed he wrote and revised it, but the piece got bumped from its culture pages for one about a hardback book being published with blank pages. Since then I hadn't had a nibble in New York.

I had a good time walking the vast park, admiring the sleek fast-moving women. I ate a street hot dog and that night had supper at the Ginger

Man. After first training in a little town up the Hudson River, Kenny had moved his training to a gym in Harlem. In Don King's double-header promotion, Kenny's bout was the undercard of Ali versus Chuck Wepner. That fight would come off in a suburb of Cleveland, King's home base, but in New York the Norton-Quarry fight was the main event.

Kenny was now ranked fourth and Quarry fifth, but King was paying Quarry $185,000 while Kenny's purse was $100,000. King's first offer of a fight with Quarry was going to get him $250,000. Adding to that irritation, Kenny disliked Quarry, who had been America's favorite heavyweight when Ali was in his draft limbo. Quarry maintained that *he* was always the top dog in Los Angeles. In the elimination tournament to succeed Ali he had won a narrow decision over Floyd Patterson, but had lost a decision to Jimmy Ellis, and he'd been stopped by George Chuvalo and stopped in all four of his fights with Frazier and Ali. With a record of fifty wins, seven losses, and four draws, Quarry had to win this one to stay relevant, but he was still dangerous.

Kenny was furious that Quarry chose to make an athletic contest into an issue of race and color. Quarry had claimed Ali, Foreman, Frazier, and Kenny were trying to "leave the little white boy out of it." In fact, he'd been busy against black contenders, taking a lopsided decision against Ron Lyle, undefeated until then, and he took out the fearsome puncher Earnie Shavers in the first round. Foreman got on Kenny's nerves by saying of the Shavers fight, "Quarry showed me he's a real tiger." At the press conference in Cleveland Kenny said of Quarry, "I respect him as a fighter but I don't like him one bit. I don't like him because he's a prejudiced man."

I wrote one press release that had Kenny reflecting on the old-time gunslinger Bat Masterson, his hatred of Jack Johnson, and now Quarry as the self-anointed Great White Hope. Given Quarry's complaints about blacks monopolizing the big money fights in the heavyweight division, the piece got Kenny a greater share of the publicity. But the reporters and photographers continued to congregate around Quarry's gym workouts. I didn't have all that much to do. When the press wasn't around, I hung out with Mike Weaver. I liked the guy. "Hercules," Kenny had nicknamed him, and if you saw him with or without a T-shirt you understood why. "How's your career going now?" I had asked him.

Mike spoke with a shy wag of his head. "Ah, I don't know. I'm just six and six. Got stopped my last time out by Duane Bobick, but hell, his record was twenty-three and zip. I'm thinking I should give it up, but Kenny stays after me, tells me to train harder and stop taking fights on short notice. The hardest I train is when I'm working for him."

Mike told me that Bill Slayton had trained Quarry in the amateurs and early in his pro career, and Kenny got mad when Slayton hugged members of Quarry's family at the press conference. "Slayton said, 'Hey, man, I've known the guy for years. We're friends. I wasn't telling him any secrets. This is what boxing is all about. Fight tonight, friends tomorrow.'"

Kenny's fight with Quarry was for twelve rounds, but nobody expected it to go that long. Though Kenny looked good in the gym, the no-contest with Rico Brooks had shown me nothing about his ring rust. Quarry was two years younger than Kenny and had a big-name trainer in Gil Clancy. Both Kenny and Quarry had to win this fight. It would be the end of the line for the loser unless he wanted to be a designated victim of up-and-comers. I fretted that Kenny might well lose. Then I saw the weigh-in. With auburn hair and sideburns, Quarry had been something of a pretty boy when Ali was in exile. Now his nose was ruined and his eyebrows and cheeks and brows wore ridges of scar tissue. Barrel-chested, thick around the waist, he raised his arms and flexed his biceps after stepping off the scales at 207. Kenny weighed 218 in his undershorts and he had an *eight-inch* reach advantage. Unless Kenny got careless, I didn't see how Quarry could overcome that.

In the dressing room Kenny seemed as calm as somebody going to the post office. Quarry had a person in the room to watch Slayton tape Kenny's hands. Weaver warmed Kenny up with the mitts. When they got that going it sounded more like bats connecting with baseballs than impacts of gloved hands. Slayton moved around them, not saying much. "Keep your right up," he said. "Remember his hook."

In the arena I had a chair beside the corner post with Slayton and the cut man. Kenny wore the blue robe he favored and blue shorts and white shoes. Quarry's robe was green and had "Irish Jerry Quarry" and a shamrock in white on the back, and he got a roar when he came through the ropes. The boos that greeted Kenny were mixed with a fair amount of cheers. I figured most of the people rooting for him were black. Madison

Square Garden had a seating capacity of over twenty thousand, and it looked full to me.

When they met for the ref's instructions Quarry fixed a glare on Kenny, who kept his head down, shifting weight as he always did. Jolts of Kenny's jab took a toll from the start. Quarry winged punches but couldn't seem to catch a rhythm or set his feet under them. He wasn't loose. But toward the end of the round Quarry landed a left hook to the body that sent Kenny backpedaling across the ring to the ropes. The crowd went wild and Quarry attacked, but Kenny defended himself well and took over again with a loud right uppercut and more hard jabs.

In the second round Quarry was landing body shots. In response to one, Kenny scored a chopping right that swayed Quarry and got a roar from the crowd. Quarry may have won the round on the cards but he was taking too much punishment from a bigger and stronger man. Kenny gave him a glove bump of acknowledgment after the bell.

In the third Kenny jarred him with a jab and a right cross, then one of his lefts sliced open the scar tissue at the end of Quarry's right eyebrow. It was a bad cut and the blood pooled in his eye. Quarry threw combinations in desperation, but Kenny was giving better than he got with short left hooks and the best right uppercuts I'd seen him throw.

The ring doctor came up and looked on as Clancy tried to close the cut. Quarry's left eye had started closing as well. Kenny seemed to tire just from the exertion of landing so many shots to Quarry's head. In the next round Kenny backed against the ropes and let Quarry whale away. It was the best defense I'd seen from Kenny, and he was winning the exchanges inside. He stepped away and scored with a right lead followed by a hook, then a jab and a right that drove Quarry back on his heels. At one point I heard one of the broadcasters' shout, "I don't think Norton's missed a single punch this round. They're *all* getting in."

By the fifth Kenny could have been just having fun pounding a heavy bag. Two minutes into the round he threw a four-punch combination that buckled Quarry's knees with every blow. With thirty seconds left Kenny followed a jab with a straight right that almost put Quarry down, and at last the ref jumped in and stopped it.

They embraced twice in what seemed a genuine way before Quarry left the ring. Kenny told me later that his hostility toward Quarry vanished the instant the ref stopped it.

But as I watched the fight, I kept thinking about Sarge's remark at Camp Pendleton that Kenny wasn't a cruel fighter. I wondered if that was true anymore. If it ever had been.

Slayton went over to Quarry's locker room after the fight and found him busted up, as Kenny promised. Sitting on a massage table, Quarry had to squint through swollen eyelids to see his old trainer. Quarry said, "Did I disgrace myself?"

Slayton told him, "You fought like a true Irishman."

Quarry retired after the Norton fight but couldn't stay with it. He fought four more times, losing his last one, a six-rounder, in a Holiday Inn Trade Center in Aurora, California, against an opponent who had won three of eight fights. Quarry lapsed into dementia, living with help of family and Social Security. He died at fifty-three of complications of pneumonia and brain damage. His gravestone in Shafter, California, reads "The Great White Hope."

After the fight I had delivered Kenny to the lead TV broadcaster, who asked him how he thought Ali's fight against Chuck Wepner would go. "Oh, I'm an Ali fan," Kenny said. "I like Ali." The man said his team had heard from Ohio that the champ had been watching his fight with Quarry. "Well," Kenny said, "I hope he was impressed."

In Richfield, Ohio, Ali made $1.6 million in his first title defense since upsetting Foreman in Zaire. Wepner was thirty-six, stood six-five, and weighed 225. He'd then won thirty-one of forty-three fights. The face of the Bayonne Bleeder bore scar tissue from the beating that Sonny Liston and many other heavyweights had given him. Yet against Ali it was Wepner's night in a weird way. Ali punished him lazily and was booed for covering up and letting the big guy bang away on his arms. In the ninth round Wepner stepped on the champ's foot and knocked him down, which shot me back to my foul of Kayron Coger in the Texas Golden Gloves. Coger was now on the downhill side of a B-minus career in the pros. Embarrassed, Ali turned up the volume and pace, and the ref stopped it with twenty seconds left in the fifteenth.

Word went around that Sylvester Stallone got his inspiration for the *Rocky* script from watching Wepner fight Ali. I wondered if Stallone cut him in on the movie money. A buzz was stirring in Hollywood about

Kenny's approaching debut as an actor. At first Kenny said he'd play Stallone's character Apollo Creed in *Rocky,* but then he begged off, saying he had too many scheduling conflicts. I figured the real reason was that he couldn't stomach playing Muhammad Ali, even a fictionalized one.

In the year since the disaster in Caracas, in addition to Kenny's new sideline of acting, he stopped seven straight opponents with credible records. Only his defeat of Ali matched the Quarry fight in sealing his reputation. George was still out there, but Kenny stated his preference for a third fight for Ali. If Ali was reluctant, Kenny thought that sooner or later he could force one of the commissions to declare a mandatory title defense against him.

The champ was elusive, though. His promise to retire after beating Foreman had gone away the minute it left his mouth. And how could he quit? Don King and foreign potentates were throwing millions of bucks his way. Ali and Joe Frazier had beaten each other, and for the money and pride and ego they *had* to fight again.

In October 1975 the "Thrilla in Manila" actually came off in the crowded Philippine suburb of Quezon City. Harder for King to work his rhyme schemes into that. So it could be telecast prime time on American TV, the fight began at 10:45 in the morning. Ali was one week away from his thirty-third birthday. At the start of the seventh round, as Frazier burrowed inside, Ali tied him up and said, "Joe, they told me you was all washed up."

Frazier said, "They lied."

Joe dominated the middle rounds. Ali had trouble holding him off with his jabs and combinations and a brief trial of rope-a-dope. Joe wasn't buying it. He bobbed and weaved and battered Ali's head, ribs, and midsection. The tropical heat was intense, and Ali hadn't trained hard enough. But in the tenth round Joe started to wear down from the pace, and in the eleventh Ali's punches had both of Joe's eyes almost closed. Joe wanted that fight so badly that he had gone ahead with it knowing he had a cataract on his left eye. Ali realized Joe couldn't see through that eye anymore. Ali went after it with straight rights, his feet set firm beneath him, before dancing away again. In the thirteenth round Ali put together a combination that sent Joe's mouthpiece flying. Kenny's former trainer, Eddie Futch, told Joe on the stool he couldn't go out for the fourteenth round. Joe yelled, "I want him, boss!"

"It's all over," Futch said. "Nobody will ever forget what you did today."

Ali rose from his stool, raised his arms, then collapsed and lay on his back a long time. He said afterward that he never felt so close to dying. *The Ring* magazine declared it the best boxing match of all time.

It took a while for *Mandingo* to reach an Austin theater. I told Sabine I was off to rehearse with the band when I went to the movie. I knew she'd hate it. *Mandingo* was the brainchild of a California writer named Kyle Onstott. A judge of dog shows, he first wrote a book with his son about breeding dogs. Wanting to make some money off his writing, he turned to the breeding of slaves. He found a small Virginia publisher that would publish his novel in 1957. *Mandingo* was a surprise bestseller and adapted into a play in New York. Onstott didn't live to see the movie produced by Dino de Laurentis, whose credits included the much-praised *Serpico* starring young Al Pacino. This one starred James Mason, the Brit with the elegant voice in *A Star Is Born, 20,000 Leagues Under the Sea,* and *Lolita.* To me, this performance was one more lesson that actors can and will do anything they're paid for.

Mason played a Louisiana slave plantation owner named Maxwell in the 1840s. He had rheumatism and found that sitting in a rocking chair and resting his feet against the bare torso of a slave boy relieved the pain in his feet. His son Hammond fell for a cousin Blanche played by Susan George, best known then as a half-willing rape victim in Sam Peckinpah's *Straw Dogs.* Like Mason she was British, and together they massacred accents of the American South. Hammond bought himself a "bed wench" played by a beautiful black actress, Brenda Sykes, whose role required her to be pawed on naked by Hammond. There was a great deal of nudity, most of it black. On finding their wedding night that she was no virgin, Hammond declared he would have nothing more to do with her. She pounded her hands on a bed and screamed, *"Never! Never! Never!"*

Trapped on the plantation, Blanche turned into a miserable drunk. Kenny didn't enter the movie as a slave named Mede until its midpoint. He appeared on a slave dock clean-shaven, looking almost boyish. A stocky woman with a sunbonnet and bad German-English accent stuck her hand down Kenny's shorts and made awestruck comments about his equipment. Hammond outbid the woman for $3,500 and brought home Mede. The word "Mastah" appeared in almost all of Kenny's lines.

In most scenes he had his shirt off, and he played a slave fighter in the movie. His bouts were of the wrestling, gouging, and rolling in the dirt variety. He won the climax battle by ripping out another man's jugular with his teeth.

Blanche sent for Mede and ordered him to come in her bedroom and she locked the door. "I want you to listen to me 'cause I'm a gonna tell you a story. Listen good. You hear me? Sit down," she said, pointing at the bed. "See, one day I was a walkin' along in the woods. Just a walkin' by myself. And then you came up behind me, real sweet like. And all of a sudden you attacked me."

Kenny cried, "Miz Blanche, I nevah . . . "

"Shut your mouth. This is my story. You attacked me. You raped me. And I'm a gonna tell my husband."

"He won't believe you, Miz Blanche."

"Oh, he'll believe me. He won't believe a nigger. And he won't sell you. He'll kill you. So, 'lessen you do what I want, I'm a gonna tell him the truth. Mede, ain't you ever craved a white lady before?" She began to unbutton his pants and shirt. Most of the nudity involved Kenny, but there was one explicit scene of their pantomimed screwing. He told me that doing that over and over for the director and crew was very strange and got old.

The story line had Mede getting Blanche pregnant that day. When a physician delivered the mulatto infant, the doctor killed it at once. In a rage Hammond asked the doc for the poison he used on old slaves and horses. He poured it into Blanche's whiskey. Then he blasted Kenny's Mede with a shotgun and finished him off in a cauldron of boiling water, shoving him under with a pitchfork. The movie ended at just over two hours with a rebel slave shooting Mason's old man Maxwell and his son weeping, "Papa, papa, papa."

I understood why Kenny was forbidden to say anything about the script. Though a few critics hailed *Mandingo* as a Blaxploitation classic, the great majority howled in derision. In a *Saturday Night Live* skit that Sabine and I happened to catch, O.J. Simpson played Mede and Bill Murray played Blanche in a send-up of the seduction scene. It ended with Murray French-kissing a cow. Sabine said, "That was in Kenny's movie?"

"I don't know," I said. "I haven't seen it."

CHAPTER 45

I should have known something was up when Sabine started taking a greater interest in my music. She seldom played my records after they first came out, but she began to ask to go to out-of-town gigs with us. I told her she wouldn't be entertained by long hauls in our van and funky motel rooms. We didn't exactly travel in the style of the Rolling Stones.

The building where we rehearsed was a place of obscene grime and clutter. The easy chairs and sofas were split and leaked stuffing. When we opened the door, we were often greeted by odor from an untended pizza box. Large wood roaches scuttled. When Sabine said she'd like to just watch us rehearse, I tried to discourage her. "You'd never think the same of us again. It's a dump."

"Oh, bosh," she said with a laugh. "I've seen campaign headquarters."

"Our digs make them look like palaces."

When I relented and told her I'd take her, she insisted on driving herself. She arrived in a filmy dress, bare at the shoulders, pearls and earrings, and higher heels than she usually wore. "Good god," she said, taking in our habitat.

"I warned you," I said, offering her the sofa.

Sunken deep in it, she couldn't help showing off her legs, and when she crossed them, she tossed the right slipper, gold in color, in time with the drummer and bass. She was a definite distraction. Jake was over the top that day, goofing around with solos that weren't part of our repertoire, and he cracked dumb jokes that only she laughed at. The other Rip Chords lost interest and grew disgusted. The rehearsal was a waste of time.

She called from her office a few days later and invited me to lunch. She said there was a new Italian place downtown that the dining-out zealots raved about. The place inside was dark and toney. She suggested we share an entrée of eggplant Parmesan. She knocked down her glass of pinot grigio pretty fast. I could never again stand eggplant Parmesan.

"I have something to tell you," she began. "I'm infatuated with Jake."

My mind spun through her legal associates and then I blinked. "Jake? Our Jake? The guitar player?"

"He's not *your* Jake. You don't own him."

I put my fork down hard enough it skittered on the table.

She said, "We're having an affair."

"Well, that's just fucking great—"

"It is great lovemaking, as a matter of fact."

"All right, I knew I'd never measure up to the English teacher who turned you on to Ambrose Bierce and abused a minor in grand style."

"Fuck off."

"You keep saying that."

"You ran around on me."

"You're right, I did. Once. I can never be sorry enough."

"Who was she?"

"Her name was Clarinda. Ask around if you want; she's moved on from Austin. You might have seen her, but you wouldn't have noticed because you're not interested in anyone but yourself." I gave my hands a loud clap, and a few people glanced at us. "So, there you have it, my confession and shame. Your turn. How long has this been going on?"

"Since you went to Venezuela."

My voice rose and drew more looks from the lunch crowd. "You're not just breaking up our marriage. You're breaking up my goddamn band!"

She sighed. "I'm not necessarily breaking up our—"

"Oh. You're just *trying out* this jerk that gets paid by me."

"I like the way his eyes crinkle when he laughs."

"God, you're shallow."

"And you're violent and mean. You get your rocks seeing men punch each other."

I tossed my napkin on her eggplant goo and stood. "I'm gone is what I am."

When she came in our front door it was past six o'clock.

"Where's Emily?" I asked. "She didn't come home from school."

"I called Russ and asked him if she could spend the night there. I knew how it was going to be with you."

"Thanks for letting me know. I worried."

She made herself a scotch and sat at our dinner table, looking at the live oak trees that sloped down to a creek beyond our fence. I laid a check in front of her and said, "Tell your lover boy he's fired."

"You'd better not hurt him."

"Hurt him? What makes you think I'd do that? I can't speak for the others. We just had an album go down the sink."

"You have an awful temper. You scare me."

"Bullshit. Have I ever once in anger laid a hand on you?"

"You spent a year trying to kill people. You must have liked it, because you keep those dog tags in our chest of drawers."

"I thought maybe someday I'd get them bronzed, like the little shoes of that baby we wanted to have."

"Oh, you," she said. "You asshole." She went in our bedroom, came back out, and with a clunk laid the Brazilian-made .38 revolver on the table.

After a moment I said, "You looked hard to find that."

"I was telling an intern at the office who's into quilting that your grandmother made one out of your baby shirts. She said she'd like to see it." Her pause was deadly.

"How could you? Emily lives in this house. *My child.*"

"Okay, you're right. Call the police."

"What?"

"I said call the cops. You've got me. Felon in possession of a firearm. That'll get me two to ten years."

"What are you talking about? A felon?"

"You heard me. I was court-martialed and convicted of aggravated assault when I was twenty years old. The marines sentenced me to four years in the brig, hard time. Vietnam was their idea of parole."

She put her face in her hands. "How can you hide all these things from me?"

I stuck the muzzle in the web of flesh in my reconstructed hand and pulled the trigger. She shrieked and spun away. I broke open the gun's cylinder and slid it across the table. "There are no bullets in the house. Never have been."

"You kept that wrapped in your granny's quilt!"

"I didn't know you pried. There's a reason I went to Venezuela while you and Jake got down to business. Kenny asked me to come down there and protect his parents from harm. He didn't trust the security guys assigned to him, and he was right. I would have been shot and killed if it wasn't for George Foreman. Kenny asked me for the kind of help you'd only ask of a friend."

"What you just said makes no sense at all. George Foreman? Are you a boxers' groupie? I'm disgusted by all the testosterone in your life."

"You keep a meter on Jake? Does he sleep with his Serpent? I've wondered."

"Why don't you just *go away?*"

"No, you get the hell out. You're the one leaving me."

CHAPTER 46

Don King and Bob Arum, who now wielded enormous power in boxing, knew that with talent so deep in the heavyweight division, money could be made promoting non-title fights. They loved Eliminator bouts that came with unenforceable promises that the winners would get title fights against the champions they promoted. King was especially smitten by Oscar Bonavena, who had become a favorite in New York. He almost always went the distance, whoever he was fighting, and he put paying customers in the seats.

Oscar nicknamed himself Ringo and bragged that he was the Argentine Beatle. Pretty young women were seen with him on the streets of Manhattan. He fought with feet planted wide on chunky legs and slugged away in the old-time style of, say, Max Baer.

He beat up George Chuvalo. But he had been beaten twice by Joe Frazier and once by Ali's Louisville friend and former sparring partner Jimmy Ellis, who put Oscar on the canvas twice and took the decision in a tournament to succeed Ali when his titles were withdrawn. When Ali's banishment ended, he fought Oscar in Madison Square Garden. The Argentine whaled away gamely but Ali knocked him down three times in the last round, an automatic technical knockout. The aging ex-champ Floyd Patterson overcame a knockdown by Oscar and rallied in the last two rounds to win that decision. Oscar's record was fifty-eight wins, nine losses, and a draw. He belonged in the room of the top heavyweights but was never really a player.

Still, King announced an Eliminator bout pitting Oscar against Kenny, with the winner earning another bout with Ali. Kenny couldn't have been more disgusted. Oscar had already missed his chance, pulling out of a fight with him over a professed liver disorder, which was plausible given his intake of booze. Now King positioned Oscar as yet another obstacle to a third fight with Ali.

One afternoon as I was preparing to pick up Emily at school, Kenny called. We talked briefly, then he said, "I've got something to tell you that's funny but it's not."

"Knock me out, please."

"Oscar Bonavena was shot and killed outside a whorehouse in Nevada."

"What? How?"

"You sound like Tonto and the Lone Ranger." He said Oscar had moved his base and social life from New York to Vegas, which brought a small-time gangster and brothel owner named Joe Conforte into the picture. Conforte had immigrated from Sicily back in the thirties. He was a cab driver in Oakland who pimped prostitutes for sailors and marines and saw the real money was in owning the premises. He moved his operation into Nevada, and his first whorehouse was a house trailer. When local cops and sheriffs got after him, he just moved the trailer to another county.

He tried to blackmail a district attorney that was giving him trouble. The DA had Conforte's whorehouse burned to the ground, gave his evidence to a US attorney, so the Sicilian did two years for income tax evasion. But when he got out, a county outside Vegas let him open Nevada's first legal whorehouse.

The Mustang Bridge Ranch had a hundred rooms and a five-hundred-acre compound. Oscar was then living in a double-wide, but he made the party when the brothel opened. Oscar had a big head and a big mouth and smoked big cigars. He waved one around that night and asked people, "How you like my joint?"

He thought he could do that because he had taken up with Conforte's wife Sally, a plump onetime looker with a helmet of heavily sprayed platinum hair. She was twenty-five years older than Oscar. He named Sally his business manager and was under the mistaken impression that banging her negated Joe Conforte's community property rights.

"Oscar wasn't afraid of her husband being a gangster?"

"Nah. Oscar's parents were Italian immigrants to Argentina, and anybody who'd gone fifteen rounds with Ali wasn't afraid of some old Sicilian."

He went on that Conforte sent word for them to get out of his whorehouse and stay out. When they didn't heed his advice, a Conforte bodyguard wrecked Oscar's trailer house and burned everything he had, including his passport. A couple of days later Conforte sent a courier to Oscar with six thousand dollars in cash and a one-way ticket to Argentina. Oscar was a hero in his homeland, but he had to have a passport to re-enter. He could have gone to a consulate and gotten a replacement, but his mind didn't work that way. He got drunk and blew the six thousand playing blackjack and roulette in a Vegas casino.

And with King's Eliminator against Ken Norton already announced by Don King, in late May 1976, he and Sally rolled out to the whorehouse in Sally's Mustang. The perimeter had two prison-like security towers and fences with enough juice to electrocute the wildlife that sometimes tried to bang or wriggle through it. Willard Bryner, the bodyguard who had burned Oscar's trailer, was on duty that morning with a hunting rifle. He called out, "You two better clear out now."

Instead Oscar swaggered away from the car, dropped the airline ticket on the ground, and pissed on it. That was his last act. He died where the rifle slug dropped him, and officers found a pistol in his boot. In hysterics, Sally claimed the cops planted it, but the pistol belonged to her. Joe Conforte wound up deported to Italy, and a jury would aquit Oscar's killer on grounds of self-defense.

I said, "How do you know all this, Kenny?"

"Oh, there's already a movie pitch going around. Talk of Helen Mirren playing the madam. See? I keep feeding you all this material. If you'd just write the songs, you'd be packing them in at Caesar's Palace."

I sang *Just goes to show, Ringo shoulda been working on his mojo . . .*

His laugh was quiet and easy. "That's cold, man."

"Not as cold as you. This is good news for you."

"I hate you put it that way. I got my standards. But I think I've got Ali cornered now. The only way out is for him to retire. And he won't do that."

As always, he asked about Sabine. I told him we were separated and likely headed for divorce. "*What?*" he said. "Oh, man, I hate that. I like that girl."

"So do I, most of the time. But there's not much I can do about it."

"Separated—does that mean you talk to her?"

"Just about Emily, my stepdaughter, who's staying with me some of the time, and when we do talk it's always strained. She left me for another guy. Member of my band."

"Well, fuck," he said. "But don't give up on her. I was around her enough to think she's worth it. I bet there's plenty of blame to go around. There usually is."

He called again a week later and again asked how Sabine and I were doing. "Hard to be optimistic," I said.

"Well, listen, I've got an intuitionist out here. He tells me not to worry too much about you two."

"An intuitionist? Where do you find these people, Kenny? But tell him thanks. I'd take help from a Ouija board."

"Listen, I gotta run. Things are happening here. I think I've got Ali cornered."

Bob Arum wrestled the promotion from Don King, who negotiated a title match for fifteen rounds in Yankee Stadium. At stake was Ali's undisputed heavyweight title. He was guaranteed six million while Kenny got one million. Kenny told me the split didn't really bother him. This one was for more than money. But when?

As soon as the contracts were signed, Ali took off on a junket to Japan. Introduced at a convention of the Japanese Amateur Wrestling Association, he popped off, "Isn't there any Oriental fighter who will challenge me? I'll give him a million dollars if he wins." Ali talked himself into a spare six million for a farce against a wrestler in Tokyo. He may have imagined himself jabbing and tormenting a sumo wrestler into exhaustion, but he got Antonio Inoki, who spent the bout diving on the canvas and kicking. In the eleventh round Ali got tired of it and kicked him back. The Japanese ref gave *Ali* a warning.

When corner men press ice bags to stop a fighter's swelling, usually it's around the eyes. That night they applied the ice to the backs of Ali's thighs. He was kicked so much that Ferdie Pacheco, the ring doc on his team, feared he was going to get blood clots. People die from phlebitis; the clots can break up and destroy the lungs.

Kenny's big fight was on hold until the champ recovered and could train. Kenny had already started training in Massacre Canyon and didn't stop because of the fight's postponement. He said one night he just wanted to drive in, pay his respects to Ali in his Santa Monica hospital, and make sure he was okay. They both had been assigned the same publicist, a man named Irving, who insisted on getting involved. Irving passed on the request to Ali and said he wanted to bring Kenny up with maybe a few photographers.

Ali said, "Bring that sucker up here tomorrow, but I don't want no press around me when you do. No press. You hear?"

The publicist worked out a deal with writers and photographers who could gather on the first floor. Kenny would give them a couple minutes' time, go up and visit with the champ, and then Irving would come down with a report on how the fighters' meeting went. Kenny drove into the city, got to the hospital, and the press guys were all over Irving, begging him to take them up. Kenny and Irving shook loose of those guys, ducked in a gift shop and bought a Snoopy stuffed toy, handed it to Kenny as a gift for Ali, and they waited on the elevator with Kenny feeling like a fool, holding Snoopy.

They found Ali sitting on the edge of his bed in his pajamas and a bathrobe. Ali said, "Hey, Ken, baby, nice to see you." He cocked an eyebrow at Snoopy.

Kenny said, "How you doing, man? How they treating you?"

"I can't complain. Can't complain."

But Ali had too much nervous energy to rest easy in a hospital. He asked Irving, 'Where's the press?'

"Well, downstairs waiting on your statement. You said they couldn't come up."

Ali told Kenny, "C'mon. Let's go show those mothers we're still alive." As nurses gasped, Kenny pushed him down the hall in a wheelchair. Ali started in on Kenny's movies. "I'm not only twice the fighter you are, I'm *three times* a better actor. What am I going to call you? I know. I'll call you *Mandingo.*"

When they got off the elevator and the TV lights came on Kenny knew what to expect. "Bring him here!" Ali hollered. He rose from the wheelchair, hobbled toward Kenny, and yelled, "Let's see what you got!" He snapped out a real jab, though he aimed it over Kenny's shoulder. Ali steadied and started his routine. "I want a mike in the ring when we fight. We'll fight and we'll talk, and I'll destroy you."

Kenny knew the drill, as old as show business. He said, "Every time he takes a breath, I'm gonna put a fist in his mouth."

Irving was overjoyed. He thought he'd orchestrated a riveting story in the press.

"Hear that? Ken's really worked up a hatred for this guy. It's a vendetta."

They left Irving downstairs and Kenny wheeled Ali back to his room, where they found Ali's wife Veronica and her younger sister waiting. Veronica was Ali's third wife, and her sister was just as pretty. Kenny walked over to Ali's sister-in-law, held the champ in his gaze, and murmured to her, "Hey, Puddin'. You and I could make it good."

Ali unleashed a tirade of threats that ended when they all started laughing. They shook hands again and Kenny said, "Get well soon, Champ." He dropped off Irving and was driving back to Massacre Canyon when he turned on the radio to an LA station that aired sports programing. Ali was yelling, "I'll destroy Norton! You hear what I say? I'll destroy that man! He got knocked out by George Foreman and *I'm George Foreman's daddy!*"

CHAPTER 47

I dragged along lower than a skunk. The band was blown up, I feared for good. The Rip Chords were flummoxed by the development but musicians learn to roll with punches in the business. When somebody breaks a guitar string they improvise while he fixes it fast. Bands form, bands break up. I called Johnny and asked him to meet me for a drink.

"Jake's gone, period," I told him.

He nodded and said, "I get that."

"It's up to you guys what happens now. We've put in a ton of work, recorded two good albums, and the gigs are paying more and giving us a higher profile. Do we give that up? And if we don't, should we look for another guitarist or let you play all the lead? It would be more money for everyone." Johnny got back to me after a couple of days and said they wanted to hang together. They liked the sound we had. But on one condition—they wanted no part of my soap opera. Some wanted to remain friends with Jake. Others didn't care.

"Okay," I said. "It's a deal. But you guys have to find the other guitar player. I'm not thinking very well right now."

I was hearing music when I drove, when I fed Emily's cat Daisy, when I ate my lonely dinners. I was deep into questioning myself. Playing my harmonica or singing along with singers better than me brought no comfort. One afternoon the phone rang. I picked it up with my pulse racing, hoping it might be Sabine. It was Emily.

"Haid?" she said. She had called me that from the start.

"Hey, baby, how's it going?" I said.

In a small voice: "Have you heard from Mom?"

"No," I said. "Have you?"

"Yeah. But . . . can I come back and stay with you?"

Tears filled my eyes. "Of course you can."

"Dad loves me and I love him but he has too many rules. I miss being home. I miss Daisy. I miss you."

When I picked up Emily, Russ carried out her clothes and some toys and gave me a look that said: More than you'll ever know, *I understand.* Emily and I settled in, and it got better for both of us. I roused her in the mornings, made her breakfast of eggs scrambled with grated cheddar cheese, made sure she had her lunch money when I dropped her off at school, and in the evenings made dinner, helped her with homework if she asked, and when she said she was finished we watched whatever she wanted to watch on TV until bedtime.

As soon as that happened, my working life started to come back together. Joe Ely had gotten his start in his hometown of Lubbock, and the press and record producers were calling him the second coming of Buddy Holly. He always hired terrific guitar players. The Rip Chords and I convinced one, Phil Hauptman, to join us. Though Phil couldn't showboat like Jake, he brought us the dobro, a sound I loved, and from the start he and Johnny played like they'd grown up together. But we had to deliver a record to Cow House Creek in a hurry. We were doing all right in gigs, but we weren't ready for the recording studio.

One weekend we had a gig in a club on the Jacksboro Highway in Fort Worth. The club was big and rowdy but didn't feel dangerous. In a way the gig made me feel I'd finally arrived. I hadn't seen my parents in several months, so the next day I had the band drop me off in Dallas at Love Field, where I rented a car and drove the hundred miles of so to Daingerfield. It's pretty country up there in the nexus of Texas, Oklahoma, Louisiana, and Arkansas. Eleven years had passed since Pioneer Oil shut down its refinery in Deerinwater and forced the transfer away from the house Virginia and I grew up in. In Daingerfield Daddy was at last able to retire from that work and the night shifts he despised. The company gave him a fake gold watch, a paperweight, and an engraved beer mug, this to a lifelong teetotaler. He told me he was just going to fiddle around and play golf with friends he'd made there. Mom had worked her way into a job buying and stocking ladies' wear, as she put it, in a small department store. She talked about them going on a church cruise to Alaska. I thought they were doing well.

One day I drove Daddy over to Texarkana and north from there to the Ouachita Mountains. A winding scenic parkway had been built through the mountains into Oklahoma. Now the seasons were edging into fall, and I knew the leaves would be turning on the high slopes. After their bad luck in Deerinwater, it had been nice to see them fall back in love in a new start in another place. But as we wound through the hills Daddy started talking about Mom. "She's done so much, helped so much, I can never . . . " I looked over at him, and his eyes were full of tears. Such an open show of emotion was out of character. In hindsight that was the moment I knew the life of the gruff and often fiery refinery hand and baseball coach I'd known was changing.

I stayed with them three days, then drove back over to Dallas to catch a flight home. Love Field had become a frenetic place because it was the hub of Southwest Airlines, the only one that used it. Stewardesses in shorts cracked jokes when they took their turns greeting passengers on the mike; they handed out peanuts and pretzels if you wanted them, but there were no first-class accommodations or bad airline meals. It was just a half-hour flight to Austin, but it was late afternoon on a weekday, and across from the gate's plate glass a cluster of people with briefcases milled or sat or stood at a large bank of silver-colored pay phones that reflected the glare of the sun's descent. I laughed, for leaning against a wall and smoking a cigarette was Russ Million.

My puzzlement about Daddy receded as we greeted each other. "What are you doing here?" I said.

"Oh, I had an audition for a movie part. What about you?"

"Over east of here seeing my folks. What's the movie?"

He grimaced and shook his head. "It might be good. The part of the script I saw said it's going to be called *The Great Waldo Pepper.* It's about biplane circus pilots in the twenties that are back from the First World War, bored with doing anything else. Big-name director, and one of the grips told me it's got Robert Redford, Margot Kidder, and Susan

Sarandon, who freezes up having her clothes blown off while standing on a wing hundreds of feet up. He said it's going to be a sexy climax scene. Doesn't matter. I won't get the work."

"Why? What was the role? What happened?"

"Oh, some of it takes place on an Old West movie set. I was doing some lines as a director. Ordering silent movie actors around. 'More volume,' the assistant director says."

"So I keep doing while the AD's yelling *'Cut, cut!'* He tells me, 'Can the drawl, will ya?' I'm thinking, the movie inside the movie is a cowboy flick. But you're not supposed to talk back to people in the movie business. Also, he made me do the lines barking through a megaphone. It distracted me."

Russ shrugged. "Waste of time and their airplane money, but you gotta show up."

We took our boarding numbers from the clerk at the gate and found seats together next to a window. With the plane circling over the office towers downtown, I said, "Russ, how did you get to be an actor?"

I had seen the folk trio in which he sang and played the guitar and ukulele, but the appearances were mostly for small crowds of their Austin friends. Russ could sing well, but that didn't seem like fertile ground for him to meet casting and location scouts. He looked out the window with a soft laugh. "Do you remember the Shoal Creek flood?"

My turn to laugh. "Do I ever. There's been more than one. I proposed for the second time to the mother of your child that night and almost drove us off into one of them."

The stewardess brought us our whiskeys in plastic glasses with paper napkins and packets of the peanuts. When she moved on, he said, "A few people were swept away and drowned. Found their bodies in Town Lake. An old buddy of mine was the probate judge for one of them. A Hungarian man who managed to get out of the country when the Russian tanks put down the revolt in 'fifty-six. It turned out the man had family in Budapest. He left a will that named them as his sole legal heirs, but there wasn't much information on how to find them. I talked my buddy into appointing me executor of the man's estate. So I went over with a briefcase, one suitcase, and my fiddle."

"Why the fiddle?"

"It's why I wanted the gig. I listen to different kinds of music, and I got hooked on some recordings of Hungarian gypsies. Fantastic fiddle players. I wanted to look some up and find out how they did that. I got lucky in my search and did all right by that immigrant and his kin. And in the process of finding them I started asking around Budapest, which is a damn pretty place. But this was behind the Iron Curtain, and the response I got about the fiddle playing was, 'You can't just come over here and start asking questions like that.'

"Hungarians in general and gypsies in particular have learned to be careful. The Nazis were as eager to send gypsies to the death camps as they were the Jews. The Russians don't like gypsies either. But I stayed there long enough and asked the right questions. And sure enough, a gypsy taught me how to play the fiddle in that style. He traded his instrument for mine. It was a great time, let me tell you. There are some good-looking women over there. Anyway, when I came back to Austin I was at a party one night, and got to talking to this young fellow who had just written a play, and it was going to be produced here. He said, "We've almost got it cast. All we need is someone who can play the fiddle like a Hungarian gypsy.'"

Russ grinned at my laugh and fumble of the ice cubes in the plastic glass. "You know how it is," he said. "One night the moon shines bright enough for a lifetime."

That week I listened to Russ play and then brought him to our rehearsal hall and introduced him to the band. Shack wisecracked before Russ got the fiddle out of its case, "You gonna run a banjo in on us, too?" The guys were pretty united in pulling back the reins of country music I tried to bring to our sound. But Russ handled it with aplomb. Holding up his instrument and bow, he said, "First thing you need to know is that it's really an insult to call this violin a fiddle. This instrument has been played in the recordings of the Vajdaszentivy Band."

The guys hooted, but they had never seen a violin *or* fiddle player work the frets like that, and the bow was flying. Russ didn't want to be a permanent member of the band. He didn't want the travel, and he wanted to be good to go when he got any calls to audition for movie roles. But he gave us the flavor of our next record. We threw out some of what we'd been working on and adapted the rest. We were late getting the demo done, but we had great fun in those sessions. With a chorus of young women backup singers, we recorded at a small studio in south Austin with a guy who had a portable sound board that once belonged to Elvis. We called the album *Soviet Gypsies.*

Our producer at Cow House Creek loved the demo and asked if we could add two or three more cuts that emphasized the fiddle. But our record company had a distribution deal in Los Angeles, and the guy who'd been so high on us when we played the Troubador said the demo was fine but he wouldn't green-light the album if we called it *Soviet Gypsies.* All of the Rip Chords said he was dead wrong and we ought to stand our ground. I talked to the young man again and said, "I don't see the problem. Ever heard the song 'Back in the U.S.S.R.'?"

"Yeah, but you're not the Beatles and this is *so very* not 1968. The Republicans are in power and they're keeping score."

I asked if he hadn't noticed that Nixon had been chased out of office over Watergate. "You think Ford's not the same?" Gutless, I thought as he rang off, "Ciao."

The people at Cow House Creek came to our aid, and we supplied the two more cuts our producer wanted. The best one was a cover of a song written by my friend Bob Brown, who'd quit the music business after his band the Conqueroo got roughed up by their reception in San Francisco's Flower Power days. Bob wrote and sang it as a simple blues tune. Sharing the songwriting credit, I added more storyline, the band did the rest, but it was Bob's song, carried by its title and hook, "Was That a Kiss (Or Did You Try to Bite My Hand?)." The distributor eventually relented, the album came out, and Bob's song got almost as much airplay as "Two Bubbles Off Plumb."

I didn't know where Sabine lived. I'd take Emily to school with her backpack on a Friday, and Sabine picked her up. The next Friday we reversed the procedure. I asked Emily once if Jake lived with them. She rolled her eyes and didn't answer. Sabine was Emily's mother, and she could raise her however she chose. I was waiting for word that she had filed for the divorce and I wouldn't be seeing Emily anymore. One night I was making hamburgers for dinner when the phone rang. Emily answered, stuck the receiver out to me, and fled. "Hello," I said.

"Hi," said Sabine. "What are you doing?"

Here we go, I thought. I turned off the burner and watched sundown shadows growing on the woods along the creek below our yard and house.

"Just being your nanny."

"Don't be an ass."

"I'm sorry. That was a cheap shot. I'm sorry."

Sabine started to speak but fought to control her voice. I said, "Look, Emily wants to be with you all the time. Not with me and not with Russ. She needs you. I'll get my clothes and stuff together and I'll go."

Then came the surprise of my life. "Haid, I don't want to go over that cliff. This has been an awful mistake. I am so sorry I said all those things to you. Hurt us this way. I'm sorry for it all. I want to come home."

We tried hard to make it work. She invited me to sleep in our bed, but that was all. Sometimes our interactions were warm, other times slush. One night, Emily was at a slumber party at a friend's house. As dusk gathered, we were back at our dining table with our afternoon whiskeys, watching the sun and shadows on the woods. She said, "What are we doing this weekend?"

"I don't know. I'm free. The band needs a break."

"Kenny's movie's showing in town. Do you want to go?"

I'd seen the trailer, which went: *"It scalds. It shocks. It whips. It bleeds. It lusts. It out-Mandingo's* Mandingo!" Which meant it was an over-the-top Blaxploitation slave film with lots of nudity. In this one Kenny played the mulatto son of a New Orleans whorehouse madam. I said, "You really want to see that?"

"Well, sure. It's your friend's movie. Let's go see it. Let's go tonight."

CHAPTER 48

Across the parking lot from the theater where Sabine and I saw *Drum* was a good Mexican restaurant. We often went there after movies for margaritas and ceviche. Sabine poked a fork at a piece of redfish and said, "What did you think?"

I didn't tell her that it was twice as nasty as *Mandingo*, since I'd lied to her that I hadn't seen the first one.

I said, "I wonder if they sprung that on the festival in Cannes."

She laughed. "I liked it! How strange is that?"

"Is there some award for white trash movies? Warren Oates deserves best actor."

"Do you think Kenny sold out?"

"I don't know. I doubt they offer him parts written for Sidney Poitier. He's got a son growing up now and he has a stepson, and he and his wife are soon to be parents of another baby. Kids he'll want to send to college. He can't fight forever."

I laughed, sipped some more lime and tequila, and raised a glass to his effort. "I'm not going to tell him he could have been a star in silent movies."

"Do fighters think about the risk? Do you worry that he'll wind up addled? Like your dad?"

Those words stung but I said, "Sure. You get hit that hard, that many times, you're playing a bad hand in the long run."

"How old are they?"

"Kenny's thirty-three. Ali's a year older than him."

"They're younger than I am. The sport makes them old?"

"Not just boxers. It happens to pole vaulters. Ballerinas. Figure skaters."

She said, "But why do they . . . "

"Because there's plenty of money in it if you can do it as well as they do. Imagine being the best in the world at anything. Each one's beaten the other. Both fights could have gone either way. They have to find out which one's the best."

After we got home, she settled in beside me on the couch.

"Are you going to New York to see the fight?"

"Yeah. I wouldn't miss it."

"I want to go, too. I want to go somewhere, almost anywhere, with you. We need to get away together. Russ will keep Emily. Pretty soon she's going to reach puberty and her teens and we'd better be ready for that. I'm tired of slumber parties. I'm tired of you struggling and worrying all the time about the band and what rabbit you can pull out of the hat. We have enough money. Let's go have some fun again. I haven't been to New York since I married you."

"The fight's not for three more weeks."

"Then let's go someplace else in the meantime."

We were quiet for a moment, considering those options. Then she asked, "Is Kenny your best friend?"

"I don't know," I said. "I like to think you are."

"Thank you. I'd like to think that, too. I meant your men friends."

"I guess he is, in our way. I don't see him too often."

"I'm glad it's not my ex-husband."

"Well, Russ is the number one contender."

She laughed and poked me. I reflected a minute and said, "The best friend I had is dead. He didn't make it past twenty."

"In the war?"

"Yeah."

"I'm sorry. What was his name?"

"Chuck. Chuck Mercer."

"Why haven't you ever talked about him? I don't remember if you did."

"Maybe I didn't. It seems like a different lifetime."

"Tell me about him."

I smiled, remembering. "Cool kid, a daddy-o. His dad was killed in the Second World War, the Anzio landing in Italy. That could have kept Chuck out of Vietnam because he was an only child, but he enlisted. His mom couldn't talk him out of it. It wasn't because he was all that patriotic. He was bored. He had dark hair, an actor's looks. One year he streaked part of his hair blond with peroxide. Girls loved him. Chuck was a horny kid. He had more success with that than I did. Or better luck."

She kissed me lightly on the neck. "Do you know you're a handsome man?"

"Growing up, I thought I looked like Bugs Bunny."

"Well, get over that."

I started to unbutton her blouse. She moved my hand away because I was clumsy at that. She took it off, squirmed in my lap, and crossed her hands at the nape of her neck, pushing up her hair, which was cut shorter these days. I was better at unfastening bras, and I liked the ridges and slopes of her back. I kissed the points of her shoulder blades. Then we were in our bedroom, naked together again and more relaxed than other times since she came home. Sabine sat on the mattress and sheets with her feet on the floor. She considered and touched her nipples but then pulled a pillow to her chest.

"Are you all right with this?" she said.

"What do you mean?"

She of course meant Jake, who had been enjoying a great deal of her.

"I ran around on you first," I said, "and you at least came right out and told me. Besides, I've never stopped loving you."

She set the pillow aside and pulled me closer. We were both so scarred by what we'd done, but not in this moment. I hoisted her gently on the sheets and let myself inside her. She cried out, and once more we made us one. We made us one.

If you live in Texas and take off for pleasure on the spur of the moment, that often means Mexico. Russ agreed to keep Emily, and Sabine and I had a runaway to Zihuatenejo, a Pacific coast town in the state of Guerrero. On our connecting flight from Mexico City a tall and leggy young American woman was acting up with a scruffy fellow who looked about fifty. She wore very short shorts and a pair of fishnet hose connected to a garter belt. She appeared to long for having been alive in Berlin cabarets between the World Wars. The man's hair was long and unkempt, and his sport coat was stained. He had a broad forehead, a long bulbous nose, and dimpled cheeks. I thought he might be French until he launched into a loud harangue about all the Mexican Boys Towns he'd known. The girl thought he was hilarious, and the stewardesses treated them like they were royalty.

We'd cleared customs in Mexico City and packed lightly, so it was a quick pass through Zihuatanejo's airport. The girl flounced off to a *baño* while her guy handled their luggage, which included a saxophone case. We got a taxi to our hotel and forgot them. That first night we checked out the small naval station, and on the cobblestones we wandered from bar to bar. In one we were drinking margaritas and peeling prawns when a barman strolled through shouting, *"Señor Reevers! Con su permiso. Señor Reevers!"*

Sabine had read that the famous American painter Larry Rivers lived in Zihuatanejo when he wasn't in New York hanging out with Bob Dylan and Andy Warhol. When the barman fell silent, she laughed and pointed to a wall where a print of Rivers's *Double Portrait of Berdie* hung. It was a grotesque of two sagging and naked old women. Sabine told me it was inspired by Rivers's former mother-in-law. "It helped make him famous. And hurried along the divorce, I imagine."

"Weird way to decorate a bar."

The next day we rented a little Volkswagen runabout, and on a road up into the foothills we passed a boy standing by the pavement and holding a large dead iguana by the tail. He was offering us the lizard to eat. That night we plunged back into the hubbub of *el centro* of the town and chanced on a bar that was a music venue. The pair we'd seen acting up on the plane came out to play a set. They had one of those *chick-chick-a-boom* percussion machines, a cheap electric keyboard, and a tenor saxophone. The girl was a terrible singer and the guy didn't try that. Their routine was clever, though. He would be playing the keyboard while she sang and blew a few honks of the sax, and then he'd slide off the bench, play the sax while she danced around, slid on the bench, and while continuing to sing picked up play on a fuzzy-sounding piano. When she did that he swayed soulfully, holding the sax like a lover. Sabine and I looked at each other and it came to us. *That* was Larry Rivers. I'd read him described as a jazz musician who studied at Julliard with Miles Davis. I laughed and murmured in Sabine's ear, "Zihuatanejo's the only place he can get a gig!"

That night we went back to our *cabaña* and changed into T-shirts and swim suits and sandals. A little bar with small tables lighted by globed candles sat with stools outward on the beach. We dug our toes in the sand, drank Sol beer, and ate *pulpo,* octopus, the first time for me. It had been banged into tenderness and grilled and served with halved avocados and wedges of lime. I took to the flavors at once.

"You know what?" she said.

"What?"

"You are for me a guaranteed good time." Then she pointed and said, "Look."

I looked out to the surf, where blue luminescence began dancing in the waves as they rolled in and crashed. We left our beer and sandals and ran down to see if we could swim in it. It seemed to vanish as soon as we jumped in and came up mopping the water from our hair and faces. We were in just deep enough that we were standing, then a wave would lift and move us. The current was flowing at an angle to the dunes and each wave drifted us closer to the lights of town. "Look again," I said. At a distance in both directions the lights of small beings like blue neon still danced.

"I can feel them," Sabine said. "Can't you?"

"I'm feeling you," I said. Her skin was so smooth and cool. We splashed and rolled getting rid of our bathing suits and shirts. Treading water, she reached and guided me home. I thought if I was going to drown it ought to be this way.

We came back to our ordinary senses and paddled about looking for our clothes. Sabine caught one T-shirt and pulled it on. Out in the shallows of the surf, we walked away from town with our arms around each other to the *cabaña* and the mosquito netting where we wouldn't sleep, not for a while. It wasn't far.

In New York, when I came back up to our room at the Mayflower I brought the newspaper and two cups of coffee. Sabine had put on jeans and a pullover and was sitting at a makeup table. I read some of a *Times* feature that began:

> *He is tall, lean and blond, with dazzling white teeth, and he looks ever so much like Robert Redford. He rides around town in a chauffeured silver*

> *Cadillac with his initials, DJT, on the plates. He dates slinky fashion models, belongs to the most elegant clubs, and at only thirty years of age, estimates that his worth is "more than thirty million."*
>
> *Flair. It's one of Donald J. Trump's favorite words . . .*

Must be nice, I thought. "Hey, it's time for the car," I told Sabine. "Please don't make us late."

"Don't be snippy. I'm putting on my eyes."

For the ride I had gotten the Mayflower's concierge to arrange for a car and driver. She picked up her jacket and laughed when we headed for a black limo that pulled up to the curb. "I think it's an old one," I said of the limo. "It lives in Queens."

As the driver ushered us out of the city and up the Hudson valley she looked out and gripped my hand. "What a gorgeous day." The fall was farther along up here, and the leaves were edging into bright color, and we said little, just looked out. Kenny trained at a hotel in the Catskills outside the town of Liberty called Grossinger's. The restored Victorian hotel and its grounds were a golf resort in the warm seasons and a ski resort in the winters. Rocky Marciano must have liked kosher food and borscht, for that was the pride of the restaurant's menu. The Rock came from Massachusetts and his birth name was Rocco Marchegiano. There are all kinds of reasons to change one's name.

We found Kenny strung as tight as a new fence of barbed wire, but I didn't know it at first. John Norton and I embraced on seeing each other again. Wearing a blue velvet workout suit and slippers on bare feet, Kenny greeted us with a big smile. He and Sabine chatted about their fifth graders. "Kenny Junior's in the city with his grandma," he told her. "I try to keep him away from boxing as much as I can. But his tenth birthday's the day after the fight. Couldn't keep him away for that."

He added, "Jackie couldn't come. Six weeks ago we had my first daughter. They're doing fine. We named her Kenisha Eronda."

"Congratulations!" Sabine said. "Occasion for a hug?"

"Any time," Kenny said and slid me a wink.

Ali would be over two hours late, no doubt by plan. He was irked that Kenny and his team had booked the training favorite of Marciano first. Sabine said she thought she'd go for a walk, it was so pretty outside. John Norton pointed out people I ought to know about. "Kenny's got three trainers for this one," he said. He gestured at a fellow who looked like a heavyweight enjoying his meals now. "The one there is Bossman Jones."

"Ah," I said. "The Hoover Street Gym."

"That's right. Kenny's learning in LA began with the Bossman there."

John complained that Ali was getting six times more money because Kenny was like a racehorse that had only run at Del Mar and Santa Anita.

"How you figure?" I said.

"Well, except one time across the Nevada line in Lake Tahoe on one of Ali's undercards, he didn't compete outside Southern California until his thirty-second fight." He put his hands in his pockets and said, "Ruth and I'd never seen New York until he fought Jerry Quarry. We came up thinking Chicago was the class of the nation, but now Ruth's gone crazy over New York. That momma is shopping up a storm."

Kenny's longtime sparring partner Mike Weaver came over to say hello. "How's it going with you now?" I said.

"Oh, I'm up to eight and six now. But a few weeks ago, I upset this guy from Dallas. He'd won twenty-seven but I chopped him up."

Kenny came out of a meeting with his trainers, and I could tell he was trying to control his temper. He told the New York State officials that he wanted to go ahead without Ali. When they and Arum rejected that, he muttered and paced. He and I stood together a while. I told him about my diminished estimate of Marciano. He shrugged and said, "The winners get to write the history books. Dempsey, Tunney, Louis, Marciano. Everybody except Jack Johnson." He glared at what appeared to be a figure in his mind.

"I deserve this fight, Haid," he said. "I'm going to win it. I've sparred two hundred twenty-five rounds and done more roadwork than I ever have before. I've been waiting on this three years and sixteen days. It's showtime."

Ali at last arrived with a large entourage that included the comedian Dick Gregory, who had been dosing him with a special recipe of carrot juice. Most of the reporters and photographers had gone first to Ali's upstate camp and then followed him here. He wore a black suit, black shirt, black socks, black shoes. In case anyone wondered who had the black fan base. He was barely inside when his carnival barking began. "I'm gonna blow Norton outa Yankee Stadium! I am the Six Million Dollar Man! In money, genius, personality, and charisma! The whole world's coming to see this fight. We can't have a champion who parades around buck nekkid like he did in those nasty movies. It's undignified. I'll take this sucker out inside five rounds."

Kenny didn't take the bait, just let him posture and ramble. Ali started pushing toward us with a threatening look, and the crowd surged with him. Kenny was smiling until he got shoved from behind by Bundini Brown. Kenny whirled around and snarled, "Don't ever touch me, punk! Unless you want to live the rest of your life in a *corset.*"

Sabine flinched and stepped back. Bundini bristled and stuck out his lip but had the sense not to raise his hands. When Ali reached us, he leaned over and said something in Kenny's ear. The weigh-in began. Kenny peeled down to his undershorts and weighed 217. On the scales at 221 Ali didn't look like he'd been sparring hundreds of rounds. He yammered on about his greatness and Kenny's "Uncle Tom" roles in *Mandingo* and *Drum.*

Kenny said he wouldn't take part in a press conference, not this time. When we were outside, I asked, "What did Ali say to you after Bundini shoved you?"

Kenny grinned and shook his head. "He said, 'Don't make him big. Don't make him big.' What he meant was, *We're the show.* Don't let him crowd in and make any of the story about him. They broke the mold when they came up with Ali. They broke the mold."

He looked at Sabine and said, "What did you think of his entrance?"

"It was pretty grand."

"Yeah. No wonder he and Elvis adore each other."

CHAPTER 49

Halfway around the world, Cuban doctors had first come in the eastern Congo on a humanitarian mission. The Simbas inspired Che Guevara to follow because they claimed to be Maoists, and Che knew what would happen to him in Cuba if his celebrity continued to irritate Fidel. So he decided to export their revolution abroad. The Simbas' ideology was unlike any Maoism Guevara knew about. They smoked ganja for courage and believed that if they drank the shaman's porridge of hallucinogenic herbs any bullets fired at them would splash on them as water.

The Soviet Union and Britain and the US were fighting a proxy war in Zaire. But no matter how far away the rebels were from Mobuto and his capital Kinshasa, and no matter how inept his army, that belief in fields of battle meant the breakaway People's Republic of Congo rose and fell in twenty-three months. The Belgian priests and nuns and low-level American emissaries and agricultural advisers got out of the eastern Congo as soon as Mad Mike Hoare rescued them in Kisangani, the former Stanleyville. One group of foreigners was already gone. Field radio intercepts in Spanish had all at once ceased.

The CIA sent in an ex-Navy SEAL, Jim Hawes, with his own command of mercenaries. In Africa's string of Great Lakes, topography pulls water from Lake Kivu and sends it via the Ruzzizi River into Lake Tanganyika, where the mercenaries led by Hawes conducted an inland naval war that routed the Cubans and sent Guevara on to his demise in Bolivia.

Defeated in their war of secession, diehard Simbas in the eastern Congo took to the woods for raids against Mobuto's army and civilians in the remote provinces of Nord-Kivu and Sud-Kivu. The older Simbas were exceeded in their brutality by homegrown militias, the Mai-Mai. Swahili for "water-water," their name perpetuated the belief that with enough drugs and witchcraft, they could make themselves immune to gunfire. Many were deserters from Mobuto's army. They adopted the new-fashion dreadlocks and wore exercise suits sporting the logos of the Los Angeles Lakers and New York Yankees. Interviewers with an international mental health agency found the Mai-Mai eager to talk about themselves.

"Magical beliefs are the rule," said one, "and it is our foundation. Our biggest support is witchcraft. Because when we started fighting, we didn't have the money for firearms, so, after you got the scarifications, they would provide you with a machete or a knife, and you'd go to war. When you killed an enemy fighter, his firearm would become your weapon." A boy soldier said, "After taking a spoonful of the medicine, as soon as you hear a gunshot, you become crazy and seek it out, like a dog chases a hare."

The Simba diehards set up camps in the forest on and around Nyiragongo. The worst of them were the young ones, the Mai-Mai. For women and young girls, the Mai-Mai made Nord-Kivu into one of the most dangerous places on earth. Often when they were done raping, they jammed knives and machetes into vaginas. They made their victims in the kraals swallow the flesh of humans they had seen murdered. "To rape?" one said to a missionary interviewer. "Well, rape for a Mai-Mai is Satan's work, because as people walk, Satan follows behind them. This means raping may happen to you when you are not prepared for it, but all of a sudden, the Devil fools you."

The Simba chief on Nyiragongo had been involved in the violence that closed Virunga Mountains National Park. He told the youths to look for a combative park ranger thought to be living somewhere in the locale. Soon enough they found Mwykiza and his family. Virginie, aged six, now had a sister, Honorata, who was two. Mwykiza saw the six Mai-Mai coming. These had the dreads and welted scars on their faces, and they carried light backpacks and wore warm-ups advertising the New York Yankees. From three of the packs Mwykiza could see the handles of machetes. He slipped his machete in easy reach on a cross timber of the goat pen he was tending.

At first their tone was jovial and flattering. They said they had heard Mwykiza had been a great warrior but on the wrong side, and now they wanted to enlist him in the right one. "I was no warrior," he said carefully. "I had a job." The leader pulled a plastic thermos out of his pack and said, "Drink from this, and you'll see the correct way." Mwykiza thanked him and said he wasn't thirsty. A switchblade clicked and with practice and speed a Mai-Mai cut the throat of a goat. Mwykiza got his machete down and invited them to come on, if dying was what they were after. Instead they scattered and chased Sifa and Virginie and her little sister Honorata out of the hut. The Mai-Mai who had offered the drink smirked at Sifa and said, "Your wife and girls are going to pay for your stupidity."

Two guns were now aimed at Mwykiza. "We hunger for your bitch," said the leader. "And the tight little one, too. It doesn't have to happen. All you have to do is drink this bottle of porridge."

"Give it here," said Mywkiza after a long moment. He opened the cap expecting their mix of fermented juice and psychedelic plants but recoiled from another odor. "Drink it, ranger," said the leader. "Drink it down and we'll leave your woman and girls alone."

The Mai-Mai spared Sifa and Virginie and her little sister Honorata the rapes. Their torture was watching Mwykiza choke and retch as the Mai-Mai laughed and squatted on their heels. They murdered Virginie's father by making him drink bleach.

Sifa had always been keen on Christianity. When the Belgian priests and nuns left, they were replaced by American missionaries who came up in the mountains from Goma and called themselves Episcopalians. On getting the story out of Sifa, the missionaries took the family into their care. All roads out of Goma were impassible. The missionaries had Sifa, her daughters, and others ferried on the lake to a sprawling camp for displaced persons, refugees, and asylum seekers outside Bukavu, a city in Sud-Kivu. In the camp they lived in a tent that leaked and turned the bare dirt underfoot to ankle-deep mud when the heavy rains came. They ate with their fingers *fufu,* casaba melon cooked into sticky goo. Sometimes they received small sacks of brown grain that smelled sweet and made a passable porridge. One of the missionaries told them that where they might be going, herders fed it to their cattle.

In the camp, praying and singing in the church tents made their long days endurable. All the occupants of Bukavu camp needed help, but Sifa and her two daughters became favorites of the Episcopal Migration Ministries. That led to the exhausting Refugee Determination Process of countries enlisted by the United Nations. Sifa could only estimate the birth records the Determination Process required. An official wrote down three dates on a document and asked her to confirm them with her signature, which she had learned how to do. Then came evaluation by men and women who spoke French and ruled on something called adjudication on behalf of the UN's High Commissioner on Refugees.

When the Episcopalians and a barrage of medical exams signaled that they would be leaving the camp, they hoped for Australia or New Zealand, countries they knew nothing about, only that the Episcopalians teased them that other possibilities were Sweden, Norway, Finland, Denmark, and Canada. Their jests about bitter cold frightened them almost as much as the Mai-Mai. Then came the news they were going to the United States.

They had no passports and didn't really know what passports were. The Episcopalians told the asylum seekers to put their fears away because they and their colleagues would accompany them all the way. Sifa protected her daughters fiercely but would be a frightened soul the rest of her life. The battered DC-3 that carried them from Bukavu to the capital renamed Kinshasa sent her into a paroxysm of praying. But the Ethiopian Airlines jet that whooshed them up from Kinshasa's runways was the most thrilling thing that had happened in the lives of Virginie and Honorata. Virginie was agog at the features of the big airplane and passengers and stewards who just got up and moved around. Their feet weren't on the ground—how did they know they wouldn't fly about like the airplane itself? They glued themselves to the windows, staring at puffy white clouds that cast dark moving shadows on the earth below them. The Episcopalians walked them through the customs and airport transfers in Addis Ababa, Ethiopia, then the flight stretched west across Sudan,

Chad, Nigeria, and finally down to Abidjan in the Ivory Coast. It was the last of Africa they'd likely ever see.

The flight across the Atlantic made Lake Kivu seem like a small gourd of water. Virginie's mother and sister slept at some point, but from her seat by the window, she watched it all. When night fell, a stewardess handed her a tray of food that looked interesting but was tasteless to her. The woman came back and handed her a pillow and blanket. After a while she thought she might as well sleep, but it startled her that the night's rhythm was all off. Daylight returned to the wing outside her window before it should have. She watched it all, and she was very tired when the Episcopalians came back from where they sat, awakened Sifa and Honorata, and in French told them they'd soon be landing. They were not to be afraid, the missionaries said. Virginie was exhausted, and the sight before them set her jiggling with anxiety. So many people standing all crushed together and speaking in languages that sounded different, but she couldn't understand any of them. One of the missionary women saw Virginie's state, put her arm around her shoulders, and gently pulled her thumb out of her mouth. It embarrassed Virginie. She didn't realize she'd reverted to that.

At last the longest day and night and day again ended. Two Episcopalians put them in a van that sped and then halted amid an endless blare of horns. She was so dazed by it all. The Episcopalians jabbered and laughed in their English, then remembered them and their fright. Back to French they told them to look out at this amazement of a place they seemed to call *noo yoke siti.* Sifa and the girls had never been inside a hotel before. The missionaries put them in a small one in lower Harlem for cost and, to ease their culture shock, they would see other dark-skinned faces. Virginie fell on a bed and watched her mother untie the laces of her shoes. She had no idea how long she slept but it was daylight again. Outside she heard groans of trucks lifting Dumpsters, then smashing them back down on concrete. Jackhammers sounded like vicious tireless woodpeckers. It was so loud!

What could they be *doing* out there?

CHAPTER 50

Sabine and I awoke the morning of September 28, 1976, to a more dangerous New York. When Bob Arum had gotten promotion of the Ali-Norton title fight away from his nemesis Don King, the Reverend Al Sharpton tried to organize a boycott because Arum was white. That went nowhere, and neither did security offered by an outfit calling itself "Fruit of Islam." A year earlier the city had tottered on bankruptcy. The city's politicians claimed it was now pulling out of its swoon, but two thousand cops had been laid off, and the lucky ones claimed they were being told to work shifts without pay. The police force picked that day to go out on strike.

The first week of fall sent temperatures skidding into the fifties, and a stiff wind blew off the Harlem River. It was the first heavyweight title fight in Yankee Stadium in seventeen years, since that night Ingo Johansson knocked out Floyd Patterson and thrilled me at age sixteen in Deerinwater. The stadium had been fixed up nicely, all the newspapers said, but it was still in the Bronx. I was familiar only with parts of Manhattan and a smaller part of Brooklyn, and getting to Yankee Stadium by subway seemed impossible. The guy I'd mocked at the Mayflower at last flagged down a cabbie who said he'd consider it. The hotelier stepped aside and with a smile invited us through the rear door. The cabbie looked back through the plexiglass and said, "Four hundred cash. You ain't got it, we ain't going." I seldom had that kind of money on me, but on reading the papers I had gotten a thousand. I counted it out to him in twenties and tens. Striking cops were picketing the fight, shouting, banging trash can lids, and blocking traffic. Kids and streetwalkers openly smoked weed and crack pipes. Muggers and pickpockets were hard at work. Once more Sabine and I had to wonder what I'd gotten her into.

The cabbie got us close enough to the stadium that I thought we could make it if I held her arm tight and we walked fast. Naturally she tried to jerk free. I was ready to fight some kids that started toward us if I had to. It felt like Caracas two years earlier.

I breathed easier when we got through a turnstile, showed our passes, found the junior publicist Kenny sent me to, and she got us to our third-row seats. On the other side of the ring I saw a friend of Kenny who'd been at the weigh-in usher John and his grandson Kenny Junior to their seats on the first row. John and the child sat across the ring from us. I started to go over and say hello, but my better sense told me to stay where I was. Celebrities on hand ran from Walter Cronkite to Joe Louis, from Jean-Paul Belmondo to Sugar Ray Leonard. Some were denied their seats by hooligans who had pushed through the gates or climbed fences into the stadium because no one tried to stop them. The associate promoter with the TV rights had insisted on blacking out the telecast in the New York area, thinking that would enlarge the live crowd to capacity—fifty-four thousand.

Only thirty-four thousand people paid for tickets, and to me it looked like there might have been twenty thousand in the stadium. I saw people running *toward* the exits. Bob Arum said they expected ten thousand fans to buy walk-up tickets that night. They sold ten.

After Kenny warmed up, put on his blue robe, and entered a tunnel to the field, fight officials warned him he might be walking into a riot. He had a long chilly wait in the ring, and this time it wasn't Ali's mind games. The champ couldn't get inside the stadium until forty-five minutes before the telecast went on the air. Kids jumped up and down on the hood of his limo and tried to turn it over, not caring who might be inside.

When at last Ali made his entry with his big entourage, I got out a little notebook I had brought along. I had no systematic way of knowing how to score a fight but thought I'd see if my unsystematic way might turn out to be correct. Assuming neither one knocked the other out. In the ring above us Ali thrust his lower lip out in a pose of menace and came over and stood beside Kenny like a buzzard sitting on a tree limb. Kenny turned away laughing. Ali, who looked soft around the waist, made a circuit of the ring pumping his gloved hand up and down as he had in Zaire. Now the cry was *"Norton must fall! Norton must fall!"* It was just not the same as *"Ali bomaye!"*

Kenny no longer had quite the pretty face that he bragged on that day I met him. He was still a good-looking man, but counting the amateur bouts in the marines he'd been taking punches from heavyweights for thirteen years. Ali talked all the way through the referee's instructions at mid-ring. Kenny wagged his head back and forth. *Yeah, yeah.*

When the first bell rang, Ali slung his right arm like a windmill and leaped out and landed a right-hand lead, but Kenny fended off the three-punch combination behind it. For this one Ali had decided stay put, toe to toe. He probably didn't have the reflexes to slip punches like he had as a young champion in his prime, but it was more than that. As time ran out on his body and reign, he seemed more and more set on demonstrating he could *take* a punch. Kenny held his left hand and arm low, as he always did, and he had his right out before him and covered up quickly and counter-punched when Ali threw the combinations. Ali planned to surprise Kenny with powerful right-hand leads instead of his usual dominance with the trademark jabs.

Ali stood between rounds with his back turned and his forearms on the ropes, and this fight Kenny decided to do the same. Neither one took his stool the rest of the fight. Ali tried to get the crowd going again, acting as his own cheerleader. He went into his windmill routine again, but not many fans were buying. They had battled past the thugs and were not here for vaudeville. Kenny kept deflecting Ali's blows with his right glove and forearms. He didn't have to work at cutting off the ring. Ali stayed right in front of him.

At the start of round three Ali flung his arm in the windmill once more and almost ran into a right Kenny had waiting for him. After that Ali changed strategy. He started skipping through his dance moves, which drew a roar from the crowd. Ali ignored the body except when they clinched. He landed a hard jab and another overhand right, but Kenny was fast enough to double up with hooks, one to Ali's ribs, the other to his head. Seconds later one of Kenny's looping rights buckled Ali's knees. I thought Kenny had him badly hurt, that he might be able to end it, but Ali fought back with four scoring rights. Kenny yelled as he headed back to his corner. *"You ain't nothin'!"*

Sabine yelled at me, "What do you think?"

"Too early to say, but it's Kenny's fight so far."

He was scoring well with his own jabs, and his overhand rights had the crowd roaring and into the fight now. Ali feinted a jab and landed his own resounding right. Kenny went downstairs, throwing lefts and rights, and Ali didn't catch all of them on his arms. He fought off the ropes throwing more fast rights, making Kenny cover up Archie Moore-fashion for the first time. Headhunting, trying to put Kenny down so hard he couldn't get up.

Ali had predicted a fifth-round knockout, but he seemed to lose interest in his bet with himself. Kenny backed him into the ropes and pounded away with hooks to the body and head and with uppercuts, both hands. Ali went to the rope-a-dope, only he didn't come off it in flurries as he had against Foreman. He wiggled his hips to convey to the crowd that he was toying with Kenny. A chorus of boos greeted this stunt. It was a weird round, and Ali gave it away. At the bell, Kenny yelled, *"There's* your fifth round!"

Joe Frazier was at ringside, a few chairs from where we sat, yelling support to Kenny. In the sixth round the champion's fans started trying to get Ali going. He looked toward their chants and pumped his right arm. Kenny leapt at the opportunity and just missed with a hook that would have staggered a cow. Ali started holding his left out like a running back's stiff-arm. Kenny first batted the arm away then threw uppercuts at the arm and elbow.

Kenny seemed in command until early in the eighth when Ali countered with a right that sent Kenny into a juking routine that just made it look like he was indeed hurt. But later in the round Kenny landed his hardest punch yet, a left hook to the body. When the bell rang as Kenny watched Ali pass, he yelled, "You don't want it bad enough tonight, Ali. *Fuck you!"*

I noticed something I hadn't seen from Kenny before. His jabs and body shots and uppercuts landed hard, but his straight right disappeared. *All* the rights he now threw were over-the-house. Some landed with much force, but he had given up the element of surprise.

"I hate this," Sabine announced. "Let's go."

"No!"

"All right," she said and started to rise from her chair. "I'll see you at the hotel."

I pulled her back down. "Are you crazy?" I said. "You wouldn't last sixty seconds trying to get a cab alone out there. In twenty-five minutes this thing will be over. Don't quit again on me now." Fuming at my choice of words, she crossed her arms and for most of the ninth round she wouldn't look at me or the fighters in the ring.

Ali wasn't playing at anger now. He came out dancing, landing jab after jab. He was moving left, moving right again. When Kenny tried to cut off the ring the champ brought out his old shuffle, getting a roar from the crowd. In the eleventh Ali came out throwing combinations. Kenny answered with a left hook that rocked him back on his heels. But then Kenny backed against the ropes, spread his feet wide, and spooning out some of his own showboat medicine, he dropped his hands to his side and then clapped his gloves together. He rolled his arms like somebody in a disco. That wasn't his style or personality. And he let Ali steal the round.

In the twelfth Ali thumbed Kenny in his left eye. Kenny stepped back, raised his glove to the eye in a gesture to the ref, but he nodded at Ali, who nodded back. Kenny had told me once that Ali was never a dirty fighter. Why would anyone be with all that talent? The fourteenth was the fiercest battle of the night. Ali moved but didn't dance. He kept his feet planted, ducking his shoulders and head slightly, looking for ways in. Kenny picked off jabs with his right. Above the crowd noise the punches that both were landing sounded like large rocks dropped from a height. With almost the speed of old, Ali threw several combinations. Kenny weathered them with his arms crossed in front of his face and from the Archie Moore-style defense fired right back. The last fifty seconds were an all-out slugfest.

Kenny had been talking to him throughout the round, and now his drag-footed advance forced Ali into a neutral corner. With fifteen seconds to go, Kenny landed an overhand right that pinned Ali against the post. Kenny mugged him high and low, then at the bell stepped back and yelled another taunt. With a curt weary nod, Ali headed for his corner, where his seconds brought out the stool for the first time. Ali didn't sit but he propped his right foot on it and rested with his arms on the ropes.

It looked like there was blood under his nose, and Angelo Dundee wiped his face with a towel. Ali had a glum expression, and his chest heaved up and down.

They touched gloves at the start of the last round, and Ali went back to dancing, playing to the crowd and the judges. He moved and jabbed well with a few power shots behind them. Kenny had been told for three years that he lost the second fight by either running out of gas or easing up in the last round. In his stalking pursuit of Ali, Kenny threw some weary and wild punches, and at one point he stuck out his tongue. But he cut off the ring at the end and flung back Ali with one more thudding overhand right. When the bell rang, he bellowed, "I beat you, you son of a bitch! I beat you!"

Kenny had come a long way from the Hoover Street Gym. Bossman Jones rushed out and hoisted him. Kenny's arms were raised in triumph. Ali's corner was quiet and subdued. The swelling of Ali's right jaw was pronounced, a gift of left hooks like the one that once knocked me unconscious. The ring was a madhouse. I found it hard to believe that all those people had passes to be inside the ropes, but the outmanned security guards couldn't keep them out. As we waited for the decision, I got my reading glasses out and looked at what I had scribbled in a little notebook. I had no systematic way of scoring it, and when I didn't know about a round, I had marked it even. I checked my math a second time, and my card had it six rounds for Kenny, five for Ali, with four rounds even.

All but one of four top veteran boxing writers at ringside believed I was too generous to Ali. One writer had it a draw, with six rounds each and three rounds even, but Red Smith had it ten to five for Kenny, Dick Young scored it nine to six for Kenny, and another man called it eight to six for Kenny with one round even. You could hear and feel it. Almost everyone in the stadium thought the world had a new undisputed heavyweight champion.

At last the ring announcer brought down the mike, and in deadpan he read the cards eight to seven, another eight to seven, and eight to six with one round even: *all for Muhammad Ali.*

There was an instant intake of breath, a shudder, as if an aircraft had hit the stadium, then the crowd exploded with boos. There was no celebration in Ali's corner. Bundini helped him into his white robe and his entourage started pushing people out of the way. Ali waved off one reporter with a tired flip of his hand. For the television audience the British correspondent Ian Darke found his way on camera. "I find this absolutely shameful," he said. "Ali doesn't deserve to be the heavyweight champion. One man does and his name is Ken Norton." Across the ring from Ali, Kenny's shoulders were stooped, and at first his large hands were on his head. Then his hands moved to his face, and he jerked as one of his seconds put a towel on his head. "He's sobbing," the lead broadcaster said, shocked. His partner said, "I don't believe I've ever seen a fighter weep at the end of a match."

Seeing that broke my heart.

CHAPTER 51

One day Daddy had driven off from their home in Daingerfield, and after Mom's panicked calls, a state trooper found him bewildered and out of gas forty miles away. My sister and I insisted that she take the car keys away from him, and his last Chevy collected dust in their garage. Daddy started telling the same stories over and over, often in the same conversation, and at some point, he realized that. And he stopped talking at all. I don't know if it was Alzheimer's or some other kind of dementia, but it came on fast. A doctor in Tyler told me the condition was "organic brain syndrome." It was the first time I'd heard that medical euphemism for Alzheimer's or other kinds of dementia. I thought that doctor was a prick. Daddy would reply when I spoke to him, and he always knew who I was, but we'd had our last real conversation. I was grieving for someone who was still sitting in the room.

Mom wrecked her health trying to care for him at home, and in the end it was impossible. He spent the last weeks of his life in a wretched small-town nursing home that smelled of Lysol and urine. Mom had learned to drive enough that she went to see him every day. It was anguish for me to watch him in the chair where they had him parked. I sensed him trying to will himself out of that prison of a body. Then one day he spoke her name and his chin dropped. A heart attack let him go.

Mom wanted Daddy to have funerals in both Daingerfield and Deerinwater. Wanting no part of the long-haul logistics of that, Sabine booked flights to Dallas-Fort Worth for Emily and her, and I rented a van for the drive to Daingerfield. It was the first funeral that my stepdaughter attended. Mom and her relatives honored the tradition of open caskets. I had told Sabine to slip off to the side with Emily when the ritual walk past the coffin began. Mom and I made the walk first, followed by Virginia and Oran and Angie and her young family. I stood beside her before his body until Mom signaled in some way that she'd seen enough. His ruddy face looked like it was caked with powdered sugar, but in shaving him the undertaker had missed a patch of red whiskers that poked through the makeup like weeds.

When I was a kid, sometimes it leaked out of Mom that she thought all this playing of ball games by males in her kin was frivolous, almost sinful. In a town obsessed with high school football and summer league baseball, Deerinwater was also a hotbed of fast-pitch softball, and one of those years the Pioneer refinery fielded a team. Though Daddy was a decade or more older than the other guys, in their first game he fielded at first base with style. He threw right-handed, but when he came to the plate, batting eighth, he surprised me by digging in left-handed, flexing his fingers on the bat like Mickey Mantle. A switch-hitter!

Good fast-pitch softball hurlers can throw as hard as baseball pitchers at the shorter distance, and their curve is a brutal sinker. That night he struck out his first time up, but his next time up he smoked a line drive over the leap of the other team's second baseman. The Pioneer refinery players came off the bench cheering the old guy. When we got home, Mom went into an ongoing gripe at supper that his shifts at the plant only let him be at home with us in the evenings two weeks out of three. On and on, she went, it wasn't fair for him to be out playing ball, too. "All right," he yelled. "Stop your nagging!"

I never quite forgave her for depriving him of youth's one last season.

In Deerinwater more than a handful of people came to the church where I had once been the song leader. A few had worked with him at the refinery, but most came out of respect and fondness for my mother. There were her two sisters and brothers-in-law and a few cousins from her large clan. I was grateful that the preacher, who didn't know Daddy, kept his sermon short. Except for Virginia's and Darrell Raines's wedding and the time Daddy came to watch me lead the singing, I don't believe Daddy ever set foot in that particular church.

I journeyed about two thousand miles in the course of driving to Daingerfield, then Deerinwater, then back to Daingerfield and home. When Mom and I got back to their house, in the Rip Chords' van I loaded up his old golf clubs, the bent fedora he wore at the refinery and around town, some tools and wrenches from his little workshop, and his antique baseball glove, which had just one leather strip between the thumb and index finger. It didn't bear a signature and endorsement of a major league player, as all the gloves do today. Just the imprint of a company in Kansas City and assurance it was "Genuine Horsehide."

For years I had seen the tremor in Mom's hands. After Daddy died, she told us she had Parkinson's and apologized for trying to hide it from us. Virginia lived no closer to Daingerfield than I did. Though Mom had a fine brick home and friends she had made there, she had never stopped thinking of Deerinwater as their real home. Dry Creek, where Virginia and Oran lived, was just eighteen miles from Deerinwater. Mom and Virginia and I sold their Daingerfield house to a family of immigrant Mexican people of evangelistic faith who had jobs at a chicken processing plant. Virginia said she had checked out all the senior care facilities in Deerinwater and had gotten Mom into assisted living at the best one. In no time she went from that wing to the nursing home wing because doctors said she could no longer walk. After watching her try to manage a walker I had to admit they were right. Guilt was no stranger to me—had I been selfish? The way Virginia said I'd always been? The nursing home looked and smelled like they all do. One day when I was up there visiting, Mom said, "You know they've got rats in here."

I jerked alert in the chair. "You've seen them? Where?"

"On the walls."

Later that visit she started snatching at something in the air. Angie was now a nurse in El Paso. I called and told her how upsetting my visit with Mom had been that day. "Grandma's dying, Haid," she said. I asked what Mom's eerie snatching at the air meant. "Maybe she's seeing angels."

I asked how much longer it might go on. She said it might be the next day and it could be weeks or even a few months. She said I ought to go on with my life—just let Virginia or her know at all times how to contact me. She snatched at the angels, if that's what she believed they were, like tufts of cottonwood flowers and seed set loose in a breeze. I sat outside the nursing home a long time before I started the car, put it in drive, and started home.

Two weeks later the Rip Chords and I were loading the van in Colorado Springs to continue on to a gig in Cheyenne, Wyoming, when Sabine found me and said I needed to call my sister. During the night Mom had died. "I am sitting in the office of the mortician," Virginia began, "on the speaker phone with a very busy gentleman. You get yourself on a plane or on a highway wherever you are and get back here this instant!"

Since her infancy I'd been very fond of Angie, and Oran had steered me toward a musician's life as much as anyone did, but if there was anything left in my relations with my sister, that phone call finished it. When I reached Deerinwater, Virginia and I went to do business with the undertaker. Neither of us spoke on the way. Mom wanted her funeral to take place as Daddy's had in the little church at Seventeenth and Keeler. The mortician was the kind of man whose after-shave filled up a room, who had his fingernails done. Virginia carried on in her best haughty voice about all the experience she had in the hours and days of these sad events and the honor of grief. The undertaker carried on his part of the chatter in his most comforting way. As I listened to them my gaze came to rest on a chromed letter opener that lay on the man's desk. I could stab her with that, I thought. I could stab her.

Mom was buried beside Daddy in a little cemetery near the onetime cotton gin town of Cottonmouth Creek, where she had been valedictorian of her tiny senior class. That school was now a hay barn. Despite the forbidding name the cemetery was a handsome spot enclosed by pasture and groves of post oaks. Virginia had gotten Joey Carrigan to sing at the funerals of both our parents. When Mom was buried, he stood beside her grave and sang "Precious Memories" and "O They Tell Me of an Unclouded Day." He asked for two hundred dollars. I paid him a thousand.

After the burial I went for a long solitary drive. I was thinking that these rolling plains had once been the risky limit of settlement when the Comanches ruled the plains. After that, for a few decades you would have seen unbroken fields of cotton. A seven-year drought ended that in the fifties. Most of the oilfield pump jacks were still now. The sight of the stock tanks still amused me. The water in them was pink because of the underlying red clay.

I didn't expect to see much of Deerinwater anymore. The second night after Mom's funeral and burial, Joey and I went to a bar and drank red draws—tomato juice and draft beer, the local concoction. I didn't say much about Vietnam, but I opened up to him about my time in the brig. And his prison stories opened my eyes to what the state did with its outlaw youths. Texas prisons occupied the same sprawling cotton and sugar cane farms on the same coastal plains that had been slave plantations before the Civil War. Trusties called building tenders ran them inside the walls more than guards did. They were warlords who had free run and enjoyed a cheap kind of luxury in food, tobacco, and drugs. If you jacked with them, you wound up dead. The convicts wore thick white cotton coveralls, some with flop hats, and heavy brogans. They marched out to the fields with ten-pound hoes called aggies on their shoulders. Trusties fed and cared for the dogs that ran the convicts down.

"They called us dog boys," Joey said. "We turned the dogs off their leashes and ran behind them. I turned them loose on guys that bunked in the same cellblock, ate in the same cafeteria. Turnip greens. They fed us lots of pork and greens."

"The building tenders protected you?" I said.

"More or less. Being a dog boy made enemies, but any one of them would have wanted the job, and armed robbery gives you a little stature. Like everybody else I had a shiv. I only had to use it once. I didn't kill the guy. Just cut him and made him go away."

"What happened to your partner Jeff?"

"Still out there somewhere." He laughed softly. "His name is Cecil. I turned state's evidence against him to get a little less time. He was older and had a prior record, arrests for burglaries, assaults, that kind of thing. The prosecutors disliked him more, and the church elders and Brother Borbino spoke up for me. But Cecil and I planned those robberies together. He might come calling on me some day."

Joey sipped his pink foamy drink and studied me. "When I pointed that gun at people, their hands shook every time." Joey said his path since getting out of prison had been as straight as a length of oilfield pipe. He had a residential repairs company and cherished being the song leader at the little church on Keeler Street. "It keeps me grounded, you know?"

CHAPTER 52

In his Yankee Stadium dressing room after the fight with Ali, Kenny had sat on a table and asked reporters, "What do I have to do to beat him?" There was some clearing of throats but none of the reporters spoke. They looked down and leafed through their notepads. They thought he was emotionally unstable and might again embarrass himself.

The other locker room in the bowels of the stadium was uncommonly subdued. Ali told his corner men and others in his inner circle, "I think it's time for me to call it quits. I mean, if I can't even beat Norton . . . " His voice trailed off. "I don't have it anymore. I wasn't myself out there. I see the things to do, but I can't do them."

When the reporters were allowed in, a black reporter shoved up front and berated Ali. "How long do you think you can keep fooling the American public?"

Ali bristled. "I'll beat your black ass right now, and we'll see who's fooling who."

In the days that followed, the officials were stung by the blowback. One highly respected judge, Harold Lederman, blamed the loss on Kenny's three trainers. "I've never seen such an experienced corner in all of my profession, and their telling Ken that he had the fight was preposterous. I think I was the only guy who gave Kenny Norton rounds two through six. Five rounds in a row. I had him with a huge early lead, and then Ali started to turn it on. Then Kenny won the eighth round, so that made him six-two after eight rounds. Then Ali turned it on again, and those three guys told him to coast in the last round, and that just killed him."

But the public verdict was a landslide against Ali. The champ's trainer Angelo Dundee would only say, "I thought all three of their fights were close, but Kenny had a style that would give Muhammad trouble every day of the week and twice on Sunday. I used to call Kenny the Hopalong Cassidy of boxing due to his unique style and rhythm. He had a style that just put Ali off-kilter and kept him off balance."

A month after the fight, in an interview with the TV producer Mark Cronin, Ali would own up with humility, class, and grace. "Ken's too difficult for me. I can't beat him, and I sure don't want to fight him again. I honestly thought he beat me in Yankee Stadium, but the judges gave it to me, and I'm grateful to them."

At 1:30 that morning after the fight, Ferdie Pacheco had come over to the locker room to see Kenny. Kenny had always liked the doctor in Ali's corner. Pacheco told him, "It was a hell of a fight, and after three fights I still don't know who won any of them. If it's any consolation to you, I think you retired Ali."

Pacheco may have believed that. He doubtless hoped it was true. But Ali was never one to seek opinions of others, and even in his disheartened mood he wound up hedging bets about his future. But Pacheco's remark made Kenny hold back more tears. "If he retires, I retire. I don't want to fight anyone else but Ali."

"Kenny, stay in the game," the doc said. "You've still got a few good years in you. Pick up the big money. That's the name of the game."

After his own Waterloo in Zaire, George Foreman had holed up on his ranch near Marshall. Divorced from his first wife, he later said he tried to sleep with a new woman every night and walked the pastures with a lion on a leash. "I'd never lost before," he said, "so I didn't know how to lose." He blamed his trainer Dick Sadler for rubbing his legs between rounds and telling him to keep slugging—it was just a matter of time until he caught Ali with those punches. But what happened to the right uppercuts he used to destroy Frazier and Norton? They could have blown right through Ali's arms and gloves, and well-thrown uppercuts are the hardest punches to slip. Several sportswriters at ringside thought the ref was going to disqualify Ali for refusing to fight. What if George had stepped away, held his arms out and laughed at Ali, working the judges and crowd?

But that's not what he did. He slugged away and wore himself out. Ali kept stealing rounds by coming off the ropes with lead right hands. The eighth round brought the combination and then the lead right hand that sent George floundering and down. Archie Moore was supposed to call out the count to him in the unlikely event Ali floored him. Just seconds to the bell, he would have had a minute on the stool to rest and recover. The Mongoose was still calling numbers to George when the ref counted him out.

In his most ominous suspicion, George said the water they gave him in the corner tasted like "medicine." When he asked them for ice, it tasted right, so he decided he'd been drugged. George fired his friend the Mongoose, who had actually called out the seconds right. The ref ended the fight when the count was really nine. What was George to make of that? He fired Sadler, and then Sadler wound up in Ali's entourage! Maybe George's own trainer was in on it? George said he and Ali had one conversation about a second bout. "Ali called and said he heard I wanted a rematch and that was fine, but I had to rehire Dick Sadler as my trainer. I said Sadler would never work my corner again. Ali got mad and said there'd never be a rematch."

George's bitter isolation and Kenny's big win over Jerry Quarry had allowed Kenny to edge back into the heavyweights' number one ranking, but everyone who watched boxing knew what the huge money fight was. George's record was forty and one; just three of his victims had gone the distance with him, and he was only twenty-seven years old.

When he finally got back in the ring for real it was not against a soup can. At age nineteen Ron Lyle had shot and killed a member of a rival gang in Denver and gone down for seven and a half years for manslaughter. He almost died on a prison operating table after being stabbed by an inmate. When Lyle got out, he gained a large following in his hometown and climbed fast in the pro rankings. After knocking down George and then struggling against Wepner, the Bleeder of Bayonne, Ali had given Lyle a title fight. If the champ thought this was going to be an easy payday, he was wrong. Lyle had stopped thirty of thirty-three fighters who got in the ring with him. Ali found out right away that the rope-a-dope that humiliated George and a new defense he ballyhooed as "the mirage" didn't work with Lyle. Behind on all the cards after six rounds, Ali had once more become the dancer, jabbing and stinging, and Lyle had no answer to his speed. In the eleventh round Ali landed a thunderous right and once more was the finisher of old. Lyle was on his feet but in such poor shape that Ali frowned at the ref and waved him in to stop it.

Yet four months after that, Lyle rebounded with a sixth-round knockout of Earnie Shavers, whose chin didn't always measure up to his reputation as a sensational puncher. In taking on Lyle, George Foreman cast out the rumors that he was afraid to fight in the United States. It came off at Caesar's Palace in Las Vegas in January 1976. George's new trainer was Gil Clancy, who had moved on after Kenny's manhandling of Jerry Quarry. Dapper in a tux with a lacey white shirt, Kenny was there at ringside to join Howard Cosell for the commentary. If the sight of George in the ring unsettled him, his voice didn't betray it.

Getting instructions from the ref, Lyle pushed so close to George that he touched him with his nose. It must have been one of the most baleful center-ring faceoffs ever. At the bell, Lyle rushed out with a right that missed by three feet. But with fifteen seconds left in the round he almost floored George with another right. George staggered about the ring and wobbled to the stool. "Lyle got a little excited at the end and couldn't take care of it," observed Kenny. "He has no fear of Foreman, no fear at all."

George came out in the second with punishing jabs, and Lyle answered with counter rights. Then George landed a hook followed by a right and, cornered, Lyle tried to fight back but looked ready to go. The bell rang a minute early and likely saved him. In the fourth round George jabbed, tried to land hooks and rights, and gave Lyle shoves when he got too close. Midway through the round Lyle landed another right that toppled George. As his knees hit the canvas Lyle just missed him with a vicious right uppercut.

After the standing eight-count, George retreated. Then *he* landed a right and sent Lyle head first to the canvas. George pounded Lyle as he leaned against the ropes and occasionally shot out a counter in return. In weariness they both missed exhausted left hooks, and George allowed Lyle to escape. With less than ten seconds left they engaged again. Lyle took a hard hook, fired one back one in return, then his right sent George down on his shoulder. George made it up and stumbled toward his corner while Lyle wandered in search of his own.

Early in the fifth Lyle's left hook and uppercut sent George falling forward, but Lyle was too weary to step out of the way. George avoided the knockdown by grabbing hold of him. "Here we go, Howard," said Kenny. "Foreman's got his arms down, and he's wide open for Lyle's rights." George steadied himself with eight straight jabs, but Lyle rocked him again with another right uppercut and overhand right. Then George's left hook sent *Lyle* falling back along the ropes. Backed in the corner, Lyle took twenty-eight punches, the last one a right uppercut that put him face down on the canvas. He tried to shove himself up but collapsed on his back as the ref counted him out. It was voted 1976's Fight of the Year.

Afterward George was unusually good-natured and talkative. It happens when you're happy. He told Cosell, "I was off, I was rusty, but I'm still a champion at heart. This is what happens when you stay out of boxing, and I've got to give all credit to Ron Lyle. He took some hard punches and gave some. That's a hard-hitting low-down young man. I'm rusty, so I'm gonna get knocked down, I'm gonna get hurt if he *slaps* me. But I'm not gonna give up. I'll die before I give up."

"The heart of a lion!" Gil Clancy interjected.

George laughed. "Next time I fight, 'Heart of a Lion' is gonna be on my robe. There's no substitute for action, whether you're a piano player or a boxer."

During the Lyle fight Howard Cosell declared that George's psyche had been "materially damaged" by the loss to Ali in Zaire, and five months later, at the outset of George's rematch with Joe Frazier in Uniondale, New York, he offered that opinion again. Cosell often confused himself with a clinical psychologist. He speculated that all sixteen thousand ticket holders in the arena were pulling for Joe, and loud boos indeed greeted George when he came in the ring. He had decided against the "Heart of a Lion" robe, and he replied to Cosell and the boos by putting on a clinic.

Joe was too short, too disadvantaged in reach, and bulking up to 224 pounds didn't help. Nor did his surprise of a shaved head when he took off his hooded robe on entering the ring. It didn't look like he would survive the first round. George backed him to the ropes, pounded him with jabs, right hand leads, right uppercuts, left hooks to the body and head.

Scorning Joe's celebrated bob and weave, he found the head wherever it went. Joe would bang his forehead with his gloves to signal his enthusiasm, then step forward to get blasted again. Though Joe fought on into the fifth, he went down twice in that round and Eddie Futch didn't just throw a towel—he lurched through the ropes to stop it. Smokin' Joe became the first of the seventies' four great heavyweights to call it a career, although bored with retirement and unable to get any traction as a soul singer, five years later he pulled his trademark green trunks back on and embarked on a comeback that only managed one embarrassing draw.

With seven able heavyweights in the hunt, Don King, Arum, and the reigning boxing commissions had been delighted to keep them battling back and forth. Seven months after the "Thrilla in Manila" Ali had taken on Jimmy Young of Philadelphia. Young was a tactical fighter. He'd won the unanimous decision over Lyle, but his record was only seventeen and six and he'd stopped just six opponents. Though Young was plenty big, at 213, he lacked much power in either hand. But he defended himself well, gloves held high. He had good hand speed, he knew how and when to clinch, and he had a reputation as the best counter-puncher in the division. But the question in the sporting press was how much Ali had left in his tank after the epic third battle with Frazier.

Angelo Dundee put a sign in Ali's locker that read "Remember San Diego," a reminder of the trainer's belief that Ali lost and got his jaw broken by Ken Norton because he was over-confident and out of shape. Nonetheless Ali weighed in at 230, the heaviest of his career. Of the fight with Young, Ali's fans expected little more than an exhibition. They thought Ali was being thrown red meat.

I watched the bout on home TV that night. Emily had jumped up, sending her cat Daisy flying, and run to her room when she realized people were going to be hitting each other. I thought it was about the strangest fight I'd ever seen. Young would duck so low to the canvas that Ali had to pull back or be penalized for rabbit punching. Other times Young stuck his head outside the ropes, so Ali again had to stop punching. When Young did that in the eighth round, the referee took a point away on the cards. In the ninth Ali punished him with jabs and combinations, but Young won the war of wills with the ref, who gave up and let him use the ropes however he wanted. Young poked his head through the ropes to stop action again in the twelfth, thirteenth, and fifteenth rounds, but he fought hard in spurts. The Associated Press scored it in favor of Young, and the crowd booed the unanimous decision awarded to Ali. I thought they would have booed Young for finding ways not to fight.

On the telecast team, Kenny scored the bout even on his unofficial card. "Ali looked pitiful," he said. "I kept hollering to him, 'Don't blow the money, Ali, don't blow the money!' But the Ali you saw tonight is not the guy I have to fight. I wish it was, but it won't be. He'll be ready for me. You can count on it."

The gears of money and demand rolled for a rematch between Ali and George. The boxing commissions awarding the crown wouldn't let the king avoid it much longer. If Ali didn't agree to it, he'd have to retire, and that would signal loss of courage. As a presumed warmup to that huge fight, in San Juan, Puerto Rico, in September 1977, George's bout with Jimmy Young didn't attract a closed-circuit telecast, though the ABC network carried it. At the press conference announcing the fight Jimmy Young boasted, "If I don't get hurt in the first five rounds, he's mine." A reporter said few people thought he had the heart to stay in the ring *two* rounds with George. "What do you know about my heart?" Young shot back. "I let my heart speak for me in the ring."

Young had now won two decisions over Ron Lyle, but he got the fight against George thanks to his weird performance against Ali. No one outside Young's corner and marriage thought he had a chance against George. Young had a puzzled expression before the fight began, like he wondered if he belonged there.

In a clinch toward the end of the first round Young cried to the ref that George had hit him in the back of the head—so George popped him with a soft right as they broke the clinch. Young and his corner complained to the ref every chance they got. One of George's effective weapons was the hard shove with his gloves or forearms if an opponent got too close—in the pocket, as boxers put it. In harm's way. The tactic was used by many fighters, including Ali, but this ref warned George that they were infractions.

"What he's been doing," Howard Cosell said, "is what any veteran fighter will do." Early in the third round Young went to a knee in the course of another clinch. George gave Young a shove as he stepped back.

"There was nothing there," said Cosell, then he cried, "Wait a minute, the ref is taking away a point!"

The ref's explanation was "unnecessary roughing," like he was throwing a flag in a football game. George grew more frustrated and annoyed. In clinches he'd get the heel of his gloved hand under Young's chin and give his head a neck-wrenching shove. The ref warned him for raking Young with the laces of his gloves, and some observers thought George tried to break Young's arm during one clinch. At times Young counter-punched well. But early in the seventh Young was trying again to clinch when George landed a left hook that sent him stumbling and almost down. With two minutes left in the round George nearly dropped him again with a right uppercut. It looked impossible for Young to make the bell. But with thirty-five seconds left he came off the ropes fighting back. The crowd responded with a standing ovation for Young. *"Jeemie! Jeemie Young!"* they chanted the rest of the way.

Young later said, "George didn't know it, but while I may have been standing, I was out cold. He could have pushed me over with his little finger."

By the twelfth and final round Gil Clancy looked panicked in George's corner. Midway through it, Young threw a punch that appeared to miss. George got his feet tangled or was just too weary and went down. "The ref called that a knockdown!" Cosell yelled in disbelief. George attacked and tried to land the punch that could end it, but with fifteen seconds left he looked at the timekeeper, something a weary boxer is never supposed to do. If it hadn't been for the questionable point taken away from George and his weary fall being called a knockdown, the scorecards would have declared it a draw, but the decision for Young was unanimous. In celebration of the momentous upset the fans threw garbage at the ring. Latin American fight crowds are prone to strange behavior.

According to Clancy, George plunged into despair on leaving the ring. George said he'd died, and a giant hand was carrying him through emptiness. He said his head and hands were bleeding, and he yelled, "Jesus Christ is coming alive in me!" He ran in the shower, still wearing his trunks and shoes. *"Hallelujah, I'm clean!* Hallelujah, I'm born again!" Clancy said, "It was hot as hell in the ring. He was hallucinating from dehydration." In any case George Foreman had just retired from boxing. He went back to Houston and became a fat, happy street corner preacher.

CHAPTER 53

In Austin the band and I were at a crossroads. Our addition of Phil Hauptman pleased us—we thought his bottleneck guitar, dobro, and mandolin delivered more than Jake Spoon had, even with his Serpent, songwriting, and singing. Still I was glum when I shipped the demo to our new executive at Cow House Creek. It contained a song I'd drawn from my conversation with Joey Carrigan. But you just never know. The distributor who had wanted to veto the title of *Soviet Gypsies* and suggested we lose the Mexican clarinet player was once more our pal. They loved where we were headed, he said, and instead of going back to a studio they and the Cow House Creek people wanted our next album to be *Dog Boys: Haid Pecos and Rip Chords Live at the Lone Star Café.*

Okay, if they could pull that off, let's go.

At Fifth Avenue and Thirteenth Street in Manhattan, the music club was so misplaced it couldn't help but be cool. The offices of *Forbes* magazine were just down the block, and resident neighbors were not amused by the new tenant. The club occupied a squat building wedged between high rises, and its look would be forgettable if it hadn't sported a forty-foot-long sculpture of an iguana on the roof.

From his hometown in El Paso, Bob Wade had arrived in Austin and the university in the 1950s as a frat guy and hot-rodder whose nickname "Daddy-O" stuck. Daddy-O went on to graduate from distinguished art institutes and became known for his sculptures of great size and offbeat irreverence. A two-story pair of cowboy boots in front of a big clothing store in San Antonio. A troupe of mariachi-singing bullfrogs perched on a hillside beside a truck stop on an interstate highway south of Dallas. A New Orleans Saints helmet that the sculptor and his crew fashioned from the shell of a junked Volkswagen and placed on the roof overhang of an Austin saloon that specialized in Louisiana soul food. But the Lone Star Café's iguana was the brainstorm that made Daddy-O famous.

In three sections of wire mesh and polyurethane foam, his image of the spiked but harmless lizard had first come about for a works-in-progress exhibition on the New York side of Niagara Falls. After the exhibit ended, Daddy-O had to decide where to put the thing, so he called an owner of the Lone Star Café, a stranger, at two in the morning and said he had a great idea. The owner, who recalled being stoned at the time, answered, "Why not?"

Daddy-O's modest commission was $5,000, an open $5,000 tab in its bars, and a secret enclave to which only the artist had a key. Beneath the beast at the entrance was a wall that proclaimed "Too Much Ain't Enough," and a poster inside promised "The Best Honky-Tonk North of Abilene." Neighbors and the city sought for years to have the iguana taken down on grounds it was advertisement, not art, a violation of city codes. Pro bono lawyers and the endorsement of Mayor Ed Koch beat the spoilsports back. The club took off at once with bookings that included Merle Haggard, Waylon Jennings, James Brown, the Band, and Roy Orbison. In the crowds John Belushi, Dan Rather, and Andy Warhol made the scene.

Once our Cow House Creek producers got fired up about the concept of the show, they handed off most of the work to me. I got along well with Kinky Friedman, who was then deciding if he was a musician or novelist or both. He grew up in Austin, son of a university psychology professor, and he claimed that during his Peace Corps tour he taught villagers and farmers in Borneo the joy of sailing Frisbees. He was unlike Austin's cosmic cowboys. He was what I'd now call at anti-alt-cosmic cowboy. Under his hat Kinky looked like Groucho Marx with a cigar in his mouth. Kinky's first album, *Sold American,* was outrageous and controversial. He meant it to be. He satirized women's liberation with one called "Get Your Biscuits in the Oven and Your Buns in the Bed."

Another held that Charles Whitman, the UT Tower sniper, was just another Eagle Scout, which angered a great number of people, among them an Associated Press reporter who was wounded and filed his story from a hospital bed. But I thought Kinky's debut, recorded in Nashville, was an impressive piece of work.

In Austin he called his terrific show band the Texas Jewboys. Now as the eminence of the Lone Star Café he fronted a new group called the Shalom Retirement Village People. For the *New York Times* he would reflect on the club's mystique: "It had a very strange ambience, people trying to be Texans and Texans trying to be people. People made love inside the iguana. Drug deals went down all around it. The iguana was the perfect symbol of the times; it was an otherworldly, next-door-to-evil creature."

Kinky was hard to know but harder to dislike. I tracked him down and told him the idea about our live show and album. He said he'd pass on the word. The plan took on life, but the club was booked weeks and months ahead, which was fortunate for us. The reborn Rip Chords, our part-time gypsy fiddler, and I pitched into rehearsals, trying to come up with enough material for an album with two LP's worth of material.

I wondered but didn't ask Kenny how his son reacted after watching Ali fight his dad and waking up on his tenth birthday the morning after. For eight months Kenny stayed out of boxing's limelight. He told me he was spending much more time at home and doting on his infant daughter Kenisha. We talked about music, movies, our wives.

Kenny kept his eye on Ali, who said those nice things about him but was hardly acting like a retiree. And George's shocking loss and retirement was a godsend for Kenny. His career bugaboo was gone. So was the only obstacle to another fight with Ali.

Kenny had already decided he had to take Ferdie Pacheco's advice. He accepted a return to New York, this time in the Garden against an undefeated youth named Duane Bobick. Kenny would get $500,000, and third-ranked Bobick would get $300,000. Jimmy Young could make all the noise he wanted, but with George out of the picture, Kenny was the uncontested top contender. If Kenny kept winning, and Ali didn't lose or retire, one of the boxing commissions would inevitably declare a fourth match between them mandatory.

Duane Bobick was a twenty-seven-year-old who grew up in Bowlus, Minnesota, which had a population of 268 in the 1970 census. Bobick had taken up boxing during an enlistment in the US Navy. He won ninety-three amateur bouts in arresting fashion. In the US he had been a national Golden Glove and AAU champion, and he beat Cuba's hero Teófilo Stevenson and won the 1971 Pan American Games. The next year in the Olympic trials he won another big decision over the future heavyweight champion Larry Holmes. But the Munich Olympics turned sour when in the rematch Stevenson stopped him in the third round.

Bobick came back with his Bronze Medal and first set up in Little Falls, Minnesota. After sixteen straight knockouts, he moved to Philadelphia to be schooled by Kenny's former trainer Eddie Futch and managed by Joe Frazier. That was big news in boxing. When Bobick signed to fight Kenny in Madison Square Garden, he was undefeated in thirty-eight pro fights and had stopped thirty-one of them. He succeeded Jerry Quarry as boxing's Great White Hope and garnered other tags—among them "The Golden Boy."

But who had he overcome in ten or more rounds? Larry's erratic sparring partner Mike Weaver proved to be the best of them. Nonetheless, while Bobick was training for the Norton fight he popped off to a writer for the *Minneapolis Star.* "I've never felt so good, trained so hard, or felt so prepared for a fight as I have this one. I feel a lot quicker. My left jab is better. He fights flat-footed and can't move back. He proved that in the George Foreman fight. So I'm willing to go toe to toe with him and slug it out with him. Once the bell rings, everything will be great."

Eddie Futch still resented the circumstance of his parting with Kenny, and he tried to wreak havoc with Kenny's psychology and emotions. Futch told the press, "Norton's not as quick as he thinks he is. Outside of Ali and Foreman, he hasn't fought anybody better than Duane fought. Jerry Quarry came out of retirement to fight Ken and had only ten days to get ready." Which was untrue; Quarry had just beaten Scrap Iron Johnson, no pushover. Futch went on that he arranged most of Kenny's matches, so he knew about the quality of opponents. "I think Norton's chin is more suspect than Duane's. I've had to pick Norton up off the floor a couple of times. And that's not easy."

Kenny's old friend and mentor called him fat!

He shot back in the press: "I love Eddie Futch. He taught me everything I know about boxing, up to a point. I'm sorry he thinks he has to resort to insults to inflate this boy. Give Bobick credit. He's unbeaten and he's the WBA's number three contender. Cut out the baloney. Let's get it on."

The Rip Chords thought I was paying too much attention to that boxing match. But a coincidence of scheduling had brought our big nights together. If Kenny's fight in the Garden came off on time, I could watch the fight even if it went the distance and still have time to get a cab to the Lone Star Café—Kinky and his band were playing an opening set. Sabine chose to stay home, practice law, and keep up with Emily. I flew up, checked into the Mayflower, and paid for the secure storage garage. The trickiest part turned out to be getting the band there on time. We had traded up from our two cramped vans to a one-owner bus. Seven musicians and a roadie transported thirteen prized instruments, if you counted Howie's drum set as just one, and they thought they'd take their time enjoying a springtime roll through the Smoky Mountains and the Blue Ridge Parkway.

They hadn't planned on Jehovah's Witnesses transporting themselves to a national convention and grand revival in New York the same weekend as our gig. Our guys wouldn't have thought anything about it if they'd known. The Witnesses were perfectly polite, saying grace before their pancakes in I-Hops, but motels from Texarkana to Baltimore were booked full of them. The Rip Chords were ragged and dazed by the time they reached the Mayflower. When the van and their instruments were safely locked away, they staggered to their rooms and when they woke up, they knew it was irrational but were irked at me because I'd flown.

I skipped the fight's weigh-in because of our endless sound check at the club. The major difference I saw was two mikes where usually there was just one. Our sound man Shack was pushed out while Cow House Creek's experts squabbled with their counterparts at the club. I got tired of saying, "Testing, testing, one two three, rub a dub dub, my girl's throwing up drunk at the country club." The lack of control made us nervous, but we thought we'd finally arrived, whoever jiggered the board.

That evening I put on Levi's, my elk skin boots, a black mock turtleneck, and a fur-collared leather jacket for the cold. In the dressing room of the Garden, John Norton and I watched as Weaver warmed Kenny up. Despite all the bravado, there were trouble signs in the other dressing room. Joe Frazier had that week shocked Bobick by telling a reporter he wouldn't attend the fight. One press account said Joe predicted his fighter would lose.

Joe's friendship with Kenny wasn't the reason for his boycott of the fight. "Duane also was represented by a lawyer and a financial manager," Joe said. "I was his manager and sparring partner, but he listened to those guys over me. The lawyer and manager thought Ken Norton was too old and over the hill, yet still had name value. I asked these guys, 'How in the world do you figure Ken Norton's through? He kicked Ali's ass last September.' I told them Duane wasn't ready for Ken, but they voted me down."

And now their fighter made Eddie Futch nervous. "Bobick had a lot of his navy buddies in the locker room," he said, "and they were talking old times when he should have been warming up. I told Bobick, 'Come on, knock off this conversation, let's get busy. I want you to come out really warm against Norton because he's gonna come out after you because he wants to pay back me. He'll be on a mission.' For that fight, we had monitors in the dressing rooms so we could watch what the other fighter was doing. We could see them and they could see us. I was watching the monitor in Ken's dressing room when he started out toward the ring. He was sweating like a horse, and Bobick was bone dry."

Bobick stepped through the ropes wearing a hooded white robe. He had been in the Garden twice before, and he got a big roar of welcome back. He performed a lazy dance with his big arms raised. When he took off the robe, he had a gold floral wreath around his neck. I supposed it was a good luck charm and reminder he was the Golden Boy. A corner man relieved him of the wreath. Bobick gazed at Kenny like he was a passerby on the street. He jogged easily, foot to foot, not really moving around. He was so calm and relaxed he looked drowsy. Though Kenny had gotten respectful cheers there were plenty of boos.

They both stood six-three. At 222 Kenny outweighed Bobick by five pounds. Bobick wasn't cut and chiseled like Kenny, and his upper torso and Minnesota origin made me think of a snowplow, not Paul Bunyan. The bell rang and Kenny measured Bobick with his jab. Bobick was known as a quick and heavy puncher with his right, and he shot out a couple that missed. Kenny was wary of the right but saw that Bobick carried his left a shade low. He ducked inside and shot a right to Bobick's body, watching where his eyes went. Kenny then threw a straight right off the jab, which Bobick caught on his gloves and forearms. Bobick was starting to launch a counterpunch when Kenny took one step left and his overhand right fell on Bobick like a battlefield mortar.

His gloves came up, his knees buckled, and he stumbled toward Kenny. Bobick said later that the punch caught him in the throat and he couldn't breathe. Kenny maintained that the force of his blow to Bobick's chin sent his *jawbone* crashing into his adam's apple.

Kenny backed Bobick into a corner in a calm fury of left hooks, right uppercuts, and four more overhand rights, nineteen punches in all. He loaded up the last right that put Bobick down. The youth landed on his right side and tried to push himself up. From my vantage point all I could see was the broad backside of his light-colored trunks. He made it to his feet just before the ref's count reached ten. But then he drifted sideward, crossing one foot over the other. "No, no, no," the ref yelled and jumped between them.

CHAPTER 54

At the post-fight press conference Bobick had the composure and brass to say, "Guess you guys had some time to kill, huh?" Kenny cut it short, took a quick shower, and dressed for the rest of the night. He was tired of being booed in New York. From the wings of the Lone Star Café's stage he and I took in the mix of black guys in sunglasses, hippie chicks, and bogus shitkickers. I shed the jacket and put the *frattoir* on. The club's lighting guy had said he'd make the rubboard shine like a brand-new dime.

After congratulating Kenny and chatting with us a few minutes, Kinky walked to the lead mike and took his stogie out of his mouth. "If any of you folks missed the big fight tonight," he said, "don't worry about it—we all did. This man here finished off Duane Bobick in Madison Square Garden tonight in fifty-eight seconds. I wish I could get paid half a million for work like that. You gotta love Muhammad Ali, but let's hear it for Ken Norton. After his last two fights, who can say this man's not the real heavyweight champion of the world?" Kenny let the noise die. It included some catcalls.

"Thank you, Kinky. How do you get away with being called that in Texas? Stay where you are. This mike is mine now. Duane Bobick is a talented young guy. He just didn't have time to show it. I wish him well. Muhammad Ali is a great fighter and a good friend, and I was honored and delighted to whip his ass a time or two."

Laughter, cheers, and a scattering of jeers rose to that.

"But enough about me. I want to introduce a guy I met in California in 1967. I was trying to get out of the marines and so was he. You wouldn't know it looking at him, but Haid Pecos was once my sparring partner. He was the best we could get at the time, and he was pretty good. Before I took my discharge and turned pro, Haid told me, 'Don't let them make you stop throwing that overhand right.' Well, I'm still throwing it, pal, and tonight it was landing. Let's hear it for Haid Pecos and the Rip Chords. Rock and roll."

He gave me an embrace as I walked out. Some people went *wooo h* and looked up with more interest when the multi-colored beams of light hit my rubboard. I admired a Delbert McClinton recording called "The Rub" that was about low-life trouble. He sang it in a drawling baritone, accompanied by jazzy horns and the harmonica style he taught John Lennon, but to my ear it was Fort Worth Jacksboro Highway talking blues. I shortened and moved around the lyrics some. I timed my version by making my tocks and strums of thimbles align with the thumps of Shack's bass guitar, in the dark behind me.

I know how you hate to wake up in the morning
But somebody's gotta make a move
There's a parking lot full of police outside
And they all ask for you
He said "I never shot him, he shot himself
While he was shooting at me"
I said "There's a pitch fork
Sticking in the roof of his car
And both headlights are busted out
These people say they saw you running away"
He said "Hell, I was just going for help"
Now all y'all witnessed what I said he done
I hope he makes bail, I love it when they run

The band let the quiet rest for a few beats then Howie's drumsticks were flying, Johnny and Phil stepped out with their guitars, and I chased after our modern Jezebel in "Two Bubbles Off Plumb." We scattered in other songs we'd written and recorded and that got some air play—"Pipe Town Blues," "Soviet Gypsies," and the best one from Jake Spoon, his vision of Jerry Lee Lewis's little girl, "Daddy Was a Killer." But we couldn't help noticing that the farther we got away from home, the crowds grew attentive about our material but response was lukewarm. We hadn't had the one big hit that identified us in people's ears and minds. So with a nod to Austin's cosmic cowboys and Nashville's outlaws, neither of which we aspired to be, we had a good time covering Delbert's big hit, "Two More Bottles of Wine," and Jerry Jeff Walker's cover of Guy Clark's "L.A. Freeway." I loved Mick Jagger's and Keith Richards's "Dead Flowers," reflections of a junkie sunk in a Louisville basement on Kentucky Derby Day. But he dug deeper in his baritone than I could go. "Listen to Keith's harmony," Johnny Stafford suggested one day, and when I did, then I knew how to sing it. We liked our version of Bruce Springsteen's "Atlantic City," about street toughs spoiling for a fight with out-of-state gangsters, though I sang it more like Levon Helm's version. We wanted the crowd to find its comfort zone. Then Ramón got out the flute given him by South American Indians and applied that breathy style to the intro of "Can't You See," a song that bridged the cultural divide between Marshall Tucker and Waylon Jennings. Any singer worth his salt can get into that one. We followed with my friend Bob Brown's "Was That a Kiss (Or Did You Try to Bite My Hand?)" The crowd laughed and cheered the spunk of that one. Then Terry Allen's "Amarillo Highway," an endorsement of life on a two-lane north out of Lubbock. *There's a girl in the back seat, asleep on the back seat, and that trunk's full of Pearl and Lone Star . . .* The real Texans and counterfeit ones howled and sang along.

We mixed in some soul favorites, All Green's "Stay with Me" and Jackie Wilson's "Lonely Teardrops." During the second set I said, "I think most good songs are love songs, though they may not end up the way you want." Demonstrating the latter, we began with the embittered "Rock Salt and Nails," which I heard first recorded by Joe Ely. Then Willie Nelson's "It's Not Supposed to Be That Way" and "Just a Waltz," a song Steve Fromholz wrote but never recorded. Then another of my favorites of broken-hearted vein, Jimmy LaFave's "You're a Big Girl Now." *This pain that stops and starts . . . honey, it's like a corkscrew through my heart . . .*

From watching Willie's live shows I'd seen that medleys can work well if they're well-paced and honed to a sheen. We'd put in hours rehearsing a short one for the encore. It began with "Dog Boys," my song and title track of the new album. The Cow House Creek guys had come up with a brainstorm; they brought in an animal trainer and an old bloodhound called Sneezy. He claimed that as a young dog it was one of the bloodhounds that trailed Paul Newman in *Cool Hand Luke.* The trainer said he'd make Sneezy howl on cue. I was afraid it would come out farce, but the trainer got the dog to speak up every time we sang the chorus.

Sounds you hear at night
Would make a free man shiver
Stabbings in the yard
Over some guy's gang tattoos
I lie here aching for the dawn
Just to breathe some outside air
Yonder goes a school bus
In the early morning haze
Our man on horseback don't care
How bad you used to be
Hoe those weeds, bad boys
Hoe those weeds

Big mean man with his twelve-gauge handy
All day on that saddle and big bay mare
Meaner by the minute, it makes a man sore

My dogs they're just hounds
They don't want to eat on no one
Noses bred to love the smell of man
Then some guy has a mind to run
Dog boy loping along after 'em
Hearing howls like canine bassoons
Knowing the sad outcome
Hoping just one time I'm wrong
Oh sweet Ann, I know I know, you're
Worn out writing, hearing nothing back
Dog boy and his dogs in the wagon shade
Sorry kind of peace in surrender

To that big mean man with his twelve-gauge handy
All day on that saddle and big bay mare
Meaner by the minute, it makes a man sore

Throughout the second set Johnny and Phil had been working in riffs and echoes on one of the best collaborations of Eric Clapton and Duane Allman on Derek and the Dominos' *Layla* album. Now they stepped out and turned that way up, Johnny's lead and Phil's bottleneck, with a percussion bridge duet of Howie's drums and my *frattoir*, and we let it go on longer than the original. The crowd pressed up close, singing along. *Any day, any day, I will see you smile ... Anyway, anyway, just for a little while . . .*

CHAPTER 55

We didn't get press like Kenny's knockout of Bobick, but the concert won us a subsequent nice short piece in the *New Yorker.* The Cow House Creek people hired a top photographer for the cover shoot. He dressed up three young guys in white coveralls and flop hats like convicts in Texas and provided them long-handled hoes and two bloodhounds on leashes. The photographer assembled the eleven of us, not counting the dogs, like he was trying to mimic the Beatles' famous *Sergeant Pepper* cover. He took photos with a Polaroid, looked at them, repositioned us, shot more Polaroids, repositioned us again, then took endless photos with a large camera I couldn't identify, and by then I didn't care to ask. The assistant brought buckets of water for the dogs to plunge their floppy jowls in. The photographer exhausted us, but he delivered an image for a striking cover.

Then I got a message to call the chief executive of Cow House Creek. It puzzled me but I expected it was probably more good news. Tour of Europe perhaps. A secretary asked me to hold for Bain Jefferson. He offered a few pleasantries, then said he wanted me to come see him in Charlotte, North Carolina. He didn't say why, just that it was important, and of course they'd cover my airfare and lodging.

Wearing a sharp suit and open-collared shirt, Bain shook my hand heartily when I arrived and insisted I have a cup of Costa Rican espresso.

I sipped a little before I set the cup aside. He led me down a winding hall to a studio where two men also hustled to greet me. They were guys who'd worked with us on *Soviet Gypsies,* as well as the concert in New York. Andrew put us in chairs around a mixing board, and one of the men handed me earphones.

He took the kind of deep breath you take when you're about to do something you don't want to do. "Haid," he said, "that was a fantastic concert in New York. You know it, the guys in your band know it. The crowd loved it. We loved it. But we've got problems."

"What?"

"Recording is getting so sophisticated these days. FM radio has followed suit. Even jukebox manufacturers have to get their heads in the game." He took another breath. "This is painful. I don't know if the guys in the band have told you. Has your wife told you?"

"Told me *what?*"

"Something's happened to your voice." He looked at the sound engineers, who nodded sadly. "You're singing a note and it's almost like you hiccup—"

"Bullshit."

He raised his palms. "I know. But I don't how else to describe it. You'll believe it when you put on those earphones. Cow House Creek is a small, class independent that we mean to keep growing. We have to meet industry standards. We have to meet our own standards. These guys couldn't hear it that night because they were so caught up in the show. But now it's there, and they can't fix it. They've tried. Done everything they could. We can't put this record out. You've always been so precise. Every syllable. But now record buyers aren't going to be able to understand you."

I started to rise out of the chair. "Well, let's see, buster. Give me the master."

Bain smiled. "You know better than that. If you put it out on your own everybody will know we recorded and paid for it. You've got to find a doctor that can help you through this. We'll help you find that doctor. When you get back this voice we love, maybe we can get all your guys back in this studio, or one in Texas if that suits you better, and do this all over again. It just won't be a live double album."

"Maybe," I repeated.

"Haid, we're your friends. You've been a very good singer, you've held a good band together, and we've been proud to have you for your albums. Sales could have matched what you did with Shelter, and you could have been more prolific, but that's neither here nor there. Let us help you get your voice back. Let us help you get rid of that hiccup."

An ear, nose, and throat specialist in Austin told me I had something called spasmodic dysphonia. "It's not going to kill you," he said, "but it's not going away. My hope is that with help and work you can learn to control it. Hundreds of thousands of people in this country develop this. They're usually older than you." I was so confused and disheartened I told Sabine and the Rip Chords I had *symphonic* dysphonia. It's a tic in the larynx or walls of my voice box, or both. My ENT said he wasn't qualified to treat it but he'd refer me to a good speech therapist and would help with the search for the right kind of specialist. The speech therapist met me once a week and gave me drills to repeat daily. I drove around saying the words on highway signs, trying to make the sounds reverb slightly on the part of my upper palate against my front teeth. As time went by, the Rip Chords peeled off to recording sessions with other bands, sitting in on their gigs. I wound up steered to an otolaryngologist, a kind of doctor I'd never heard of before then, at Johns Hopkins medical school in Baltimore. Before I flew up to see him, my ear, nose, and throat doctor arranged a test for me in Austin. Her tests recorded the sounds but also pictures of my throat that looked like the flapping hands of characters in *The Muppets,* only they weren't a soft friendly green. The speech therapist was a good-looking blonde in high heels, and she made me hopeful.

That test provided the doctor in Baltimore not only the sound of my ailing voice but visual evidence of what was going on in the mechanism. The doctor at Johns Hopkins was a tall man named Norman Roth. I could tell from all the diplomas and testimonials on his walls of his stature in his field. Most of them were professional singers I'd heard of, which buoyed my hopes.

He said, "I listened to your records, and I have to tell you I like them. A great deal. Some interesting work on what you've got is being done at a number of medical schools. They've found that injections of Botox every two or three months can basically freeze the tic, but it's classified experimental at this stage. If you say the word Botox, insurance underwriters at once assume you mean cosmetic." He paused. "You're unlike most musicians. You have good insurance."

"Yeah, thanks to my wife."

"If you can get your insurance to accept the injections every two or three months, and I'll fight for you if they try to turn you down, your wife and friends and children, if you have them, will be able to understand every word you say. So will strangers on the phone. If anyone ever tells you that you have a speech impediment, tell them to go fuck themselves."

I managed a smile.

"But I have to tell you that you're never going to be able to sing like that again."

He sighed and studied my expression. I could tell he was a nice man.

"I've never seen so much scar tissue in someone's throat," he said. "You can't see it on the outside. Has something ever happened to you? Some trauma? Like a car wreck?"

Sabine could tell from my voice on the phone that I was distraught. "I'm tired, babe. I'll tell you about it when I get home." I was flying out of an airport between Baltimore and Washington. On the way there I decided to stay over another night and wander around the Mall and monuments in DC. I caught a cab the next morning. Tulips were abloom everywhere. The flowerbeds had traces of melting snow.

The weather was windy and chilly but overnight the sky had cleared. The real reason for my delay was a sudden wish to see the Vietnam Memorial. It hadn't been unveiled long, and gathered around it was a large crowd of men and women about my age, some holding the hands of children. I moved on from the statue of the Warriors to the Wall of black granite in panels quarried in Bangalore, India. The enormity of it stunned me. Supported by a berm, the Wall is set in the shape of a stripe of rank on a military uniform. Each of its two wings looked like they were about the length of a football field. I started on the east wing and found the date my friend Chuck Mercer died the summer of 1966. I stood before his panel a long time, seeing my face reflected in the stone. It was far enough down on the panel that I started to reach out and touch it but feared I'd leave a handprint.

I moved on looking for names of people who might not have made it back during Tet in 1968. On the east wing I found the name of PFC Phil Lanzarotta and was glad I didn't see Private Henson, the big Midwesterner that laid out Private McCombs in the ice plants. I was glad for that matter I didn't find McCombs, nor more so my favorite DI, Staff Sergeant Mulligan, or Colonel Bullick, commanding officer of the brig at Pendleton. I looked for names of marines and navy corpsmen I knew in the battle for Hue and on other patrols, firefights, and slogs in the heat and downpours. I saw faces in my mind, but the experience of the Wall was overpowering, and I couldn't call back the names. My last name on it would have been Shelton, but those guys would have remembered me by my nickname, High Noon.

I came to the tapered end of the east wing and found the names stopped in late May of 1968. I went to the other end and started walking the west wing. In the panel containing the names of that August, my gaze passed, then like a force of nature it jerked back to one: *Geoffrey Edwards.* The hero of the "Chosin Few" in Korea who murdered my voice with one swing of a chow hall tray.

I spun away and wound up on my hands and knees. A man came up behind me and paced a comforting hand on my shoulder.

"It's not what you think," I said.

Startled, he stepped back and gave me room.

I was at the airport turning in the rent car. Like a fighter hanging up the gloves, I turned off the mike.

CHAPTER 56

Kenny was riding high, thinking he had Ali cornered once more. Then Don King and the World Boxing Commission, which was run in Mexico City by Jose Sulaiman, struck again with another Eliminator. Before the WBC would mandate a title fight against Ali, Kenny had to fight Jimmy Young, despite Kenny's far superior record and the fact that he had once beaten Ali while Young lost his only attempt. Rumors reached Kenny that Ali *ordered* Sulaiman to heed King's wishes, hopeful that Young might be able to beat him. Kenny cursed and made his family miserable for several days, then started getting ready.

Four months after his big night against Bobick, intent on staying in fighting shape, he had been preparing to take out a quick but light-hitting Italian, Lorenzo Zanon, when he arrived in a locker room to get dressed and taped and paused to watch a televised interview of Young, who had won a lackluster decision over a young journeyman on the undercard. Young was saying: "I was ready for Norton tonight. I could've gone fifteen rounds easily. By the tenth round I was just getting started. Norton can't fight; he's just an experienced amateur. Look at all that jewelry he wears. Who does he think he is, Sammy Davis Junior?"

Kenny was usually businesslike in his attitude toward rivals and opponents, but here was one he could dislike. He considered Young a "garbage fighter" who complained to the refs about how poor Jimmy was being treated, and in Kenny's opinion, he showed utter cowardice by sticking his head through the ropes to keep from being hit by Ali.

The fractured and competing boxing commissions had ushered in a time when almost no fighters of any weight could claim to be champions of the whole world. Pro boxing had become like the schisms of popes who excommunicated each other in the fourteenth century. More boxing commissions and title belts were on the way. Ali was an exception because he held the crowns of both the World Boxing Commission, the WBC, and the World Boxing Association, the WBA. But Jose Sulaiman granted Don King's wish of a Norton-Young Eliminator with a significant caveat. Within eight months of that bout, Ali had to fight the winner or the WBC would strip him of the title.

Unlike the Eliminator canceled by the bullet with Oscar Bonavena's name on it, Kenny's fight against Young made boxing sense—Young after all had retired Foreman. And King made it worth their while. Kenny's purse was $1.75 million, and Young got his first million. That night at Caesars Palace in Vegas, Young counterpunched crisply and pulled ahead with his right-hand counterpunches. Kenny had trouble figuring out Young's tricky defense. Young would land a punch and then dive into a clinch before Kenny could hit him back. Kenny knew he was not looking good.

Twice, when he landed a left hook to the body and later one of his overhand rights, he thought he could finish Young. But in the tenth Young shook Kenny with a counter right, a hook, and two more rights. Before the fourteenth round Ali stood and hollered for the TV audience, "I'm tired of fighting Norton. *Win, Jimmy!*" Kenny overpowered Young for the next three minutes, but then Young rallied and controlled the fifteenth round. Two judges had Kenny winning 147-143 while another judge gave it to Young 144-142. Over his career Kenny had now won two out of three split decisions, all in major fights.

At the press conference afterward, Young was angry about the decision. "Do I think I won the fight? Of course I do. I disagree with the whole scoring, but what can I do about it?" Kenny had no use or sympathy for Young, but the press conference sobered him with the human cost of their pursuits and dreams. "This is just a temporary setback," Young's wife sobbed to the reporters. "Jimmy will still win the title someday. You watch."

But it had been Young's last chance. He fought twenty-seven more times. His record down the backstretch was thirteen wins and thirteen losses, not counting a bout in São Paulo, Brazil, where the ref disqualified both fighters for "faking." Young retired with a record of thirty-five wins, eighteen losses, and three draws. After his retirement, he found himself a defendant in criminal court charged with felony drug possession, and he had to listen to a Philadelphia public defender plead to a judge that he was not responsible for his actions because boxing had left him with traumatic brain injury. Young was dead at fifty-six.

Ali didn't like all the praise Kenny was getting for his knockout of Bobick. Days later he answered, though, by awarding a title shot to stocky young Uruguayan Alfredo Angelista, who had won just fourteen of sixteen but battled Ali for fifteen rounds. Ali said, "Did you see me overweight and not conditioned and didn't have no real trouble? Still moving, my legs are there, my reflexes. I'll lose the weight. I got time. . . . I'm thirty-five years old and I danced fifteen rounds. It's a miracle."

Howard Cosell grumbled, "I'm sorry we televised it."

Stung by the criticism, Ali prided himself on never ducking anyone, so he took on a genuine contender. Some boxing fan organization had honored Earnie Shavers as the hardest punching heavyweight all of time. When Shavers at last got a title shot against Ali, the thirty-three-year-old had won fifty-four of sixty and was perceived to be running out of time and incapable of lasting more than six or seven rounds. The fight aired on NBC home TV with Dick Enberg as the lead announcer, and Kenny again was the pro on the telecast team.

Ali kept Shavers waiting in the ring a long time. Enberg asked Kenny if that would bother Shavers. "Not really," he said. "You're more or less in your own world, so to speak." As they moved around the ring, Ali mugged and made faces at Shavers, and during the ref's instructions he kept rubbing Shavers's shaved head with the palm of a glove. When the fight began, Enberg explained that the unending hollers came from Bundini Brown, the cheerleader in Ali's corner. Kenny said, "I think Bundini's more like his spiritual adviser."

Kenny didn't even talk like other fighters.

Trying to demonstrate he still had the hand speed, Ali right away cut loose a combination of eight punches and a feint. Shavers caught each one on his gloves, and when Ali stepped back, Shavers grinned and turned his thumbs outward in a shrug. Ali's greatest loss to age was his ability to slip punches with movement of his head; now he seemed determined to prove how well he could *take* a punch. With a minute left in that first round Shavers found the range for his right. Ali's knees collapsed and he almost went down. He clinched Shavers around the shoulders and offered the crowd a jaw-drop of mock awe at the power of the blow. Seconds later, though, Shavers caught Ali again with the right, and this one sent him stumbling and grabbing at the top rope to keep from going down. Shavers almost knocked the champion out.

Ali knew he'd better start fighting and stop showboating. He took over with jabs and combinations, but Shavers jolted and staggered him again and again. Ali landed a left hook that would have finished many fighters in the tenth round, but at the end of the fourteenth Angelo Dundee had to steer his wobbly charge back to the corner.

In a play for ratings the networks had started posting real-time scoring of the judge's cards at the end of each round. The short-lived experiment robbed viewers of the suspense of boxing and played into Ali's hands. Dundee had a TV on in the dressing room and a runner who informed him exactly where they were and what Ali had to do. Ali had won enough rounds that he only had to avoid a knockout in the fifteenth. He did that and more, battering Shavers around the ring the last thirty seconds of the fight. For the slugfest the crowd gave them a standing ovation. Ali won easily on the cards but said afterward, "Earnie hit me so hard it hurt my kinfolk back in Africa." He'd used the same line when Henry Cooper put him down early in his career. Ali's fifty-seventh pro fight was his last hurrah.

After that close call, Ali went back to shopping for easier opponents, and Bob Arum offered one. Ali expected to fight Alfio Righetti after that undefeated Italian disposed of "Neon Leon" Spinks. In the 1976 Montreal Olympics, the older Spinks brother had won the light heavyweight Gold medal, and his younger brother Michael won the middleweight Gold. They were a great story out of East St. Louis. But going into the fight with Righetti, Leon had won only five as a pro and managed just a draw with so-so Scott LeDoux. Then Spinks won a unanimous decision upset of Righetti.

This was not the title fight Arum intended to promote. Leon favored a wild haircut and beard and had lost both his upper and lower front teeth while sparring in the marines. At a flabby 224, Ali outweighed Spinks by twenty-seven pounds. Leon's style was to square off and bang away with whoever was in front of him. The twenty-five-year-old mugged Ali for fifteen rounds, leaving his face swollen. One scorecard gave the bout to the champion, but the other votes weren't close. The world had a totally unexpected heavyweight champion.

Shocked by what they'd been dealt, the WBA and WBC tried to hold the unified crown together. But instead of taking a first title defense they offered against Kenny, Spinks opted for the bigger-money rematch clause in his contract with Ali. The WBA caved in, hoping to stick with Ali, but Jose Sulaiman and the WBC yanked their heavyweight title and awarded it to Kenny because he had won the Eliminator against Jimmy Young.

After a career of eleven years, forty wins, and four losses, Kenny disliked being cast as a "paper champion," but he would have been a fool to turn it down.

The WBC gave him scant time to enjoy his dream coming somewhat true. In eighty-four days, he had to defend it against the commission's new number-one contender, the hungry Larry Holmes, who had a record of twenty-nine and zero with nineteen knockouts. It would happen at Caesars Palace in Vegas in June 1978. In the buildup for the fight, Kenny couldn't understand why Holmes was so angry. Holmes was angry because he'd struggled to find financial backing for his pro career after losing to Duane Bobick in the Olympic trials six years earlier. The anger came from growing up poor on a tough side of a Pennsylvania town called Easton, from working for three dollars an hour in a blistering steel mill, from starting out as a boxer making sixty bucks a fight, from trying to escape the enormous shadow of Ali, who took him on as his favored sparring partner, and from trying to evade the connivances of Don King. When Holmes began to gain a foothold in his career, Don King took over as both promoter and manager. King's son was Holmes's manager on paper, but in a conflict of interest common in boxing, King double-dipped into his purses. Holmes would have been angry at a pack of Yukon wolves.

To let Holmes prove himself against a high-caliber opponent, King suggested Earnie Shavers. Shavers was then ranked third, Holmes fourth. "Perfect," Holmes said. Holmes's corner men clamored, *"Yikes!"* when his trunks split in the first round of the national telecast. A man sprinted for another pair. In the second round Shavers landed one of his thunderous rights. Holmes shook his head to clear it, then fired back a fast one-two. After that, Shavers lost stamina round after round. The twelve-round fight wasn't close on the cards.

Holmes was twenty-nine when he finally got his title shot. Kenny was making $3.7 million off this fight. Holmes got half a million. At the press conference announcing the bout Holmes erupted, "I'm not fighting for a title. I'm fighting for respect. Once you have respect, everything else falls into place: titles, money, everything else I need. Norton thinks he's God's gift to the world. He thinks he's so pretty. I won't win any beauty contests, but I'll win this fight."

Kenny thought Holmes was obnoxious and liked the contrast drawn by a sports columnist: "Norton is introspective. Holmes wears his emotion like a badge. Norton, the only child of middle-class parents, is well-educated. Holmes left school at thirteen to help support a family of twelve children. Norton has parlayed his ring career into acting roles while Holmes, until recently, toiled away in obscurity. The two men are as diverse in their beliefs and lifestyles as one can imagine. The one thing they have in common is a desire to be the heavyweight champion of the world."

Partly true. Kenny had been a lazy college dropout who gained his philosophy and intellectual direction by reading a book recommended by his shrink. Holmes's insults and hostility inspired Kenny, who said he sparred two hundred rounds. The Tuesday before the fight, Holmes had a workout that was supposed to end at four o'clock, when Kenny's would begin. On the blaring sound system of the casino's Sports Pavilion, Kenny's people put on the Bee Gees or some other disco group, and he made an appearance befitting a champion and movie star. Holmes and his crew hung around, which wasn't in the script. When Kenny started warming up, his challenger came close and jeered, "Look at the pretty boy jumping rope."

Watching the loop of his rope zing over and down, Kenny said, "Larry, the only reason you're so jealous of me is that you're so damn ugly and skinny. Anything next to you looks pretty." People in the gym laughed, not the response Holmes had in mind.

He rushed Kenny and said, "What did you just say to me, pussy?" Then he gave Kenny a hard shove. Kenny knew trash talk was a standard promotion ploy, but the shove enraged him. Bill Slayton got between them before the fight got going five days early. Slayton said, "It was stupid for Holmes to do something like that. One punch and the fight might have been called off. I've never seen a fighter act in such a low-class, cheap, lousy manner, especially when both fighters were going to see a nice paycheck that could easily have been blown all to hell."

Since that didn't happen and nobody got hurt, Don King loved it. He tagged Kenny's first title defense "The Battle of Bad Blood."

CHAPTER 57

I didn't go to Vegas for Kenny's fight against Holmes. Money was a lot tighter since the gigs and album were gone, and I was blue and in the limbo of unwanted retirement. And Sabine and I often failed to coordinate our social calendars. I had no memory of her saying we were having two couples over for a dinner party that night. I couldn't reschedule Kenny's fight, and she wouldn't reschedule the dinner party. Okay, keep the peace.

I had heard much about Sabine's rearing by her Basque grandmother in Utah. We had a Basque cookbook, and in addition to sliced baguette and sheep's milk cheese imported from the Pyrenees, I made tapas that could be served cold or room temperature—mussels and shrimp in avocado vinaigrette and blender-made mayonnaise with roasted *pimientos,* as sweet red peppers are called in Spain. Then I made a paella of seafood and rabbit. I busted my ass in the kitchen that day and hauled in the bottles of liquor and wine. Sabine was moved by the Basque menu and my effort, but when the couples arrived and we were having drinks she rolled her eyes and said, "Haid has this fight he has to watch tonight."

I smiled and said, "That's right. I am going to watch my friend's heavyweight championship fight, in my office if it's an inconvenience. At most it lasts fifty-nine minutes, then a minute or two for the decision, if it goes to that. You all can go ahead without me. When it's over I'll hop back in and be the best company of all time."

One of our guests was a garrulous sociology professor from Houston. "Why don't we all watch it?" Bill said with a smile under his thick gray mustache. "I've long wondered what it would be like to be beat upon by black men."

Outvoted by the guests, Sabine said, "Oh, all right." I set the oven on low to keep the paella warm. We took our drinks and bread and cheese into the living room and chose places in front of the TV. I turned on the fight just as Kenny shed his purple robe and twisted his neck and shoulders and champed his mouthpiece. "Which one is your friend?" said the professor's wife, Donna.

"The one with the mustache."

"Oh," she said. "He's handsome. And quite a physical specimen."

"The mustache speaks well of him," said Bill. He saw that I had opened a notebook and was clicking a ballpoint pen. "Are you going to write about this?"

"No," I said. "I've started liking to score them. It's for fun. I don't really know what I'm doing." The other woman, whose name was Beth, had been Sabine's friend since law school. She was an ace basketball player. "Are you going to give us a blow-by-blow?"

"Um. No."

"Kenny's actually a very civilized man," Sabine said. "He took us for a lovely drive and had us for steak dinner before his first fight with Muhammad Ali. We saw him in a movie not long ago. He's a little stiff but he could learn to be a good actor. Haid used to spar him. Is that the right verb?"

"You did?" said Bill.

"There wasn't much to it," I said with a glance at Sabine. "We were in the marines, they had Olympic hopes for him, and I was the only sparring partner available."

After the National Anthem, I noticed something unusual. Kenny was introduced first, Holmes second. In the sport's protocol, champions were introduced after the challenger. I wondered what was that about? Because of the way Kenny won his title and Holmes was undefeated? Or a ploy and hint by Don King? He never really had his hooks in Kenny.

According to Holmes's trainer Richie Giachetti and *Sports Illustrated*, the fight almost didn't come off at all. A day or so before the shove and near-fracas at the gym, Holmes had been sparring when he suddenly bent over and came through the ropes holding his left arm. "It feels funny," he told Giachetti. The trainer packed his fighter's arm in ice and rushed him to a hospital. A doctor and therapist told him the muscle of Holmes's bicep was torn, and he shouldn't fight again for four months. "No way," said Holmes. The Vegas doctor suggested ultrasonic water treatment and diagnosis by a specialist who often worked with injured football players. Giachetti called his wife that night and told her, "Larry says he can fight Norton with one arm, but if this guy from Phoenix says no, it's no."

The next day Giachetti asked the specialist, "Can he fight?"

The doc said, "If he wants to. When the fight starts his arm should be one hundred percent. It's later the trouble will come. In the late rounds he'll lose six to eight percent effectiveness. And if he gets hit on the tear he could lose as much as forty percent."

Not an enthusiastic green light.

Kenny and Holmes came together listening to the ref. Kenny moved his feet a little and kept his gaze down, as always. Holmes was a shade taller and was much thinner at 209. Kenny weighed 220 and looked as solid as he ever had. Holmes leaned close, glaring and trying to taunt. "You just got in there and did that?" said Beth, who was intrigued, being an athlete. "Like off the street? Is that how you say it?"

"Oh no," said Sabine. "Haid was the Golden Gloves state light heavyweight champion."

"Sweetheart," I said, preferring to watch the fight.

Bill laughed and clapped me on the shoulder. "Well, tell us about that."

"I was on the team of my hometown, Deerinwater. The tournament's in Fort Worth. I won four fights in four nights and knocked a guy out in the finals."

Bill laughed. "Could you go with me to faculty committee meetings?"

The lead broadcaster in Vegas was Bob Sheridan, who had called Kenny's split decision loss to Ali and the blowout against Foreman. Sheridan made a point of calling this one "The Battle of Bad Blood" and mentioned the incident in the gym. From the start, he was a cheerleader for Holmes. Maybe he just liked pulling for the underdog. It didn't matter—he was articulate and called a fight well. I was no less a homer for Kenny.

"Haid and Kenny are quite a pair," Sabine was saying. "Kenny hired him to bodyguard his parents one time in Caracas, Venezuela."

"Honey," I said. "Let me listen to this and pay attention."

"Of course," she said. "He's your friend. I hope he liked me, too."

"He did. He does."

The fight began. Kenny landed the first punch, a jab. Holmes danced and flicked out jabs that were very fast. Sheridan must have used the word "lightning" a hundred times during the bout to describe Holmes's hand speed. The younger fighter kept moving, jabbing, throwing out straight rights. Kenny drove off his right foot, his right glove held beside or in front of his face, and tried to establish his own jab. Sheridan remarked that Kenny was vulnerable to a right uppercut because he held his left so low. Indeed, Foreman had turned out Kenny's lights with right uppercuts. He flattened Joe Frazier with them, too. But as Sheridan was saying that, Kenny juked right and led with a left hook that must have sounded like a thunderclap when it caught Holmes on the ear. Because of that punch I gave the first round to Kenny. Sheridan said it was even.

Holmes put on a show in the second and third rounds. He threw volleys of punches, and some got through Kenny's crossed-arms defense invented by Archie Moore. Holmes glided like Ali in his younger days and doubled up jabs followed by straight rights. He pivoted and landed a right cross that jerked Kenny's head to the side. When Kenny got to his stool his left eye had already started swelling, and Slayton pressed it with an ice pack the rest of the fight. When the third round began, Holmes began to showboat, dropping his hands low and daring Kenny to find his chin. It took an effort to tune out the cheerleading of Sheridan, who always called Holmes by his first name. Norton was Norton in his call. Holmes was busy and throwing a lot of punches, but he missed a lot of them. Increasingly. So what, I remembered it the other way. Kenny had more strength in his upper body, and he started reaching Holmes with his powerful jab. Late in the third he overtook Holmes with an overhand right that rocked him back on his heels. But as in the second bout with Ali, he and Slayton thought he had given away two or all of the first three rounds.

Just as well for my nerves, I stayed busy in the breaks between rounds. I made sure everyone had a drink of whiskey or gin or glass of wine if one was wanted. I arranged the tapas on our living room table and they got compliments from our guests. I dodged back in the kitchen and splashed some white wine on the paella to keep it moist. It's amazing what you can do in sixty seconds.

Slayton told Kenny to quit trying to match Holmes jab for jab. "Start counterpunching," he said. "Let him make the first move, then make him pay for it." In the fourth round Kenny's power began to offset Holmes's speed. They went toe-to-toe at one point with the crowd out of the chairs and roaring.

"Who's winning?" asked Beth at the end of the fifth.

"Holmes so far," I said, looking at my notebook. "I've got three rounds for Holmes and two for Kenny. But that's not exactly how they score it. A guy gets ten points if he wins the round or it's even. The loser gets nine points or it can be a ten-eight round if there's a knockdown or . . . "

I shut up, having lost them. Watching this fight with them was like going to a movie and everybody in the theater is talking, and not about what's on the screen.

Kenny's left eye kept swelling, and Holmes started dancing in a different way. He mimicked Ali, but Ali in his youth threw knockdown punches and combinations out of that side-to-side prance. Something may have hurt Holmes or reminded him that his injured arm might not hold up for fifteen rounds. Now when Holmes danced, he bounced up and down and just ran. Maybe he was taking a breather, but it signaled the fight had turned to Kenny.

Aggression and ring command are key components of judging, and I thought Kenny was relentless, even when he lost the exchanges. He never took a round off. In the seventh he landed a right that flung Holmes's head and neck as far around as the punch that I thought broke Ali's jaw. I later saw a photographer's capture of that blow. Holmes's open mouth looked like a storm wind had ripped through it, his knees buckled, and the seat of his trunks was on a plane well behind his heels. It took great will and strength in his legs to keep him from going down.

Kenny followed with another jolting right. Sheridan conceded that either one of those rights would have put most fighters down, but to him they were proof Larry could take a punch. At the end of that round Sheridan said for the first time he had Larry ahead. I thought Kenny was pulling away, despite his eye being almost swollen shut.

Slayton kept pressing the ice pack against Kenny's eye and rubbing Vaseline on the eyebrow. I don't think Holmes threw a body punch the whole fight, and while he could dance and glide and please the crowd doing it, he couldn't match one thing like his mentor Ali had at the same age. He couldn't slip punches with his reflexes and movements of his head.

Over the next stretch I thought Kenny won five rounds, with two even, while Holmes won none. But then in the thirteenth Holmes landed five straight jabs, and then amid a blitzkrieg of punches and the crowd on their feet he almost put Kenny down with a right uppercut. "All right!" Sheridan exulted. "Now Larry's taking the fight back!" Almost knocked down twice, Kenny wobbled, stumbled, and gasped for wind when the bell rang, but he was standing. I scored that one a 10-8 round for Holmes.

If Holmes and his corner men and the crowd thought he was about to score a knockout, they were in for a surprise. In the fourteenth Kenny at last cornered Holmes, and he punished him with hooks to the body, two ripping right uppercuts, and the overhand rights that had demolished Bobick. Holmes couldn't fight his way out of the assault, but he wouldn't go down. Now the crowd was up bellowing over the blows landed by Kenny.

Early in the fifteenth Kenny caught Holmes with two rights that started blood pouring from his mouth. He backed Holmes into the ropes, banging him with left hooks to the body and head and right uppercuts, straight rights, overhand rights. "Larry can't let this continue—he's going to lose this fight!" cried Sheridan.

Both had their feet planted now. They were landing blow after blow, not like hooligans in an alley brawl, but with the fluid if weary expertise the years had taught them. In one exchange Kenny landed a right uppercut and something resembling a small white bird flew and landed in the ring. The veteran ref Miles Lane snatched it up.

"What was that?" said Bill.

"Holmes's mouthpiece," I said.

"Isn't the referee going to make them stop and give it back to him?" Beth said. "Or get him a clean one?"

"No," I said. "Right now, Larry's trying not to bite his tongue off."

That was too much for my wife and her women friends, who gasped and recoiled.

The Vegas crowd rewarded the heavyweights with three straight minutes of standing ovation. They were taking the very best the other one could deliver. Kenny landed hooks and rights to Holmes's head and the challenger fired right back. "Larry has to explode!" Sheridan cried, and

Holmes did. He twice staggered Kenny in the last thirty seconds, but my friend landed the last punch, a left hook upstairs. Kenny gave Holmes a shoulder tap at the bell, and they wobbled to their corners.

There were no embraces now that it was over. Sheridan remarked that Kenny's corner looked very confident. "Who won, who won?" all were asking in my living room.

"Let me see," I said. I ran through the arithmetic fast and did it again. I had scored only three rounds even. Despite Holmes's 10-8 round in the thirteenth and because of the last thirty seconds, I had given the fifteenth to him, my card had the score 144 for Kenny, 143 for Holmes.

At last the bell sounded again, and the ring announcer said, "We have a split decision! Judge Harold Buck: 143-142 for Holmes. Judge Lou Tabor: 143-142 for Norton. Judge Joe Swessel: 143-142 for the winner and new heavyweight champion of the world, Larry Holmes!"

Pandemonium engulfed the ring. Bill reached over from his chair and gave my shoulder a sympathetic squeeze. "Good god," Sabine said, standing to refill her glass and mine, "that was incredible." I was too numbed by booze and what we'd seen to dwell on my disappointment. The fighters didn't approach each other again, and neither stuck around to be interviewed. Don King with his electric gray hair came on the screen, gleefully saying this is what happened when you took a troubled youth out of a ghetto and set him on a righteous path. Afterward Richie Giachetti said of his champion and the last round, "It was the greatest display of courage I've ever seen in a ring. Both of his arms were hurting so bad it was agony just to keep his hands up. How he was able to throw punches and win the round I'll never know." Without showering, with the gaudy WBC title belt wrapped around his middle, Holmes ran outside and jumped in a swimming pool.

In his locker room Kenny said, "Sorry, Pop. I tried."

"You fought a great fight, son."

The ref Miles Lane told Kenny, "That last round was the greatest I've ever been a part of." *The Ring* magazine declared it the all-time best heavyweight round. But there was this. Ken Norton became the only heavyweight champion who never won a title fight.

CHAPTER 58

HERCULES

Mike Weaver loved Kenny Norton, who gave him his nickname, but he got tired of being perceived as Kenny's little brother. He was eight years younger than Kenny, and it was true their profiles were close to a mirror image. Born in Texas when his dad was in the army, Mike grew up in the LA suburb of Pomona and was a star high school fullback. In track meets he consistently timed 9.8 seconds in the hundred-yard dash, which at his size was plenty fast for college football. He got a scholarship offer from an area junior college but instead enlisted in the marines in 1968. He landed in Vietnam not long after I left. He survived his thirteen months in Vietnam without serious physical injury, but though we became friends, that was one thing he would never talk about.

When he came back, he still had a couple of years to do, and the marines sent him to Camp Lejeune, North Carolina. One afternoon he was in a club for junior enlisted marines called a geedunk. Nobody knew why they were called that. Mike wanted to play a favorite hit song of the Motown boom called "It Should Have Been Me." A big black guy shouldered him aside as he was digging in his pocket for a quarter in the jukebox.

Mike said, "Hey, man, wait your turn."

The black guy said, "Get outa the way."

An argument ensued, and it didn't end with the usual shouts and shoving. With one straight right, Mike put the marine flat on his back on the concrete, unconscious. Only after he was thrown out of the geedunk did someone tell him the guy was Lejeune's heavyweight champion. How could you not like a fighter who got into the sport over a song by Gladys Knight and the Pips?

He discharged out of the Corps in 1971 and returned to LA. In eighteen amateur fights he won the California Golden Gloves and a national AAU tournament, but in the US trials for the Pan American Games he drew the navy's champion, Duane Bobick. They knocked each other down, but Bobick won the decision.

Mike was odd-jobbing, in construction and on shipping docks, when he turned pro with unpromising results. Then one day he walked in the Hoover Street Gym, took off his dusty clothes and work boots, and geared up to spar Eddie Bossman Jones, who in retirement was one of the trainers in Kenny's third fight with Ali. Bossman left his best fighting in the gyms but was renowned for toughness that outmatched his size. A hush fell over the Hoover Street gym when Mike knocked *him* out that day. The only other fighter who'd done that was George Foreman, also in a sparring session. Awed by what he'd just seen, Bossman's trainer called Don Manuel, who took over Mike's training.

Kenny didn't witness Mike's feat against Bossman, but after that Mike became his sparring partner, understudy, and all-around pal. But their career alignments ended there. Kenny had just upset Ali and broken his jaw. His record was thirty and one with twenty-two knockouts. Mike at that point had lost three out of his first four pro bouts and in his latest outing had been stopped in Fresno. Mike thought finding a real job with a steady paycheck was a sensible course of action. Kenny hectored him for his indifferent approach to training and talked him out of quitting three times.

Apart from his sputtering career, Mike was thrilled by those years of sparring and traveling with Kenny. Then came the crushing decision that went against Kenny in the third bout with Ali. After Christmas that year, Mike met him at a Denny's out where Kenny and his family lived. "What are you gonna do, champ?" said Mike, diplomatically.

Kenny sighed and stirred his coffee. "I don't know. I might be through and I might not be through. It comes down to money and what Ali decides to do.

"Mike, how old are you now?"

"Twenty-seven."

"You can't wait on me, bud. You gotta do what you gotta do."

Mike rejoined Kenny and worked hard with him when Kenny decided to fight Bobick. In the amateurs and pros Mike had tried but failed to beat the big hunk. He wanted to help make sure Kenny succeeded.

Mike became the house heavyweight of the Sahara Hotel in Reno. You can't get much farther out in the weeds of big-time boxing than that. Then he got a fight against once-beaten Bernardo Mercado, a one-time sparring partner of Oscar Bonavena. The big Colombian had won twenty fights and lost just one. Kenny's record then was fifteen and eight. Mike had sparred Mercado and was well-acquainted with his power. It bounced him off the canvas in one session. And in the money fight he carelessly dropped his gloves when he heard the bell ending the fourth round. Mercado already had a punch coming and once more he took Mike down hard. When the next bell sounded, Mike walked out and dropped the big Columbian with a resounding left hook. Mercado got up but claimed he'd been thumbed in the eye and chose not to continue.

The upset of Mercado boosted Mike to the number eight ranking of the WBC. Eight months later Don King offered him $75,000 to take on Larry Holmes in his third title defense. Mike was so lightly regarded that all three major networks declined to air the bout. HBO picked it up and King put it in Madison Square Garden, but the promoter told Mike his purse now could only be $50,000. Most of the fourteen thousand fans there that night came to watch Roberto Duran against Carlos Palomino.

Holmes controlled the first three rounds with the quickness of his jabs and rights. Then Mike started bombing Holmes with his own right hands. The crowd realized this was a genuine fight, and the unknown challenger became an instant crowd favorite. The rest of the way they chanted *Weaver, Weaver.* The ninth round brought them all to their feet. At the start of the tenth Holmes said, "I'm the champion. There's no way you're gonna beat me."

"I'm gonna try," Mike said.

They slugged into the eleventh, with each fighter hurt more than once. With twelve seconds left in that round, Holmes unleashed a desperate right uppercut and Mike dropped like a sack of hog feed, though he beat the count. At the start of the twelfth Holmes pinned Mike on the ropes. Mike couldn't fight his way out of the fog, so the ref stopped it.

But because of that fight, Mike's moon waxed while Kenny's waned. Still the number-one contender, Kenny knocked out Randy Stephens, the sixth-ranked contender, and then in March 1979 he took on Earnie Shavers. Knowing Shavers would come out gunning, Kenny planned to play defense, counter-punch, and let him run out of gas after a few rounds. Instead Shavers nailed Kenny with a left hook the first time they got in each other's range. Kenny went down, got up, but almost fell again without being hit. Out of respect for Kenny, ref Miles Lane let the assault continue. Kenny tried to fight back but a blur of punches put him down again. He regained his feet but not his senses. Bill Slayton signaled to Lane that he wanted it stopped, and the ref made his move with just over a minute left in the first round.

Ruth Norton couldn't bear to watch Kenny's bouts, but she knew her son, and she said of his loss to Holmes, "That fight took some of his soul away from him." After the knockout by Shavers, Kenny had sat on his stool a long time as the ring doctor and Bill Slayton tried to bring him around. "Kenny's heart wasn't in that fight," Slayton said. "He had a real bad rib and he didn't like heavy punchers. He didn't even like to train with heavy punchers. He was leery of 'em. Before the Shavers fight Kenny said, 'This is going to be it for me.' But then he decided to buy a new home for $850,000. I told him, 'You got the money. You got all your marbles. Why do you want to fight anymore?' He said, 'Two fights. I'll make a million dollars.'"

For his rematch with Leon Spinks, Ali trained harder and slimmed down to 221 for a fight that drew a crowd of sixty-three thousand in New Orleans's Superdome. Neon Leon was only four pounds heavier than in their first fight, but he looked flabby. Leon's team neglected certain details. No one had brought him a water bucket, water bottle, or his protective groin cup. One of his co-trainers yelled, "For god's sake, get Leon a cup." The PR guy turned to another Top Rank employee and said, "Go get Leon a cup of ice." The trainer yelled, "Not that kind of cup! A *cup cup!*" Spinks's trainers had feuded and decided they would alternate making suggestions between rounds. One of them walked away after the fifth. "My god," he said, "it's a zoo." Leon again took him the distance, but as Howard Cosell warbled Bob Dylan's song line "Forever Young," Ali won the decision and reclaimed the WBA's title.

Leon was still a hot commodity, but he next fought in Monaco against a big South African, Gerrie Coetzee, who knocked him out in the first round. Leon was a classic case of too much, too soon. He claimed that all of his $3.75 million purse for the second Ali fight wound up with his lawyers. He got one more heavyweight title shot and was knocked out by Larry Holmes. He dropped to cruiserweight and lost a title fight in that division. He finished with a record of twenty-six wins, seventeen losses, and three draws. He then worked for Frontier Martial Arts Wrestling and at thirty-nine won its Bare Knuckles Heavyweight Championship.

His younger brother Michael fared much better, winning ten title fights while losing none in a strong light heavyweight division, then put on weight and won back-to-back decisions over Holmes, stopping the embittered champ one win short of tying Rocky Marciano's all-time undefeated record. Michael was undefeated in thirty-one fights until he came through the ropes looking pale and aghast at what money had gotten him into. Mike Tyson took him out in ninety-one seconds. But Michael had a Hall of Fame career and put enough away to live quietly and well on a sprawling estate in Delaware.

Meanwhile, Leon married and divorced three times. His son Cory won a version of a world welterweight title; another son was shot and killed after a street fight. Leon got busted for possession of cocaine and marijuana. He got dentures; someone stole them as a souvenir. But a woman who owned the oldest bar west of the Mississippi served him his favorite fried chicken gizzards and brought him affection and a better quality of life in Columbus, Missouri. He cleaned up the local YMCA and helped unload shipments for a McDonald's, where he got a fifty percent price break for his Big Macs. "I can eat, sleep, breathe," Leon said. "I ain't gonna pressurize my brother for money."

Ali said he retired after he won his title back from Leon, but despite his racial pride and sense of mission he really didn't know what to be except a heavyweight champion. Looking toward the future, Bob Arum wanted to promote a fight for the vacated WBA title pitting young undefeated heavyweights—John Tate of Knoxville, Tennessee, and Gerrie Coetzee, who knocked out Leon. Moneyed interests in South Africa wanted a major title fight featuring Coetzee on their soil. After two years as an exploited businessman, Ali had begun sounding vague about whether he was really retired. Exasperated, Arum paid him $300,000 to release a public statement that he was through. The South Africans got their title fight in Pretoria, and Tate won a hard-fought decision over Coetzee to claim the WBA title.

Ali had meanwhile started running before dawn on country lanes where he wouldn't be recognized, and he trained in secluded gyms until he worked himself back into what he thought was fighting shape. Tate, the WBA, and unifying the title could wait for now. Ali announced a grand comeback and in October 1980 he challenged Holmes for his WBC title. *Sports Illustrated* predicted Ali would win. As the fight progressed Holmes yelled at his mentor, tormentor, and hero to *please, please quit!* One judge gave Ali a round, but the other two cards had Holmes winning all of the first ten. Then like Sonny Liston eighteen years earlier, Ali endured the humiliation of sitting on the stool and letting the bell ring.

Even that didn't persuade him. After a few months he convinced himself he would beat Tate and win the WBA title in celebration of his fortieth birthday. Bob Arum began discreet discussions about such a fight. Meanwhile, Arum thought John Tate needed more exposure in the States. Behind-the-scene negotiations for another Ali fight were gaining steam when the WBA and Arum awarded Tate a first title defense in his hometown of Knoxville. For an opponent, Arum wanted someone whose reputation could help sell the fight but wouldn't spoil the big payday with the star attraction, Muhammad Ali.

That role fell to Hercules, Mike Weaver.

"I'm not like Kenny in one way," Mike told me once. "I'm religious. I've always gone to church." After fourteen rounds Mike was far behind on the cards, and his trainer said, "You've been telling people in church you're gonna knock out Tate. It's now or never, so you better do it." Mike recited the Lord's Prayer to himself, and at the bell he attacked. Their fighting was so close inside, with so much clinching, that it didn't look like Mike could get off a punch with any power. But with forty-five seconds left, Mike threw a short left hook and knocked Tate face down, out cold. Mike tried to perform a flip and landed flat on his back.

Someone just tuning in on TV would have thought they'd knocked each other out.

Having used Mike for some past sparring, Ali was *certain* he could win another title now. While Ali trained, Arum talked Mike into defending his new heavyweight title against Coetzee in a resort of hotels and casinos in remote Sun City, South Africa. Arum offered $2.2 million if he'd take the fight down there. Activists in the States chastised Mike, saying right-minded Americans now boycotted all things South African over apartheid. "I went to see my pastor," Mike said, "and he said, 'Yes, go fight.'"

In South Africa, black people came up to Mike and said, "Please win for us."

"I promise I'll win," he said. "I promise."

Mike called Coetzee "Big Red" because he was six-six, weighed 240 pounds, and had a reputation as a very strong puncher. As the fight progressed, lineament that Coetzee's corner men kept spreading on his chest mixed with their sweat and got in Mike's eyes, and Coetzee kept calling Mike "boy."

Mike said, "This boy is gonna whip your big behind. In your backyard."

In the eighth Coetzee unloaded a right that made Mike see three of him, but he stayed on his feet. Mike's trainer now was Ray Barnes, who asked him how he felt after taking that punch. "Fine," said Mike, seeing just one trainer.

"Okay," Barnes said, "it's the second half and he's fired his best shot. Pick up the pace, he's done." By the thirteenth round Coetzee was bleeding from the bridge of his nose and had a badly bruised left eye. At the start of the round Mike jabbed hard through Coetzee's defenses several times and then landed a jolting right. Seconds later his next right, as perfect as the hook that finished John Tate, put Coetzee down and unable to beat the count.

Mike might be a so-called world champion with a record of only twenty-nine and eight, but he could throw devastating left hooks and straight rights, punches that claim the most knockouts in boxing. Any heavyweight had better be wary of them. Even Muhammad Ali.

Ferdie Pacheco and another physician said Ali's speech had slowed and was at times slurred, leading them to believe he had taken too many punches to the head. Worried about that himself, Ali submitted to CT scans and other neurological tests conducted by thirty doctors from institutions that included the Mayo Clinic and the UCLA medical school. The lead doctor announced, "There's absolutely no evidence that Muhammad has sustained any injury to any vital organ—brain, liver, kidneys, heart, lungs," and said he had the blood vessels of a young man. The doctor shrugged off his vocal difficulties. "If the slurring were due to permanent damage, it would be there all the time."

Ali should have listened to his fears and Ferdie Pacheco. Ali's choice of a tune-up opponent in a warmup fight before the title bout with Weaver was an expatriate Jamaican who fought out of Halifax, Nova Scotia. Trevor Berbick's career had been up and down. Promoting the fight was a man named James Cornelius, who later changed his name to Ali Muhammad and was convicted of bank fraud. Cornelius staged "The Drama in the Bahamas" with caution. The bout of Ali and Berbick in Nassau would precede fights featuring several upcoming young fighters, among them Tommy Hearns. Bleachers capable of holding ten thousand people were put up in great haste. Only Ali, Berbick, and Hearns had private dressing rooms—the other fifteen fighters had to get ready in one tiny room. Ticket prices plunged to five dollars. Berbick complained that the promoters' letter of credit for $100,000 was $250,000 short of what they'd promised. The promoters meanwhile had to come up with $1.1 million for Ali. The night of the fight, Cornelius's lieutenants couldn't locate a bell or gloves or water bottles for the fighters. Two judges had Berbick winning nine of the ten rounds, while another judge gave the Jamaican-born Canadian seven rounds.

Berbick was briefly a champion, then got in the ring with Mike Tyson. He was convicted of assault for sticking a gun to the head of his business manager on accusations she stole his money. He went down again for forgery and raping a babysitter. Imprisoned for fifteen months, he dodged back and forth across the border of Canada until he got caught and deported to Jamaica. Over a property dispute, his nephew and another youth beat him to death with a tire iron and pipe and left his body in a churchyard.

The thirty doctors who signed off on Ali's health didn't emphasize that on their resumés. Going out with a loss to a middling fighter and man like Berbick was a sad finale for a man as beloved as Muhammad Ali.

I asked Kenny if there was any talk of *him* challenging Mike for his WBA title. “No, no,” he said. “Mike didn't really want to fight Ali, because word of his condition was going around. But that fight would have been old-age security for Mike. He and I joked about a fight between us, but sparring's one thing. A title bout's another. That would have been like fighting the little brother I never had.”

CHAPTER 59

In November 1980 Kenny lay with his hands behind his head on a bed in a classy old hotel in San Antonio. The interior had been restored, and it was out of the way of the River Walk and Alamo traffic. After the Shavers disaster, he had briefly retired, announced a comeback, had to settle for a draw with mediocre Scott LeDoux. Then his San Diego patron and financial adviser died in surgery, so Kenny retired again, saying he didn't have the heart to continue. Then he announced yet another comeback.

He was going to fight his forty-ninth bout in the Hemisfair Arena. He'd asked me to come down, hang out with him before the fight, and after it was over, we'd go somewhere to have enchiladas and margaritas. It was only eighty-five miles. Of course I agreed to come. Kenny was calm, almost nonchalant. His suite had two double beds. We each stretched out on one and talked about marriages, children, and boxing. He could no longer make any bones about his role as "the name opponent." Kenny was thirty-seven now. San Antonio was a fight town, and not wanting to cut into Kenny's purse, Bill Slayton had hired local guys to work his corner. Kenny's opponent that night, Randall "Tex" Cobb, had a record of seventeen and zero. Cobb, who was thirty, had been born in a refinery town on the Gulf Coast, but in the mesquite plains where I grew up, he played high school football in Abilene. As a freshman he was an offensive lineman for Abilene Christian College, where he lasted one year and left over some behavior that did not seem very Christian to the deans. After football, he won nine kickboxing bouts and earned a black belt in karate. Hoping to make more money he moved to Philadelphia, where he caught on at a good gym and started learning the boxing version of martial arts. That led to a friendship with a local newspaper columnist named Pete Dexter. He had written what he considered a sympathetic column about a youth who'd been killed over gang or drug violence in a rough part of Philly known as Devil's Pocket. The dead kid's brother, the owner of a bar, called and promised to break Dexter's hands sometime, making it harder to write hurtful stuff like that. Dexter decided to go over to the bar and apologize personally, and asked Cobb to come along. "When we got to the bar," Dexter recalled, "about thirty guys with baseball bats came through the back door. Cobb turned to me and said, 'I hope this is the local softball team.'"

Dexter would go on to be a major American novelist, but he lost most of his teeth and suffered a serious concussion, among other injuries. One of Cobb's arms was so badly broken that its way of healing allegedly made him a lesser fighter. But in his major accomplishment he had stopped Earnie Shavers in the eighth round on the undercard of a Tommy Hearns title fight. Joining the lead announcer and Kenny that night was Gerry Cooney. They bantered lightly whether Cobb or Cooney was the Great White Hope. Cooney seemed shy and didn't have much to say, though he surprised the others in the sixth by saying Cobb was winning the fight.

Cobb showed off his past as a football lineman, shoving with his shoulders and the 230 pounds behind them. Shavers unloaded many of his feared shots and a choice elbow now and then. By the seventh round they were so tired they could barely keep their arms up. "These guys are really tired," observed Kenny. "It's 'I'm going to hit you for a while then rest, then you hit me for a while.'" Cobb won the fight with good but slow left jabs and round house rights that usually landed on the top of Shavers's shaved head, for he tried to protect himself with the crossed-arms Mongoose defense and added to it by ducking. At the end of the seventh Shavers was so weary he could barely walk to his corner stool. The ref asked him if he'd had enough, and Shavers shook his head. The end came with Cobb bludgeoning him with rights that looked like he was throwing bales of hay.

It turned out that Shavers's jaw was broken. The crude tag that nagged at Kenny's self-esteem once again became the can tied to his tail. The ten-round fight between Kenny and Cobb in San Antonio was billed "The Battle of the Jaw Breakers."

Cobb was not an exceptional fighter, but he was one of boxing's great characters. He was big, curly-haired, colorful, ugly, and funny. Once he said, "Don King is one of the great humanitarians of our time. He has risen above that great term, prejudice. He has screwed everybody he has ever been around. Hog, dog, or frog, it don't matter to Don. If you got a quarter, he wants the first twenty-six cents."

When he advanced to a record of twenty and two, he would get a title shot against Larry Holmes in Houston. The judges' cards in favor of the champ were 150-135, 150-135, and 149-136. Howard Cosell washed his hands of boxing in the course of calling that fifteen-round target practice. Cobb said the beating was worthwhile if it got Howard off the air. Years later Cobb claimed that the morning after the fight, Holmes came in his hotel room moaning about how sore he was. Cobb said, "That's all fine, Larry, but I can't *chew.*"

The Coen Brothers saw his comic potential and cast him as a motorcycle-riding hooligan in their breakout movie *Raising Arizona.* He had a good career in the movies playing himself.

"The Battle of the Jaw Breakers" was the first time I didn't see Kenny try to be the aggressor in a fight. At times he came out to center ring and battled Cobb in his old style, but for the most part he adopted his own version of the rope-a-dope. He covered up and counter-punched while Cobb whaled away. At the bell after every round Cobb gave Kenny's hip a friendly bump with his glove as they headed for their corners. I can't remember which round the crowd started throwing quarters. Something Latino, evidently. The damn things hurt.

Kenny tripped in weariness heading for his stool after the ninth round. But when the next bell rang, he walked out to center ring and in the middle of the last round, he put together a six-punch combination that brought the fans howling to their feet. Cobb had no defense for the uppercuts. Once more it was a split decision—97-94 for Kenny, 97-95 for Cobb, and 96-95 for Kenny. He had now won three of those and lost two.

Some of Cobb's friends and backers came in Kenny's dressing room afterward and seemed happy with the outcome. Now Tex was going to get some big-money fights, one said.

Kenny said, "He's not gonna make another nickel off me."

When they had gone, he asked me, "What was the deal with the quarters?"

"I think they were saying, *'Te quiero,* I love you.' You okay?"

"Yeah. Let me clean up and let's get out of here."

Downstairs in the hotel lobby, Kenny and I were discussing where to go eat and drink with a young woman on duty that night when we saw a large man with wet curly hair coming in a deep-voiced rage. Kenny stepped back. Cobb yelled that he was going to kill him, break his neck, stomp his head in, right here in the lobby.

"What's wrong with you?" Kenny yelled.

I knew about Cobb's black belt in karate. So did Kenny. Cobb's fists were clenched. An artery stood out in his thick flushed neck. What happened to the sporty taps on Kenny's hip at the end of every round?

With my usual good sense I got between them. "Hold on here!" I said. "Are you out of your mind? Oh, I see you are."

Cobb gave me a hard thump on my chest with the heel of one hand. "Who are you, pilgrim? Get outa my way, you fucking little twerp!"

Kenny was not coming around me to help. I reached and tapped the bell on the check-in desk, where a young clerk with eyes wide and blinking had removed herself from the possible fray. The thump on my chest had driven me back a step, but I rang the bell on the counter, then got in Cobb's face. "I'm no pilgrim but I am a twerp," I told him. "And if you touch me one more time, this man here"—I gestured at Kenny over my shoulder with my thumb—"and this scared young woman there, and that man over there, and those two shocked women in the chairs behind you, they're going to be my witnesses that you assaulted me. In fact, you already have. And you're gonna spend the night in the Bexar County jail, where the men in their wing and women in their wing sing songs to each other in *español*, and the guards don't have aspirins or much sympathy for the aches and pains of their guests."

I once heard a caged lion throw an annoyed roaring cough at a lawn keeper that got too close with the whine of a weed eater. Cobb's response sounded something like that. He glared past me at Kenny. "Somewhere, sometime," he promised the paper champ, then turned and stomped off. With my heart racing, I looked at Kenny and said, "You weigh two hundred twenty-five pounds! *Where were you?* What was that about?"

He put his hand on my shoulder to calm me down. "I got no clue," he said. "I'm sorry. He scared the shit out of me." I walked over to a lobby chair and sat with my arms rigid on my thighs and my hands gripped around my knees. After a moment Kenny took another chair, crossed his legs, and said, "Good work, bodyguard."

I looked at him and we started laughing. "There's a great bar near here called the Esquire," I said. "Before we go eat, let's stop in there and dive into a bottle of tequila."

Two or three days later, when Kenny was home in California with his family, he called and said, "Now I know what that was about with Tex. In the hotel."

"Yeah?"

"His purse was two hundred thousand dollars. He bet it all on himself."

The win over Cobb left Kenny sixth in the rankings of the WBC and WBA. *The Ring* magazine downgraded him all the way to tenth. But Kenny decided that with hard training and much resolve he might upset the number-one contender and force a rematch with Holmes. I hadn't conducted my own life with enough distinction to argue against it.

The top contender, "Gentleman" Gerry Cooney, stood six-six, weighed 225, and he was twenty-five years old. An Irish Catholic from Long Island, Cooney was a natural left-hander who fought right-handed, and he had a very strong straight left jab and hook. Cooney was then undefeated in twenty-three pro fights and had stopped nineteen.

Kenny had trained for his fight with Cooney to come off in Vegas in February, 1981. Harold Smith, a former rock promoter, wanted to chase Don King out of boxing with a promotion titled "This Is It!" The "Greatest Boxing Card in History" would have Kenny and Cooney and an undercard deep in major talent: Tommy Hearns, Wilfred Benitez, Alexis Arguello. But then Harold Smith vanished as a person of interest when $21 million was discovered missing from a Beverly Hills bank.

"This Is It!" collapsed, the undercard fighters scattered, and Kenny's ten-round bout with Cooney had to be salvaged at Madison Square

Garden four months later. The term "Black Irish" refers to hair color on scalp, beard, and chest, and with his zigzag nose and shy smile, Cooney personified the characterization. When the robes were off, Kenny was announced as a former heavyweight champion of the world. Cheers were respectful, not many boos. When Cooney was announced, he put on a showboat routine of fast shadow boxing that he picked up from Sugar Ray Leonard. The crowd of about ten thousand roared.

At the bell Kenny walked out to center ring. From a crouch he threw three jabs in a businesslike way. Then Cooney rushed with a stiff-arm of a jab and buckled Kenny's knees with a right, his first real punch of the fight. Cooney wasn't supposed to *have* a right. Kenny tried to slug his way out of trouble and managed to turn the battle out of a corner, but Cooney maneuvered him back around with a thudding left hook and forced him to a corner post. Cooney threw thirty-six straight punches, and it appeared they all landed. Kenny's back was against the post and he sagged until he was almost sitting. Cooney later said, "I got a little bit frightened because I kept hitting him and he was unconscious."

Well, how about step back *and stop?*

Tony Perez was a small man. Cooney's back was so broad that the ref couldn't get around him. At last Perez wedged between the two and waved off Cooney to an arms-raised dance of triumph. As the ref stooped before Kenny, Bill Slayton and three New York Athletic Commission doctors rushed to the scene of the massacre. Kenny's chin drooped, his lips parted over his mouthpiece, and his eyes appeared to be seeing nothing.

"Payback in the Garden," Kenny put it. Against Cooney he lasted exactly as long as Duane Bobick had lasted against him in the arena. I was flung aghast to my first conversation with Kenny at Camp Pendleton, California. The doctors decided he was okay, but the ref told him he was four seconds away from the fate, in the same ring, that nineteen years earlier ended the life of Benny "Kid" Paret.

PART V
SWEET VIRGINIE

CHAPTER 60

Nine years later, in the summer of 1990, I was working out one morning at Richard Lord's Gym. It had no air-conditioning, and I was no longer thrilled at seeing the needle of his thermometer reach 103 indoors at my favored exercise time, three or four in the afternoon. Two Dallas Cowboy linebackers in the bigger of the two rings were veterans in the NFL. It was midsummer off-season for most Dallas players, before they reported to training camp. But Richard had this pair jumping in squats like frogs, picking up and pitching back to him a heavy medicine ball that he dropped before them. He'd been pushing them with that and other torments for the hour and a half I'd been there.

They seemed to like Richard well enough, but as sweat poured off them, their grunts, scowls, and grimaces registered their displeasure at being singled out this way. Under head coach Tom Landry, whose regime had drafted both of them, the Cowboys had registered three straight losing seasons, capped by a dismal record of three wins and thirteen losses in 1988. The second owner of the franchise found himself mired in a national savings and loan scandal, so in February following that season that owner sold the Cowboys to the Arkansas natural gas tycoon Jerry Jones, who at once fired Landry and hired away from the University of Miami Jimmy Johnson, an ex-Arkansas Razorback teammate of Jones.

In private, Landry was said to have a dry sense of humor. He wore the iconic fedora because it was 1950's business attire; he had been educated and expected to spend his life as an electrical engineer, and he was bald. Aloof though he seemed, you had to respect him. When his older brother was shot down and killed over the north Atlantic early in World War II, Landry suspended his football scholarship at the University of Texas and, barely in his twenties, flew thirty bombing missions in Europe and crash-landed once in Belgium when his B-17 ran out of fuel. Back on the University of Texas campus in Austin, he meant to be the passing and running tailback and field general of the Texas Longhorns, but he couldn't match the throwing arm and accuracy of Bobby Layne, or the way he charmed coaches. Landry adjusted as a hard-running fullback and was the team's star safety. The Texas coach sent him out one Saturday with a heavy plaster cast on a broken arm because he was capable of covering and tackling Layne's high school pal Doak Walker, SMU's great runner and receiver. Some believed Landry's collegiate slight affected his treatment of quarterbacks when he was in a position to boss them. Landry was a combination safety and defensive coach for the New York Giants when he took the head job of the expansion franchise in Dallas. Now with one churlish seizure of the Cowboys' headquarters, gone were the twenty straight seasons Landry had led them to the playoffs, their two Super Bowl wins, and the three they reached but lost. "America's Team," all that jive.

Unlike Jerry Jones, Jimmy Johnson had grown up in Texas, a Port Arthur high school classmate of Janis Joplin. He played college ball at Arkansas, and his coaching led the trash-talking University of Miami Hurricanes to two undefeated seasons and a national championship. But his brash, razor-cut style did not endear him to Cowboy fans. It didn't help that his first team finished with one win and fifteen losses. Jones knew he needed to soothe unhappy Dallas fans. So, gone along with Landry were the cool breezes when the Cowboys ran through training camps at a Lutheran college in Thousand Oaks, California. Jones moved camp to the sweltering heat on the campus of St. Edward's University, which occupied a striking hilltop in south Austin.

Like Landry, Jones first made his name in coaching as a defensive innovator. He wanted linebackers who were big and strong enough to throw off the blocks of three-hundred-pound linemen and still be quick and agile enough to run with NFL backs and stretch the field from sideline to sideline. He wasn't sure these two could do that, and having heard about the training regimen Richard imposed on his most committed fighters, Johnson had a contract drawn up and ordered the linebackers into our gym so Richard could get them conditioned.

Eugene Lockhart was a six-year starter at middle linebacker, and in Johnson's first season he had led the NFL in tackles. Starting his third season, the other was a past UCLA All-American and second-round draft choice, Kenny Norton Junior.

I had asked Richard not to tell him about my acquaintance with his dad. I hadn't spoken to Kenny in four years. My forced retirement as a singer left me with a lot of time on my hands. A young woman physical therapist who got hooked on the workouts taught me how to wrap my left one in a way that didn't expose it to more hurt and harm.

That day as noon approached no one was there but Richard, the linebackers, and me. With sixteen-ounce gloves, I was having a good day on the heavy bag, making noise. Between squat jumps and chasing the medicine ball Kenny Junior grinned over at me and snorted, "Hey, listen to Pop! He *got* some pop."

"That's what your dad called your grandfather," I said.

If I could go eight rounds on the heavy bag it got my heart racing, and I called it a good day. Having done that, I sat on a bench near the ring, wiped off my face and hair with a towel, and was taking off the hand wraps when the players' workout ended. Lockhart slipped through the ropes and sped past me without a glance. Richard called after him, "There goes 'Mean Gene, the Hittin' Machine.' Off to get his Falstaff."

"They don't make that shit no more," he yelled over his shoulder, and was gone.

I looked up at the young giant who stared down at me. He was maybe an inch shorter than his dad, but he was much thicker in chest, shoulders, and legs. I heard later that his playing weight was 236, but he looked more like 250. He said, "Are you gonna tell me what you meant there? Pop?"

"Sure. You got a minute? Have a seat."

CHAPTER 61

Four years before this, Johnny Stafford and Shack Brown had invited me out for a drink. They were the two band members I couldn't remember ever having cross words with. Having two friends and talented musicians pull and help me along had been one of my life's rewards. We chatted a while about families and girlfriends and what bands they had been playing with and where. Then they looked at each other and Johnny said, "Haid, there's something we need to talk about."

I gave them a curious look. He said, "You know we have to make a living. There's not enough session work here to keep us afloat. At our age we can't keep scuffling from band to band. We want to bring back the Rip Chords."

I winced inside but smiled. "I tried to convince you guys you can sing."

Shack said, "Now don't get mad, but when we go out with this it's going to be Jake Spoon and the Rip Chords. We've already got a record deal with—"

I sputtered my gin and touched my napkin to my mouth.

"He's straight and sober now," Johnny said. "He went back to the well and found a good rehab place that turned him around."

As if I cared about that. I think they expected me to blow up. "I'm all for letting bygones be bygones, but I'd like it more if you just called yourselves the Rip Chords."

They traded more glances. "Jake's our lead singer and the writer or co-writer of a lot of our songs," said Johnny. "Jake's a showman. The rest of us aren't."

I wondered how Phil Hauptman would fit in this arrangement. With Jake leading the band, they would have three lead guitarists. There might be trouble making that work.

"If it helps," Shack said, "we all want to relocate to New Braunfels. The rent's cheaper and it's a nice town. We'll have easy access to gigs in Austin and San Antonio. We've talked it over with the folks at Gruene Hall, and they're pretty pumped. We'll have regular gigs there."

I shook my head. "I'm not going to have any part of running you guys out of town. I'm a grownup. So's Sabine. But you understand there are business considerations."

I wanted to make sure I got what I had coming from this rebirth of the band, especially with Jake out front. I went to LA for meetings with a royalty consultant and an entertainment lawyer. Kenny had listened to my schedule on the phone and said one night we might be able to get together. He said he had something social to do that night of February 22, 1986, and I might find it entertaining. He told me to dress up a little, not in jeans.

At my fairly seedy hotel Kenny picked me up in the most astounding car I'd ever seen. It was a silver hardtop two-seater with a clip-on hardtop for the rainy season, fenders separate from the hood, headlights positioned between them retro style, likenesses of some great fish's fins flaring on fenders behind the front wheels. A spare wheel was mounted on the back. The interior had red leather seats and walnut panels that looked genuine. The cabin sat so far back in the chassis that when I got in and looked down the hood, I thought it must be like driving an aircraft carrier. "What the hell?" I said. "Now your name's Gatsby?"

He laughed and gave my jaw a soft push with his fist. "No, but I'll tell you who else has one. Farrah Fawcett, Julio Iglesias, Rod Stewart, Sylvester Stallone, and Jordan's King Hussein."

"You and Rocky, huh," I teased. "What do you think of those movies?"

He took off fast and ran through the gears. "The first one was good and deserved the praise it got. I've faked making love to a beautiful naked woman on a movie set. I guess I could have played Apollo Creed but decided not to. If I had, I would've tried to coach Stallone better than they did. People that don't know any better would watch those movies and think every boxer carries his gloves down by his knees and takes every punch slinging his head side to side like the Three Stooges getting slapped. He's got the talk and body language down, but put him in a ring, he turns into a bad take on Oscar Bonavena. And every sequel is worse than the last one. But Stallone's got an industry going for him, and I'm glad for him. When I run into him, I won't let him get started about Mike Tyson. That routine turns me off. Somebody buy the guy some socks. I like the smaller guys when I watch the fights at all. Hagler, Hearns, Duran, Arguello. Sugar Ray Leonard's good, but he tries too hard to be another Ali. Stallone's all right. We talk about our cars."

"What is this thing?" I said.

"A '78 Clénet Excalibur," he said. "They manufacture them in a cool coachwork in Santa Barbara. Damn well made."

"You're the guy that used to handle car frames. You'd know."

"Yeah. The good old days." Kenny wore a dark pinstriped suit, white shirt, and a floral tie. He was bigger than I'd seen him but still looked fit, about 240. When he reached the freeway, he pulled out an ashtray made of crystal and lit a cigarette. I'd never seen him smoke before. He sped and weaved through the traffic. I smiled and recalled his racing up the firebreaks of Pendleton in that Jeep the marines let him use.

He said, "Hey, you know who I met last year?"

"Who?"

"Your man Nino Benvenuti. Jackie and I went on vacation in Italy, and we had a great dinner and talk with him at his restaurant in Trieste. That is one smart and good-looking dude, considering he had ninety pro fights and won a 120 amateur bouts without losing one. His conqueror was the great Argentine fighter that Oscar never was—Carlos Monzon. Here's a guy Ursula Andress was hot for. Now he's in prison down there for killing his wife. Threw her off a balcony. Nino sends him money so he can get by all right in there."

"Do you and Ali talk like that? Or Foreman?"

Kenny frowned and drew on the cigarette. "Muhammad's struggling now. There but for the grace of God, as they say. Joe Frazier and Mike Weaver are the ones I stay closest to. I haven't seen George, but he's called me a couple of times. I thanked him for what he did for my parents and you in Caracas. I'm the one that should have made that call. He told me maybe his greatest sin was thinking he ought to kill me in that fight. He's the Christian shepherd now looking out for his flock. I don't doubt it's genuine."

"Tell me about this business you started," I said.

"The Ken Norton Personal Management Agency. I have a partner, a guy named Rodney, who helped Bob Biron stay on top of my finances before Bob died. I was in the Bahamas last year and met Eric Dickerson. Plays for the Rams, you might have heard. The guy was rookie of the year and All-Pro, and then in his second year he broke O.J. Simpson's records for single season rushing and the number of hundred-yard games in a season. He decided, hot damn, that rookie contract ain't gonna cut it. His agent renegotiated that for him. He and I'd stayed in touch, and when the big contract came through, he asked us to manage his money. He's our only client so far, but it keeps us busy."

He glanced at me. "How come you laugh?"

"I live in Texas. Did he tell you about the Trans-Am that Texas A&M alums gave him when he was a senior in high school? And the Aggie ex who trashed it with a ball peen hammer when he reneged and signed with SMU?"

Kenny sniffed. "He says that story's bullshit. His grandmother took it on a trip to Mexico and the car didn't make it back."

Kenny and Jackie lived in a part of Los Angeles County called Ladera Heights—well-spaced mansions in the hills east of Culver City. They shared their home with a daughter and two sons of their own now, along with her son from her prior marriage.

"What's up with Kenny Junior?" I asked.

"You ought to watch some football in southern California. Kenny averaged nearly nine yards a carry running the ball his high school senior year. UCLA decided they needed him more at linebacker. He just finished his sophomore season. They won eight games, lost a couple, and tied one. They were underdogs in the Rose Bowl against Iowa, but they ran up forty-five points on them. He's as gentle a kid as you'll ever find, but he's a beast in cleats and helmet and pads. He's gonna make All-America, wait and see."

"Good for him, Kenny. Where are we going tonight?"

"Political fundraiser for a friend of mine, Tom Bradley, just the second black mayor of a big city in the country. He ran for governor four years ago and lost to the Republican, but he's gearing up for a rematch now, and he'll get the Democratic nomination. You'll see lots of men in tuxes and beautiful women in dresses showing a whole lot of skin. Roll with it, pal. Tom asked me to come by and I told him I would. We won't stay for it all."

I wore a linen sport coat, mock turtleneck, and khakis but felt underdressed at the party in the downtown Biltmore Hilton. Kenny was haunted by his terror of being in the ring with George Foreman and his razor-thin loss to Larry Holmes. He was most famous, of course, for his battles with Muhammad Ali. In all they fought each other for three minutes short of two hours. Neither one could knock the other down. The scorecards gave Ali wins in two out of their three bouts, and he won fifty-six rounds to Kenny's fifty-three. But Ali was the one who wound up in surgery with a broken jaw. Kenny earned his ticket to the dance.

At the fundraiser some of the prettiest women with bare backs and generous views of their bosoms pivoted on high heels and carried trays and goblets of wine. Kenny took a glass of red and when he was done with that, he carried only a glass of ice water. I downed three glasses of the Chardonnay and tried to be on my best behavior. He didn't introduce me much, and I didn't mind. I recognized Willem Dafoe and Kim Basinger. Mayor Bradley was a handsome, balding black man of about seventy. He talked smoothly about being born in Texas, the grandson of slaves. They couldn't hold on to their sharecropper acreage there, so they came to Arizona picking cotton in other people's fields. His dad found work in LA as a railroad porter, and his mother was a maid. He talked about winning a track scholarship at UCLA and then the years he spent as a beat cop working downtown and in a segregated community known in the police department as the Newton Street Division. That when he married, he and his wife had to have a white friend sign for them so they could buy their first home in an integrated neighborhood. How he worked his way through law school as a cop.

Before he got to the meat of his campaign pitch, he introduced Kenny as a heavyweight champion and pride of the city. "We've got a lot of things in common, and I don't mean boxing," said the mayor. "The closest I got to that was trying to get some guy in handcuffs. Kenny went through many struggles when he came here. He was trying to find his way in boxing while working in an auto plant and raising a son all by himself. Ken Norton, Jr. is now a starting linebacker for my alma mater,

UCLA. My friend here was honored as Father of the Year in 1977 and was the first African American to win that prestigious award."

People applauded. Kenny grinned and told the mayor, "They've given it to me twice. Let me tell you, those awards spoke volumes and meant the world to me, and I hope it was a wake-up call for those fathers who have abandoned their responsibilities." More applause. His own birth father had been such a man.

When we reached his car and he pulled out on the freeway he said, "Hang on, let's take this for a ride." Though I'd been in LA many times I'd never gotten the hang of the place. Kenny was reminiscing about his pleasure when he knocked out Jose Luis Garcia, who gave him his first defeat and taunted him in Caracas. He said he got even with a hook to Garcia's liver in the fifth in St. Paul, Minnesota. I saw an exit that said CHINATOWN.

I said, "Hey, take this exit. I'd like to see that."

"Why? There's nothing there."

"You're the movie star. I never could follow the plot, but I like that movie."

Kenny hadn't lied about LA's Chinatown. I expected it to be like San Francisco, but here I saw little but empty parking lots. I said, "Where are the Chinese?"

"Moved somewhere, I guess. Real estate values must have forced them out."

"I don't believe this," I said, staring at the few blocks of buildings lit up with words in neon that looked so exotic to me. "It's the movie set. That's all there is to it."

Kenny lit another cigarette, drove slowly, and took it in, too. I cracked a window and said, "Whoa. Listen to that."

I have had my fun, if I never get well no mo'
Oh my health is fadin' on me, oh yes, I'm goin' down slow

"That's Howlin' Wolf," I said. "Best cover of him I've heard. He's been dead a while. Let's go see."

"Haid, I'm kind of careful where I park this thing."

"Oh, come on. Listen how loud that is. You can park under a streetlight right beside it. Please. You used to be a fighter, I used to be a singer. I'd like to see who that is."

He parked, locked the steering wheel so the car couldn't be stolen, and then the doors. It felt like walking into the movie. The club was up some stairs, and playing tonight, we learned at the door, was the Charlie Chan Band. The crowd was modest, for the hour was early. It was a five-piece band and I thought they could be northern Chinese, for they were tall. From Korean War stories I'd heard about the characteristic height of ones from the north. They were all over Howlin' Wolf's "Killing Floor" and "Back Door Man," Muddy Waters's "Got My Mojo Working" and B. B. King's "Paying the Cost to Be the Boss." At the bar I got a double Bushmills on the rocks. Kenny asked for club soda with a twist of lime.

Four or five songs after we arrived the singer said they were going to take a short break.

With my back against the bar I said, "We've found it, man."

"Found what?"

"The melting pot. Here's this cracker with a Texas accent drinking Irish whiskey with a black friend and listening to these Chinese guys nail Mississippi Delta and Chicago blues. All we need is a Guatemalan bartender."

"Come on, Haid," said Kenny. "Let's get out of here. I need to get home."

"Go on. I had a great time, Kenny. Thanks for asking me along. I'll catch a cab."

I hadn't seen Kenny that mad at me since he knocked me out and put that crackle in my jaw. "This is not New York, Haid. You can't just walk out here and *hail* one."

I shrugged. "It's a tourist place. I'm a tourist. I can get back to my hotel."

Kenny muttered and walked to the woman working the door. He gave her his card and some bills. He pointed at me and she nodded, agreeing to get me a cab when I was ready or when the bartender decided it for me. Then he came back, shook my hand, and with a light clap on my shoulder left me to my folly and called it a night.

Somehow, I made my flight out the next morning. I got a pillow and napped until the plane started the descent into Phoenix. In the layover I was directed to a gate where a host of unhappy passengers milled. A man sent me back to a gate three numbers down from where I had left the first one. I missed my connecting flight, and it was dark by the time I got home. Sabine picked me up at the airport. I kissed her and slumped against the door.

"Are you all right?" she said.

"Yeah. Long day today. Too much fun last night."

"Did you hear the news about Kenny?"

I looked at her. "What news?"

"He was in some kind of bad accident last night."

"No, he wasn't."

"I don't know, honey," she said, sounding exasperated. "Someone that knows you're friends called me at the office. He's a client that listens to radio sports shows. He just said Kenny was in some bad kind of accident."

"No, he wasn't. I was with him last night."

CHAPTER 62

Kenny never knew how the wreck occurred, for when he came out of the murk of trauma and sedation his brain injuries spared him the horror of remembering. If other drivers saw his car go off the entrance ramp they elected to keep going. What's certain was a colossal noise of metal being shredded as the Clénet Excalibur crashed through the barricade and, with all those lavish features turned into flying junk, the wreck spiraled and tumbled through brush into a deep ravine, crashing upside down into a tree big enough to take the impact.

Because of the massive breadth of highway construction and the steepness and depth of the ravine, no neighborhoods were close around. If it hadn't been for the tree and a phone call from a ten-year-old girl, he might have died unnoticed far down the ravine until buzzards swirled and his remains had been snatched and pecked by coyotes and crows.

Radioed about the girl's 911 call, an LA traffic cop spotted the guard rail, turned on his lights, skidded down the ravine, and was shocked and scared by the remnants of the car, the smoking hunk wedged against the tree, and the reek of gasoline. He didn't believe any human could have survived such disaster, but upside down, suspended by his seat belt, was a large bleeding black man who appeared to be alive.

The cops, firefighters, and paramedics who ran and scooted on their backsides down the slope knew the car's gasoline could explode at any time, incinerating the man and them as well. Within minutes a Jaws of Life crew with their bolt and metal cutters ripped away enough of Kenny's steel trap to give him a slim chance to survive. The EMS crew lashed him to a stretcher and fought to keep their footing so they could reach a point where a helicopter MedEvac crew could deliver him in extremely critical condition to the Cedars-Sinai Hospital. Kenny had a fractured skull and all manner of internal injuries and bleeding. The emergency room doctors and nurses were horrified when this possibly dying man lurched up and for a moment made it to his feet, further injuring a broken leg. It was as if some recess in his brain made him keep trying to get up from those uppercuts of George Foreman.

They strapped him to the sterile surface where trauma patients first lie so that couldn't happen again. They couldn't give him any morphine yet. He screamed and wept. They gained enough information about his blood loss and injuries that they could finally sedate him and surgeons could begin. They first had to stop the internal bleeding, but the most dangerous condition was the fractured skull. If the brain's swelling increased and they couldn't stop it, he would die or at best survive in a vegetative state. The surgeons labored on him for three hours. The lead physician told Kenny's wife Jackie he might not make it.

As his identity spread, doctors and nurses braced for that Code Blue call that would bring them running and mean all the effort and medical expertise and technology had failed. Kenny was in intensive care, but the doctors provided a closed space so next of kin could slip in for just one minute, and they alerted hospital security to keep friends, professional associates, and the press away.

Kenny's daughter Kenisha, a newborn infant when Kenny fought Ali the third time, was now ten years old. Before she got her minute with him, her sobbing mom had told her and her siblings that the doctors said he might never be able to walk again. Her dad, this oversized person and personality whose photos and other mementos of achievement were spread throughout their large home, now lay bandaged like a mummy, she thought. His eyes moved like he knew his daughter but restraints kept him from moving his bandaged head. He couldn't have said anything to her if he'd had the capacity. Among the other impediments his mouth was wired shut. The Jawbreaker had a broken jaw.

I was frantic and guilt-stricken, though I didn't know what blame was rightly mine. But if I hadn't called him and accepted his invitation that night, maybe he would have left the campaign party, headed straight home, and not touched his brakes too hard trying to miss a doe or raccoon, or whatever made him miss that curve.

The numbers I had for him were clogged with messages, and eventually when I called, a recorded message of the phone company informed me the numbers were no longer in service. I tried to call John Norton and got another message that the number had been changed, and the new one was restricted. I called the Jacksonville, Illinois, police department. The cop who fielded the call said, "He's retired," and hung up.

A spokesman for Cedars-Sinai said Kenny had come through the surgeries well, considering. In response to a reporter's question, a spokesman for the police said they had not requested access to the hospital's laboratory blood work for Mr. Norton. Given his fragile condition, they believed such an intrusion would be indecent. The privacy of Cedars-Sinai's patients was protected by law and hospital policy.

I started to write Kenny a letter but got no further than a greeting and paragraph before I crumpled the page and threw it away. He'd never get it, and besides, I didn't know what to say. At last I got a number in LA for the Ken Norton Management Company. All the man said on the recording was "Leave a message." I couldn't talk fast enough to get my contacts stated before the machine or service cut off. I kept trying and was startled one day when a man picked up and said, "Ken Norton Management. Yeah?"

It was the partner Rodney, and he sounded wildly stressed. I persuaded him to just hold on and hear me out. "Listen, pal," he responded. "You wouldn't believe the volume of requests I've been getting. It's a frigging avalanche. I see here on his rolodex—last guy on the planet, certainly this town, that uses one—that the name you gave me does have an entry. But I gotta tell you, I've known and worked with Ken Norton since he was just a contender, and I don't recall hearing him mention you. Not once. I can tell you he's gonna live but he's never gonna be the same. So tell me fast, what can I do for you? What do you want?"

I was taken aback. "What do I want?"

"Yeah. Hurry up. What I said."

"I want to hear from him or someone in his family how he's doing. Pal. He's been my friend since we were in the service together in 1967. In ringside seats that he provided I've seen him fight Muhammad Ali in San Diego and Yankee Stadium, George Foreman in Venezuela, Jerry Quarry and Duane Bobick in Madison Square Garden, Tex Cobb in San Antonio, and Rico Brooks in Oklahoma City. I managed his publicity against Quarry."

"Yeah, so?"

I sighed. "I was with Kenny at the Bradley fundraiser. I saw him drink one glass of wine and the rest of the time he had nothing but a glass of ice water in his hand. When we left the hotel, I harassed him into going in a music club with me in Chinatown. He had nothing to drink but club soda and lime. I got drunk but Kenny Norton was sober."

A pause on the other end. "Then you oughta be talking to the papers, not me."

"Say again?"

"'Hero comes forward,' is that what you want?"

"You think I want publicity? Do you know what a dickhead you are?"

He heaved a sigh. "Yeah, I know, I know. But you got to understand I'm flummoxed by all this. I'm not equipped. There ain't enough hours in the day. Eric Dickerson's people are freaking out, man, and they're ditching stocks and pulling money out. We didn't get their business because of me."

"All right, I apologize. I get the picture now."

"Tell you what, amigo." He read my contacts on the rolodex card and asked if they were accurate. I said they were. "I'm writing on this legal pad—our secretary quit—and I'll get your story to his wife or his son the football player. That's the best I can do."

As Kenny Junior and I talked, we had moved to the ring apron because it was more comfortable than the wood bench. "I remember Rodri's mention of you now," he said softly. "I wrote it down like all the rest. You're not the only one I didn't get back to. I'm sorry."

I waved that off. "I just wanted someone to know he wasn't drunk or high on drugs. I saw him smoke a couple of cigarettes but that's no crime. I guess that speculation's gone away by now. I just wanted him to know I care about him."

"The speculation was Hollywood gossip. *National Enquirer* stuff. Dad was screaming from the pain when I first saw him. You wouldn't think you could do that with your jaws wired shut but you can. It was like a high-speed metal saw."

"Jesus."

"Do you know what all he's been through?"

"No. I read the stories in *Sports Illustrated* and the *Sporting News.*"

"His whole right side was paralyzed. It was like the opposite result of a bad stroke. He couldn't move his right arm or leg. The man's right-handed. He couldn't dress or bathe himself or shave. He lost sixty or seventy pounds. Water therapy was the physical breakthrough. It takes away a lot of gravity and lets the body remember how it's supposed to move. He made it from a wheelchair to a walker but with frustration, dark moods, rages. You know, I get tired of telling the story. I'm sorry, but I do."

He was quiet for a moment, holding back his mix of emotions. "When he started trying to talk again, he couldn't make us understand him. He knew what he was saying but to us it was jabber. Speech therapists have worked wonders with that. One thing he's never lacked was pride. I thought he and Jackie had a fine marriage. I've got two half-brothers, a half-sister, and a stepbrother from their years together. Now everything's changed between him and Jackie, and it's neither one's fault. His life's consumed by doctors and therapists, and he's got a gym and trainer tailored to his needs. They've got him working on strength, balance, and flexibility. Dad's fought through it, though. Was he a good marine?"

I shrugged. "He didn't love it. Big smart athletes tend to get through their boot camp all right. He sure didn't want to go to Vietnam. He washed out of service football faster than he did in college. The rest of the time they mostly asked him just to be a fighter."

"Dad's a tough son of a bitch."

"Lots of guys would second that. When he was still changing your diapers."

"And I've had to change his. Maybe that's part of the problem now. Our relations are kind of strained."

"I'm sorry to hear that."

He wagged his head. "These things pass. We'll work it out."

"When you were little, do you remember all the girlfriends?"

He laughed and said, "You bet. He could have gotten tickets for that traffic. I thought all boys had a cast of pretty women cooing over them. A shrink told me I shaped them all into one big mom."

"All this must have been hard on you. I'm surprised you could keep playing ball."

"The coaches and most profs at UCLA were understanding and flexible. I'm glad I didn't sign with Illinois. Grandpop pushed hard for that because he wanted to see the games. I don't care for cold. I'll say this about the experience. It made me grow up in a hurry."

"And you made All-America and now you're a starting linebacker in the NFL."

He looked at the gym and seemed to take in the odor. "Well, maybe I'm starting."

He got down from the ring and walked into Richard's office. When he came back, he gave me a piece of paper with phone and fax numbers for his dad. "I'd tell him to expect you, but we're not exactly speaking now. You should call him. He cut people off because he was humiliated that he couldn't make them understand him. It was hardly ever personal."

He offered his hand and I shook it. I said, "You must have your dad's conviction. You've sure got his genes."

CHAPTER 63

Usually by bus, sometimes on a train, on one leg another airplane, after New York the Episcopalians had ushered Virginie and her mom and sister to stops for several weeks in Scranton, Pennsylvania, then Lincoln, Nebraska, and finally Los Angeles, California. The Episcopalians got them handed-down clothes and shoes for the growing feet of the sisters and apartments where they might find waiting for them bath towels, soap, a gallon of milk in the refrigerator, and one mattress on the floor. State government workers channeled federal funds that kept them from going hungry, but they had to learn how to spend it and what to buy.

Each stop presented a new set of nurses and social workers who might be courteous or might be cold. Learning English and "job training" for Sifa consumed their days. What did she know how to do but cook and collect wood and bathe children and garden with her hands? English came easier for Virginie and Honorata because they were children, and they already spoke several languages. The Episcopalians and other aid groups provided them with a phone, paid their rent and utilities, and in Los Angeles they enrolled the children in a grade school with a program for teaching immigrant children. Honorata at least started in the first grade with children her age. Virginie had to overtake four years of schooling to catch up. Many kids in her class had brown skin and black hair and their first language was Spanish.

At the school, in an English as a second language class, a woman told Virginie that her name would now be Virginia. That way Americans would understand her when she told them her name. The teacher told her how to spell it, called her to the blackboard, handed her chalk, and told her to write this name that was now hers, in this new life in America. In her first act of defiance she wrote *Virginie.* The teacher scolded her, but Virginie refused to yield.

Discarding the name her father and mother gave her would have been rejecting all they had been through. Learning English was no different from others, though it wasn't any more musical than German to her ears, and it was strange and confusing that so many sounds coming out of her mouth could be identical and yet have completely different meanings. When Virginie was on the streets she noticed something about the white Americans, especially the men. They stared at her then quickly moved their eyes away. They didn't do that to American speakers of English who were called black but their skin mostly registered gradations of dark brown. They gaped at her because she was so very black, as black as coal.

Virginie's mother was in a constant fret because of one obligation of their status. Six months after their arrival she was supposed to start paying back the cost of their airfare from Zaire—almost $3,000. If she fell far behind, their asylum request could be denied or reversed. She found work in a house-cleaning crew run by a small pretty woman from a little town in Mexico. The Mexican woman's Spanish and Sifa's Portuguese allowed them to communicate in a basic patois. But Sifa had no bank account and for proof of employment, she had no paycheck stubs. The Mexican woman paid her only in cash.

The worst of it for Virginie, one night her mother heard an exchange of gunfire, and after that she forbade her daughters to go outside the apartment at night. Virginie at ten knew about television, her teachers at school had begun to praise her, she had a Taiwanese friend, and they had a sudden interest in boys. For Virginie, going to school felt like being let out of a jail cell. All they had for entertainment in the apartment was a radio, and her mother kept it tuned to a station whose disk jockeys spoke Swahili and played African music. Some kids at school had portable radios, and at recess on the playground and waiting for the bus with Honorata, Virginie's learning of English let her respond to very different music.

The Go-Go's' "We Got the Beat," the Pointer Sisters' "Should I Do It."

Late one night she got in a bad argument with her mom. She grabbed a light jacket and ran out of the apartment with a loud door slam. She jogged down the steel stairs from the second-floor and fled with Sifa calling after her. From bus rides that carried her to school, a deep ravine had caught her eye. They passed it right before the bus chugged into a mass of freeways. She wore jeans, T-shirt, the jacket, and sneakers that let her keep her feet as she skidded down the grade. On Nyiragongo at night she feared lions and long-tailed spotted golden cats that weren't true leopards but were just as dangerous. Near enough the hut to scamper back inside, she liked to sit out and ponder the stars and the red and pink glow from the summit's lake of fire. Her escapes in the ravine were the closest she could get to that. Different were the dry brush and very different smells, the soughing passage of cars, the shrill whines of motorcycles, and the distant wail of ambulance sirens. But it was her haven.

Then came the noise that shook her to her newly painted toenails. She thought a plane had crashed and the wreckage was coming right at her. Not fifty yards away she saw a loose wheel bounding like Dik-dik and pygmy antelopes on Nyiragongo's plateau. A long low car came apart as it flipped end over end, taking brush and small trees with it. What was left of it came to another loud crash against a large tree. It was over before she had time to move. Two spinning wheels still on the wreck made a noise like ululations. When she heard that, she knew the God of the Episcopalians was real and had saved her. She prayed and gave God her thanks, and when she opened her eyes, she saw the wreck smoking. She had not had a close look at a dead person since the bleach in her father's stomach and lungs ceased his screaming and frantic jerking and he lay still. Death fascinated her.

She inched down the slope to the wreck, knowing the gasoline smell and smoke ought to send her running. She wanted just one look and then she'd be gone. Then she heard the man groan. He was suspended upside down in the wreck. She squatted and sat on her heels and twisted around trying to see the man. He made another sound.

"Do not die," she said. She wasn't sure which language came out.

"Can't … unfasten … the belt," he said.

On the tumbling mats in the school Virginie had discovered that she could stand on her head and with her hands making the adjustments, she could balance that way for a minute or two. The big wounded tree had put its roots out on fairly even ground. She looked around, put her hands on the soil, and stood on her head beside the wreck. The large black man looked her way and his eyes widened. "Please," she said, "do not die."

He took some breaths and said, "Sugar, I'm sure I am."

"No, please. I'll get someone."

He seemed to think she was an apparition. "Why are you here?"

"I was sitting on the ground. Looking at the stars."

He struggled some, then extended a hand past the shattered door glass. "Take these. So my wife and children . . . they'll know. Give them to a cop. He'll know what to do. And maybe do the right thing. Take them, child. Please."

Her legs and sneakers had begun to waver like tall grass in a wind. She was losing her balance and it was time to come to her knees. The bad thing about standing on her head was when she quit, it made her dizzy and breathless for a moment. She took the rings from him. There was a simple gold band and a large ring that looked cluttered but possibly had diamonds in it. She thought the man had very large hands and fingers.

Virginie reached past the jagged glass and put her hand on his shoulder. "Do not think you're dying. Please, do not. I find someone."

He breathed out and made another sound. She stuck the rings in the pockets of her jeans and raced back up the slope, across the freeway access road, and along it until she came to the two-story public housing apartments. Someone was playing Latino hip-hop. She ran up the steps and banged with her fists on the metal door. Sifa unlocked it and tried to shake her in anger, but Virginie tore free, got to the phone, and dialed 911. In English she managed, "There is a car crash and the man is alive, he's bleeding, but I heard him. He talked."

"All right, child, calm down. Where is it?"

She drew a blank until she remembered their bus driver was always grumbling about traffic. "The Santa Monica Freeway," she said.

"Well, there's a lot of that."

"The car left the road and went down a mountain."

"Mountain on the Santa Monica Freeway. How old are you, hon?"

"I'm ten. They can see where his car came off the road. It's like a . . . like a bridge. Like he ran off a bridge. Please, hurry."

CHAPTER 64

I thought a sorry spectacle called the smoker had passed into our history with poll taxes and Jim Crow laws. Ralph Ellison had described a black teenager's experience of one at the start of his 1952 novel *Invisible Man.* Suckered into believing the town's white leaders wanted to hear him read a graduation speech that he'd written at his segregated high school, instead he was blindfolded and had boxing gloves pulled on his hands. Inside a boxing ring he was forced into a battle royal with other blindfolded black kids while the white men jeered and cheered. Some of the youths got pretty badly hurt.

One night I was stunned to find a variant lived on in smug liberal Austin. I had been working out at Richard's one afternoon when he was preparing for an annual event that made the gym a little money. He and a volunteer crew of helpers tore down, transported, and reassembled his largest ring in a hotel ballroom in the affluent northwest hills of Austin. And he delivered a card of pro fighters for the night's entertainment. Richard had a handful of guest passes he offered to gym regulars. He told me Ali would be there.

"Bullshit," I said.

"What they say, they're flying him in," he said with a shrug, and I took one of the passes. He said the dress for others was formal but that didn't apply to us. I put on a suit, dress shirt, and tie. That night the doorman eyed my pass and motioned me through. The ring sat in the middle of a ballroom under glitzy chandeliers. The fighters on the card had passed physicals and made weight; their bouts had been approved by the state boxing commission, and the outcomes would count on their records. None were far along in their pro careers, nor would they ever be. The main event was an eight-rounder, and all the others were six or four rounds. At our gym I had befriended a Hispanic fighter who'd be in the main event. The guy's ring handle was "World Famous." We all called him that.

No sportswriters covered the bouts, and just one photographer had set up in front of the table where people could stand in line to get autographs by Ali. The scarcity of takers surprised me. Men and women, all wearing tuxedoes, stood about talking to each other and smoking cigars. Some women puffed them as eagerly as the men. About a dozen young women had been hired for the occasion. Wearing long black dresses, they moved about bearing silver-colored trays with glasses of wine, cigars, and butane lighters. Unlike the mob in Ellison's novel, these people stood with their backs to the fights, and when one went to the judges' scorecards or was stopped by the ref, they didn't applaud and few even looked around. They were realtors, real estate brokers, and developers. They were here to talk about Austin commerce, about how they might turn the tide from fanatics who only wanted to save that cold swimming hole, Barton Springs. Turning their backs on the fights and fighters and what they represented was a pointed code of behavior. They shunned the boxers brought in to entertain them with contempt.

One such developer had won a seat on the city council, and now he was trying to get elected mayor. The developer thought Ali's attendance at the smoker might boost the turnout and generate contributions. I'd been close enough to Ali to hand or toss him a tennis ball, but now he sat far across the room from the wall that our gym contingent leaned against. Richard sat with him and a young black man who had flown in with the ex-champion. They meant to keep the line of autograph seekers orderly and moving, which wasn't hard to do. Ali wouldn't have looked much more isolated in that crowd if he'd been a Guernsey milk cow.

At forty-eight Ali believed he inherited the gene for common Parkinson's, not the "dementia pugilistica" bandied about in the press. He loved publicity but he had no interest in being the poster boy for that. Watching him, I remembered an interview on the British network, BBC, that aired in 1971, when he was twenty-nine.

He had recently failed to take back the title from Joe Frazier, and in the interview, he tossed out a few insults to Frazier. Laughed at the notion Joe could go out with a band and sing. Ali had then fought thirty-two pro fights, and he didn't have one tell-tale mark on his handsome face. The BBC interviewer was a white man. He went by the single name of Parkinson, as it happened, and he may have annoyed Ali in his introduction by saying he was a "figurehead" in the black power movement in the States.

Their exchanges grew testy at the start as Ali argued against integration and interracial marriage. "God made us different," Ali maintained. Bluebirds flew with bluebirds, redbirds with redbirds. Eagles flew over mountains, buzzards across deserts. "Tell me when I'm wrong. Pigeons gonna be pigeons. You can't take no Chinese man with no Puerto Rican woman that say they're in love"—he curled his lip slightly at the notion—"but they're not happy because he's gonna want to hear Chinese music, she's gonna want to hear Puerto Rican music. It's just nature to want to be with your own. I want to be with my own. Life is too short to be catching hell over something like that. I want a beautiful wife, beautiful children. They all look like me, then no trouble."

To Parkinson's clear relief and probably that of the live audience, Ali then leaned back, smiled, and turned on the charm. "I'd say, 'Momma, why is everything white? Why is Jesus white with blond hair and blue eyes? Why's the Lord's Supper all white men? Angels, they're white, too.' I say, 'Momma, when we die, do we go to heaven?' She say, 'Naturally we go to heaven.' But what happened to all the black angels in the picture?"

Ali raised his eyebrows as Parkinson and the audience laughed. "I say, 'Oh, *I know,* black angels are in the kitchen making the milk and honey. Why do I want to die to get milk and honey? I don't want no milk and honey. I like steaks. Milk and honey's a laxative anyway. They got lots of bathrooms in heaven? I always wondered why Tarzan was king of the jungle. I see a white man swinging in Africa wearing a diaper and yelling *'Ahh ah eeh ah yahhhh.'*" More laughter from the audience.

"'All the Africans hear him yelling this way. And here's Tarzan talking to the animals, and the Africans that have been there for centuries, they can't talk to the animals. I always wondered why. I always wondered why Miss America is always white. Nice tan, pretty shape, good complexion, but why is she always white? Miss World is always white. Miss Universe is always white. And we got White House cigars, White Swan soap, White Cloud tissue paper. And Angel Food cake is white, and Devil's Food cake is chocolate. Momma, I always wondered. And the president lives in the White House. And Mary had a little lamb and its fleece was white as snow. And there's Snow White. Santa Claus is white. But the Ugly Duckling is black. And seeing a black cat is bad luck. If I threaten you, I blackmail you. Momma, why don't they call it *white-mail?* White men lie, too!'

"I was always just curious, and that's when I knew something was wrong."

At the time, when I watched that interview, I imagined Ali standing in the schoolhouse door with George Wallace. Segregation now, segregation forever. Yet that was just one side of Ali. In Austin I knew a tall novelist and screenwriter named Bud Shrake. He had been one of the early stars of *Sports Illustrated.* Early on, when Ali was trying to stay out of prison for refusing the draft, he had a federal court hearing in Houston. Bud got an interview with him that day in Ali's hotel room; they talked long enough that the champion in limbo feared he was going to be late. They hopped in Bud's rental car, Ali in the back seat. A big crowd of Ali's young black admirers had gathered at the courthouse. They expected Ali to arrive in a limo with a black driver and entourage. Their expressions clouded and they began to growl in anger that their hero showed up in a mere Chevrolet driven by a tall white man. Ali rolled down a window and shouted "Leave this man alone! He's my *chauffeur.*"

The most voluble man of my generation was silenced now, unless he trusted you enough to let you lean close and hear his murmur or whisper. At the Austin smoker, the bouts of young pros, most of them black or Latino, began and ended unwatched by the cigar smokers. I saw Ali tilt his head at his young handler, signaling he'd had enough of this. He didn't want to sign any more autographs. The mayoral candidate claimed a microphone and drawled a brief tribute to Ali. There was a polite round of applause as Ali came walking with care around the ring. The young man walked close beside him, poised to catch his elbow if he stumbled.

The developers and realtors made way for him as they would any cripple. Some stared, others ducked their heads and looked away.

"Aaa*lii!* Aaa*lii!*" I raised the cry that stirred fight fans and people who cared little about boxing all over the world. Vince the FBI agent, Billy the insurance executive, and others in our bunch of gym rats joined in. Ali made a sharp right turn and walked straight to us. His gaze roved from face to face. His illness barely let his smile move his lips, but light and humor still danced in his eyes. The handshake he offered me was gentle, but when I gripped his bicep with the other hand, his arm felt a lot firmer than mine. Billy clapped him on the shoulder and said, "Go get 'em, Champ."

Musicians and writers tend to bunch together. We're of the same tribe. The friendships came my way at first because of the music and the band. Some deepened after my moment in rock and roll ceded to the past. Sabine and I vacationed and roamed in Oaxaca and Tuscany with Gary Cartwright and his lively wife Phyllis, a prospering realtor who wouldn't have been caught dead at that smoker. Gary was nine years older than me. He aimed to write a magazine feature at some point about George Foreman's attempt to regain the heavyweight title after a layoff of over twenty years. One night he and Phyllis told us to do ourselves a favor some Sunday when we were in Houston: Go watch George preach.

Dr. Simmons, my voice physician, booked all his Botox injection appointments on Fridays. They were weird but painless, and I was in and out in ten minutes. It was 165 miles to Houston. Sabine went with me on one trip; we had decided to stay over, try a couple of new restaurants we'd heard or read about, and on Sunday we'd visit George's small church on the city's northeast side. The neighborhood was well-kept and didn't look impoverished, but the small homes didn't look prosperous either. They looked forgotten.

The Church of the Lord Jesus Christ was small and unimposing out front. George didn't evangelize the neighborhood for fear of turning his church into a circus. Inside, it was well-furnished but spare. There were about sixty people in the pews, all but four or five of us black. George's nephew, an assistant pastor, stood and sang and played an electric guitar. *Glory, glory, hallelujah, I'm gonna lay my burden down . . .*

When the music ceased, George walked in resplendent in brown Italian loafers, dark trousers, a camel blazer, a white dress shirt, and a bright red tie. As he approached the pulpit, he kissed a child in the first pew on the top of her head. He walked with an odd funny step, like his feet hurt. George didn't write his sermons. He selected a passage of Scripture, read it, and riffed on whatever came to mind. This day his sermon was drawn from the Gospel of Luke, Chapter 12. He opened his Bible and read Christ's parable in that chapter.

"The ground of a certain rich man brought forth plentifully; And he thought within himself, saying, What shall I do, because I have no room where to bestow my fruits? This will I do; I will pull down my barns, and build greater, and there will I bestow all my fruits and my goods. And will say to my soul, Soul, thou hast much goods laid up for many years, take thine ease, eat, drink, and be merry. But God said unto him, Thou fool, this night thy soul shall be required of thee: then whose shall these things be, which thou hast provided? So is he that layeth up treasure for himself, and is not rich toward God."

The gospel carried George's thoughts and sermon to miserable times in his life. He talked about the torment he had caused his mother. He said when he was fourteen, too much poverty, too many children, and especially his misbehavior hospitalized her for an emotional collapse. He pulled down his lip now and mimicked a man with no front teeth. "Wake up from being dead drunk and my best friend says, 'George, look what you did to me!' 'I did not do that!' 'Yeah, you did . . . but it's okay!'" The congregation burst out laughing.

George read some more of the apostle Luke, then talked about how his troubles followed him wherever he was. He described a low point in one of his five marriages. "Sometimes they just don't want you. I mean *you.* I went up to my ranch, and all I could think to do was cut grass. Mow and mow and mow. I ran my tractor over a stump. I was trying to fix my mower with a sledgehammer and come way up over the top. *Whomp!* Hit myself right below the knee." He danced across the church on one foot. "Thank you, baby Jesus, thank you for all this pain. Take my mind off the mess I have made of my life."

He limped on as the laughter subsided. "Amazing grace," he said, shaking his head. "That saved a wretch like me."

There was no baptistery in the church, no invitation hymn, no call to come down front and be saved on hearing his words. Confessions and affirmations of faith in his congregation were private affairs. George stood by the door and greeted people who'd blessed his church by sharing the morning with him. He called many by name. On seeing Sabine and me, his face broke into a pleased smile. He asked us our names and where we were from, and I felt the soft handshake John Norton had described that night on the outskirts of Caracas. I was wearing a gray mohair blazer Sabine had bought me early in our marriage. George, who was quite a clothes horse, rubbed the wool of my lapel with fingers and thumb and said, "That's a mighty fine coat."

Never one to hold back an impulse, Sabine said, "You two have met before. You called him Bodyguard."

George's brows and forehead furrowed. "Beg your pardon, ma'am?"

"He believes that one night in Caracas, Venezuela, you saved his life and the lives of Ken Norton's parents."

George blinked and leaned back in surprise. "That was you?"

"You remember that?" I said.

"Why, sure, I do. I got enough brain cells left for that." He put a large hand on my shoulder and told her, "I didn't save nobody that night. The Good Lord saved us all."

He glanced at other people who had begun to slip past without being greeted. "Listen," he said, "could you wait a few minutes? I'd like to talk to you, but I need to say God bless to these other folks. It won't be long."

CHAPTER 65

We had a nice chat with George that day after his family and the other churchgoers had gone. He told me that his youth gym was just a couple of blocks away from the church. He said he often went up to his ranch in Marshall on weekdays but when I was in Houston, I was welcome to drop by and see the gym. A couple of Friday trips for my Botox treatment offered me excuses to do that and stay over for his church services. Truth be told, I was fascinated by the man he'd become.

I was trying to fathom a man that I considered my guardian angel. Was that more than just a saying? How could anyone be sure? I know those few moments on a dark road in Venezuela brought me face to face with my mortality. I'd survived prison and a year of war, and now this was it? I was never as godless as I made myself out to be. George's preaching made me more at peace with myself.

The gym was small enough to fit on a residential lot. It had the heavy and speed bags but no boxing ring. Much of it was taken up by a half-court polished wood basketball court with three hoops and backboards positioned around it. It was a gym for kids, not competitive fighters looking for a place to work out and spar.

One day when I walked in, I was greeted by George's old friend, stablemate, and now his trainer. "How's it going, Bodyguard?" called Charlie Shipes.

I smiled and responded with my diffident shrug.

"That's what George calls you," he said.

"Because he can't remember my name."

"No, no. George likes you. You've come to his church more than once."

Charlie had come close to winning the welterweight title, his hopes undone by Curtis Cokes, the champion I had seen all those years ago in the 4-H Barn in Deerinwater. There were just three in that stable in Pleasanton, California—Charlie, George, and Sonny Liston. That day at the gym, George and Charlie reminisced about their time in Pleasanton. "Sonny had to be the angriest fella I ever met," said George. "He could scare you. Stare a hole right through you. I thought if I was going to get success in boxing, I had to channel anger in myself like that. Charlie, now, he had these red shoes, red trunks. He just looked like a boxer. Everything he did in the ring was perfection. I thought, I don't want to turn pro until I can learn to box like Charlie."

They were really talking to each other more than me. George told another story about Liston. "We were out walking one night and came on this office building that was shut down for the night. It had three tiers of long steps made of some kind of polished rock, like marble. Sonny went up on the top step and balanced right on the edge. Then he bent his right leg at the knee and stretched his left leg and shoe straight out. Then he stretched his arms and hands and held them straight out to the side. He just stayed there like that, could have been a statue. Never seen anything like it."

Sonny Liston enjoying his athleticism. Having fun.

Another day Charlie invited me to come over to his house for supper. He made his living with a small company of dump trucks parked around his house that night on Houston's east side. He met me at the gate and, puffing on a cigarette, led me and a pit bulldog, which walked close to my side, eyeing my backside. I watched it with friendly glances from the corner of my eye. The only evidence of Charlie's position in boxing was a couple of heavy bags under a shed and a few photographs on the living room mantel. Charlie's affable wife told me she had been a friend of one of George's cousins, and the friend introduced her to Charlie one Sunday at George's church. She said she'd never seen a pro fight. "I hope George will quit now," she said. "He's got his health and all those kids still at home." She laid out a classic supper of pork chops, black-eyed peas, cornbread, sliced garden tomatoes, and sweetened iced tea. Charlie asked me if I'd like to say grace. I bowed my head and called up the short rote prayer that got me through my boyhood.

Barbara wouldn't hear of me helping clean up the dishes. When Charlie and I took easy chairs in the living room, he reminisced more about their small team of fighters in California. "Sonny was good to George," he said. "George would bloody his nose, and Sonny wouldn't unload on him like a lot of fighters will. He was just bringing him along. George got his puncher's reputation because of the way he took apart Joe Frazier. But, hell, he did it with jabs, hooks, rights, and uppercuts. The man can box."

We fell to considerations of who George was up against. Basically, Mike Tyson and the rest. "Well, yeah, Tyson's good," said Charlie, "quick on his feet and shadowboxing. Great hand speed, and he's kind of a switch hitter. He'll step to the left and double hook, high and low, then do the same thing to the right. Ain't ever seen anything like it. But if a man's still got his legs under him, and there ain't no *nerve damage,* I'll take the experience. See, George came up with Ali, Frazier, Kenny Norton, Jerry Quarry, George Chuvalo. That's like going to Harvard. This young crowd now, they just been to junior college."

The town of Marshall in northeast Texas is on the western edge of the Old South. Somewhere in that farming country George came from a bloodline of slaves. He never dwelled on that in my hearing. He made his peace with his father in Marshall and later preached at his funeral. He donated his Olympic Gold medal and the gaudy world championship belt to the county historical museum in the town. The ranch outside Marshall, run by the oldest of his five sons, was George's refuge. Up there he could think and read and fish. His ranch contained two homes, one of them built for his mother, two stock tanks, stables for his Tennessee Walker horses, and a gym modeled on the church in Houston.

Then one day George's accountant and financial adviser had come to see him and said the youth gym had to go. George's church was exempt from property taxes, but that didn't apply to the gym. Those taxes kept going up, plus the utility bills every month. He told George he had to let the gym close or his church would go down with it.

George said, "Why, I know how to get money."

At thirty-eight George started shedding pounds and stopping well-picked opponents in out-of-the-way places—the ARCO Arena in Sacramento, the Oakland Coliseum, the Hitchin' Post USA in Springfield, Missouri. One night in Phoenix, two thousand souls and a USA Network TV audience saw George take on Bert Cooper, who then had a record of twenty and four. Cooper had power in both hands and had been trained early in his career by Joe Frazier. He would fight and mostly lose to opponents that included Mike Weaver. Mike and Cooper fought in an unusual venue, the Capital City Gymnasium in Beijing.

At 253, George outweighed Cooper by forty-two pounds. Some body shots made Cooper wince in the first round, and in the second George wobbled him with a right to the head. When the bell rang for the third Cooper stayed put on his stool. It would take more than boos to make him go out for more. The Arizona boxing commission withheld his purse because the ring doctor could find no sign of any injuries. Cooper explained his poor showing by saying he hadn't slept in three days. He said two prostitutes, twin sisters, had taken him on a nonstop binge of booze, cocaine, and fucking. "They set me up," he maintained.

Most sportswriters and commentators derided all this as farce, but for two years George fought every six weeks on average—a strenuous schedule for fighters half his age. In his second career, unlike his first one, he was attentive to reporters who might give him some benefit of the doubt. When the time was right for Gary Cartwright to write about George's second ring career, he described his training.

> Watching Foreman move around the ring, you were reminded of a circus elephant. He was ponderous, yet graceful and finely balanced. His expression was one of determination. The rage of youth had smoothed out, though it hadn't entirely vanished. There was still something menacing about the man, something barely suppressed and potentially deadly. His shaved head was circumscribed by a narrow strip of terry cloth, and the sleeves of his silver warm-up suit bulged as though there were enormous boa constrictors in there lunching on live pigs. He wasn't as quick on his feet as he once was, but then fancy footwork was never Foreman's weapon. He still had that relentless, merciless knack of stalking an opponent, of cutting off the ring and forcing the other boxer to take six steps to his two. And his punches still rattled the eyeglasses of onlookers at ringside.

In my company George exuded praise for many of the fighters he'd beaten. One afternoon he told me, "In boxing we got this saying, 'I'm gonna put my head on your chest.' Means I'm gonna come through all your defenses. Joe Frazier *did that* to a man as great as Muhammad Ali. After that, Joe never was quite the same. What else did he have to prove?"

George was obsessed with doing that to Mike Tyson. If he had opinions about Tyson's character, he never expressed them to my knowledge. Tyson was an obstacle, a man who had what he wanted back—the heavyweight crown.

One chilly morning at home I put on a bathrobe and flip-flops, started a pot of coffee, and went outside to get the newspaper. Sabine had an affection for the obituaries that I found curious. I took the sports section out and grimaced at a story about how the university volleyball coaches started courting girls as possible recruits when they were still in junior high. I turned to other pages and saw a brief filler ending a column that made me say, "Oof."

"What?" Sabine said, looking up over reading glasses perched on her nose, which I found charming. She had pulled up the sheets but she was still nude from our lovemaking, a Sunday morning habit when Emily was gone that likely saved our marriage.

"George is going to fight Gerry Cooney."

"Oh," she said, trying to sound intrigued. Her thoughts didn't jump like mine to the night Cooney ended Kenny's career and came close to killing him. Several talented heavyweights were maneuvering to challenge Tyson, and George was by far the oldest. He ranked high only in public opinion. Cooney would be a money fight, and beating him would stake a claim that the prior victims in his second career had not. "This is a dream fight," George told the press. "When people close their eyes, they dream about fights like Ali-Frazier, Liston-Clay. But those fights can't happen. This fight can, and it's the kind of fight that people dream about. I'm not fighting Gerry Cooney. I'm fighting time."

Cooney's first-round knockout of Kenny nine years earlier had vaulted him past contenders who thought he was getting all this attention because he was white. After Larry Holmes's tenth title defense, a knockout of Leon Spinks, Holmes was being interviewed by Howard Cosell. Holmes saw Cosell's assistant bringing Cooney their way. Holmes said, "If you bring him over here, Howard, I'm gonna slap you." The assistant and Cooney kept coming, and in the scuffle Holmes accidentally cut Cosell's lip with a bang of his elbow. In the postfight press conference, Holmes went off again on Cooney. "Who the hell is Gerry Cooney?" he jeered. "I've proved time over time again that I'm the baddest heavyweight in the world. I've beaten everyone. He's the Great White Dope. Who's he ever beaten? He ain't ever beaten anybody. If he wasn't white, he wouldn't be anywhere. If he was black, nobody would know who he was."

Among other things, the rant was a flabbergasting insult to Kenny Norton. In the run-up to the fight, Holmes received death threats and his house was vandalized. The Ku Klux Klan demonstrated in support of Cooney. He appeared on covers of *Sports Illustrated* and *Time*, one with Sylvester Stallone posing beside him as the hero in his movie *Rocky.* Though Cooney fought hard, getting up from an early knockdown to win some rounds, by the thirteenth he was hanging on the ropes, trying to stay upright, when his trainer slipped through the ropes to stop it. Since then Cooney had fought only five bouts in five and a half years, and in the most recent one he'd been stopped in the fifth round by Michael Spinks. Cooney was now thirty-three and had been inactive a long time. Still, he had a record of twenty-eight and two, and twenty-four of his victories were knockouts. Bob Arum promoted George's fight with Cooney in Atlantic City, styling the event "The Preacher and the Puncher." The *Los Angeles Times* countered: "A Fight for the Aged." The UPI: "Geezers at Caesars."

Cooney was now trained by Gil Clancy, who had guided George well in his unsuccessful quest for a rematch with Ali. Charlie Shipes did the real training of George, but George had forgiven Archie Moore and brought the Mongoose back as the second in his corner. I watched the fight at home on HBO. I hoped Kenny wasn't watching, because the program began by airing back-to-back clips of George and Cooney knocking him out in brutal fashion. As it was about to begin, one of the announcers wondered why George would risk a fight with such a powerful foe as Cooney. "He's got millions of dollars at stake here. George didn't need this fight to get a fight with Tyson. He was going to get it anyway."

Whatever the press thought of the bout, the prizefighters were each getting a million dollars, and in the first round they got right to business. While Cooney circled and fired salvos of punches, George used the arms-crossed defense patented by the Mongoose, and he kept coming with those thudding jabs and hard shoves. Toward the end of the round Cooney countered with a left hook, then another one. The second blow staggered George so much that a left and right he had started flew so wild and wide they looked like haymakers in a cowboy movie. Clancy yelled at Cooney to *believe it* and finish him!

George collected himself quickly after the bell, but when asked later who were the hardest punchers he'd ever faced, he said they were Ron Lyle, the old-timer Cleveland Williams who was brought in for sparring one time, and Gerry Cooney. In the second round HBO's broadcasters were belittling George's round-house rights, but he was landing heavy body punches and lead rights, and his arsenal now included a short punch that was part left hook and part uppercut. Near a corner he landed one of those and staggered Cooney. George was fast on him with a jab and another right, then three rights dropped him in a corner. Cooney made it to his feet, passed the ref's inspection of his eyes, rubbed a glove against his bleeding nose, and prepared for more battle. In two long businesslike strides George reached him with a sweeping left hook; then a right sent Cooney into a head-first heap. The ref waved a halt to it as George calmly walked past.

I'm sure it was the last thing George would have thought about, but I found some satisfaction that just as Cooney's power had ended the career of my friend Kenny, George's power was the end of the line for Gentleman Gerry.

A couple of days after his knockout of Cooney, with makeup not quite masking a black eye, George appeared on a TV interview guaranteeing that he would knock out Mike Tyson in the first or second round. "I own the center of the ring against Tyson. The only way it'd go any longer would be if he pulled some *boxing thing* that let him get away for a while."

But George's dream finale was a mirage. A month after George's disposal of Cooney, in Tokyo a 42-1 underdog named Buster Douglas got off the canvas in Tokyo and ended Tyson's aura of invincibility with a knockout that left the champion more concerned with getting his mouthpiece back between his teeth than standing up to beat the count.

Later came the news that Tyson had been arrested in Indianapolis and charged with raping an eighteen-year-old Miss Black America contestant in his hotel room at two in the morning. The boxing establishment never took the charge as a serious matter. Tyson was supposed to convince the grand jury that the sex was consensual. What was she doing in his hotel room at that hour? Jesse Jackson voiced a public prayer for the defendant; Donald Trump vouched for him; Don King launched a "Free Mike" public relations campaign; and the celebrity-loving Harvard appeals specialist Alan Dershowitz joined the defense team.

The lawyers expected Tyson to carry the day when they put him on the stand, but he mumbled through it, and in cross-examination the lead prosecutor gave him the dress she wore that night and asked him to explain a tear in a beaded seam. Tyson growled something and flung the garment, which fluttered on the work space of the court reporter. The jury convicted him of rape and two counts of criminal deviate behavior. The judge sentenced him to ten years in an Indiana penitentiary, and at least three of those years had to be served.

It would take George three title fights to make his dream come true. He did it with a short right that finished young Michael Moorer, who until then had a record of 35 and 0. It was the kind of punch he could never land against Ali, now his friend, and everyone knew he wished Moorer could have been Tyson.

One day George invited me to come to his office at the gym in Houston. It was late in the afternoon, and he closed the door against the noise of a pickup basketball game between kids who were razzing each other loudly. The sound of the ball thumping reminded me of bass lines with the band. George was talking about his fight with Ali in Zaire. Even after the cut in sparring and the dead time down there waiting for it to heal, he was so sure he was going to knock Ali out. "Then in the eighth he came off the ropes, hit me with a hook and then a good right, knocked me down, and my whole life changed. I was devastated. I hated Ali for years. Little did I know I'd made the best friend in my life. Muhammad got a second chance to be the greatest show on earth. And it turned out he was. Those second chances, they're important in life."

"When did you realize he was your friend?"

"The late seventies. He called one time and went on about half an hour about how great I was. I thanked him and thanked him and finally asked why he called. 'George,' he said, 'I got this contract to fight Leon

Spinks, but the WBC's gonna strip my title if I don't fight Ken Norton again. I want you to get back in shape and beat him, George.'

"I said, 'Muhammad, I can't do that. I'm an evangelist now.'

"He said, 'Please do this, George. I can't beat him, but he's afraid of you.'"

I nodded and laughed. "That's true. You terrified him."

George stretched his mouth. "Yeah. I tried not to let people know it, but looking across that ring, I was scared of Kenny Norton."

I laughed again. "If you recall, I was at that fight."

"They didn't call him Body Beautiful for no reason. You were in the ring with him enough to see him in just shorts and shoes, maybe a T-shirt. It wasn't Hollywood inside that ring." He paused for a moment. "How is he now?"

"I'm not sure. I just know it's been a hard road back."

"Fast cars," he grunted. "Tell you something else about him. In his rivalry with Muhammad, he could have easily presented himself as the Patriotic Veteran against the Draft Dodger. He never said a word of that, to my knowledge."

I thought about it and nodded.

"Joe Frazier had some success with Muhammad because he could get inside and bang with him. But when Muhammad established his distance, he had too much speed for Joe. Kenny, though, had as much height and reach as Muhammad. He could match him jab for jab. And he had that way of picking off punches with that right hand in front of his face. And Muhammad didn't have enough power to knock him out. Kenny not only won that third fight. I believe he won all three of them."

CHAPTER 66

It never made sense to me that the Los Angeles police and a legion of reporters couldn't find the girl who called the lifesavers out for Kenny. I wondered how hard they tried. My solo record continued to sell a little because of the musicians who produced and played on it, and some dear hearts were nostalgic about so-called Texas music of the period. Leon Russell had licensed it so that when I parted company with Shelter, the rights to *Two Bubbles Off Plumb* came with me, and from Cow House Creek I got a fair deal for its reissue on their label and rights to *Pipe Town Blues, Soviet Gypsies,* and the never-released *Dog Boys*.

I told Sabine I could use a travel. I said I was going to drive out to Los Angeles, rent a cheap apartment, and find that girl who saved the life of a friend I never would have expected to have. She'd be fourteen now, the same age as Kenny's daughter Kenisha.

"It's been years," said Sabine with her habitual logic, "in a huge city you don't really know. Won't it be the needle in a haystack?"

"Could be. I need to try. What else am I doing except cooking every other week and trying to build guitars?" I planned to start with people I knew in the music business and boxing world and see where that led. I drove out Interstate 10 and followed it through Texas's part of the Chihuahua Desert, admiring the dust devils that Comanches believed were ghosts and made Tony Pereira think the Air Force landed him on the moon. I kept going past El Paso and stopped for the night at the approximate midpoint,

Deming, New Mexico. That night a thunderstorm with some awesome bolts of lightning passed through as I watched from a bench outside my motel room. Across the highway one strike turned a scrub pine into a flaming cinder just before the thunder boom nearly knocked me off the bench. It inspired me to go inside.

I was out of Arizona by noon the next day, and in California I detoured and picked up Highway 101 so I again saw the brown hills of Pendleton and the beaches where Kenny and I had plugged along in our boots twenty-one years earlier. My emotions on seeing them again were mixed and strong.

In LA I found a one-bedroom apartment beside Tongva Park. I picked it because the park was a pretty place to walk in the cool mornings. My triangulation strategy got shot down at once. In the offices of the people I had talked to about my financial interest in the reborn Rip Chords, I got blank looks. "Ken who? You mean that old fighter?"

LA is all about today, baby.

In the two newspaper morgues I got people to let me read the files about Kenny's accident. I knew I wouldn't find the answer there, but they felt like places to start. I saw in one clip that Mayor Tom Bradley, who lost his second race for governor, had offered a reward for anyone who found the girl and a matching one for her and her family. I tried to get an audience with the mayor, but an aide rebuffed me. Now, the aide said, the mayor was pushing measures against AIDS and HIV discrimination, trying to battle the emergence of crack cocaine, and looking for answers to the outbreaks of road rage. The aide added helpfully that the expression originated in LA.

I was about to give up and go home when at a gym in the San Fernando Valley I tracked down Mike Weaver. In a ring and the middle of a round of sparring, he raised his chin and grinned on seeing me and told me to stick around until he was through.

His sparring partner that day was sure to be of the opinion Mike still had power in his straight right and left hook. Mike carried a little flab around his middle now but he still had the shoulders and bulging pectorals. He now had a mustache. When he got through with the workout he pulled on a dry T-shirt and led me to a torn sofa to talk. As he unwrapped his hands two kids geared up for a ring workout drifted by and with reverence called him Champ.

We started out talking about boxing. Except for the time he briefly remarked on his faith, that was all we'd ever talked about. Mike held the WBA heavyweight title from 1980 to 1982. It didn't do as much for him as he hoped when he knocked out John Tate with the desperate last-minute hook. After he stopped Gerrie Coetzee on South African soil in his bruising first defense, he won a verbal agreement to defend it next against Gerry Cooney. The fight was supposed to come off in either Vegas or Madison Square Garden six months after Cooney almost killed Kenny in the ring. "Woulda been my biggest money fight," Mike said, "and I'd have had the psychological advantage."

That was news to me. "What happened?" I said.

"Oh, the WBA said I had to fight James 'Fighting Cowboy' Tillis, young guy out of Tulsa. His other ring handle was 'Quick,' and he was fast. Had a record of twenty straight wins but he hadn't fought nobody." He shook his head. "The fights. My manager Don Manuel, who'd started out as my trainer, told them, 'Look, you got Tillis ranked number three. Cooney's ranked number one. Explain it to us.'

"'Don't matter,' they say. 'If you don't fight Tillis we'll strip you of the title.' So Bob Arum puts the fight in a little town outside Chicago called Rosemont. Nice enough people, seemed like, but there might have been three thousand of them. Top it all we were the undercard. Tillis got his title shot, and I beat him up. Marvin Hagler got all the press and a million bucks for stopping Mustafa Hamsho. Make you happy, WBA? There went Cooney and another shot at big money."

I watched him unlace his shoes. "Do you see Kenny?"

"Now and then, when I can. He didn't want to see anybody but family at first."

"How is he now?"

He looked up. "You haven't talked to him?"

"No. I stopped trying to get through."

He tilted his head and gave me a curious look. "Sane man woulda been done in. It's like his minute with Cooney got stretched into four years and they ain't never gonna ring the bell. The skull fracture is what about got him. Know what they did to keep the brain from swelling? They put him on ice, almost gave him frostbite. He's had to learn how to speak all over, and you know how that man liked to talk. Therapists and trainers and a good gym have got him back on his feet and in pretty fair shape. I get the impression it's pretty much ruined his marriage, though, and that's a shame."

I hesitated to push further. I knew Mike had spent much of his adult life answering questions about Ken Norton, not himself. I asked him what happened to his career after Tillis. He said the WBA next offered him another undefeated gunner, Michael Dokes.

"This one was a Don King show at Caesars Palace. Dokes came out of his dressing room throwing roses to the crowd. I thought this guy's lunch, but he surprised me. Twenty seconds in, he got me good with a hook and then put me down with another one. I can dig it. I've always started slow. I took the eight-count and we were trading hard shots when the ref jumped in and stopped it with a minute left. I wasn't hurt! I couldn't believe it. The crowd was booing and yelling, *'Fix! Fix!'* Manuel said, 'Start the fight over, Dokes can have the ten-eight first round.' Then come to find out the ref laid substantial money on Dokes with a bookie. I'm still working at forgiving that worm. It's my Christian obligation."

He looked around like he was wondering what we were doing sitting on a split couch in one more boxing gym. "He give you a rematch?" I said.

"Yeah," he answered. "Six months later, outdoors at a Vegas palace called the Dune. Dokes looked like he'd been eating roses and Snickers and anything else he could get his hands on. I got him good with the first punch of the fight, a right that came around the first base side. His jab did lose its zing. Fourth round, he threw some punches so low that the ref gave me half a minute's recovery. But he only gave the guy a warning. Dokes got a little second wind and had a spurt about round twelve, but most of the way he clinched. I had cuts over both eyes and had to have one sewn up, but he was cut, too, and the right side of his head looked like a water moccasin bit him. I hit him with jabs, I hit him with rights, I hit him with hooks, I got tired of hitting him. That point the ref should have taken away for the low blows would have decided it. But you got to *take* the title from the guy that holds it. Two judges had it dead even. The other judge gave it to Dokes by a point, so the title stayed with him, a majority draw. I should have quit after that. My legs were going. I knew."

"How old are you?"

"Thirty-seven."

"What's your record now?"

"Thirty, thirteen, and one."

"So . . . "

"So what?" he answered.

"Why keep doing it?"

He grinned. "Because I'm hot stuff in Africa. They pay me to keep coming."

I laughed. "Why's that?"

"Oh, it started with me giving my first title defense to Coetzee and beating him down there. Then I beat this guy named David Jaco in Yaound, capital of Cameroon. Last fight I had, I upset this young guy, Johnny du Plooy, back in Sun City where I fought Coetzee. I like it over there. In my hotel I could hear hyenas at night. Until du Plooy got me, he was seventeen and zip. He didn't come out for the sixth. Next one's a rematch with him. I'm their American in Africa. People saying I'm on the payroll of the CIA."

I started to get up. "It's been good seeing you, Mike. Good luck in your fight. I guess I'm heading back to Texas. I tried to find the girl that called help for Kenny but didn't get anywhere."

"Virginie."

"What?"

"Virginie. Her name's Virginie Nalula."

"You *know that?* How do you know?"

He shrugged. "Jesus loves me, this I know."

"How'd you find her?"

"Oh, I had a lady friend at church that got me into trying to help refugees. She's got a new fella now. But one of those refugees was Kenny's guardian angel."

"Have you taken her to meet Kenny?"

"No."

I was puzzled and asked why. He shook his head. "You got to understand how shy that girl is. She's got reason to be. Her mother's scared to death her girls will do something that gets them sent back to the Congo."

CHAPTER 67

Mike told me to stick around till Sunday if I wanted, and after church he'd try to take me to meet Virginie. The sign outside Mike's church didn't stipulate a denomination. There was a lot of fine music from a small choir, accompanied by a piano and tambourines. Mike's bass singing was unabashed, off-key. The beauty and simplicity of it carried me back.

I drove us through corridors of lonesome-looking palms and followed his directions. He said, "Virginie's mother's doing better now, but English has been hard for her. It's hard to know what all she understands. Just be careful what you say."

"What does her mother speak?"

"Portuguese, French, Swahili, and another tribal one, I think."

The apartment building where we arrived was dingy and stark on the outside, but the woman who answered the door was dressed like she could have been heading out for an upscale job interview. The mother, whom Mike introduced as Sifa, was very small. She had a toothy smile and wore medium high heels and a dress of fabric cut just below the knees that looked like swirling wraps of crimson and white. She was beautiful. "Welcome, our home," she said and gestured. "Mike, our good friend."

"I gathered," I said. I could tell from her expression that the idiom confused her.

The younger girl, Honorata, had tight dreadlocks decorated with several bows of multi-colored ribbon. Still wearing her dress for church and a pair of spotless white sneakers, she lay on her stomach on a sofa and watched cartoons on TV, the soles of her sneakers aloft. When Sifa summoned Honorata, she rolled off the sofa, stood before me with a solemn expression, and extended her hand. I shook it and said hello. Her sister came forward and stood before me with perfect posture. Virginie's hairstyle was simple—a brushed-out but otherwise untamed mass of black curls swept back by a red scarf tied over the nape of her neck She had on a pair of dangling red earrings that matched the scarf and looked tribal.

"I'm Virginie," she said.

"Pleased to meet you. I'm Haid."

Pubescent breasts poked through the trim navy-blue dress she wore. She wore a delicate chain with a cross resting in the hollow of her throat. She asked me to sit down with as much formality as her mother. She took a chair next to me. All the questions I thought to ask sounded stupid. "How do you like your school?"

"Fine," she said. She kept her head turned in the direction of the television but I could tell the cartoons Honorata was watching didn't interest her. She slipped quick glances at me and jiggled her knees. Trying to help, Mike offered that Virginie was a very good student.

"Your mother must be proud of you," I said. Her glances measured me, the way a wary fighter does. With another inner groan I said, "What are your favorite subjects?"

"Reading and music," she said.

"Oh, well, they're the best. Would you like to sing or play an instrument?"

"Both, but sing," she said, turning her face to me now. Her knees continued to jiggle. "Mike told us you're a singer."

"I used to sing and made a few records, but it was time to quit. My voice got where it wasn't worth hearing anymore."

"What kind of songs did you sing?"

I still carried one of my harmonicas tucked in my pant pockets beside the wallet, more for luck and out of habit than anything else. But instead of "Two Bubbles Off Plumb" I blew other notes that came to me. *Just as I am, without one plea . . .* Virginie lit up with a look of pleasure, and she and her mother and Mike came to their feet. Sifa grabbed the control from Honorata and turned down the volume of the cartoons, and they took off singing the hymn so fast I could barely keep up. I put the harmonica away. "There Is a Fountain Filled with Blood," "O They Tell Me of a Home Far Beyond the Skies," "Shall We Gather at the River," "Blessed Assurance, Jesus Is Mine," "Sweet Hour of Prayer," "What a Friend We Have in Jesus." I remembered some of the lyrics but always the tunes, but Mike and Virginie were the strongest voices in our acapella chorus. Sifa sometimes sang in another language, I wasn't sure which one, and I directed with the hand motions that once served me in the pulpit of that little church on Keeler Street. We were out of wind when we ended with "Softly and Tenderly Jesus Is Calling."

Virginie and her mother laughed and clapped their hands and beat their hands against their thighs. A hunch had broken the ice. Virginie seemed to me as Americanized as hamburgers and baseball. I said, "Do you ever wonder where gospel songs come from?"

"The gospel?"

"Well, sure. But songs are easier to sing and remember if the words have some rhyme, and the melody has to carry them. Let me tell you about that last one we sang." I told the invitation hymn's story slowly, with glances at Sifa, wanting her to understand. "Mike tells me that the Episcopalian Ministries did a lot to bring you here. The town where I live has an Episcopal seminary, a kind of college where people study the Bible and creeds of the faith. It has a nice library where I like to go sometimes. Just a good-feeling room, smelling of books. One of the best parts about singing for me is finding out the stories behind songs. For instance, the one we just sang.

"'Softly and Tenderly Jesus Is Calling' started as a poem in England in the 1830s. A sad mess of a man was a clerk for the English House of Lords, kind of like our Congress but the seats are inherited by white men who still wear powdered white wigs. Have you ever seen a rat or mouse caught in a glue trap? Good, you don't want to. The work was so boring and the lords were so arrogant it made the man as crazy as a rat stuck in a glue trap. He decided to kill himself. He thought he'd do it by jumping off the Tower of London, then he got a good look at the tower, and was afraid he couldn't get high enough that the fall would kill him. Or some Samaritan would come grab him when he was trying to jump. So he got this stuff called laudanum. It was alcohol mixed with raw opium, powerful stuff. Anybody could get it then in these little bottles called miniatures. The clerk started to drink all of his miniatures, lost his nerve, and threw a bottle against a wall and smashed it. He changed his mind again, got out a pocketknife with a fair-sized blade, and jumped off his bed with the blade aimed where he thought his heart was. The knife broke when he landed and the blade wound up sticking out of his stomach, but not deep enough to do anything worse than make him bleed a little. So he got a thick elastic strap, tied it around his neck and the hinge of a tall door, and jumped off a chair. He relaxed his knees, and was blacking out when the band snapped and he banged his head on the floor. That's when the poem came to him. Poets call it an epiphany. Someone added a melody later."

Virginie and Mike were laughing by the time I got through the tale. Sifa looked happy but confused.

I said, "Virginie, do you know why I wanted to meet you?"

She nodded.

"I haven't talked to Mr. Norton in a long time," I said. "I call him Kenny. Mike and I believe you were his guardian angel. I know he'd like to meet you."

With a cautious glance at her mom she said, "He doesn't have to thank me."

"He knows that. He'd just like to know you. He has a daughter your age. Mr. Norton is a good man, a nice man. We were good friends before he got hurt so bad in that wreck, and his getting better has made staying in touch difficult. I just want you to know I'm grateful you gave him a chance to go on living."

She had quit jiggling her knees. I said, "Can I give you something before I go?"

She looked at her mother, who nodded. I had played another hunch. She was a teenager in America, so her ears would be pierced. From my jacket I handed her a small box that I'd gotten the jeweler to gift-wrap. She removed the paper, opened the box, and gasped. They were just small gold earrings in the shape of leaves. Not very expensive, but they were gold. She showed the earrings to her mother, who gave me a glorious smile, took the red tribal ones out of Virginie's ears, and fixed the new ones in her child's earlobes with care. Virginie said, "Can I hug you?"

"Of course."

I told Mike that it was for us time to go, but she said, "Wait. I have something I'd like to give you." From another room she brought out a small velvet bag. She handed it to me, I pulled the drawstrings, and brought out Kenny's plain gold wedding band and a big ring that was elaborately carved, set with four small diamonds, and the face of it read "WBC World Heavyweight Champion 1978."

The ring made me smile. Players on teams that win the World Series and Super Bowl get large gaudy rings. Fighters that win world titles get belts like the one Larry Holmes wore when he ran out of Caesars Palace still in his trunks and shoes and jumped in a swimming pool. They don't get rings. Out of pride, Kenny had it made for himself. Just in case somebody wanted to know what he'd done with much of his life.

"Can I take these to Kenny?" I asked Virginie.

"Yes. Please."

As I drove Mike away from the apartments I said, "How'd I do?"

He laughed. "How'd you do? You made a friend. Room full of them."

"Did you know she had these?"

"No."

"I wonder why she didn't give these to you."

"A pretty little bird sat on her shoulder and told her to wait to hear your song."

CHAPTER 68

Sabine and I made love again that morning. It was our favorite time for it. There were no lights to turn off or down. It wasn't filtered through booze or my weed. It was just us in the altogether. She let me grip her hands in mine and hold them against the pillows. She made her soft cries and twisted her head back and forth against the pillows when she came. Later we let our breathing return to normal. I wiped sweat off her collarbones with an end of the sheet and kissed her again. Sabine was always telling me about her dreams. In times good and bad it was part of our ritual. They hadn't been this good in a long while. Some mornings I found her dream stories interesting and sometimes I didn't. But they were part of her human experience, and I respected it. My dreams were usually erased from memory thirty seconds after I woke up. But this morning one had stuck, and I told mine first.

"I was in a separate arrangement. I wouldn't say universe or reality because who knows what those are. I saw people who looked familiar but most of them didn't. I knew I was a visitor in this. I was accepted but forever apart. It was possible to have a relationship with the others, but only if they agreed to it. And there was a price to pay. It was good for no more than three encounters. They could express love or hate, anything in between, but there was a catch. After that it was erased on their parts. If I wanted to continue I had to start all over and spring fifty more bucks.

You were one I wanted more of. Then I woke up."

She blinked her big brown eyes. "That makes me a fifty-dollar whore?"

"I don't think dreams mean anything. Dogs have them, too. What do they mean? I was just glad you were here when I woke up. It might have scared me if you weren't."

"How could we have almost gone so wrong?" she said.

"But we didn't. Something made us come to our senses."

I couldn't imagine why anyone would want a wedding outside in Texas in August. But Emily and her young architect Anthony, whom we liked a great deal, had their reasons, and I kept my mouth shut. I had left LA without seeing Kenny, but since then he and I'd talked three times. The last call, he said he'd been studying the Dallas Cowboys' training camp schedule, and he thought he'd come to Austin, watch them scrimmage the Broncos, and start trying to patch things up with his son. He told me the date, and I said, "Oh. That's my stepdaughter's wedding day."

"Well, maybe the day after then, before I head back . . . "

"No, wait. Do you know what time the scrimmage is?"

A pause as he looked at something. "Three o'clock," he said.

It was the worst time and place they could impose on young guys weighed down by all that armament. It made me think of my hapless two-a-days when the high school coaches gave us salt tablets instead of water.

"Perfect," I said. "I'll pick you up, we'll do the wedding, and then I'll take you over to the little college where the Cowboys are training. It's close to the home of friends who are hosting the wedding. I won't be able to stay for the scrimmage. There's a party with a band where I'll need to be. But we'll have some time together."

"You're sure I'm invited?"

"Of course you are. Sabine will be delighted." And she was.

I had gotten into my tuxedo early and packed a bag with other clothes that would be more comfortable in the heat. The garage of our home that I'd had remodeled into my studio had morphed into a workshop. I had been trying to transform myself into a luthier, a builder of archtop acoustic guitars and mandolins. I had gotten better at it as the months accumulated, and I'd sold a few of both instruments. They were pretty. But I couldn't help calculating that I made about thirteen cents an hour. I was hanging out in my office chair, listening to an old Ry Cooder album and his instrumental "I Think It's Going to Be All Right." I picked up the envelope and reread the letter that had come in the mail three days earlier. On blue stationery, it was in a young girl's hand.

> *Dear Haid, You asked me to call you that, you said you'd rather not be Mr. Pecos. I'm looking forward to starting a new school. Your records sound different to me but I like them. I like the way you sing. Music brings me joy. I sing soprano in our church choir and I hope one day I will play the cello in an orchestra. How is my English, please? How are you?*
>
> *I have been thinking about what you told me. That I am Mr. Norton's guardian angel. I asked our pastor what you meant and he said in Exodus that when the Israelites ran away from the Egyptians and wandered in the wilderness, God told Moses, "My angel shall go before thee." I pray every night for my mother and sister and you and Mr. Norton and people we remember on our mountain Nyiragongo. I hope their lives are safer now. I'm afraid they're not.*
>
> *I pray for myself too. I am not anyone's angel. I have read about Mr. Norton now. In Swahili and my old country he is bingwa, a champion. A warrior and defender. On Nyiragongo Papa tried to be bingwa for people of my tribe and the gorillas and elephants but the Simbas were too many. Mama has a new job in a laundry now. She likes it there, though she says the odors are strange. She's not so afraid now.*
>
> *You told me Mr. Norton is a good man. I have so little to offer, but if he would like to know me, I would like to know him. Call me when you want to. I like it very much when you do. Your friend, Virginie Nalula*

Sabine jingled the bell through the walls. Since getting up, she had been in an efficient frenzy all morning, dealing with the florist, the caterer, her dress. I thought I could best help by staying out of the way. But I found her calm, dressed, and scented with my favorite perfume. In our bedroom she sat in front of her makeup table and mirror with her legs crossed, as she always did. I took off the patent leather slippers of the tux and lay on my back watching her, with my hands clasped behind my head. She was "putting on her eyes," as she described application of her eyeliner. I loved watching her ritual.

"When are you going to pick up Kenny?" she said.

"I'll head out to his hotel soon." She glanced at me.

"Trust me," I said. "I'm on top of it."

"I have a suggestion. Don't get mad."

I stiffened a bit and said, "Okay."

"I could hear the record you were playing. That Ry Cooder instrumental, 'I Think It's Going to Be All Right.' Why don't you apply yourself and learn to play bottleneck guitar? You've talked about wanting that as long as we've been married. We know about your hand. So. Figure it out. You've got plenty of friends who'd help you."

"And then what? Sit around playing 'Four Walls'?"

"Stop feeling sorry for yourself."

"Are we having an argument?"

"I hope not. We started off the morning making love."

I let my breath out slowly. "I don't know, babe. It's just hard to start over. Sitting in with other people's bands . . . "

She swung around in the chair. "Sweetheart, you are forty-seven years old. While you're learning the guitar, start singing again."

"I can't, Sabine, that's over with. I can't sing anymore. It's terrible."

She blew me a kiss, holding the eyeliner brush. "I hear you in the shower. It's not the same, but maybe it's more interesting. Don't be such a perfectionist. Have you ever listened to Tom Waits? Leonard Cohen? Kris Kristofferson?"

After a moment I said, "You really think?"

"You'd be so much happier. And I liked your space better when it was a studio. When it didn't smell like varnish and glue. I could come join you. Hang out and listen to music, like we used to do. Workshop, it's just not the same."

She looked at the mirror and considered her eyes done. "Let's call your comeback record *Sawdust.*"

CHAPTER 69

Emily's wedding took place outside a Victorian home that our friends had restored. It had been built with leftover pink granite used in constructing the state capitol. At one point in its history it had been a boys' school. At another, right before our friends bought it, the place was so run-down it was the set for a couple of low-budget horror movies.

So that the summer heat wouldn't frazzle the whole deal, fans blowing cool mist had been set about. Emily had said she wanted both her dad and me to walk her down the sidewalk that was the aisle. Russ and I both looked stiff in our tuxedoes. The aisle was a long sidewalk lined with beds of red and white amaryllis. As we waited, a pretty blonde woman was playing a viola. I remembered one Halloween night when she put on a body suit so form-fitting she looked fully nude and rode a white horse down Sixth Street as Lady Godiva. Austin as it was back then, when I was a cocky young singer courting Sabine.

Among the seated guests I watched Kenny. He was much thinner than I'd seen him, maybe 195 pounds, but he stood out among the others as tall athletes do. He wore a brown fedora. Sabine leaned toward him, and as they talked, she held his hands.

As the judge, Anthony, and the attendant friends assembled, Emily joined us, looking fabulous and somewhat spooked. I sang the Nick Lowe line *I knew the bride when she used to rock and roll . . .*

"Hush," she said.

Russ and I had cooked up a bit of mischief. He said, "When the judge asks who's giving her away, who's going to answer?"

"You, of course," I said.

"No, it has to be you. You raised her more than I did."

"Not so. You're her father."

"Doesn't matter," Russ went on. "I insist."

"No, I insist."

Emily had enough of it and shrilled, *"You guys!"*

The young judge had gone to law school with Sabine. He cued us with a slight nod, and we stepped away after both answering, "We do." Give her away from what to what? What a notion. Then it was done and the wedding was over. People mingled in the shade of live oaks, some went up into the house, and bottled water, beer, and wine were being brought out in large iced tubs. The caterer and crew were laying out trays of appetizers on the rear patio. The Lost Gonzos were coming in with their instruments. I changed from the tux into the clothes I'd brought along. "Damn," I said. I'd forgotten to add the deck shoes I usually wore. The round-toed patent leather slippers that came with the tux would have to do.

As I wound through Travis Heights toward the St. Edward's campus, Kenny looked at the homes and trees and said, "Austin's a good-looking town."

"They're ruining it as fast as they can," I said.

"Grumble, grumble," he teased.

The traffic had clogged around the campus, which had suspended summer classes to land the training camp. This was all about the Dallas Cowboys. On South First I poked around and found a parking place behind a Mexican restaurant that had tables with fans blowing mist on a patio. The waiter brought us queso, guacamole, chips, and margaritas on the rocks.

"You wonder about my hat," Kenny said.

I shrugged. "My dad wore one like it."

He put his hand on the fedora's crown and raised it. He still had hair, but the skull fractures and surgeries had left his head scarred and somewhat misshapen. He had some gray on his temples. "No casting calls for Ken Norton," he said, then put the hat back on.

"Lots of movies can use a big black guy who wears a hat. One of those old cop and private eye crime movies they call *noir.* I never knew what noir means."

I gave him the envelope with Virginie's letter. When he read it and looked away, his eyes glistened. "That's really her?"

"Yeah."

"What kind of name is Nalula?"

"East Congolese. I don't know her tribe."

"How did you find her?"

"I didn't. Mike Weaver did."

Kenny was quiet for a moment. "Son of a bitch didn't tell *me.*"

"Virginie was too afraid."

"Of what?"

"They're legal refugees. I guess that feels precarious."

"My man, Hercules," he said, a bit overcome. "You know what he's doing now?"

"No."

"Training for a fight with Lennox Lewis. That Jamaican Canadian Englishman will knock him stiff. That's crazy. Crazier than me fighting Gerry Cooney."

I reached in a side pocket of my jeans and gave him the velvet bag with his rings.

"Good God," he said, looking at them. "I gave them to her?"

"Yeah."

"I guessed they'd just cut them off in the surgery. Jackie told me I was swollen."

"How are you and her?"

"Ah, I don't know. She's a beautiful woman and the mother of two of my children. But I don't know if we'll make it. This has been too hard on her. It's my fault."

"Why? How do you figure that?"

"That's the hell of it. I don't know."

"You'll call Virginie, won't you?"

"Of course I'll call her. You think I'm that cold?"

Kenny's speech was more halting than before, but the sounds of it were the same. Voices. In different ways our bond and challenge. He told me the story of his reclamation. He said at one of the hospitals, before he regained speech, he had a room on a top floor. The bed was beside a window, and he could see all the way down into a deep construction pit. He flinched on hearing the explosions of dynamite as they blasted the bedrock. Then the steel girders started going up, floor by floor. From all the right angles, he could tell how the offices and corridors were going to be laid out. The hardhats never worked like they were in a hurry. They were careful, but the building that would be taller than his vantage point in the rehab hospital kept steadily going up. The crane bringing them materials was an acrobatic act.

"Watching that helped me in ways no docs or shrinks could. Even the therapists. I chased out the preachers right away. I was going to sort out all the things that were wrong with me and start working on them systematically, without panic. People would come to see me and I'd point at the construction site and try to make them understand what I said. Some did, I think. I said, 'That's where I work.' The ones that heard me probably went home thinking the rumors were true—I was crazy along with everything else."

He nodded at the waitress that he'd like another margarita. I raised my palm to her and shook my head. "I hated the morphine," he said. "Terrible dreams, and in every one of them I didn't know a soul. When I was coming out of it, I realized I was belted to the bed. The nurses unhitched them when they came to turn me over on my sides. Precautions against bed sores. But they hitched me back in when they left. I thought Jackie and Kenny Junior had gotten me committed. Things got better and my mind cleared a little when they put me beside that window and I could see the construction pit."

"George Foreman says he pulls and prays for you."

Kenny nodded. "I don't doubt it. He's a good man."

"And Ali?" I said, turning my head to look at him directly.

He smiled. "Ah, Ali. He sends me short little notes. Illustrates them more than he writes. I've got a shoebox full of them. Joe Frazier's come out to see me three times."

As Kenny talked, I began seeing them. I mean I didn't, but I did. They stood in a line about ten yards away. Ali was taller than the others but would have stood out anyway. Part of his shirttail had gone untucked in his dress trousers. He was smiling at something like he didn't seem to want the rest of them to know. Grinning with his new teeth, Leon Spinks fidgeted and stood as far away from Ali as he could. At the other end, he swung his head back and forth, looking for all the world like Stevie Wonder. Between them were Floyd Patterson, Ingo Johansson, Jerry Quarry, and Jimmy Young, ones who'd lost their way in life and maybe died not even knowing who they were. Sonny Liston at peace at last in the vapors of his overdose. Oscar Bonavena and Trevor Berbick, astonished in the instants of their murders. Kenny asked me something and I looked back to him. When I glanced again, the heavyweights were gone.

"Do you think about getting back on stage?" Kenny had said.

"Oh, maybe. Sabine wants me to."

"Do it," he said, like he was still my boss.

He paused and sipped his drink. "You know, as much as it's cost you, you were right to pay back that DI. He could have killed you. And gotten away with it. And kept on taking out his demons on kids who had no defense against him."

I chose not to tell him Geoffrey Edwards was dead or where he died. "I don't know," I said. "I could have just called him out in the piranha bar. Embarrassed him in front of the other old salts before they threw me out. Saved myself a lot of grief." I smiled. "But I never would have known you."

"Haid, I want to tell you something I've never told anybody else."

I blinked in surprise. "Okay."

"After you and I went our different ways, I almost got in more trouble than you had. After Jose Luis Garcia knocked me out, I thought it was over for me. Eddie Futch was pushing me, putting me in sparring with Joe whenever he could, but I was still making three or four hundred bucks a round. Except I wasn't. My backers in San Diego used my purses to pad the paydays and get me fights with guys like Jack O'Halloran, so I'd still have some visibility. My paychecks at the Ford plant were never enough. I was desperate for money just to buy food for Kenny Junior. I was a walking sack of guilt. I had a liquor store picked out I was going to rob. I bought the gun from a guy at the plant. I had it all staked out. You know what stopped me?"

I was so startled I couldn't answer.

"Pop. The shame I'd bring on him and Mom if I got caught. And I would have. I called Pop and told him, 'I can't make it out here. I want to come home.' He said, 'Son, you won't like being back here. This little town has more pride than it's got coming. Abraham Lincoln made a two-hour speech here one time about ending slavery. The Underground Railroad came through Jacksonville. Several local boys—white boys—got to go off and play major league baseball. But you were the best athlete this town had ever seen. If you come back here scraping for money, in this state of mind, people here be shaking their heads. How could a boy with all that talent be moping around here a failure? What's happened to your courage, son? You can only get hold of it when you're in a boxing ring? Just once you got to finish something you started.'"

I watched Kenny slip the rings back on his hands.

I said, "What did you do with the gun?"

"Went for a run and threw it in the Pacific Ocean."

"Don't let your crimes overload you."

He ducked his head and grinned. "Say what?"

"Oh, just a riff on a line of a holler we sang on the rock pile."

"All right." He looked at his watch and set his hat brim lower. "Guess I'd better go start making amends with my son."

As we came out of the cantina on South First, the traffic on the broad street was backed up because of the Cowboys' training camp. I punched a button on a utility pole to put up a light for pedestrian crossing. Waiting on the curb for the light to change, I looked down at my feet. Beneath the hem of my jeans, the patent leather slippers looked dumb.

Across the street on our sidewalk, a young woman in a T-shirt and thin clinging shorts was jogging in the heat. She had her blonde hair rubber-banded back in a pony tail. I said, "Look at that girl's hair. Isn't that beautiful? Tossing left, tossing right."

"You know me. From the rear I'm used to aiming my gaze a little lower down."

Because we were transfixed by that girl, we didn't notice that the light that let us across was changing. Kenny walked without a limp, but the high school track star's pace was slow now. We were only a third of the way across when our ten seconds on the crossing light expired. A kid in a pickup appeared to have no air-conditioning, for he propped his arm and elbow on the door. The traffic clot was getting on his nerves. He gunned the truck, which had a loud set of pipes that shot out clouds of black exhaust. I bet he was one of those yahoos that hung to his bumper a dangling pair of iron testicles. Then he weighed down on his horn. Kenny turned his head and pointed with his long arm and index finger, like George had done to those men in Caracas who meant to kill me, and he shut that rude noise down.

AFTERWORD

The storm that created the published version of Jan's final novel spanned five decades, and thundered between two deaths. The novel bridged the author's experience from bleak, blue-collar boyhood to young, rebellious man—Jan looking over his shoulder to his youth, to his family, to his faith, and to the Texas town and turbulent times that had molded him. The veteran writer worked steadily throughout the fatal illness of his wife, throughout the lockdown of his city, carrying on alone in an empty house during a global pandemic and most volatile presidential election since Lincoln rose to office. As far as I know, there was only one more mission left for Jan Reid. And he was going it alone.

Well, Jan did have a dog.

On Christmas Eve 2019, after a protracted bout with cancer, and a lifelong campaign against anyone whom she believed deserved it, Dorothy Browne, Jan's wife of thirty-seven years, suffered her last and only defeat. I was among Dorothy's herds of friends. She was as unique, passionate, and fiery a human being as I've ever known. I adored her. So did everybody else. In her last days, she hid herself from the world. I don't know why. I happened upon her, in her kitchen, just days before we lost her. She, deep brown eyes like syrup, was still absolutely beautiful.

About eight months later, in the teeth of your standard 120-day Austin August, a group of Jan's closest literary brothers (loosely and accurately known as "Knuckleheads," now unofficially mandated as a *cabal*) gathered in the breezeway at his West Austin residence to celebrate the end of a long journey to bring *The Song Leader* home. Six weeks and two days later, after a lifetime of fifteen-round bloody split decisions, Jan's prodigious heart finally played out. Seventy-five years old, partially paralyzed from a robbery attempt in Mexico City, when a thug bounced a .38-caliber slug off his spine, Jan had just completed a workout at his beloved Lord's Boxing Gym when his heart fired the first round in what would be a three-hour battle to settle on who calls the shots. Even a man as tough and stubborn as Jan finally reached for the phone. Weakened as he was by so many years of struggle, battling so many serious and nuisance health conditions, along with the standard daily desperations of a working writer's life, it still took a good ten days of intense warfare to end Jan Reid.

In Jan's body of work, *The Song Leader* appears exactly in the succession he himself chose. His very existence those last few months hinged on seeing this last novel through. After Dorothy's death, knowing what I knew of Jan's personal and health struggles, I presumed I was about to witness his quiet but relentless decline. Who was there for him now? To be sure, his stepdaughter, Lila, and his family, and his legions of friends. But what could any of them do for him during Covid-19's reign? For over a year, those of us who understood the viral process and believed the CDC and Dr. Fauci, recognized that all of us were on our own.

To me, Jan's situation alone in that house with his memories looked unimaginably grim.

My own connection to Jan Reid even predates his marriage to Dorothy Browne. As a kid at middle-class Sharpstown High, I absorbed the fledgling *Texas Monthly* magazine from cover to cover. For a small-town Arkansas preacher's kid, 1970s Boomtown Houston seemed to resemble the Armageddon of Paul's fevered Revelation more than anything I'd seen driving through Little Rock or Lubbock. We all needed help making sense of a transforming Texas. In the earliest days of the magazine, the voices in *Texas Monthly* rendered structure, context, and understanding. Sort of. The clearest of them, to me, belonged to Jan Reid.

I had no image of him in my head then. He was only a byline to me. But I *heard* him.

The Department of History at the University of Texas at Austin. 1977. A new discipline emerges—*American Studies*. I see the course listed, *The*

History of Rock and Roll. I figure that's a blow-off of a class for a jackass of my hip, cultural sophistication, all of those hours of Memphis, St. Louis, and Houston FM radio stations echoing in my head. It becomes my favorite course, spawning my first encounters with Jack Kerouac, Tom Wolfe, Joan Didion, and a return to Hunter Thompson's work, among many others—all to the soundtracks of their dynamic but tempestuous times. The class was held in the then newly constructed Thompson Conference Center, on the northern edge of UT's ever-emerging campus, complete with media room, theater-quality screens, and concert-grade sound system.

One required text for the course was *The Improbable Rise of Redneck Rock*, by Jan Reid. I knew his writing well, but I didn't know he was in it for book-length work! Taught now in *college* alongside legends! Jan's groundbreaking book on the Austin music and progressive "outlaw country" scenes laid the foundation for what I was hearing in those bars and honky tonks all around town. The mid-1970s was still a magical time to be young and alive and living on borrowed money, youthful fantasies, longshot dreams, and cheap beer. There were also topless chicks sunning at Barton Springs. This damn town was made for me.

The Improbable Rise of Redneck Rock has been in print, mostly, since it was first published. That's how good and rich it was in its time and place; how perfectly Jan had captured and celebrated a now lost epoch. And the writer who understood the music that defined that era well enough to throw the floodgates open to the wide world beyond, would one day become my friend.

Jan Reid's vision, as expressed in two entirely different mediums, had influenced my own thinking about my own time and place, and I had never met him.

Flash forward another twenty years. I publish something. Get invited to something. It happens to be on the University of Texas campus. I'm an awkward usurper in the Austin literary scene—most everybody knows I crashed through the back screen door of publishing. I enter the gala, acquire my name tag, avert my gaze in order to avoid potential small talk as I approach the bar, order a gin, speak to the assured man with the buck teeth leaning against a pole. He appears to get along okay with gin, too. He reads my name tag, draws a blank. He tells me who he is. I am struck Arkansas dumb. Jesus Christ, this is Jan *Freakin'* Reid standing right there in front of me! In an instant, I re-assume the guise of reader rather than an author. Let the fan-boy ass kissing begin.

Within a year of our introduction, Jan Reid is shot in Mexico City. An armed robbery that Jan couldn't abide. Jan swung. The criminal fired. The violence erupted into an array of emergency medical and surgical procedures—some performed by Texas icon, Dr. Red Duke—that would save his life. All of this experience Jan Reid captures himself in *The Bullet Meant for Me.* And when that stunningly raw memoir ended, Jan returned to the fiction career he had begun so many years before, piped right out of Wichita Falls, Texas. He published epic nonfiction titles, as well, during those years, including his landmark biography of Governor Ann Richards, the best collection of writing from Grover Lewis (co-edited with W.K. Stratton), and a collection exploring the Rio Grande. Once Jan hit bank with his nonfiction, he crafted yet another award winner in the grittiest fiction version to date of the Quanah Parker legend.

Daily life for Jan was an ordeal: Botox injections in his voice box, serial infections, radiation treatments for cancer, phantom pains, and tortuous cramps. I can't supply a complete list, because Jan never bitched about his health issues. Or about much of anything else. Instead, Jan, accustomed to a life of suffering, quietly took out one opponent after another. He sparred with each book project, in its turn, no matter the obstacle, until he knew in his heart that he had completed the journey he had begun all those years ago, from so damn far away. *The Song Leader*, by Jan's own intention, would be his last and perhaps most character-driven work. It would also be his most personal. The closest, perhaps, to his heart, and even it would soon fail him.

Strange things happened during the Covid-19 Pandemic. Dolphins swam in the canals of Venice for the first time in centuries. A pack of coyotes prowled the hungry streets of the near-abandoned Chicago business district. Carbon in the atmosphere dropped to levels not seen in decades. All of humanity locked itself down in an eerie calm. While we learned the new Draconian rules of daily existence, the most pervasive reaction in my poll was a sense of fear and dread. Was this the beginning of the end of our times?

Not for Jan Reid.

Midway through another Austin August day (and there are 120 of them), I was delivering supplies to Jan at his residence. Entering the compound, I encountered Jan and his large black and white collie, "Biscuit," when, at that exact moment, a three-foot garter snake emerged from under the deck and serpentined straight for Jan's office. Man, dog, and snake confronted each other and immediately recognized that they'd never make it work. We kept garter snakes as pets when I was a kid in Arkansas (only much smaller), so I wasn't worried about the snake. But it became a problem for us all when it slipped through Jan's office door, heading for the endless cracks and crevasses that defined Jan's working space. A reptile's vacation destination, basically. Meanwhile, in the middle of the commotion, me trying to catch the snake, Jan pivoting back-and-forth on his cane like a whirling Dervish, Biscuit—ever an opportunist and at least a foot longer and taller than your "Best in Show" collies—saw his shot at freedom and crashed through the cedar gate to the street. In the panic, I looked to Jan.

"Is Biscuit a runner?" I asked, forlornly.

"Oh, yes," he said. "You have to remember that Biscuit's just a two-year-old dog." And also that the Lord hath blessed him with almost as many vertebrae as the snake. Biscuit is unwieldy, as canines tend to go. I've noticed that he also leans against the wall, like Lee Marvin's horse in *Cat Ballou*. Biscuit's a weird dog, but separation anxiety is not among his complaints.

"Unfortunate," I said. And, the hell with the snake, off we went, running. Me trotting after Biscuit in triple-digit heat. Behind me, I could hear Jan's cane pecking the deck following behind us. Once out in the street, I saw the dog trotting up the blacktop, already a block away. I yelled for him. He turned. Looked at me with an expression that conveyed that I held no authority whatsoever over him. I know the look. I've gotten it from my stepdaughters. The dog turned, reared like a mustang, and raced on.

Thankfully, two much younger, much faster women, in separate cars, (not my stepdaughters) allied with Jan and me on the fly to corral Biscuit. I had to pick him up and carry him home. (Biscuit weighs a good eighty pounds.) But what I remember most about the entire episode was, in the middle of all of this, looking back downhill at Jan, leaning in to the hill with his cane, topaz-blue eyes sparking, wizened Covid-hair tossing in the scalded breeze, steadily coming for his dog, hell or high water, which he couldn't possibly catch. To me, it was the very image of Jan's fortitude and indomitable spirit. He kept on a-coming, and a-coming—just like those old Texas Ranger legends Jan loved for the whole of his life—all of it uphill on a pock-marked street, chasing a dog that was capable of eating us both. This was happening on Eleventh Street in Tarrytown, but had it been Mount Kilimanjaro looming between him and Biscuit, Jan's fierce determination would've been the same. Jan loved his dog. Their relationship was not going to end in the same year that he'd lost Dorothy.

Jan summoned those very same powers to complete the novel that's before you now. From whence they came, no mortal can say. I am so encouraged, battling my own struggles during our most tempestuous, disheartening, leaderless times, to have been a witness to how Jan martialed his most primal energies—as a writer; as an unflinching artist; as a man well-accustomed to the hunger of poverty, the sting of rejection, and the wounds of perennial adversity, willing his battered body and aging mind ever onward. What he mustered that one day to catch his dog, he mustered a lifetime for you to experience in his fiction. I am twelve years younger than Jan. My health challenges pale in comparison to his. So far, nobody's shot me. (Four misses, as a matter of fact.) And still, I can't claim that I ever faced the daily struggles of this life with the relentless courage, resilience, and grace I witnessed in Jan Reid.

Later that same day of Biscuit's jail break, a cryptic email pinged my inbox. "Hey, Bud!" Jan wrote, "What kind of snake did you say that was?"

I don't know what happened to the goddamn snake. But, oh, how I loved being Jan Reid's friend. It's been an honor, really. Thank you, Jesse. Thank you, Knuckleheads. Thank you, Austin.

So, anyway, Dorothy's memorial at Sagerrunde Hall (which was SRO of old, liberal Austin) occurred before the pandemic hit. All humanity soon shut down, as we've said. Jan had now turned to what would be the final revision of *The Song Leader.* According to Jan's running mate from those days—journalist, academic, and authority Uncle Roy Hamric—Jan had started to ruminate on a "coming of age" work, with a Texas accent, maybe akin to McMurtry's *Horseman, Pass By,* as early as 1976.

Deerinwater (published 1985) represented Jan's experience with the oil industry as he'd known it. He then turned to encompass all the rest of life in a small Texas town. *The Song Leader* grew slowly, in snatches and bits, many originating from the author's most intimate, and sometimes painful places, as the foundation for his novel. Jan cranked out a solid first draft while he and Dorothy clawed at cancer. After her death, he reconsidered his earlier draft, and now that we all lived like lepers, committed himself to an ambitious overhaul of the manuscript to tighten, enlarge, focus, and expand the story of his journey from boyhood to man. Texas, by God.

My wife, Jan, and I formed a bond. We ate together. Ran errands together. We went grocery shopping at Central Market, which resembled a scene from the film, *Contagion,* in its intimidating viral protocol. Jan just kept tapping that cane on the floor, wearing a Walmart hoodie like a night shift Druid priest (which he was), and filled his basket. I hate to be disparaging about a deceased friend, but Jan thought he was a good cook. I'm here to tell you that he wasn't. My dog already knows that. But my dog doesn't read, and I know he wants justice. Jan loved Martha's bone broth soups, her posole from scratch, homemade Ramen, her fried chicken, Marfa stack enchiladas, venison chili, whatever the hell kind of Thai cuisine she took a stab at, and on and on.

Always, Jan returned Martha's container with a recipe of his own. That's the kind of grace you experienced daily with Jan Reid, definitely widowed, supposedly in decline, literally on his last leg. He thought enough of others to make an Irish stew, and share it with the only friends currently available. Even if it was, indeed, a wretched stew, Martha and I loved him a little more each time he delivered it.

Jan's manners and bearing reminded me so much of my father's congregations when I was a child. How it felt to be part of a community. To *belong.* To understand that there are certain rules and customs that must be observed for humanity to persist for even one generation longer. That was the wisdom I saw in Jan's life. And I'm certain that it came from his rearing, in those fiery, fundamental churches where you sipped Welch's grape juice for Communion under the glare of an Angry God, often a perturbed mother, and for certain, your scabby, burr-headed, fidgety cousin whom you damn well knew to be a little sketchy on *The Beatitudes.* Naturally athletic, Jan was also blessed with a golden voice. He had actually been the song leader of his congregation at a very early age. As the son of a Presbyterian minister myself, I want to suggest that his time among those people, of that intense faith, anchored Jan through the storms of his life. He didn't speak much of the Christian faith to me. I just saw him *live* it.

I credit the creation of the "Knuckleheads" to hyphenate Jesse Sublett. Jesse's an empath and artist to the bone, but in today's newspeak he's also one hell of a "connector." We met at the Texas Book Festival, where my "career" as a professional started for me as much as it ever would. I love Jesse like a big brother. If he suggests I do, or don't do, something, I usually comply. Jesse invited me to lunch with some other writer friends of his, usually back then at Hoover's on Austin's East Side. Over muffalettas, I started to socialize with Tom Zigal, Christopher Cook, W.K. Stratton, Roy Hamric, and, to my delight, Jan Reid. (And, if I've left out a name or two of the Knucks, it's not because I don't like them. It's because Jan didn't like them. And Jan liked everybody.)

Later, Jesse took on the memoir of Austin impresario Eddie Wilson. Eddie, we soon learned, had qualified as a "Knucklehead" by an idiosyncratic, indefinable, and potentially illegal process. (It's all up to the Supreme Court now.) Eddie's also kind of pushy. He's never really wanted for entertainment, but the Knucks needed a chicken-fried steak. The "Knucks"—now an unofficial, quasi-sinister cabal, with mysticism and dogma known only by our most dedicated members and their moms, migrated to Threadgill's. There we were joined by author and journalist Joe Holley and author and Wittliff Center conservator, Steve Davis (the youngest, nicest, and most sophisticated Knuck); New Mexican novelist and member of the Choctaw Nation Ron Querry, who blew in with his distinguished photographer wife, Elaine; *Texas Monthly* alum and prolific author Joe Nick Patoski; mystery writer Ben Rehder; and some dude who emailed in artistic vignettes involving him and his mules—hopelessly beyond the understanding of even the most out-of-state, hickoid knuck. Obviously, we don't turn them away. Frequently, we were joined by an assortment of on-hand Austin characters, media types, politicos, old hippies, new money, and your standard groovers and gangsters that inhabited both Threadgill's locations. Often, things spiraled out of control, and it was still noon. We couldn't possibly have been good for Eddie's business, but that seemed a secondary concern.

Readers: See me among these writers as I see myself—seated at the table at the Algonquin in the days of Dorothy Parker. Know also: all of this has ended.

And if Jan's voice had weakened, his command of language thrived. Jan's emails resonated his ballistic train of thought, delivered in staccato beats, like he'd shot all that at you with a Thompson. His freight train intent and his journalist's choice of efficient verbiage was clean, direct, and powerful. You understood him very well. Lots of Knucks are quick on the trigger with those emails, and all of them are in need of medication. Just keeping abreast of what comes in each day is a full-time job. My favorite writer, hands down, was Jan Reid.

Before I became Jan's friend, we met at some festive occasion when I was living in Alpine (the Big Bend). Jan carried himself, as he always did regardless of where he found himself, like he lived there, too. I was about to publish a new book. For lack of a far better term, this one was generating a little buzz. Some controversy surrounding the subject matter. I had come to believe one way. Jan, closing on negotiations for a funnel cake, believed the opposite. He circled me like a coyote does a jackrabbit snared in a goat-wire fence—which is silly when your face is dusted with powdered sugar. "Are you prepared to defend your position?" he asked me. "You're goddamn right," I said, adding: "How about a bite of that funnel cake?" Looked pretty good. Being Jan, he tore off a well-dusted chunk, but pressed on with the inquisition. I wish somebody had that exchange on film.

I had just met Jan Reid the professional journalist, and maybe a little bit of the Golden Gloves boxer. Jan was a handsome man. He spoke softly, with an accent that sounded more Southern to me than North Texan. Women liked him. Lots of them. He kept his word. Told fabulous, mostly true stories. He was kind to most everybody. Had a grin like a cartoon mule. Around me in our last days when nobody was watching, he could actually act kind of goofy. But he was nobody to cross, either. I've seen him when he was riled. You will see it, too, in the *The Song Leader*'s Haid Pecos and his at times lightning temper. Jan understood self-discipline. But Haid's a free-wheeling dude. What Jan shares with his protagonist is coming up hardscrabble in Wichita Falls, literally "a boy named Sue," watching his daddy punch a clock in khakis worn smooth like chamois, topped by a sweat-stained fedora. A place inhabited by characters with more in common with Steinbeck's cast in *Grapes Of Wrath* than with contemporary Texans. People with money love to talk about their past seasons of poverty. People who bleed for a living just want to forget about it for a little while.

Not so for Jan Reid, who, at times in his early career, lived feral, he was so fierce in his ambitions to write! Jan worked as the sports writer for the New Braunfels *Zercher Zeitung*, fresh and emboldened by his successful *Redneck Rock* book, when he realized he had collected all the fixin's for one of those "coming of age" novels we all like to publish if we can. Especially if it's successful—or so I've heard. *The Song Leader* was threaded into Jan Reid's DNA as early as the 1970s. The pain and paucity of life on the working side of Wichita Falls began to glimmer like a rough gem. The world and the people in it that Jan had known in those days had also vanished from the cracked Texas earth. Jan had to look long and hard from his home in West Austin and see what he had once been. And still, for me, that's the beauty of the character of Haid Pecos—he was born not belonging, and he still had to fight his way out of town. The rules he learned in Wichita Falls, and in that church on the mean streets where the stray, raw-bone dogs run, no longer apply in Haid's world. Like everybody else, he's got to figure it out, and there'll most certainly be betrayal, heartbreak, and blood. Watching him on his journey, and the fascinating, eccentric characters that people his path, is what makes *The Song Leader* so adventurous. I really don't know what's true, and what isn't. Jan never told me. But, would you be interested in my opinion?

Haid Pecos looks, sounds, acts, and creates situations a lot like the flesh and blood Jan Reid. All of him as Texas as a mesquite tree. If they ain't blood kin, they're from the same county.

So Jan proudly announces that he's delivered *The Song Leader* to the level he'd demanded of his body, heart, and soul. Growing in his powers that last summer, he felt energized upon reaching his goal. He decided, within reason, to get back in shape. He worked out. His heart had other ideas. Jan battled his initial heart attack for some three hours before he thought maybe this particular issue was one he could no longer endure. During that interval, Jan spent 70 percent of his heart function. By Jan's account, Biscuit howled inconsolably the entire time.

I visited Jan often in Seton—as I had done when Dorothy was there, because I loved them, and I could not bear for them to be in the hospital without some outside snark and inside contraband. All one had to do was egg them on a bit. Jan asked me to bring him his laptop. Really? He had edits to make for TCU Press. And, as so often happens, while he was laid up, he thought differently about a beat in the plot here and there; an extra detail to attribute to a supporting character; a more evocative way to phrase a line. While Jan was dying, he was still writing. Or, rather, while he lived, he wrote.

After a few days in the ICU, Jan called to ask if I could take him home. I came. I was stunned at the sight of him, how diminished. My heart broke when I had to pick him up and set him in my front seat. Men don't want to ask other men to do that shit. I knew it hurt his pride. I made a joke about it. His body felt desiccated, his bones rattling like unmatched club shafts in a rented golf bag. We drove to his Eleventh Street home.

I bet it took a good ten minutes to wheel him from his driveway to his bedroom. We moved slow. Pained. But no garter snakes. He lay back across the foot of his bed, like he was just home from afternoon two-a-days football practice, and sighed loudly.

"Hey, Bud, maybe tell them other boys not to wait three hours when the pains hit," he said. I told him any idiot knew that. Even Biscuit knew it was a real bad idea, but I'd be glad to pass it along to the Knucks. (Jan did himself, in an email.) But I was thinking, how the hell can this man stay in this house alone in this condition? I went home, but my worry, and my dread, stayed with him.

Sure enough, he'd gone back to the hospital that very same night. He needed the laptop again. When I went in to see him one evening, he told me joyously over a cup of green hospital jello that he had sent in the FINAL edits to TCU Press! He clapped shut the laptop, and with that grin, he said, "I believe I'm going to write me another novel." A sequel to *Sins Of The Younger Sons.*

I told him no self-respecting Knuck would sit still for it. Give somebody else a chance, for Christ's sake, and it better not be W.K. Stratton. Kip's murdering us all, you see, one notice at a time. I also wondered what the hell Jan saw in that nasty hospital jello.

The next night, I watched in silence as the nurse concluded Jan's permissions. Then she wrote "*D.N.R.*" in a red wax pen on the board above his head. Jan had just confirmed there were to be no heroics if/when his heart took another cheap shot. Something had changed, but you wouldn't sense it from Jan's demeanor. As soon as the nurse shoved her supply cart out the door, Jan said, "I don't think I'm gonna get to that next novel, Bud." He went on to tell me that it'd been a "dark night of the soul," which I took then to mean that Jan had for hours been fighting for his life. But on his face: calm and resignation.

I've seen a lot of hurt from the underbelly of the publishing biz. I lived through the ruthless rise of the chains, the death of stalwart independents, the obsolescence of the book pages in major market newspapers (and the obsolescence of print media itself), and the domination of online platforms where every idiot has the same say as a lifelong fiction devotee. We sometimes see poor ratings based on the reader's shipping and handling experience. Makes it tough. I see a lot of "content" out there, but much of it should never have been choking the road forward for those old school writers. At every turn in my time in publishing, writers have been marginalized, their livelihoods strangled, with little chance to retool and regroup for another shot at the ever-dwindling population of readers. Even Oprah couldn't save us from a nation that refuses to read.

For the last ten years, I watched most every writer I know—even Jan Reid—squirm under the lifetime struggle with an economically unsustainable art form. Even the people who love us most just do not understand why we're so goddamn stubborn. And so goddamn sad. It's because we invested everything of ourselves in our work before we sent it out in the world, and almost *nothing* came back. I don't know if Jan felt that way. I just know that he had to worry about money for most of the time I knew him. We all do. The wolf is always waiting out your front door.

But the saddest thing a writer ever said to me was the night Jan Reid told me that *The Song Leader* would be his last. He didn't deliver the words for dramatic effect—which, to be honest, was kind of a disappointment. But he broke my heart just the same. It was the howl of the lone coyote, too old and too broken to hunt with the pack, watching the full moon rise.

D.N.R. Jan looked at the board as the nurse wrote the blood-red letters with the same gambler's stare he used for a Threadgill's menu. He gave me nothin'. I assured him that I had organs that I couldn't trust anymore, too. Pretty sure I lost it on the drive home.

I expected to hear from Jan the next day. I didn't. With escalating dread, I reached out to our network of Knucks. An email finally hit my in box, from Lila, Jan's stepdaughter, "Jan didn't make it."

I went numb. I'm still numb. Jan had no idea how much a part he was of our Pandemic Response, Bitch, and Debate Team. I was with him two or three times a week. I'm restless. I pace. When I can't stand the confinement another minute longer, I eat tacos. Lots of times, I ate Jan's tacos. That's exactly how Jan handled situations like this. I knew the perfect food truck to stay socially distanced but still enjoy interior cuisine. I knew Jan had cash these days and often over-ordered. All I had to do was deliver him there to win big!

I don't go anymore. When I drive toward downtown, or to the lake, it takes me right past Jan's house. I always look up Eleventh Street. I know he's not there. I look anyway. Hoping maybe to see the Jan Reid on the eerie cover of *Bullet Meant for Me* trade paper edition, fading from his friends into the Italian fog.

Now he's faded out of the frame. I see only a void that my friend used to fill. I could tell that man anything! So I did. What he didn't understand is that none of the things I did for him where actually *for him*. They were always for *me*. Because I needed a friend, and I could not have had a better one, at this troubled time in my life, than Jan Reid. We ran errands, told lies, and kicked up shit all over town. And that's why, no matter how stupid or impulsive Haid Pecos lives his life, he lives it with everything he's got, and most of it Texas gave him. And now, the pages that contain Haid's story represent all I'm ever going to see again of my mentor and friend.

"Say, Bud, what kind of snake did you say that was?"

It was going to be the *last* snake, Jan. For a fiction writer, better if it'd been a spitting cobra or a black mamba. That'd up the tension, and the stakes. Garter snakes are just kind of nice, like Jan was. I honestly don't know what ever came of the one that assaulted Jan's compound. Jan's office was like the debris field after a jet crash. Always a wreck. Always hopeless. Trees de-masted. But full of mystery, evocative images and artifacts, and a rich, well-lived, hard-used past.

I want to remember him this way: In the middle of the massive revision of *The Song Leader*. April or May, 2020. As I've said, I expected to see Jan Reid in a slow, ever-declining downward spiral. The very same I'd witnessed in so many die-hard writers just like him. Just like me.

I saw just the opposite. Jan Reid was no longer the widower, the cripple, the potentially "has-been" writer. I watched him take his stance on *The Song Leader*, in impossible circumstances, fighting out of his class. By the spring, Jan had already found his rhythm. I've been there. We all have. I knew he was going to finish that novel on the sheer momentum of its mass. But I didn't expect to see Jan *thrive* like he did. One night,

I told him what kind of eatin's we had on hand. And he texted back to say something like, "I'm fine. Knocked out twenty pages today! I like it! Kicking back now, enjoying the weather, listening to the Stones." Later, when I told Martha that I'd been over to see Jan, she asked how'd he look? And I answered, "He's *glowing*!!!"

And so, that second death I told you about at the beginning—we didn't expect that one. I actually thought Jan might try out for the Cowboys in the fall. He just looked and acted like he'd lost twenty years. He was seventy-five, and still wore jeans without a belt, and nobody can help the Cowboys. His stare trained on his laptop monitor like he was trying to stab it. In a word, I saw *contentment* in his deep, glistening blue eyes. But, also, *fire*! I was looking at a man who had gone the distance, beaten the odds, had money in the bank, plenty of old friends, a young dog, and a "coming of age" novel he'd planned as early as 1976 spreading before him like a grass fire. When it was done, Jan emailed the file to his editor, and thought he'd give the speed bag a few jabs. At the end of a combination, a heart attack tapped him on the shoulder.

As they roll credits at the end of Frederick Wiseman's documentary film, *Boxing Gym*, a solitary man, credited as the "elderly boxer," works the heavy bag. We observe the concentration on his sweaty face, the heavy, plodding footwork as he positions himself for the powerful next punch. One hears the thud of the bag, and the grunt of the boxer who yielded it. Again and again until his image fades out.

That is Jan Reid. That is precisely the way I envision him spending his last spring and summer on this earth, breathing life into this novel. One punch at a time. Slow. Deliberate. Powerful. And fucking relentless. All of his energies he gathered in *The Song Leader*, an effort born of pain as the great writers of an earlier age used to say, crafted with as much skill as he'd learned in over seven decades as a born writer, native Texan, and natural storyteller.

But this is no courtesy read. Jan had the time, the peace, the money, the mindset, the skills, and the ideal lair from which to crank out the novel he'd been writing his whole life. Most importantly, he also mustered the requisite passion to make it as good and true as he knew how. He lived and worked within his own rawhide confidence and solitary grace. Self-doubt never a contender. Jan knew he had nothing to lose. He aspired with everything that remained.

Jan's won all kinds of awards for his work. When it's all said and done, I still believe that future readers, critics, and academics will recognize the quality in the writing and the value of Jan's experiences, and assay his classic trajectory over the arc of his work, earned by time, risk, pain, the absurd, and plenty of his own blood, punctuated with a novel he cobbled together over forty-five tumultuous years. Jan's stated intention was that *The Song Leader* be his very best—the punctuation to a life fully invested in literature. Friends, that last summer went his way. Cosmically so. Like it was *ordained.*

And maybe it was. From the moment Jan Reid set foot behind that plywood pulpit, and led his family, friends, and neighbors in "In the Garden." He sang his heart out, because there was no one else among that congregation with the talent and conviction to lead them ever so well—up to the point where they broke his heart, and shoved him out into the heat and the burning wind. And even then, for the whole of his life he led the rest of us who aspired to be what he was. He left it all in his last novel. And I assure you that he left this world grinning about it.

He... was... glowing! And that is why I still can't accept that he's dead.

I'm more selfish than to remark on the quality and importance of Jan's last novel. I say, to hell with the book. I'd just like to call up my friend, tell him, don't mind the excuses, I'm on the way, restrain Biscuit, and we'll go swap lies at the taco truck.

Jan's were *always* better.

He told me he wanted to buy a new cowboy hat when he got out of the hospital. I wasn't sure how that was going to go. Not with that bean head and those buck teeth. Dorothy would no doubt have shot us both. One week longer on this earth—or, at least, near enough to Lockhart—and he'd have had it. We'd all have seen him in that hat. And we'd know.

"Anything but black," Jan said. "I don't look good in black."

I bet he looked okay in black, but I was thinking buckskin. "Low Gus" crease, maybe. Jan sort of carried himself like Gus McCrae. A flesh and blood man. A great Texas writer. My dear, irreplaceable friend.

DAVID MARION WILKINSON
High Divide Ranch
Tom Green/Coke County, Texas
January 2021